W9-CEJ-068

cp 1 9/95

LARGE PRINT

F
STA   Staples, Mary Jane

           The trap

THE TRAP

Jamie Blair had managed to survive the trenches in the First World War and when he came back he ended up in the house of Henry Mullins and his four stepchildren.

The lodgings were cheap, but Mullins was a mean, brutal man. When, in a violent altercation with seventeen-year-old Kitty, he fell down the stairs and died, no-one was sorry. Jamie, just for a few days, stepped in and helped the kids where he could. Too late he realized he had walked into a trap—for Kitty saw their lodger as the answer to all their problems. While he was there the family could stay together—Jamie would look after them, help them from one crisis to the next. Kitty, who began to look quite pretty when she was well fed and neatly dressed, was quite determined that Jamie shouldn't get away.

THE TRAP

THE TRIAL

THE TRAP

by

Mary Jane Staples

Magna Large Print Books
Long Preston, North Yorkshire,
England.

British Library Cataloguing in Publication Data.

Staples, Mary Jane
The trap.

A catalogue record for this book is
available from the British Library

ISBN 0-7505-0707-1

First published in Great Britain by Transworld Publishers
Ltd., 1993

Copyright © 1993 by Mary Jane Staples

Cover illustration © Nigel Chamberlain by arrangement with
Transworld Publishers Ltd.

The right of Mary Jane Staples to be identified as the
author of this work has been asserted in accordance with
the Copyrights, Designs and Patents Act, 1988.

Published in Large Print 1994 by arrangement with
Transworld Publishers Ltd., & the copyright holder.

Magna Large Print is an imprint of
Library Magna Books Ltd.
Printed and bound in Great Britain by
T.J. Press (Padstow) Ltd., Cornwall, PL28 8RW.

Chapter One

Jamie Blair's parents had been a daft pair all their married lives. Lovable but daft. His father, Hughie Blair, was a Scot who had left the slums of Glasgow at the age of nineteen to try his luck in London, only to finish up in the slums there. At twenty-one, however, just when he was thinking of returning to Scotland, he landed a job as a welder with ship repairers in the Port of London. He moved to comfortable lodgings in Bermondsey when he was twenty-two, and there he met Nell Shaw, his landlady's daughter and as bonny as any Scottish lassie. He married her when he was twenty-five and she was twenty-one. That was in 1897.

They both had visions about a workers' Utopia, and by the time Jamie was born in 1898, they were quite barmy in a political sense. They'd discovered Karl Marx. He'd been dead for fifteen years, but they still went dotty about him. They were among the downtrodden workers of the world, and Karl Marx was in favour of a workers' revolution. That meant dispossessing the bosses, chucking out kings and queens,

9

and doing away with lords and ladies. They were very much in favour of that and took up the cause with enthusiasm.

When the Great War began, Mrs Blair did all she could to try to persuade her husband to bring all the dock workers out on strike. It was a capitalists' war, she said, and everyone ought to be against it. Hughie Blair, a fiery and articulate Scot, did his best. But he still had a broad Glaswegian accent and had grown a huge beard, which he swore he wouldn't shave off until Buckingham Palace had been turned into flats for the workers. Accordingly, most of his fellow dockers couldn't make head or tail of what was coming out through all that hair, and even if they had they wouldn't have taken any notice. They needed their wages.

Mrs Blair was a different kettle of fish. Any London worker could understand her. So she made some fiery speeches herself, exhorting workers to set fire to their bosses' factories out of respect for Karl Marx, their immortal champion. The workers, much to her disgust, told her to shove off and go back home to her washing. Disgust, however, didn't mean defeat, and she repeatedly appeared at factory gates with her soap box and her red flag. Inevitably, of course, she was dumped one day into a large container of oily waste.

'Oh, yer capitalist minions!' she yelled.

'Tck, tck, lady, be yer age. 'Ello, she's sunk, mates, pull 'er out.'

That sort of thing was a chronic aggravation, but still didn't defeat her.

In 1916, when Jamie was eighteen, he was called up. His lovable but dotty parents knew their duty, and they exhorted him to become a conscientious objector. Jamie, a young and personable Anglo-Scot, had managed to grow up with a sense of proportion and to find his parents' political antics amusing. No, he said, he didn't fancy being a CO, he'd go and do his bit.

'Well, you won't find King George doin' his bit, nor the Prime Minister, nor the bosses,' said his mother, who still looked fairly bonny but was off her chump. 'You'll end up as cannon fodder,' she said darkly, and she wasn't far wrong about that. 'Blown to smithereens, that's what you'll be. There's yer dad, doin' his own kind of bit down at the docks, a bit of honest sabotage, and you're goin' off to 'elp win the war for the capitalists that 'ave got their boots on yer neck. Jamie, we grieve for you.'

'Aye, laddie, it's a sad day,' said his father.

'Look,' said Jamie, 'suppose I promise to do what I can to get the German army

11

to go on strike, will that cheer you up? It'll cheer me up if it happens.'

'Jamie, I couldna be prouder,' said his father.

'Jamie, I'll make a little red flag for you,' said his mother, 'and you keep it flyin' high so that them Germans can see it. They're all workers of the world, like we are, and I'll explain to me Socialist brethren you've only gone into uniform to 'elp bring the German army out on strike. Hughie, if I been worried about our Jamie bein' a bit casual about Karl Marx, I'm a lot 'appier now.'

'Aye, Nellie, ye've got reason to be.'

James went off a few days later to do his bit. His parents continued on their political path. He began the tough task, after his training, of trying to stay alive while he served with the guns in Flanders. They went on with their self-imposed task of trying to up-end the established order. In 1917, soon after the Tsar of Russia abdicated, they joined a new workers' revolutionary party. Jamie received letters from them in which they poured out their enthusiasms, while at the same time slightly chiding him for the negative results he was getting in his campaign to bring the German army to a striking standstill. He told them frequently that as a member of a gun crew he couldn't get close enough to the German lines to let them see his red flag. He assured them the flag was alive and well, and simply waiting to go into action when the opportunity presented itself. Lieutenant Drinkwater, the officer who censored outgoing mail, spoke to him one day.

'Now look here, my lad, what's all this guff about a red flag?'

'Just a notion of my parents, sir.'

'Eh?'

'They're revolutionaries.'

'Don't give me that bunk, Gunner Blair, think I'm bloody barmy, do you?'

'It's a trial to me as well, sir, but I can't send the flag back and tell them to stick it on the wall. It would upset them, and you can't do that to parents who've given you free board and lodging all your life. What you do is pretend to go along with them. Actually, I'm using the red flag as a spare handkerchief.'

'Are you bloody barmy yourself?' asked Lieutenant Drinkwater.

'I'd be surprised if I wasn't, seeing what I've lived with for years, sir. Don't get me wrong, I'm fond of my parents—'

'Hoppit,' said Lieutenant Drinkwater, a grin on his face.

Inspired by the way the workers of Russia had downed the Tsar and put the fear of God into landowners, Jamie's parents began to go about on Sundays bearing placards inviting the British population to do away with their oppressors. They were dying to be arrested. At least, Mrs Blair was. Hughie, she said, you'd best keep on with your job so that you can carry on sabotaging. Once arrested herself, she could go on hunger strike until the King and Queen had been taken to the Tower of London for execution by the workers. But the police never bothered with either of them, or with their placards. They knew the Blairs were a barmy couple.

Mrs Blair had few household chores to worry about, for Jamie was the only child of the marriage. She and her husband were of a highly serious turn of mind, and Jamie often thought that in bed they probably considered anything other than a serious political discussion came under the heading of useless mucking about. He thought he himself might have been the result of absent-mindedness.

A barrage of German shells hit his battery in the autumn of 1917. He took a severe thigh wound that put him out of action until the spring of 1918. But it helped him survive because when he rejoined his unit the big German offensive had failed, and the Allies were mounting the great counter-offensive that brought the men out of the trenches at last and did away with the fearsome gun battles.

It was about the time when Jamie rejoined his battery that his father was transferred to Belfast, to work in the busy shipyards there. Other workers went with him, all by government order. Mrs Blair also went. She was her husband's political mainstay, and they were both more enthusiastic than ever. The Bolsheviks had taken over Russia, revolution looked like up-ending certain European monarchies, and Ireland was a hot-bed of trouble.

Jamie went to Belfast after the war had ended to join his parents and to see if there were any prospects for a young man of twenty-one. There weren't, although he persevered. His job before he'd been called up had been with a building firm. He liked seeing houses go up, and playing his part in that. His parents talked about going to Russia and sampling the workers' Russian Utopia. Jamie fancied that not at all. He managed to land a job in the autumn of 1920, with a builders' merchant, but it came to a messy end eight months later when a bomb planted at dawn by the IRA destroyed the premises ten minutes later. That got Jamie's goat. He was already fed up with Ireland and Ulster. Never the twain had met, and never they would in his opinion.

Further, his toleration of his parents'

crackpot activities was wearing thin. Disappointed and disgusted that the workers of the United Kingdom hadn't followed the example of the Russians by overturning the monarchy and the capitalists, Mr and Mrs Blair had turned their attention to the troubles in Ireland and Ulster. They talked about supporting the Irish Republican Army. Jamie wanted nothing to do with that. Two years of war in France and Flanders were enough to last him a lifetime.

The London police had looked upon his parents as a barmy and harmless pair. The Belfast police didn't. They came round to talk to them, to take everyone's name and details, and to warn them against engaging in activities detrimental to civic order. So Jamie announced the following day that he was going back to London.

'Did I hear you say something I didn't like?' asked his mother.

'Well, I said it, Ma, on account of liking it myself.'

'I don't know how you can like it at all, Jamie, when yer dad and me are relyin' on you to 'elp us support the starvin' masses of Ireland.'

'Sod the starving masses,' said Jamie forthrightly.

'Jamie, I can't believe me ears,' said his mother.

16

'Might I make a suggestion?'

'Aye, do that, Jamie lad,' said his father.

'Why not let the starving masses of Ireland help themselves? All the starving masses elsewhere are helping themselves. Besides, the Irish have been promised Home Rule. I don't fancy poking my nose in and getting it flattened. It's the only nose I've got, and I'm not carrying a flattened one around for the rest of my life. Suppose I meet a girl? A man with no nose is bad news to any girl.'

'Jamie, don't talk like that,' said his mother, 'you know I don't 'old with makin' jokes about workers and starvin' masses, nor does yer dad.'

'I'll no' deny it, Jamie,' said his father, 'I canna approve jokes.'

'There you are,' said Mrs Blair. 'Jamie, we've forgiven you for goin' into the army and for not doin' what we 'oped you'd do about the Germans, and we're expectin' something dutiful from you now.'

'Will ye no' stand with us, laddie?' asked Mr Blair, his beard hairier than Rob Roy's.

'Take my advice and live a quiet life,' said Jamie, 'I'm going back to London. It's my home town and I miss it.'

He left Belfast in August, 1921. He found lodgings in Bermondsey, among his old haunts. He had enough money to keep

17

himself going for a bit. He looked for a job, walking miles in search of one. But he was only one more of thousands of unemployed ex-Servicemen. By perseverance, he did get some work, work for a day here and there, work for a week sometimes, and work shovelling rubble for a few hours at other times. Mostly, however, there was no work at all.

His parents wrote. His mother was now running a canteen for shipyard workers in Belfast, and trying to make them see how much better their future would be if they blew up the ships they were building. She informed Jamie she didn't hold out much hope for them, as they were nearly all Protestants and quite nasty-minded towards the IRA. Also, they said things about Karl Marx that she couldn't possibly repeat. Jamie's father, she said, was still at his job and still doing some honest sabotage work whenever he could, out of sympathy with the downtrodden masses. Look after yourself, she always said at the end of each letter, and asked him once why he didn't join the Labour Party.

Jamie told her that he'd gone off politics when he was seven.

He reached the stage where he had to look for cheaper lodgings. Just one room instead of two. Try Walworth, someone said. It's got its street kids, but Bermondsey's got a million. In Bermondsey, Jamie fell over street kids. He took some walks around Walworth. Its streets, with their rows of compact terraced houses, were an improvement on some of Bermondsey's. He knocked on doors. Got a room to let, missus?

'I would 'ave if I 'adn't got six kids and an old man six feet wide.' That was the kind of answer he got.

In March, 1922, just after his twenty-fourth birthday, he knocked on the door of a house in Larcom Street. It was six o'clock in the evening. A boy in a ragged jersey and patched shorts appeared. He was in need of a haircut, but his face was fairly clean.

' 'Ello,' he said, 'what d'yer want?'

'Evening,' said Jamie, 'you don't have a room to rent, I suppose?'

'Eh?'

'Someone told me to call here.'

'Must be barmy, then.'

'Who's that?' A man's gravelly voice was heard.

'It's a bloke askin' for a room,' called the boy.

'What's he think this is, then, a bleedin' 'otel?' The man arrived at the open door. He was big and burly, and he had the red face of a hard drinker. He wore a labourer's thick corduroy trousers, and was

19

in his waistcoat and shirtsleeves. He gave Jamie a cursory look. 'Who the hell are you?' he asked.

'Just a bloke looking for a room,' said Jamie.

'Well, I ask yer, mate, do I look like a landlady?'

'Not from here,' said Jamie.

Henry Mullins grinned. Jamie did not know it, but he'd caught the man in an unusually sociable mood. Normally, he only had sociable moods when he was in a pub. Outside of pubs he was, for the most part, a blot on the good-hearted face of cockney Walworth. He was forty-six, a widower and a bullying step-father.

'Down on yer luck, are yer?' he asked.

Jamie, thinking he might as well present himself as a real hard luck case, said, 'It's been a struggle, I can tell you, ever since I came out of the Army.'

'Young old-soldier, are yer?' said Henry Mullins.

'I feel like an old old-soldier sometimes,' said Jamie. Not only could he no longer afford his two rooms in Bermondsey, he also wanted to get away from an over-crowded environment. The large three-storeyed house in which he had his rooms was running over with countless kids and other lodgers. It was a bedlam of noise.

'Bloody Lloyd George and 'is promises

20

to you blokes, 'e ought to be 'ung, drawn an' quartered,' said Henry Mullins. He did a bit of thinking, such was his unusually sociable mood. 'Come into me parlour. Alfie, 'oppit.'

The boy disappeared. Jamie stepped into the passage and followed the man into the parlour. He'd seen better parlours. In this one, all the furniture looked a bit tired. The sofa was sagging. And the room was cold.

'I'll be frank,' he said, 'I can't afford a large rent.'

'Course yer can't, can yer?' Henry Mullins sounded as if he knew all the hard luck stories. He thought about the kids, his step-kids, all four of them. They took up three rooms between them. That was a sight too good for any four kids. 'Well, I tell yer, I ain't ever let any of me rooms, but I was a lodger meself once and nearly broke. Tell yer what, you can 'ave the upstairs front.' That was Kitty's room. Kitty was the eldest and a bleedin' spitfire. She could go in with the other two girls and lump it. 'Three an' six a week, that suit yer?'

Three and six a week was a bargain for an upstairs front, and Jamie knew it.

'It'll suit me fine,' he said.

'But I want goodwill from yer, matey,'

said Henry Mullins, 'I want a month's rent in advance an' no trouble. Just keep yerself to yerself. I get all the trouble I want from the kids, me bein' a widower. I ain't concerned with what your 'ard luck is, you just pay yer rent weekly in advance after the first month. You give me any trouble, and out yer go. What's yer moniker?'

'Jamie Blair.'

'Eh?'

'Jamie Blair. My father's a Scot.'

'Jamie's a name?' Henry Mullins's coarse red face creased in another grin. 'Gawd 'elp yer, you'll get the street kids catcallin' yer. I'm Mullins. When d'yer want to move in?'

'Monday all right?' said Jamie, thinking three and six a week was going to be kind to his pocket. He was down to a few quid and to dole money of twelve bob a week as a single man.

'It's all right with me,' said Henry Mullins.

'Can I see the room?'

'What for? It's a room, ain't it, with four walls and a winder.'

'I'd like to see it.'

'I 'ope you ain't bleedin' fussy,' said Henry Mullins. 'Oh, all right, foller me.' He led the way. He called through to the kitchen from the passage. 'You gettin' on with that supper, Kitty?'

'Yes, course I am,' called a girl's voice.

'You better. Come on,' he said to Jamie, and led the way up the stairs, which were covered with worn linoleum. The upstairs front bedroom was a reasonable size. The bed, with its brass and iron frame, was blanket-covered. Its striped pillows were bare. There was a wardrobe, a chest of drawers, a marble-topped washstand with bowl and pitcher, and a single upright chair beside the bed. On the bed were some feminine clothes. 'That's 'er all right,' said Henry Mullins, 'too lazy to put 'er clothes away. If yer want sheets for the bed, yer'll 'ave to bring yer own.'

'I'll do that,' said Jamie, 'and I'll get someone to deliver an armchair as well.' He had a few bits and pieces of his own. They'd help to give the room a warmer and homelier look. It was fairly stark as it was. 'The room's being used at the moment?'

'Kitty can move in with 'er sisters, that's all you need to know,' said Mullins.

'Should I meet your kids?' asked Jamie.

'What for?'

'It was just a thought.'

'You just keep yerself to yerself, Blair. I'll see they don't get under yer feet. That's all, I can't spare yer no more time. I'll collect yer first month's rent on Monday.'

Jamie moved in, with his bits and pieces and his own bed linen. It didn't take him long to find out that Henry Mullins was among the bad eggs of Walworth. Most Walworth men were hard-working, boisterous and warm-hearted. They were family men of a rough-and-ready kind, their bark always far worse than their bite. In the main they were providing husbands and good fathers, handing out necessary clips round the ears to tearaway sons. Precocious little daughters could wind most dads round their little fingers. There were, however, some men whose parents had done the world a disservice by allowing them to be born. Henry Mullins was one of them.

According to those neighbours who began to take hold of Jamie's ear as soon as they realized he was actually lodging with Mullins, the man had never been any kind of a father to his step-kids. There were four of them, seventeen-year-old Kitty, fourteen-year-old twins Carrie and Chloe, and twelve-year-old Alfie. Mullins had married their widowed mother six years ago in 1915. He drove a dustcart for the council and his face had shown the red ravages of drink for years. He and the kids' mother both liked more than a drop, and when she fell drunkenly off a Thames pleasure boat and drowned herself in 1919, that put paid to even the smallest fatherly feelings Mullins might have had. He didn't like being left with four kids who weren't his and to whom he had never shown any kind of tolerance or affection. Since the death of their mother, he had twice tried to dump them in an institution for waifs and strays.

Jamie, keeping himself to himself, as Mullins had demanded, nevertheless saw something of the kids. He made his regular visits to the Labour Exchange, he went tramping in search of work, and he picked up the odd temporary job here and there. In between he got to know the kids. They all looked half-starved. Alfie, Carrie and Chloe were attending school, and Kitty, who had no job, looked after the family, doing the housework, the washing and the cooking, for which she received not a word of thanks. Mullins handed little out to any of them except cuffs, beltings and complaints. After only a fortnight in the house, Jamie wondered how long he could continue to keep himself to himself. He liked the kids, and he liked the way he could sometimes hear Kitty standing up to her step-father. What he didn't like was the sound of Mullins hitting her.

He brought a sixpenny bar of milk chocolate back to his lodgings one day. It was as much as he could afford. He shared it out among the kids before their father came home from his work. Large hungry eyes stared at him in astonishment and bliss.

'Mister, oh, yer lovely,' breathed Kitty.

'Choc'late, look, Carrie,' said Chloe.

' 'Ave we ever 'ad choc'late?' asked Carrie, breathless.

'I ain't, but I'm 'aving some now,' said Alfie, and Jamie, watching them devour it, wondered how it was that a man could not enjoy kids, whether they were his own or not.

The atmosphere in the house when Mullins was present was uneasy and unhappy. Whenever he was out and the kids were waiting for him to come home, they were quiet and subdued. Only when they were in the street, playing with other kids, did Jamie hear their natural cockney ebullience.

Something would happen one day. One could sense it. One day, perhaps, angry men of Larcom Street would descend on Henry Mullins and put him in hospital. Jamie began to feel he'd like to do it himself.

Chapter Two

It was fifteen minutes to six on a Wednesday evening in late April, and Jamie was walking home to his lodgings. He had just finished half a day's work. It was half-days for a whole week along with other unemployed men. The job was clearing the rubble and debris of houses being knocked down by the council in a street off the New Kent Road, not far from the Elephant and Castle. Eight men, half a day each for six days, at a shilling an hour. It was one way the council could share out work to unemployed men. Jamie's stints were in the afternoons.

It was ten to six when he let himself into the house in Larcom Street. He liked Larcom Street. The small terraced houses were tidy-looking, the iron railings strong enough to defy any attempts to break them or uproot them. Gates were solidly hinged and swung open smoothly. Doorsteps were clean and window curtains were clean, even if a little yellow in some cases. East Street market wasn't too far away, and was a boon to every Walworth housewife. Also to blokes like himself.

He climbed the stairs. Reaching the landing, he heard a sudden cry of pain from the kitchen below. It was followed by a girl's loud and indignant protest.

'We didn't, we didn't!'

That in turn was followed by a man's bawled curse. Shrieks succeeded that, and then came the distinct sound of a chair crashing over. Jamie knew what was going on. Henry Mullins was home from his work and his step-kids were getting knocked about again. Jamie gritted his teeth. He'd left the troubles of Belfast and Ulster in the hope of finding peace and quiet, along with a job. He'd run into Henry Mullins, who was more disturbing than the IRA. He heard him lift his voice.

'Yer lazy good-fer-nothings, I'll learn the lot of yer! An' you'll do to start with, yer little bitch!'

Jamie heard someone dart from the kitchen, someone who yelled at Mullins. Kitty. She'd slipped him. She came rushing up the stairs, still yelling. Jamie gritted his teeth again. After her came heavy feet and a roaring voice. Kitty hurled herself across the landing in the hope of getting into the bedroom she shared with her twin sisters. She could shut herself in there, if she could lock the door in time. But her red-faced step-father, on her heels, reached for her, grabbed her by the arm and hauled on her.

'Let me go!' gasped Kitty.

'Not likely, yer lazy lyin' little bitch!' he bellowed.

'Give it a rest,' said Jamie, 'what's she done this time?'

'What ain't she done, yer mean,' shouted Mullins, face livid. 'Nothing all bleedin' day, that's what she's done.'

'I have, I have!' gasped Kitty, black hair wild, huge dark brown eyes fierce, and cheekbones sharp where her face lacked flesh. 'Only I couldn't get no supper, there wasn't nothing in the larder except a bit of bread, and I told yer there wasn't—oh!' She cried out as her step-father cuffed her. Jamie, disgusted that a man could humiliate as well as hurt a seventeen-year-old girl, held himself in only with an effort.

'Yer lyin' little slut, there was eggs an' bacon an' spuds!' roared Mullins, shaking the girl.

'No, I cooked them for last night's supper, you know I did, an' you didn't leave no money to buy anything for tonight,' cried Kitty.

'Yer lyin' slut, there was enough in the larder yesterday for two suppers!'

'There wasn't!' Kitty was fierce and spitting. She was also a girl desperate with want. Her frock was shabby, her stockings full of darns, her shoes almost falling apart. If she was frightened of what her step-father might do to her, the fierceness of defiance showed for all that. It was also the fierceness of hatred.

'Down yer come,' shouted Mullins, 'down to the kitchen, where I can take me belt to yer!'

'Give over,' said Jamie. Six weeks he'd been lodging here, and if he couldn't afford to get himself chucked out, nor could he afford what it would do to his self-respect if he stood aside and let Mullins drag the girl downstairs. With the kind of temper he had, he'd finish up murdering her one day. Or one of the other kids. 'Calm down a bit.'

'Mister, don't let 'im belt me,' begged Kitty.

'Leave her with me,' said Jamie.

'You mind yer own bleedin' business,' growled Mullins, 'or out yer go, and quick. Got it?'

'Be reasonable,' said Jamie, willing to try talking the man out of his temper. 'Look, they've got no mum, can't you go easy on them? There's none of us perfect.'

'Shut yer trap, you ponce,' said Mullins, and dragged Kitty over the landing to the top of the stairs. The other kids were still down in the kitchen, and Jamie thought they were probably awaiting their step-father's return in terror. The burly man hauled on Kitty, and Kitty pulled. With a fierce little twist and jerk, she broke free and eeled away. With a roar, Mullins prepared to launch himself at her. Jamie stepped forward and blocked him. He was as tall as Mullins, but only half his thickness. Mullins was built like a barrel. Livid, he swung a fist at his lodger. Jamie saw it coming a mile off. He swayed out of its way and planted a hand in the man's chest to hold him off. It put Mullins off balance. He tottered backwards. Jamie saw his mouth open and his purple colour recede all in a split second, and then he fell all the way down the stairs. Tumbling and rolling, his head glancing the wall, he fell bruisingly to crash on the passage floor. He lay there without movement.

'Oh, Mister Blair,' gasped Kitty, 'he'll kill you—an' me too!'

Jamie went down to the passage at speed. Mullins was on his back, his red ravaged face now the colour of stale pastry. He was quite still, and Jamie had a nasty feeling that he wasn't even breathing. He went down on one knee beside him. From the kitchen there was only silence, as if the crashing sound of the fall had transfixed the frightened kids. From the top of the stairs, Kitty stared down at her

31

supine step-father. Jamie placed a hand on his waistcoat and felt for a heartbeat. There wasn't even a flicker of a beat. His mouth was still open and his eyes looked glassy and unseeing. Jamie caught the smell of the man's dustcart exuding from his clothing. He was not a man who washed himself or changed his garments when he came home from his work, he was a man who had spent too many years going downhill. And he'd tried to pull his step-kids downhill with him. Hell, thought Jamie, he'd hit Kitty for the last time. If there was one thing he was certain about after his years in France and Flanders, it was that he knew when he was looking at a dead man.

Henry Mullins, he knew, was as dead as a dodo.

Kitty came creeping down.

'Is he knocked right out, mister?' she breathed.

Jamie, still down on one knee, looked up at her, a girl who might have had the feminine appeal of her age if her dark wild hair and her shabby clothes had not been such a mess, and her cheekbones not so sharp.

Thinking there was no point in trying to dissemble, he said, 'It's worse than just being knocked out, Kitty.'

'What d'you mean?'

'Take a deep breath and look at him,' said Jamie.

Kitty, bending, took a long look. A little sharp gasp escaped her.

'He's not—mister, he ain't dead, is he?'

'I'm afraid he is, Kitty.'

'Oh, me gawd,' whispered Kitty, 'you sure?'

'I'm sure.'

'Yes, you've been a soldier, 'aven't you?'

'Yes.'

'He's gone, then?' she said. 'Oh, Mister Blair, gawd bless you.'

That staggered Jamie.

'What did you say?' he asked.

'I'm glad,' whispered Kitty in her fierce way, 'we'll all be glad. You did for him, Mister Blair. Bless you.'

'Wait a minute—'

'Don't you worry, Mister Blair, I ain't goin' to say he was pushed.'

'You're dead right you're not,' said Jamie.

'He just lost his balance an' fell, didn't he?' said Kitty, and Jamie thought there was actually a little smile lurking.

'Let's get this straight,' he said crisply. 'There was no push, I just put my hand on his chest to hold him off.'

'Course you did, Mister Blair,' said Kitty kindly.

Kindly? That was how it sounded to

33

Jamie. The young devil.

'I think we'd better start again,' he said. 'Your step-father was after taking hold of you again, I put myself in his way, he swung a punch and I put my hand against his chest to hold him off.'

'Yes, course you did, Mister Blair,' said Kitty, eyeing the body far more in curiosity than sorrow. 'But I ain't goin' to say so, I ain't goin' to say you touched him at all. He just fell. He lost his balance on the top of the stairs. I saw him, didn't I? D'you think he broke his neck?'

'Doesn't look like it,' said Jamie, 'but he might have snapped his spine. That could have done it. All the same, don't talk about not saying there was any push, because that's like implying there might have been. There wasn't.'

'Yes, that's what I mean, don't I?' said Kitty. 'It's best to say you didn't touch him at all. Best to say he just lost his balance when he was pullin' at me and I got free.'

Jamie gave her a searching look. She smiled at him. Kindly. What the hell is she up to? She's right, of course, and she knows it. To admit he'd touched the man in any way could easily make the police consider a charge of manslaughter, even though he'd acted in defence of Kitty.

'Someone's got to go for the police,' he said.

'I'll go,' said Kitty, 'I'll run all the way to the station in Rodney Road, it's not far. First, I'd best tell me brother an' sisters they don't have to worry about him no more, only about who's goin' to look after us now. It's a blessin' we've got you here, Mister Blair. I'll tell them you'll look after us for a bit, shall I? They like you, we all do, and as you're our lodger you could look after us quite easy, couldn't you?'

Coming to his feet, Jamie said, 'Now just a minute, you monkey—'

'I won't be a tick,' said Kitty, and darted into the kitchen. He heard her talking to the kids, and he heard Alfie exclaim.

'Oh, crikey Moses! Are yer sure, Kitty?'

Then they all seemed to be talking at once. Kitty reappeared after a couple of minutes.

'It's all right, I told them he just fell,' she said. She sounded very matter-of-fact. It might have shaken her in the first place, the sight of her step-father lying dead, but it hadn't distressed her. Jamie could understand that. Mullins had beaten her and her brother and sisters all too often. He'd neglected them, half-starved them, made them do without bed linen, and twice tried to get rid of them. 'They've been too scared to come out from the kitchen,' said Kitty, 'but they're all right now, they don't mind that he's dead. Now I'll run to the police station.'

'Wait,' said Jamie, a sinewy-looking young man of five-feet-ten with dark brown hair and features that nature had hewn in firm but cheerful lines. 'We need to get a doctor too. You go for a doctor, I'll go for the police.'

'But we can't leave the kids alone in the 'ouse with him lyin' dead here in the passage,' protested Kitty. 'They won't like bein' alone with a corpse. Well, he is a corpse, ain't he? If he's not, we'll all be disappointed, and I don't mind sayin' so.'

'I know how you feel,' said Jamie, 'but don't talk like that, Kitty, it's not decent.'

'Oh, sorry, I'm sure,' said Kitty, 'I didn't know I'd got to be posh and nice-speakin'.'

'It's nothing to do with being posh,' said Jamie. 'Never mind, I'll stay here, then. Who's going for a doctor?'

'Alfie!' she called, and out came twelve-year-old Alfie. From what Jamie had seen of the boy in six weeks, he seemed to own only two worn jerseys and two pairs of patched shorts, in which he alternated from week to week. If he wasn't exactly thin, he could still have done with a bit more flesh to his body. His light brown hair still needed cutting, and his boots needed mending. He took a look at his lifeless step-father, and with the same kind of curiosity that Kitty had shown.

'Crikey, is 'e really dead, mister?' he asked.

' 'Fraid so, Alfie,' said Jamie.

'Blimey,' Alfie said, and his brown eyes blinked. They all had brown eyes, except that Kitty's grew so fiercely dark at times they looked the colour of burnt sienna. 'Blimey,' breathed Alfie again, 'that just shows what can 'appen if you fall down the stairs. 'E knocked me down 'em once, but it didn't kill me, it just give me a few bruises, and I 'ad to tell me teacher I walked into a ladder. Look, 'e's got a bruise hisself, on 'is face.'

'Don't just stand there lookin',' said Kitty, 'go an' get Dr McManus. I told Chloe an' Carrie to stay in the kitchen, Mister Blair, we don't want them comin' out here and seein' him. They don't mind him bein' dead, but they won't like lookin' at him. Well, me and Alfie'll go now.'

Off they went, leaving Jamie feeling things weren't real. Henry Mullins, alive and breathing ten minutes ago, was now stone dead. And neither Kitty nor Alfie had shown any kind of grief. It looked to Jamie as if the man was going to his grave without his step-kids shedding a single tear for him. That was nobody's fault but his own. When he'd married their widowed mother he'd acquired a ready-made family. Any decent man would have made something of that. Mullins had only made a little hell for the kids. And if some of the neighbours were right, that the mother had been a drinker too, exactly what kind of a life had those kids had?

According to Kitty, they were all glad their step-father was dead. Jamie could believe that. Kitty, with her mane of unkempt black hair and her darkly fierce eyes that made her look like a young gypsy, had hated him. But the things she had said.

You did for him, Mister Blair. Bless you.

I'm glad, we'll all be glad.

I ain't going to say he was pushed.

Best to say he lost his balance and fell.

You could look after us quite easy, couldn't you?

What a hope, he thought. He had his work cut out to look after himself. Job prospects still being close to nil, he might consider emigrating.

He drew the latchcord in through the letter-box to make sure no neighbours let themselves in. They did that in cockney London, they went in and out of each other's house regularly. They'd use a latch-cord, step in and call, 'You 'ome, Mrs Smith?' Lately, some of them here had been stepping in and calling, 'You 'ome, Mr Blair?' That was when they knew Mullins was out. It was as if they'd seen the lodger as someone they could talk to about Mullins and his step-kids, as if they thought he was in a position to help the three girls and their brother. Well, he'd tried to help Kitty and the result had been fatal.

I ain't going to say he was pushed, Mister Blair.

What had made her say that? He thought about the fatal moment. Had he pushed the man? He'd avoided a blow from him and planted a hand to hold him off, no more. But it had cost Mullins his balance and his life. All the same, Jamie convinced himself there'd been no push, then went into the kitchen. Carrie and Chloe were sitting at the table. Just fourteen, the twin girls hardly looked robust. It wasn't difficult to believe Mullins had kept them half-starved for years. It beat Jamie, the fact that a man couldn't like kids, never mind whether they were his own or not.

The kitchen was fairly tidy, but there was a lack of homeliness. Most cockney kitchens were decidedly homely. Families lived, laughed, quarrelled and celebrated

39

in their kitchens. Kids grew up in them, mums and dads grew old in them. Jamie didn't think there'd been much laughter or celebrating in this kitchen. It had nothing of the atmosphere that came from parental affection, and from kids knowing there was always food in the larder. There might not be a mountain of it, but as long as there was some, as long as kids knew they weren't going to suffer dire hunger, there was always a warm homeliness to be found in a kitchen.

Carrie and Chloe both had dark brown hair and brown eyes, and if their spirit had been subdued over the years, the spirit common to most cockney kids, it hadn't been smothered. It surfaced at school, or in the street, or in almost any place that kept them out of their step-father's reach. Jamie thought that God alone knew when he had last bought decent clothes for any of his four step-kids. Everything the three girls wore looked shabby. The frocks Carrie and Chloe had on were so limp and lifeless that the garments seemed to be long dead from old age. And their hair, like Kitty's, always seemed in need of a comb and brush.

'Well, you two,' said Jamie, 'it's a bit of a sorry day.'

'Kitty said 'e's dead, but that we wasn't to go an' look,' said Chloe.

'Is 'e really a goner, mister?' asked Carrie.

'I think the doctor's going to say so. Then the police will arrange to have him taken away.' Jamie felt it was no good saying how sorry he was that their step-dad had passed on. They wouldn't respond to that. 'Listen, my bairns, when it's all over, when he's been taken away, I'll get Alfie to go out and buy us all some fried fish and chips. Will that cheer things up a bit?'

Eyes shone. They'd had little to eat all day.

'Mister, did you say fish an' chips?' asked Carrie.

'Yes, we 'eard him, didn't we?' said Chloe.

'I'm only askin',' said Carrie. 'You really goin' to treat us, mister?'

Jamie was far from flush, but he had enough for a treat, and he could look forward to collecting twenty-four bob at the end of the week, his wages for six half-days of work.

'Yes, I'm really going to treat you,' he said.

'Mister, do yer like us, then?' asked Carrie.

'Course 'e does, don't yer, mister?' said Chloe.

'I was just askin', that's all,' said Carrie. They were as alike as two peas from the same pod, except where Carrie was questioning, Chloe was positive.

'Asking is how you get to know things,' said Jamie, feeling a little chat was called for. 'Mind, you need answers. I had a friend who ought to have grown up knowing everything, because he never stopped asking about everything. But he was always so busy asking questions that he never had time to listen to any answers. So he grew up not knowing any more than when he'd started.'

'Oh, Carrie listens to answers, don't yer, Carrie?' said Chloe.

'Always,' said Carrie.

'But then she forgets what she's been told, so she 'as to ask again, don't yer, Carrie?'

'Not every time,' said Carrie.

'Keep trying,' said Jamie.

'Yes, I like askin',' said Carrie, and proved it. 'Mister, is 'e still out there?'

'Yes, we've got to leave him there until the police and the doctor get here.'

'What did 'e die of?' asked Carrie.

'Falling down the stairs.'

'Kitty already told us that,' said Chloe. She frowned. 'I 'ope we don't 'ave someone like 'im come and look after us.'

'Kitty'll look after you until some relatives—yes, what relatives do you have?'

'We don't 'ave many,' said Chloe. 'Well, we 'ad some, but I don't know where they went to. They was our mum's cousins, I think.'

'Mum took to drink,' said Carrie with a sigh.

'Kitty says we're not to talk about that,' said Chloe.

'Are your mum's cousins the only relatives you've got?' asked Jamie.

'Well, 'e had a sister,' said Chloe.

None of them referred to Mullins as their dad, Jamie noted. It was either 'he' or 'him'.

'I don't think she liked our mum,' said Carrie. 'Have you got a mum an' dad, mister?'

'As a matter of fact, I have,' said Jamie. 'Slightly potty, though.'

Carrie giggled.

'I think we're supposed to be grievin',' said Chloe.

'Kitty didn't say so,' said Carrie. 'Did she?'

'No, but we're supposed to be,' said Chloe. 'Well, you 'ave to be when someone passes on.'

'I don't feel grievin',' said Carrie, 'specially as we're goin' to be treated to fish an' chips.'

'Can we make you a cup of tea, mister?' asked Chloe.

'We got some condensed milk,' said Carrie. 'Well, I think we 'ave. D'you think we 'ave, Chloe?'

'Yes, there's still some in the tin,' said Chloe. 'We don't mind makin' you tea, mister.'

'Well, I'm no' minded to let you make it now, y'ken,' said Jamie. They liked to hear him take on a Scottish brogue. 'I think we'll wait.'

It was three minutes later when Kitty returned. With her were two uniformed policemen and a CID sergeant.

Chapter Three

Kitty and Jamie were in the parlour with the police. The body of Henry Mullins was still in the passage, but with a blanket covering it. Outside in the street, a little group of neighbours had collected. Kitty had been spotted coming home in company with the policemen.

Jamie had given his version of events, leaving out the fact that Mullins had taken a swipe at him and that he'd placed a hand on his chest to hold him off. He saw, as Kitty had seen, that that might lead to suspicions and awkward questions. In any case, he was clear in his mind that there'd been no push. Kitty had given her version at the police station. The CID sergeant now asked her to repeat what she had said.

'Oh, all right,' said Kitty in a suffering way, and recounted how her step-father, on arriving home from work, had accused her of being lazy and useless. And he'd accused all of them of eating up the eggs and bacon and potatoes that she was supposed to have cooked for his supper and theirs. She told him that that had been last night's supper. He went for her, knocking a chair over. She ran upstairs. He came after her and caught her on the landing. 'Mister Blair was there,' she said, 'and asked him what I'd done. He told Mister Blair to mind 'is own business or he'd chuck him out. He was goin' to drag me downstairs an' give me a beltin', like I told you at the police station. Mister Blair told him to calm down, an' gave him a frownin' look.'

'A frowning look?' said the CID sergeant. 'Like what?'

'Like this,' said Kitty, and fixed her face in a ferocious scowl. 'But he still kept tryin' to drag me down the stairs.' Kitty still wouldn't say 'Dad' or even 'step-father'. 'Then I twisted meself free and he lost his balance and fell. He fell all the way down. Do I have to keep tellin' this, mister?'

'We have to get things exactly right,' said one of the uniformed constables.

'Mr Blair,' said the CID man, 'it beats me how a man can fall down a short flight of stairs and kill himself.'

'It beat me too at the time,' said Jamie. 'If he'd broken his neck, that could account for it.'

'So it could, but it doesn't look as if he did.'

'Not a mark on him,' said the CID man.

46

'No?' said Jamie, with Kitty looking from one to the other.

'Except a bruise on his cheek.'

'You might find more than that when he's been undressed,' said Jamie. 'I suppose you have to wait for the doctor to do that. Mind you, he did fall from top to bottom, and I wouldn't call fourteen stairs a short flight myself.'

'Seems bad luck on the man, though,' said the sergeant. 'How did you get on with him?'

'I hardly saw him except when I paid the rent, and I've only been here just over six weeks.'

'Did it make you angry, seeing him cuff this girl?'

'Is that a serious question?' asked Jamie.

'Natural one, don't you think, sir?'

'Yes, it made me angry,' said Jamie, wondering if Alfie was having a job getting hold of the doctor.

'Well, you've said Mr Mullins lost his balance when Miss Edwards here slipped his grip.' Edwards was the kids' real surname. 'But I have to ask if you did more than tell him to leave her alone. There's the bruise on his cheek.'

'I didn't hit the—' Jamie, about to say bugger, checked himself. 'I didn't hit the man, if that's what you mean.'

'Here, pardon me, I'm sure,' said Kitty

to the sergeant, 'but I'll get upset if you go on at Mister Blair. He's a gent, he is, he don't go around hittin' people, nor kids, neither. He didn't touch—' She paused and frowned. 'Me step-father,' she said with a grimace.

'Did your step-father fall heavily?' asked the CID man.

'Like a sack of coal,' said Kitty. 'I suppose that's 'eavy, ain't it? Mister Blair went down an' looked at him straightaway, but he couldn't do him no good. He'd expired.'

One of the constables coughed.

'Expired, miss?' he said.

'Yes, he was dead. I never saw anyone more dead.' Kitty sounded cross, as if her step-father had made a thorough nuisance of himself by dying like that. 'I went down an' looked at him meself, and I said to meself oh, lor', he's expired. Mister Blair, he knew it right away, he's been in the Army.'

'In the war, Mr Blair?' enquired the CID sergeant.

'Two years and a bit,' said Jamie, 'I came out early in 1919.'

'You look very fit,' said the sergeant, and Jamie knew the man was implying he was capable of delivering a very effective blow.

'Well, tramping around London looking

for work keeps a lot of us fit,' he said.

'Are you unemployed, sir?' asked the second uniformed man.

'Yes,' said Jamie, 'although I'm doing a week's part-time work at the moment.'

'You ain't half got a sauce, keepin' on at Mister Blair,' said Kitty. 'I don't know what I'd 'ave done if he hadn't been here to take care of things. I'd have 'ad hysterics, and so would me brother an' sisters. But Mister Blair acted like a real soldier, calming things down and sendin' me to the police station an' me brother to the doctor's. That Alfie, I don't know where he's got to.'

'Well, we'd like a doctor here fairly quickly,' said the CID man. 'Meanwhile, let's go up to the landing and you and Mr Blair can show us just how it happened.'

'I don't like all this palaver on top of everything else,' said Kitty. 'I ain't used to seein' a step-father fall down the stairs in a fatal way, it's been a shock, and me an' me sisters are goin' to feel ill later, I can tell you. But all right, I'll take you upstairs an' show you.'

She led the way. One of the uniformed men detached himself and made for the kitchen. Jamie suspected he was going to ask questions of the twins.

On the landing, the CID man, Sergeant Watkins, suggested he should stand in for

49

Mullins. Jamie showed him where Mullins had been on the top stair, and Kitty showed him how he had been holding her arm and dragging at her. And she showed him how she had twisted herself free.

'Then he lost his balance,' she said. 'Well, he was pulling on empty air then, wasn't he? Mister, you ain't tryin' to blame me, are you?'

'We're only trying to get things clear,' said Sergeant Watkins.

'Well, I don't know how much clearer they can be than what me an' Mister Blair have showed you,' said Kitty, looking as if she was about to lose her temper. Jamie thought that ill-treatment and neglect, far from breaking her, had turned her into a spitfire.

'We're grateful for any help,' said Sergeant Watkins, and turned to Jamie. 'Exactly where were you standing, Mr Blair, when Mr Mullins fell?'

'Where I am now.'

Sergeant Watkins, standing on the top stair himself, said, 'Pretty close to the deceased?'

'Well, of course,' said Jamie, and Kitty made little vexed noises. 'I was trying to make him see reason, and he'd just told me to mind my own bleedin' business. He was holding on to Kitty while we were exchanging words, and I wanted him to let her go. We were all fairly close to each other, as you can see. Kitty got free suddenly, and that was it, he just fell backwards.'

The CID man turned his head, looked down the flight of stairs to the passage and gauged the extent of the fall.

'Yes, not such a short flight, Mr Blair, I agree,' he said. 'Mind if we do that again, Miss Edwards? Let me take hold of your arm again and do some more pulling.'

'Well, I don't know,' said Kitty, eyes showing a little fire, 'I've got me young sisters in shock down there in the kitchen, and me—yes, me step-father down there in the passage lyin' dead. I'm upset, I am, but all right, I'd better do what you want.' She let the sergeant take hold of her arm, just below the elbow, with Jamie close to them. The sergeant pulled at her, and she pulled back. She jerked and twisted. The sergeant's hold did not break. 'Come on, let go,' she said.

'You're sure his grip slipped?' asked Sergeant Watkins.

'Course I'm sure,' said Kitty crossly, 'it 'appened, didn't it?'

'It's not happening now,' he said, the uniformed constable looking on silently.

'Wait a moment,' said Jamie, 'you can't put yourself in the place of Mr Mullins to that extent. You can't act as he acted,

51

or react as he did. You're holding Kitty knowing she twisted free, and you're making sure she can't. You're also keeping yourself balanced. Mr Mullins, remember, was in a hell of a temper, and he was letting me have some of it, as well as Kitty.' Jamie realized it had been a piece of good sense to say nothing about the hand he'd placed on Mullin's chest. This CID sergeant would be making a real meal of that. 'I dare say my presence and my protests distracted Mr Mullins, because I assure you Kitty did slip his grip. His eyes rolled then and turned wide open and glassy, and he fell. Are you wanting a different story?'

'It's shockin', that's what it is,' said Kitty, 'he's tryin' to blame me. I'll faint in a minute, what with him lyin' dead down there and all the shock an' worry it's give me, and now a policeman tryin' to say that if I'd let meself be dragged down to the kitchen and taken a beltin', there wouldn't 'ave been no fatal fall. That's what you're tryin' to do,' she said accusingly to Sergeant Watkins. 'If you don't mind, kindly let go of me arm.'

'It's our job to establish the facts, miss,' he said, releasing her arm. 'Which is all I'm doing. An accident like this is a nasty business.'

'So it is,' said Jamie, 'especially for Kitty and her brother and sisters.' he

52

knew that what the sergeant meant was that the police needed to be sure it had been an accident.

The knocker hammered the front door. The latchcord was still hanging inside it. Kitty ran down the stairs to answer the knock.

Alfie had arrived with Dr McManus.

Another discussion took place in the parlour after the medical examination of the dead man. The discussion began with Dr McManus stating his findings.

'Heart attack,' he said.

'Heart attack?' said Sergeant Watkins.

'He was quite dead before he hit the passage floor.'

'He had a heart attack during his fall?'

'Either during it or immediately preceding it,' said Dr McManus, well-known to the whole of Walworth as a very caring general practitioner.

'Ah,' said Sergeant Watkins, and rubbed his chin. 'Could a blow have caused it?'

'What blow?' asked Dr McManus.

'I observed a bruise on his cheek.'

'Superficial, sergeant. A blow would have caused a deeper contusion.' Dr McManus refrained from commenting on the implication that either Kitty or Jamie had hit Mullins. 'I spoke to Miss Edwards and to Mr Blair before I began my examination, and you heard Mr Blair inform me that as Mr Mullins lost his balance his colour receded and his eyes rolled and turned upwards. I bore this in mind when I made my examination. My conclusion is that his heart failed him, and my opinion is that it happened before he actually fell. He fell backwards, you said, Mr Blair?'

'He did,' said Jamie, 'he went down with his limbs all over the place.'

'Yes, he did,' said Kitty.

'No control over his limbs,' said Dr McManus, 'he was dead.'

'Beats me,' said Sergeant Watkins.

Jamie thought about the fatal moment.

'Dr McManus, when he knew he'd lost his balance and was going to fall, might that have brought on his heart attack?' he asked.

'It's feasible,' said the doctor. 'He was a patient of mine, I treated him occasionally for tinea—ringworm—and found he had a heart murmur.'

'I bet that was it,' said Kitty, 'I bet he didn't like knowing he was goin' to fall, and that he might break 'is neck. I bet it was such a shock to him that he just went and expired. Don't you think so, doctor?'

'It's a possibility, Kitty,' said Dr Mc-Manus.

'His awful temper did for him,' said Kitty soberly.

'Yes, very unfortunate,' said Dr Mc-Manus, 'and I must stand by my opinion that he was dead before he fell.'

'I've never seen a man lose all his colour in a split second,' said Jamie.

'Are we sure about all this?' asked Sergeant Watkins.

'I'm quite sure myself, sergeant,' said Dr McManus. 'I'm terribly sorry, Kitty, but I'll see to everything that's necessary. I'm afraid you're in a bit of a fix now, aren't you?'

'Oh, we'll be all right,' said Kitty, 'and Mr Blair's goin' to help us, bein' our lodger. Doctor, could I get a sort of widow's pension?'

Sergeant Watkins blinked. The atmosphere wasn't heavy with grief. Jamie felt the police realized Mullins was hardly likely to be mourned, and Dr McManus probably knew he wouldn't be. And he was right, Kitty and her brother and sisters were definitely in a fix. There'd be no money coming in except the three-and- six rent from Jamie. Any help he could give would be strictly limited. As to a sort of widow's pension, he thought only Kitty could ask a question like that.

'I'm afraid that's impossible to answer, Kitty,' said Dr McManus, 'but there might be some help coming from the town hall.'

'I'll take her round there,' said Jamie, 'and see what can be squeezed out of them. Are there any more questions, sergeant?'

'None I can think of at the moment,' said Sergeant Watkins, 'but there'll be an inquest.'

'Yes, of course,' said Dr McManus, although he'd have liked to save Kitty that kind of ordeal. 'I'm ready to issue a death certificate stating Mr Mullins died from heart failure.'

'Well, there's been the accident of falling down the stairs, doctor,' said Sergeant Watkins, 'which calls for an inquest.'

'Kitty, you understand you and Mr Blair will have to attend?' said Dr McManus.

'Oh, I suppose so,' said Kitty.

'It's understood,' said Jamie.

'Thanks for all your help, Mr Blair,' said the sergeant, 'and for yours, miss.'

'It's been a lot of palaver,' said Kitty, 'I'm just thankful we've got Mister Blair here to look after us.'

I'll have to watch this little lady, thought Jamie.

It was all over. The police had gone, so had Dr McManus, and the body of Henry Mullins had been taken away, much to the gaping curiosity of neighbours. One knocked on the door. Jamie gave her

56

details of the fatal accident, then asked for Kitty and her brother and sisters to be left alone for the time being. He said he would see to them. He kept the latchcord inside the door.

In the kitchen, he eyed the boy and the three girls. Something had to be done about their situation, and something had to be done about their hungry look and their shabbiness.

'Well, what comes next?' he asked. 'Does anyone know?'

'I dunno nothing,' said Alfie, 'except *he* ain't with us any more.'

'Fried fish and chips, that's what comes next,' said Jamie.

'There, I told you, Carrie,' said Chloe, 'I told you 'e'd remember.'

'Well, I only thought 'e might not,' said Carrie.

'Mister, what d'you mean, fish an' chips?' asked Kitty.

'Cor, I like the sound of it meself,' said Alfie.

There they were, all four of them, not a sign of regret showing about their step-father's sudden drop into eternity, only the suggestion of a promise of fish and chips was perking them up.

'It's my treat,' said Jamie cheerfully. 'Would you like to go and get them, Alfie?'

'Blimey, not 'alf,' said Alfie, 'we ain't 'ad fish an' chips since old Ma Parsons 'ad one over the eight an' give me a bob instead of an 'a'penny for 'elping 'er to find out where she lived. We all 'ad fish an' chips then, didn't we, Kitty?'

'Yes, so we did,' said Kitty, looking at their lodger in a speculative way.

'Are we really goin' to 'ave some now?' asked Carrie.

'Carrie, I wish you'd listen,' said Chloe, 'didn't you hear mister ask Alfie to go an' get them?'

'I only asked because I'm 'ungry,' said Carrie.

Jamie, hungry himself, said, 'Here's the money, Alfie, for five portions of fish and chips.' He gave the boy one-and-threepence. It made the kind of hole in his pocket that caused a bit of a chilly draught. It left him, in fact, with only a couple of bob to keep the wolf from his room door. All his savings had long gone.

'Mister Blair, you're a kind gent, honest you are,' said Kitty, as Alfie went on his way. 'We're all really 'ungry.'

'So am I,' said Jamie, but he knew his problems weren't like theirs. Neighbours would rally round to some extent, but officialdom was very unlikely to knock and offer Kitty a weekly allowance. Unless she reported they were destitute, which would

58

mean them being taken to an institution of some kind, she'd be expected to find herself a job that would help to keep her and the others. 'What's the house rent, Kitty?'

'Eleven bob a week,' she said.

'Well, we'll have to sell the family treasures.'

'Some hopes,' said Kitty.

'Ain't we got any fam'ly treasures?' asked Carrie.

'Course we ain't,' said Chloe, 'that man only 'ad money that 'e kept in his pocket. He just give Kitty a bit now and again to buy food with, that's all.'

'Something'll turn up,' said Jamie.

'Don't you worry, Mister Blair,' said Kitty, 'I'll get a job, you see, I'll get one in a shop or down the market or somewhere. Mind, I don't know we could keep cheerful if we didn't 'ave you. We're thankful about that, ain't we, you girls?'

'We like you, mister,' said Carrie. 'Don't we, Chloe?'

'You gave us choc'late once,' said Chloe.

'That man never gave us anything,' said Carrie.

It was 'that man' now, thought Jamie.

'Carrie and Chloe like it that you're goin' to be a help, Mister Blair,' said Kitty. 'I said to them, I said you could be their big brother. They've never had a big brother, only Alfie. They'd like you for one, so would Alfie.'

'Big brothers ought to have jobs,' said Jamie cautiously, 'and I'm still looking.'

'But you're workin' this week,' said Kitty.

'Only for this week.'

'Oh, I'm sure you'll get a real job soon, a man like you that's been in the war,' said Kitty. 'We can manage till then. Look, I've been in his room and found quite a bit, and the police gave me what money was in his pockets. See, we've got all this to keep us goin'.'

A grubby handkerchief appeared in her hand. She placed it on the kitchen table and opened it up. Silver chinked. Jamie saw a pound's-worth at least, with several copper coins, two pound notes and a ten-bob note.

'Crikey!' gasped Chloe, eyes goggling.

'Oh, I never seen so much money,' breathed Carrie.

'Mister Blair, we've got three pounds, fourteen shillings an' sevenpence,' said Kitty.

'Well, that's useful,' said Jamie. 'If you put aside thirty bob, that'll pay your rent for four weeks, with my lodger's rent added to it. That'll leave you two pounds, four shillings and sevenpence, which'll keep you for those four weeks.' He thought about Mullins, flush with that amount of ready cash, coming home to his late wife's kids and swearing they'd eaten food that wasn't there. If the devil hadn't got Mullins down in hell, then he wasn't doing his job properly. 'Take care of it, Kitty, and spend it wisely.'

'You 'ave it, Mister Blair, you look after it for us,' said Kitty.

'No, it's not for me to do that,' he said.

'It's best you keep it for us,' said Kitty, 'you can give me some when I need to do shoppin'. You're older than me, you've been in the army and everything, and I don't know much about money meself. All this lot, oh, lor', I wouldn't know how to make the best use of it, so you look after it for us. It's been a relief tellin' the police what 'appened and not havin' them make more fuss, and wasn't Dr McManus nice about it?'

Jamie saw a little smile on her face. What was behind it? Yes, what?

'I don't know why anyone should make a fuss,' said Carrie. 'I mean, he just fell down the stairs, and it wasn't no-one's fault, was it?'

'No, but the police had to come an' find out how it 'appened,' said Kitty.

'Anyway, 'e's passed on now,' said Chloe, much as if it didn't need to be talked about.

'And they've taken 'im away,' said Carrie. 'Ain't they?' She looked at Chloe. 'I'm only askin',' she said.

'I'd faint if you didn't,' said Chloe.

'You don't 'ave to worry,' said Kitty, 'he won't come back. We've got Mister Blair now, he'll look after our money and everything.'

'Look, I'm not sure I can take on that kind of responsibility,' said Jamie, feeling he had one leg in a trap and that the other leg was going to follow it if he didn't take care. 'Don't you have grandparents?'

'Oh, they passed on years ago,' said Kitty, hair wandering about her face. 'I told Alfie once, I told him that if we had a gran and grandad, we could go an' live with them, and Alfie said it would be a blessin' if we could. Alfie was belted regular by him. Come on, Mister Blair, you take this.' She folded the handkerchief around the money, making a little bundle of it, and held it out. 'You can pay the rent for us and I can tell you when I need some for shoppin'.'

Jamie had an attack of feeble-mindedness. He shouldn't have had. The war had hardened him. That and natural commonsense should have been more than enough to make his response a firmly practical one. But feeble-mindedness jumped in where angels feared to tread,

and he took the little bundle of money.
Keep your head down, Blair, his sergeant
had told him once, when they were being
shelled, or one of Fritz's ten-pounders will
collide with it. Something had collided
with it now, and it wasn't a German
ten-pounder.

'Well, I'll help you see to things for a
while, Kitty,' he said, 'but what about
your mum's cousins? Chloe said she had
cousins.'

'Oh, they went up Colchester in the
war,' said Kitty, 'they didn't like bein'
chased by Zeppelins down the Walworth
Road. Honest, we don't mind we've only
got you, and that you'll be the kids' big
brother. Of course, at my age I don't need
a big brother.'

'Here, me and Carrie's not kids,' said
Chloe. 'We were once, but we're girls now.
D'you like girls, mister?'

'Love 'em,' said Jamie, 'and I'll be
looking for one of my own as soon as
I get a job.'

'Mary Johnson's nice,' said Carrie. 'Well,
I think she is.'

'Is she?' said Jamie. 'Where's she live?'

'With 'er mum an' dad,' said Chloe,
twisting a wayward strand of hair around
a finger.

'All right,' said Jamie, 'I'll go and see her
mum and dad when a job comes my way.'

'She's in our class at school,' said Carrie.

'That's different,' said Jamie, 'I'll give her a miss, and her mum and dad.'

'What for?' asked Carrie.

'Well, if a feller goes in for cradle-snatching, people talk about him,' said Jamie, keeping the conversation light while they all waited for Alfie to get back.

'I've just thought,' said Kitty, 'I'd best do some shoppin' tomorrow. We don't have anything in the larder except a bit of bread an' marge.'

'That won't do,' said Jamie, giving in completely for the time being. 'I'll take you out in the morning, Kitty. We'll go to the town hall first and see if they can put you all on parish relief. If they do, they'll supply you with some basic food each week. Then we'll go from the town hall to the market and stock up a bit.'

'Oh, you're a real help, mister,' said Kitty. 'I wouldn't know what to do first or second meself, specially as I'm still in a parlous state.'

'A what?' said Jamie, quite sure she was far from parlous.

'Sort of distraught,' said Kitty. 'Well, who wouldn't be? I'd be lyin' down ill if you weren't here keepin' us all calm and collected, like. What a blessin', though, that we won't have to worry about him no more, not now he's passed on an' been taken away. It's goin' to be nice with just you here, Mister Blair, ain't it, Chloe?'

'I like him lookin' after us,' said Chloe.

'Are you really goin' to be our big brother, mister?' asked Carrie.

'Course 'e is,' said Chloe, 'that's why 'e's lookin' after our money an' treatin' us to fish an' chips.'

That remark coincided with a knock on the front door to announce the return of Alfie. Chloe let him in, and he entered the kitchen with a great parcel of fish and chips wrapped in sheets of newspaper. The kitchen was at once assailed by the mouth-watering aroma of the fried food, salted and vinegared in traditional fashion at the shop.

'It's all rock salmon,' said Alfie, placing the parcel on the table.

'Rock salmon's best, ain't it?' said Carrie.

'Sit down, Mister Blair,' said Kitty, unwrapping the newspaper and disclosing five portions of batter-covered fish and a huge mound of chips. The aroma then was ecstatic to noses. 'You're goin' to eat with us, ain't you? Not just now, I mean, but every suppertime. I'll be cookin' for you as well as us. It's only right I should.'

Jamie felt his other leg was almost in the trap as he sat down at the table. Carrie and Chloe gave him shy smiles.

'We like yer better than 'im, mister,' said Alfie.

'Plates, Chloe,' said Kitty.

'What for?' asked Chloe.

'We've got company, that's what for,' said Kitty.

'Is mister company?' asked Carrie.

'Course 'e is,' said Alfie, 'that's what Kitty means.'

'Oh, I just thought 'e was our lodger,' said Carrie.

Chloe fetched plates from the dresser. Not one plate seemed to match another. They were all oddments. Kitty served the fish and chips on to the plates and handed them round. Alfie pulled open the table drawer and produced knives and forks.

'What's them for?' asked Chloe.

'You can't eat with yer fingers when there's company,' said Alfie, 'it ain't proper.'

'Yes, Mister Blair won't want to look after us if we don't do things proper,' said Kitty. She glanced at Jamie. He tried to look negative. She smiled.

With everyone getting down to the meal, Chloe informed Alfie that mister was going to be their big brother.

'Eh?' said Alfie.

'Yes, 'e's all we've got now,' said Carrie. 'Kitty said so, didn't she, Chloe?'

'Yes, except 'e's not goin' to be her

big brother as she's too old,' said Chloe. 'Just ours.'

'Crikey,' said Alfie, 'we've never 'ad a big brother before.'

'Lily Porter's got one,' said Carrie, eating chips with rapture. 'She says 'e's got a big 'ead as well.'

'As well as what?' asked Alfie, devouring rock salmon.

'What?' asked Carrie squelchingly. Her mouth was full.

'What's 'e got as well as a big 'ead?'

'I don't know,' said Carrie, 'Lily didn't say. Well, I don't think she did.'

'Why did yer say as well, then?' asked Alfie.

'I don't know.' Carrie split her portion of fish open, and white flesh shone moistly between lips of golden batter. She brightened. 'I'll ask Lily,' she said.

'I expect 'e's got big ears,' said Chloe, making hungry inroads into her chips. 'Lots of big brothers 'ave got big ears.'

'Mister Blair ain't,' said Alfie, and they all took a look at Jamie's ears.

'No, 'e's got quite nice ones really,' said Chloe.

'Will they get big when you're older, mister?' asked Carrie.

'Hope not,' said Jamie, 'or I'll get blown about in the wind.'

Carrie giggled. Not one of them, he

thought, was at all bothered by the death of their step-father. It had happened, he'd been taken away, and they were eating fish and chips with all the relish of young people who had nothing very much to worry about.

'Fish an' chips is 'eaven,' said Chloe.

'Is he up there, d'you think?' asked Carrie.

'I don't mind where 'e is,' said Alfie, 'as long as 'e don't come back 'ere.'

'He can't come back,' said Kitty, 'so don't let's talk about him.'

'All right,' said Alfie.

Yes, thought Jamie, it was all right to them. Adults might have made a pretence of sorrow, but not this boy and his three sisters. They probably felt everything in the garden was lovely now that Kitty had said their lodger was going to look after them. That young lady with her gypsy looks had pushed him into a trap. He could gnaw his way out of it, perhaps, and slink off in the night. But where to? Not back to Belfast, certainly. What Kitty and the others needed was some homely widow who'd be a mum to them. It might be a good idea to cast around for one, except that she'd need a decent weekly allowance in order to clothe and feed them, and to pay the rent. What a hope. Well, he couldn't leave them in the lurch, not for the moment he couldn't.

'Did the coppers ask a lot of questions?' enquired Alfie.

'Hundreds,' said Kitty, casting a flickering glance at Jamie.

' 'Undreds?' gasped Carrie, wide-eyed.

'Well, a few,' said Kitty, 'but me an' Mister Blair spoke up in the way we thought best, didn't we, Mister Blair?'

She was smiling again.

Best to say he lost his balance and fell.

That was how she'd fashioned the trap, the monkey. Kitty was a survivor. She'd worked out how she and the kids were going to survive this crisis, by making him the lynchpin of their security. What security? With no job, what could he do for them when he'd got the wolf at his own door? He was as good as broke, and the money Kitty had craftily loaded on to him wouldn't last long. She'd done it on him. Even though he was on his uppers, he'd been a free man until this evening. That girl really did need watching.

'Kitty, don't forget there's probably going to be an inquest,' he said. 'In which case we'd have to speak up all over again.'

'Oh, blow that,' said Kitty.

'What's an inquest?' asked Carrie.

'It's when the law enquires into the cause of someone's death,' said Jamie.

'What for?' asked Carrie.

'The law likes to know.'

'What for?'

'There, I told yer, mister, Carrie's always askin',' said Chloe.

'She can't 'elp it, she's a girl,' said Alfie, finishing his last chip. 'Cor, that was me best fried fish supper ever.'

'Yes, thanks ever so much, mister,' said Chloe.

'I dunno we ought to call 'im mister,' said Alfie, 'it don't sound right for a big brother.'

'Lily Porter don't call 'er big brother mister,' said Carrie.

'What does she call 'im, then?' asked Kitty, who seemed very satisfied with developments.

'I don't know,' said Carrie. She thought. Then, looking pleased with herself, she said brightly, 'Oh, I remember she once called 'im a bleedin' elephant.'

' 'Ere,' said Alfie, who had moments when he was proper, and moments when he wasn't, 'you shouldn't say words like that in front of people.'

'But I'm only sayin' what Lily said, I ain't sayin' it meself,' protested Carrie.

'Still, we won't 'ave any language, Carrie,' said Kitty, 'specially not in front of Mister Blair. He won't look after us if there's a lot of language. Mister Blair, what would you like us to call you?'

'Bloody barmy,' said Jamie. That didn't go down at all well. More like a ton weight, in fact. A kind of flattened silence reigned. Four pairs of brown eyes turned his way, and every eye seemed accusing. The silence became funereal, which was appropriate under the circumstances. Why did they all have to have brown eyes, like soulful cows? Jamie knew how his irrepressible mother would have broken the silence. Come on, she'd have said, workers of the world unite and let's all sing the 'Red Flag'.

As it was, Carrie found voice.

'What did mister say that for?' she asked.

'Just a joke,' said Jamie, 'and you can call me mister, that'll be all right.' If he gave them any encouragement, they might start calling him Dad. Four of them calling him Dad at his age?

'Well,' said Chloe in her positive way, 'we don't want to call yer bloody barmy.'

' 'Ere, that's language,' said Alfie.

'You Chloe,' said Kitty, shaking a finger at her, 'd'you want your ears boxed?'

'Eh?' said Chloe in alarm.

'Kitty, you never said nothink like that before,' observed Alfie.

'I've got to 'elp Mister Blair keep you in order,' said Kitty.

71

'You ain't goin' to start beltin' us, are yer?' said Alfie.

'Course I'm not,' said Kitty, 'we don't want any more of that. But you've all got to be respectful. Mister Blair don't want our neighbours telling 'im you don't behave nice.'

'I'm thinking of pushing off to Australia,' said Jamie.

Silence reigned again. Chloe broke it this time.

'But ain't yer goin' to look after us, mister?'

'Yes, we don't want you goin' off to Australia, not now,' said Kitty.

He might have said well, ruddy hard luck, monkey, but how could he when they were practically destitute, all four of them?

'Couldn't we go to Australia with 'im?' asked Carrie a little shyly.

'Or Canada?' suggested Alfie. 'They've got bears and Eskimos in Canada. I ain't never seen an Eskimo.'

'They've got them at the zoo,' said Chloe.

'What, Eskimos?' said Alfie.

'Yes, course they 'ave,' said Chloe, 'and bears as well. And penguins.'

'What do they 'ave Eskimos at the zoo for?' asked Alfie.

'To look after the bears and penguins,

I suppose,' said Jamie.

'Well, we don't need to go to Canada, then, if we can see them at the zoo,' declared Chloe.

'Is Australia best, then?' asked Carrie.

'Yes, course it is,' said Chloe, 'specially if—' She glanced at Jamie, who did a bit of muttering. 'Specially if you're goin', mister.'

I'll get Shanghaied by this lot if I'm not careful, thought Jamie. Kitty cast him a little smile.

There was a knock on the street door. Alfie answered it. Returning, he said, 'Old Ma Reynolds wants to talk to yer, mister.'

'All right,' said Jamie, and went to see what Mrs Reynolds wanted. She was one of the neighbours who'd been confiding in him. She was fifty, stout and good-natured. Another woman was with her, a younger one. Mrs Fitch was twenty-six and quite pretty. Jamie guessed she and Mrs Reynolds knew all about Henry Mullins and his fatal fall down the stairs. 'Hello, ladies, what can I do for you?' he asked.

'We couldn't 'ardly believe about Mr Mullins,' said Mrs Reynolds.

'It must've been a terrible shock to the children,' said Mrs Fitch.

'Well, a shock, yes,' said Jamie, 'but they're bearing up.'

'Was 'e drunk?' asked Mrs Reynolds forthrightly.

'Let's talk in here,' said Jamie, and took them into the parlour. It didn't have too much in common with most Walworth parlours, which were usually the best furnished rooms where housewives could receive respectable visitors like the vicar. A parlour was also the room where a family gathered on Sundays and where Sunday teas were often served, especially if aunts and uncles were present. The late Henry Mullin's parlour was hardly inviting. The ancient curtains needed a wash, and the sofa and armchairs looked in need of refurbishing. The seat of the sofa showed a rip and horsehair was sticking out. The mantelpiece was quite bare of ornaments, and the empty fireplace looked as if a few blazing coals would cheer it up no end. However, Jamie couldn't have said anything looked grubby. Kitty attended more to housework than she did to herself.

'Them poor kids,' said Mrs Reynolds.

'We thought we'd come an' see if they needed any 'elp,' said Mrs Fitch.

'We're naturally upset for them,' said Mrs Reynolds.

'And for you,' said Mrs Fitch.

'Yes, it's a real shame for you, Mr Blair,' said Mrs Reynolds, 'you not 'aving been in this 'ouse very long. We 'eard it 'appened through Mr Mullins fallin' down the stairs. Well, Mrs Wright asked one of the policemen that she knows personal.'

'Yes, Mr Mullins fell all right,' said Jamie, 'but he wasn't drunk.'

'I 'ope there wasn't no blood,' said Mrs Reynolds. 'Blood's upsettin'.'

'No, no blood,' said Jamie. 'A heart attack. Didn't the policeman tell you that?'

' 'E just said 'e died from fallin' down the stairs. Well, 'e's gone to 'is Maker now.'

'Or somewhere else,' said Mrs Fitch.

'We'd best not speak ill, Mrs Fitch,' said Mrs Reynolds. 'I can't say I liked 'Enry Mullins too much, but goin' like that, well, it's 'ard on the children.'

'Could be a bit of a blessin', though,' said Mrs Fitch. 'What's goin' to happen to them, Mr Blair?'

'Kitty's goin' to take charge,' said Jamie.

'That poor gel, just when she's of an age when she ought to be wearin' pretty frocks and goin' out with a young man,' said Mrs Reynolds. 'I know it ain't right to speak ill, but 'Enry Mullins made a slave of Kitty and never bought 'er anything in the way of nice frocks.'

'It's lucky you're here with them, Mr Blair,' said Mrs Fitch. 'I wouldn't like to think they were all alone in the house.'

75

'Kitty's up against it, and that's a fact,' said Jamie, 'and while I'm lodging here I'll do what I can to help her. I'll take her to the town hall tomorrow to see what help she can get there. My problem is that I still don't have a job.'

'It's 'ardly decent, the government not carin' about all you men that fought in the war,' said Mrs Fitch.

'Still, a fine young man like you, you're bound to get a job soon,' said Mrs Reynolds comfortingly. 'It's not as if you stand about on street corners like some work-shy 'ooligans I could mention. Well now, what Mrs Fitch and me thought, bein' yer nearest neighbours, was could we do a bit of washin' for the gels and their brother? Bed linen and that, and we could lend clean sheets if need be, and piller cases, and if there's blankets that could do with goin' in the copper for a good boil, we'd be pleasured to do them too.'

'That's very neighbourly,' said Jamie.

'We also thought about bringin' in sandwiches each morning for them to eat at school midday,' said Mrs Fitch. 'And some for Kitty too, of course. Like Mrs Reynolds, I can't say I thought much of Mr Mullins, but the children 'ave lost what he did provide for them, and I don't suppose the council or the government will pay anything to a dustcart driver's step-children. Mr Blair, d'you mind me askin' if you're meanin' to stay and give them a bit of 'elp?'

'I don't see how I can walk out on them,' said Jamie.

'Bless yer Christian soul,' said Mrs Reynolds. My Christian soul needs talking to, thought Jamie.

'You old soldiers learned goodness in the trenches.'

'Old soldiers?' Jamie smiled. 'Have I gone grey and haggard?'

'You know what I mean,' said Mrs Reynolds, 'you learned to be a real man in the trenches, Mr Blair, and them poor kids can do with 'elp from a real man after what they've 'ad to put up with from that step-father of theirs. They're good kids really, but they've got so that they don't bother about theirselves too much, nor does Kitty. Well, she ain't 'ad time to. Mr Blair, you just ask Mrs Fitch and me anytime you need a bit of partic'lar 'elp. All me own children are married and off me 'ands, so I've got time to spare most days.'

'And I've only got a little girl,' said Mrs Fitch.

All that made Jamie think his own attitude could do with a bit of improving, that he should stop thinking about escape and start thinking how to get the kids

77

in order, including doing away with their ragamuffin look.

'You two ladies are going to solve one problem by attending to the laundry,' he said. 'The next thing, in my opinion, is to get some new clothes for them.'

'New? That'll be expensive,' said Mrs Fitch.

'You can get good seconds down the market,' said Mrs Reynolds.

'Ruddy good idea,' said Jamie.

'Beg yer pardon?' said Mrs Reynolds, a church-goer.

'Yes, good idea,' said Jamie. 'I suppose—?'

'Would yer leave it to me?' offered Mrs Reynolds.

'Thanks. Shall I give you some money?'

'If you can let me 'ave six bob, say, I'll fit them all out, Kitty as well,' said Mrs Reynolds. 'She'll be sufferin' a bit in 'er worry about things, so I'll be pleasured to take the job of buyin' clothes off 'er hands.'

'Six bob?' said Jamie. 'That'll be enough for all of them?'

'Enough to make them look respectable under and over, Mr Blair. Vests for tuppence, and knickers the same—if yer'll pardon me mentioning same—'

'Oh, I'm sure Mr Blair is a man of the world,' smiled Mrs Fitch.

'I expect the world is full of knickers,'

said Jamie, showing some of his father's gravity, except that his father's wouldn't have been make-believe.

'I'm sure,' said Mrs Fitch with another smile.

'Granted,' said Mrs Reynolds, 'but it don't do to go on about them, specially as it's a mournful occasion and we don't want to be disrespectful.'

'No, not when things are mostly mournful for the children,' said Mrs Fitch, who was still young enough to give Jamie a little wink.

'I'll be able to get decent shoes or boots for fourpence a pair,' said Mrs Reynolds, 'six frocks for a couple of bob, shorts and jerseys for fourpence each, and so on, Mr Blair. None of the stuff will fall off them in a week. Knowin' the kids, and Kitty as well, I'll be able to get what suits them, and I'll go to the stall as soon as the market opens in the mornin'.'

'You're a godsend, Mrs Reynolds,' said Jamie, and dug into his trouser pocket. He fished out coins. He had the money Kitty had insisted on handing to him. He gave Mrs Reynolds six shillings.

'It won't be wasted,' she said.

'And if you'll let us go through the house tomorrow mornin',' said Mrs Fitch, 'we'll take away everything that needs launderin', your own clothes as well, if you like.'

Jamie, more than willing to be favoured by a pretty woman, said, 'I can't thank you enough, both of you.'

'It's a pleasure, Mr Blair,' said Mrs Fitch. 'We don't know 'ow the children are feelin' at the moment—'

'They're feeling relieved,' said Jamie frankly.

'Relieved?'

'Well, I never, bless them gels and young Alfie too,' said Mrs Reynolds.

'Mullins gave them a hard time,' said Jamie even more frankly.

'Don't we know it,' said Mrs Fitch.

'That 'eart attack was waitin' for 'im, I'll be bound,' said Mrs Reynolds. 'The Lord works in mysterious ways, like the vicar says. Mind, it wouldn't be Christian to say serve 'Enry Mullins right, but 'e didn't 'ardly earn any mercifulness, if yer don't mind me sayin' so, Mr Blair.'

'No, I don't mind,' smiled Jamie.

'Look, Mr Blair,' said Mrs Fitch, 'we 'ad a feelin' that Kitty and her brother and sisters might not be cryin' their eyes out, so we've both got large saucepans of hot water goin'.'

'Pardon?' said Jamie.

'Mr Blair,' said Mrs Reynolds, 'them kids 'aven't 'ad a bath for a year, and it don't do any gel or boy any good to get out of the way of takin' a bath reg'lar. It ain't good for their souls or their bodies. Mrs Fitch, she'll see to the twins, and I'll be 'appy to see to Kitty and Alfie. We thought that's the best start we could give them now they're by theirselves, specially if they've got 'eadlice.'

'Not too good, headlice,' said Jamie, 'the buggers—'

'Beg yer pardon, Mr Blair?' said Mrs Reynolds.

'Headlice enjoyed life in the trenches,' said Jamie, 'and invited their cousins to come and stay.'

' 'Orrible,' said Mrs Reynolds.

'Carbolic,' said Mrs Fitch.

'Yes, carbolic, that'll do it,' said Mrs Reynolds.

'Carbolic soap,' said Mrs Fitch.

'Sounds punishing,' said Jamie.

Mrs Fitch laughed, and he wondered if the sound made Henry Mullins turn in the morgue.

Chapter Four

Tactfully, the two good neighbours decided to wait in the passage while Jamie went back into the kitchen to advise the kids and Kitty of their imminent fate. Alfie, Carrie and Chloe looked aghast. Kitty looked as if she wanted to spit.

'Not likely,' she said, 'we're not goin' to let anyone put us in a bath.'

'We don't 'ave baths,' said Chloe.

'I ain't had one since I can't remember,' said Alfie.

'I ain't never 'ad one at all,' said Carrie. 'I think,' she added.

'Well, my beauties,' said Jamie, 'it's either going with Mrs Fitch and Mrs Reynolds or me bathing all of you myself.'

'What, me as well?' gasped Kitty.

'All of you,' said Jamie.

'Oh, it ain't decent,' cried Kitty, 'I'm seventeen, I am, and nearly grown up.'

'All the more reason to get you into a bath,' said Jamie.

'We don't 'ave any bath, so there,' said Kitty.

'I'll borrow one.'

' 'Ere, I just remembered,' said Alfie, 'I

don't need no bath, I 'ad one.'

'When?' asked Jamie.

'One Friday night once,' said Alfie. 'So did Chloe an' Carrie, didn't yer, Carrie?'

'Yes, one Friday night,' said Carrie, trying to hide herself under the table. Her smudgy face showed. 'Well, I think I did, didn't I, Chloe? Oh, where's Chloe?'

'I ain't at 'ome,' said Chloe, who was right under the table, 'and I can't 'ave a bath if I ain't at 'ome.'

'Kitty, get 'em out from under the table and I'll carry them to Mrs Fitch's,' said Jamie.

'Oh, yer monster,' said Kitty, dark eyes flashing. 'I don't know how you can be so 'orrible, specially when we're all grievin'.'

'Are they comin', Mr Blair?' called Mrs Fitch.

'Any minute now,' called Jamie. He stooped and pulled Chloe and Carrie out from under the table. They yelled. He slung Carrie over his left shoulder and tucked Chloe under his right arm. They were both pathetic lightweights. If there's one thing I'm going to do, he thought, it's put some food into all of them. He carried the twins out to the passage.

'Bless us,' said Mrs Reynolds, blinking at the sight.

'This way, Mr Blair,' smiled Mrs Fitch,

opening the front door.

'Oh, it ain't fair,' gasped Chloe.

'Oh, could I walk, please, mister?' begged Carrie.

'Me too,' said Chloe.

Jamie set them down.

'You'll enjoy a hot bath,' he said.

'Oh, all right,' said Chloe, and looked up at him. 'Are yer really goin' to look after us?'

'I'm going to do my best,' said Jamie.

' 'Is Christian best,' said Mrs Reynolds encouragingly.

'Oh, 'elp,' breathed Carrie, 'does Christian best mean we've got to 'ave another bath later on?'

Mrs Fitch laughed.

'Come on, loveys,' she said, and the twins went with her, hoping that being immersed didn't mean being drowned.

From the kitchen door, Kitty yelled, 'Don't you come back for me, mister!'

'Mrs Reynolds,' said Jamie loudly, 'I think I'll have to ask if I can borrow your bath.'

'Oh, yer fiend!' cried Kitty, and slammed the kitchen door shut.

'Give me another minute, Mrs Reynolds,' said Jamie.

'Yes, don't you worry, Mr Blair, Kitty's upset state is natural, like. Take yer time with 'er. I'll wait.'

Jamie returned to the kitchen. Alfie looked uncertain, Kitty looked flushed and rageful.

'Kitty—'

'I'll bash yer face in!'

'Mister, you ain't 'alf got 'er in a temper,' said Alfie.

'All I'm after, Alfie, is getting her into a bath,' said Jamie.

'Oh, I never 'eard anything more disgustin'!' yelled Kitty.

'Nothing disgusting about taking a bath, Kitty.'

'Yes, there is, a bloke like you puttin' a young lady like me in one, and me with no clothes on. I'll 'ave a fatal seizure, I will. Oh, you wait, the coppers'll come round again to see why I'm lyin' all dead in a bath—here, keep off—I'll scream.'

'Mrs Reynolds is going to give you a friendly hair shampoo, as well as a hot bath,' said Jamie.

'I don't want any shampoo, nor any bath,' said Kitty fiercely, and Jamie had a feeling she was sensitive about revealing her unwashed state. But the dread deed had to be done, he had to get her self-respect reborn. He swooped. Kitty screamed. He lifted her and put her over his shoulder. She beat at his back with clenched fists. 'Oh, I'll do for you, I will! Put me down! Alfie, hit him! Oh, me dignity—I hate you all over!'

The commotion brought Mrs Reynolds hastening into the kitchen.

'Oh, lor',' she said, 'I didn't want anyone to upset Kitty—'

'I ain't upset!' yelled Kitty.

'Good,' said Jamie.

'I like bein' chucked over 'is shoulder and then chucked in a bath, don't I?'

'Glad to hear it,' said Jamie. 'Lead the way, Mrs Reynolds, and if she's still giving trouble when we reach your house, I'll help you get her clothes off.'

'Oh, me dear gawd, I can't believe me ears,' gasped Kitty as Jamie carried her through the passage to the open front door.

'Mr Blair, you shouldn't say things like that,' said Mrs Reynolds, 'it's not respectable. You best put 'er down.'

Jamie put Kitty on her feet. Through wild hair, she eyed him fiercely. 'Oh, I never thought any bloke would treat me like this on me most grievous day and after all them questions and answers.'

'Kitty, are you going quietly?' asked Jamie.

'You're bossy, you are!'

' 'E's doin' it out of kindness, love,' said Mrs Reynolds.

'It's not kindness, chucking me about

86

when I'm seventeen,' said Kitty. 'All right, I'll come and look at your bath, but I'm not gettin' in if it's not big enough and unless I'm on me own.'

'There's a good girl,' said Mrs Reynolds in motherly fashion.

'Me dignity's hurtin' all over,' said Kitty, and disappeared with her neighbour. Jamie found Alfie sitting gloomily at the kitchen table.

'I dunno it's right some woman givin' me a bath,' said the boy.

'Mrs Reynolds is probably a grand-mother, Alfie.'

'Yes, but she ain't mine,' said Alfie. 'It can't be right bein' put in a bath by someone else's bloomin' grandmuvver. It could give a bloke problems 'e might never get over. Mister, I bet you'd get problems if someone else's grandmuvver put you in a bath.'

'I go to the public baths and avoid grandmothers.'

'That costs a tanner, that does, an 'ole tanner,' said Alfie. 'I ain't 'ad a tanner in all me life. Mind you,' he went on, perking up a bit, 'now I'm more me own boss, like, I can run errands for old ladies. There's a nice lot of old ladies in Walworth, yer know.'

'Well, they should be good for a few errands,' said Jamie.

'I got wishful 'opes,' said Alfie. ' 'Ere, mister, I 'ope Kitty don't kill yer when she gets back. She used to fight old Mullins sometimes, and 'e'd give it worse to 'er then. I ain't sorry about 'im, yer know.'

'I know you're not, Alfie. Has the washing-up been done?'

'No, and I betcher it won't get done at all now,' said Alfie, 'I betcher Kitty'll smash all the plates up when she gets back.'

The plates and cutlery used for the fish and chips were in the scullery sink. So were other items.

'Well, we'll do them, Alfie. I'll wash, you dry.'

'All right,' said Alfie.

Jamie put a kettle of water on the scullery gas cooker. The gas ran out just as the water began to steam, so he slotted three pennies into the passage meter.

A little while later after the washing-up had been done, Kitty returned.

'You go now, Alfie,' she said, 'to Mrs Reynolds.'

'Bloomin' 'ell,' gloomed Alfie.

'Go on,' said Kitty, and Alfie went, sighingly, to the ordeal of being put in a bath by someone else's grandmother. Kitty put her back to Jamie, but couldn't disguise the fact that her hair had been washed. It gleamed damply.

'Well, how was it?' smiled Jamie.

'I'm not talkin' to you,' said Kitty.

'Why not?'

'You did it on me. When I was in the bath, I 'ad a good mind to drown meself, only I couldn't get me 'ead under, not without losin' me dignity again.'

'Hard luck. Turn round and let me have at look at you.'

'Excuse me,' she said, 'but I just told you, I'm not talkin' to you, so I'm not lettin' you have a look at me, either.'

'Cross with me, are you, Kitty?'

'Hate you all over,' she said. 'That old Ma Reynolds scrubbed me hair with carbolic soap or something, then boiled it in scaldin' 'ot water, good as. Me at my age, I've never been so undignified.'

'Well, come on, turn round and let's have a look at you.'

'What d'you think I am? I'm not takin' me clothes off again to let you see what I looked like scrubbed and scalded.'

'Why, are you pink all over, Kitty?'

Kitty uttered a strangled cry of outrage.

'Me? Pink all over? Oh, it ain't decent, talkin' to a girl like that.'

'You smell pink all over,' said Jamie. 'Mind, it's a fresh smell.'

'I'll kill yer!' yelled Kitty. 'Oh, you're crafty too as well as bossy—you're lookin'!'

Jamie was in front of her. She *was* pink.

Her face was pink. Her old stockings were off and her legs were pink. She looked shining clean, and the wildness of her hair had been tamed by a vigorous shampoo. It clung damply around her head.

'Very nice,' he said.

'Hate yer,' said Kitty.

'All right, I'll find myself new lodgings tomorrow.'

'See if I care.'

'I'll go first thing or as soon as I've sorted a few things out. Now, about Mrs Fitch and Mrs Reynolds, your helpful neighbours—'

'Interferin' busybodies, you mean,' said Kitty. 'Oh, if I'd known you was goin' to let them scrub us all over, I'd have told the coppers—well, I'd have—' Kitty fumbled for words.

'You'd have what?'

'Mister, you're not goin' to leave us, are you?'

'No, and I'm not going to wallop you, either, you monkey, but don't try twisting my arm or I'll scrub you all over myself when it's time for your next bath.'

'Oh, you're not first thing decent,' gasped Kitty.

'And you'll be even pinker.'

'I'll have a faintin' fit in a minute.'

'All right, Kitty, it's been a fraught

day for you, so I won't go on at you. Listen.' Jamie told her what her good neighbours were going to do tomorrow, bring sandwiches for herself and the others, wash everything that needed washing, including curtains, and buy clothes for all of them. He suggested he and Kitty should help by taking down all the curtains now.

'Honest, they're goin' to do all that?' said Kitty. 'I've been out of me wits about the laundry, I've done what I could on Mondays, only we don't have a lot of spare things, not in the way of clothes or bedsheets, and that man wouldn't ever—well, he wouldn't ever put his 'and in his pocket for anything, not even for wood for the copper fire sometimes. You just can't wash things proper in cold water.'

'He'll get his dues, Kitty, and what he did have in his pocket he couldn't take with him, and he didn't.'

'Yes, it was ever so kind of you, offerin' to take charge of it,' said Kitty.

'I don't think I offered. Never mind. Let's be grateful you've got kind neighbours.'

'We've got you too,' said Kitty. 'It's like havin' a decent dad.'

'Did you say that without moving your lips?' asked Jamie.

'No, course I didn't,' said Kitty, 'I bet it was writ.'

'Writ?'

'Yes, you know, by the 'and of fate.'

'What was?' asked Jamie, thinking she wouldn't look out of place in a Romany encampment.

'You comin' among us to be our lodger,' said Kitty. 'I bet it was writ by the 'and of fate.'

'I didn't get any letter.'

'Oh, fate doesn't send letters,' said Kitty, 'it just happens. If it 'adn't happened, if you 'adn't come among us, that man would still be alive and beltin' us, wouldn't he? Mind, I don't know that the 'and of fate is always as kind as that.'

'I'm going to get a headache in a moment,' said Jamie.

'Oh, I'm not cross with you any more,' said Kitty, 'and you do like us, don't you, mister?'

There she was, shining clean, if still a bit of a scarecrow. Without any effort at all, she had dismissed her step-father and his death as if he'd been no more than an ugly piece of furniture that was always in the way. Now, thought Jamie, she was only concerned with having someone in the house to help her look after the kids. She was thinking, perhaps, that without an adult willing to take them all on, bowler-hatted authority would arrive on the doorstep and cart them off to some institution.

He couldn't help thinking again that Kitty was a survivor. Nor could he help a little smile.

'Let's get the curtains down,' he said, 'and save your good neighbours from having to do it themselves.'

'You've got thoughtful ways, mister,' said Kitty, 'and you're kind too, even if you did get a bit bossy.'

I'll seriously have to watch this monkey, thought Jamie.

Carrie and Chloe returned while they were unfixing curtains, and Alfie showed up soon after. They all looked pinkly clean, and they all had damp hair. Chloe said she didn't think scrubbing brushes ought to be allowed, because she and Carrie had nearly been scrubbed away by Mrs Fitch. Carrie said her hair smelled of disinfectant or something. Still, Mrs Fitch had given her and Chloe a nice slice of cake each and some cocoa. Alfie said old Ma Reynolds had given him two jam tarts and had let him scrub himself. But she'd washed his hair, he said, and made him feel his loaf of bread was coming off. She wasn't a bad old lady, he said, but he still felt it wasn't right to be put in a bath by someone else's grandmother.

' 'Ere, mister,' he said, 'if I've got to 'ave anuvver bath, can I go to Mrs Fitch's?'

'Why?' asked Carrie.

'Well, I fancy 'er,' said Alfie.

'You ain't old enough to fancy no-one,' said Chloe.

'Well, I will be when I 'ave me next bath,' said Alfie.

'Don't you believe it,' said Jamie. 'And hold these.' He dropped the parlour curtains on the boy's head. Kitty untangled them. 'Bedtime,' said Jamie.

'Eh?' said Alfie.

'It's well after nine. Time you were all in bed. But clean your teeth first.'

'Yes, go on, all of you,' said Kitty.

'And you,' said Jamie.

'But I'm seventeen.'

'Bed,' said Jamie, 'you've all had a long day.'

Kitty made a face.

'Mister, we've only got one toothbrush,' said Chloe.

'Where is it?' asked Carrie.

' 'Ow do I know?' said Chloe. 'Kitty 'ad it last week.'

'Last week?' said Jamie. 'That won't do. You've all got to have a toothbrush each. Find the one you have got and use it. Wash it with soap after you've each used it.'

'But there ain't no tooth powder,' said Alfie.

94

'Use salt.'

'Salt?' said Carrie in horror.

'We ain't got none,' said Chloe.

'Yes, you have,' said Jamie.

'Not for cleanin' our teeth with, we ain't,' said Alfie.

'I've got a nasty suspicion no-one's cleaned their teeth for ages,' said Jamie. 'That's got to change. See to them, Kitty, or I'll turn them all upside-down and knock holes in the floor with them. Find that toothbrush. I'll lend you my tin of tooth powder. I'll give all of you ten seconds to get started.'

'Here, excuse me,' said Kitty, 'you're not supposed to boss us about and knock holes in the floor with me sisters' heads. Nor Alfie's.'

'I don't want to,' said Jamie, 'but I might have to. You as well.'

'What, 'olding me upside-down?' gasped Kitty.

'It's the best way,' said Jamie. If they'd been grieving or mournful, he'd have treated them gently. But they weren't, they were free young beings and almost as lively as crickets. So he was quite sure that the wisest way to make a start on them was to apply a little firmness. They'd lost any inclination to take care of themselves, and that had to be brought back. To begin

95

with, they could take care of their
teeth.

'Oh, crikey,' said Carrie, ' 'e don't mean
it, does 'e, Kitty?'

'I'm not bein' turned upside-down,' said
Kitty. 'Mister, that's not like bein' a dad
to us.'

Ruddy hell, thought Jamie, she's said it
again.

'Hold on, monkey,' he said, 'I've hardly
started being your big brother yet. What's
the idea, trying to promote me?'

'Oh, it's just—well, it's just that we like
yer lots better than him,' said Kitty.

'Never mind that,' said Jamie. 'Off to
bed, all of you.'

'All right,' said Alfie.

They said good night, and Kitty led
them out. Jamie went up and found his
tin of tooth powder. Kitty found the
solitary toothbrush. Jamie went downstairs
again, and a lot of splashing, gurgling and
teeth-brushing took place at the handbasin
in the upstairs lavatory. Jamie examined
the contents of the kitchen larder. All
that came to light was half a loaf, some
margarine and two jars of jam containing
very little. Of cheap porridge oats there
were none. He wondered if instant death
from a heart attack hadn't been too good
a way for Henry Mullins to go.

Upstairs in his cupboard, Jamie had two

precious eggs and some sausages, which he'd intended to cook for his supper. As it was, he'd had fish and chips with the kids. What had he better do, treat them to scrambled eggs and fried sausages for their breakfast tomorrow? Yes, give them a treat. He'd taken on some responsibility. If he'd been an old man of forty-five, looking for a fatherly existence, he could have taken on full responsibility. But he wasn't forty-five, not yet he wasn't. He was of an age when, with the help of a decent job, he could start interesting himself in long-legged beauties of the female sex. Not a bad idea, that.

The kids called down from upstairs.

'Good night, mister.'

'We're goin' to bed now.'

'We done our teeth.'

'I swallered some of yer tooth powder.'

'Good night, mister.'

'Good night, kids,' called Jamie.

He heard Kitty then.

'Mister? We like it that you like us.'

That Kitty.

He had a restless night himself. He kept dreaming of Henry Mullins cartwheeling backwards down the stairs, his mouth open and his eyes glassy.

I ain't going to say you pushed him, Mr Blair.

97

Chapter Five

Kitty came down.

Entering the scullery, she said, 'What's that you're doin'?'

'Frying sausages for all of you,' said Jamie, 'and I'll be scrambling a couple of eggs to go with them.'

'You're doin' us sausages and scrambled eggs?' Kitty seemed astonished.

'You all ought to have some breakfast, Kitty.'

'Mister, I—oh, ain't you good to us? Where'd you get them from?'

'They were lying around in my cupboard upstairs, not doing anything.'

'You're givin' us your food?' she said.

'Just for this morning.'

'Can you cook, then?' she asked.

'Not much. Just fried stuff.'

'Let me do it,' she said, 'I'm a good cook, honest. Would you let me do it?'

'Well, you'll probably scramble the eggs better than I will,' said Jamie, and looked at her as she took over. Her hair was soft from last night's shampoo, but he didn't think a brush or comb had touched it yet. 'Listen,' he said, 'after breakfast and before

I take you round to the town hall, get your hair combed and brushed. And have you got a hair ribbon?'

'Here, what's wrong with me hair?' asked Kitty.

'Not much, if you like it looking like a broom that's been out in the wind,' said Jamie. 'Are the kids up?' It was eight o'clock.

'Yes, they'll be down in a tick,' said Kitty, rolling the sausages about. 'What d'you mean, like a broom that's been out in the wind?'

'Just a bit short of one that's been out in a storm,' said Jamie, then went to answer a knock on the street door. It was Mrs Fitch, looking April-fresh in a clean white blouse and a long green skirt. One thing about a lot of Walworth housewives who weren't down in the depths of poverty, they liked to look presentable, especially the younger ones. There was a fair amount of pride to be observed in the cockney women of South London. 'Morning, Mrs Fitch.'

'Hello,' she said, smiling, 'I won't keep you more than a minute, I expect you're gettin' the children ready for school.'

Getting them ready for school? If this kind of thing keeps up, thought Jamie, I won't feel like a brother or a father, I'll feel like their mother.

'Well, I can't sa

'You must be a blessin' to them. I said so to me 'usband last night. Anyway, I've just made the sandwiches, and I hope you won't be offended that there's some for you as well as your little fam'ly.'

'Little family?' I'm hearing things, thought Jamie.

'Oh, kind of.' Mrs Fitch smiled again. What woman wouldn't smile on a stalwart young man who was being such a good Samaritan to four lost young souls? 'As you're takin' Kitty round to the town hall this mornin', I thought I'd do some midday sandwiches for you as well. They're all in here, separately wrapped up, fresh corned beef sandwiches with pickle.' She handed Jamie a brown paper carrier bag. It felt laden.

'Well, how can I thank you, Mrs Fitch?'

'Oh, you can give us a kiss, if you like,' she said.

'Pardon?'

'At Christmas, under the mistletoe,' she said, and laughed.

'I can't wait,' said Jamie, 'but I suppose I'll have to. I'm Jamie, by the way.'

'Jamie? That's Scotch, isn't it?'

'Scottish. My father's a Scot.'

'Oh, I like the Scots, specially Harry Lauder,' said Mrs Fitch. 'I'm Teresa. I'll come in later, with Mrs Reynolds, and pick up everything that needs goin' in a wash.'

'Kitty will appreciate that. We've taken all the curtains down.'

'Yes, I noticed your parlour windows.'

'If we're out when you arrive, just walk in.' Jamie slipped the latchcord back through the letter-box. 'You sent the twins in looking very clean last night.'

'You'll be pleased to know they don't have headlice.'

'I'd be rapturous about that if I happened to be their mother,' said Jamie.

'Poor young things, not havin' anyone,' said Mrs Fitch. 'Still, they've got you now. What a blessin' you took up lodgings here. Well, I won't keep you, I'm sure you're busy. Don't forget about Christmas.'

'Christmas? Oh, yes,' said Jamie, and Mrs Fitch laughed and left. Jamie went back to the kitchen. The sausages were done and so were the scrambled eggs, and Kitty was keeping everything warm.

'Where you been all this time?' she asked.

'Talking to Mrs Fitch. She brought the sandwiches she promised. They're in this bag.'

'You didn't have to talk to her all this time,' said Kitty, putting marge on slices of bread.

'Hold on,' said Jamie, 'who's the boss round here?'

'It ain't respectable, gettin' off with a

married woman on our doorstep,' said Kitty primly.

'Somebody else's doorstep would be all right, would it?'

'That's not funny,' said Kitty, and crossed to the kitchen door. From there she yelled up to the kids. 'Come on, you lot! Your breakfast's ready, and you won't 'ave time to eat it if you don't come down now!'

'What breakfast?' shouted Alfie.

'Sausage and scrambled egg!'

'Crikey, I'd like some of that.'

Down they came, feet clattering on the lino-covered stairs. Into the kitchen they surged, ragamuffins, all three of them. But their faces were clean, although neither the girls nor Alfie looked as if they'd brushed their hair.

'Oh, 'ello, mister,' said Chloe.

'Mornin', mister,' said Alfie.

'Did Kitty say sausage an' scrambled egg?' asked Carrie.

'Course she did,' said Chloe, 'we 'eard 'er, didn't we?'

'I was only askin',' said Carrie.

Kitty hustled them into their chairs and served them their breakfast. Hungry eyes goggled blissfully. They had one and a half sausages each, with a portion of scrambled egg. Kitty had done wonders with the two eggs. The kids also had a slice of bread and marge. There was tea too, and just enough condensed milk to flavour it.

'Mister, you sit down too,' said Kitty, and put a plate in front of Jamie. It contained two sausages and a portion of scrambled egg. There'd been eight sausages, and he'd put them all in the pan.

'Mister's got two sausages,' said Chloe.

'Well, 'e treated us to them and, besides, 'e's a man,' said Kitty, with the kids eating hungrily.

'So am I,' said Alfie.

'You're not even a grown-up boy yet,' said Kitty.

'I don't mind mister 'aving two,' said Carrie. 'Crikey, ain't they scrumptious? Fancy a breakfast like this.'

'I like mister,' said Chloe.

'He was gettin' off with Mrs Fitch on our doorstep while I was cookin' breakfast,' said Kitty accusingly.

Brown eyes fastened on Jamie.

'He wasn't, was 'e?' said Carrie.

'Yes, and I told him it wasn't respectable,' said Kitty.

'I'll use somebody else's doorstep next time,' said Jamie.

'Yes, I expect that's best,' said Chloe.

'No, it's not,' said Kitty.

Through a mouthful of sausage, Carrie said, 'Lily Porter's big brother don't get off with Mrs Fitch, does 'e?'

'I suppose he's more respectable than I am,' said Jamie.

'I never 'eard Lily say he was respectable,' said Carrie.

'It's not funny,' said Kitty. 'Suppose the neighbours start talkin'?'

'I ain't goin' to worry,' said Alfie. 'I mean, gettin' off with Mrs Fitch ain't nearly as bad as gettin' pinched for nickin'. Old Mrs Green's lodger got pinched for nickin' once and she wouldn't let 'im darken 'er door again.'

'Mrs Fitch is pretty,' said Carrie.

'Yes, course she is,' said Chloe, 'that's why Mr Fitch married 'er an' they 'ad a baby.'

'You're not supposed to say things like that,' said Carrie.

'We won't talk about Mrs Fitch any more,' said Kitty. 'Drink your tea up, all of you, then get off to school.'

The kids departed for school five minutes later, scrambling out of the house in such lively fashion that Jamie thought it had to be something to do with being free of their step-father and having a decent breakfast inside them. He suggested to Kitty that with the kids now out of the way, he and she should go round to the town hall as soon as possible.

'Yes, all right,' said Kitty, and set about

104

clearing up and washing-up. Jamie dried the things for her, and she then went upstairs to get herself ready.

He called up to her.

'Strip the beds, Kitty.'

'What for? And who you shoutin' at?'

'Mrs Fitch and Mrs Reynolds are coming in for the blankets and bed linen, and I have to shout from down here.'

'All right, don't get grumpy. Mister? Mister, you there? Listen, we don't 'ave much bed linen.'

'Strip off what there is, Kitty. I'll do your step-father's bed.'

'Oh, thanks. I don't fancy goin' in his room this mornin'. Mister?'

'Yes?'

'I ain't really cross with you.'

'That's a relief,' said Jamie, and slipped into Henry Mullins's bedroom, which was between the kitchen and the parlour. The bed that hadn't been slept in was covered by an old eiderdown. He turned it back and saw at once that the pillows had covers on them. He knew there were none on most of the kids' pillows. And there were sheets, of course. Well, when they were washed, they could be transferred upstairs. He began to strip the bed. Something caught his eye, an elliptical blue vase standing on the small bedside table. Its neck was narrow. It was the kind of vase

105

in which a woman would place a single rose with a tall stem. It was out of place on Henry Mullins's bedside table. Imagine a sod like that placing any rose in any vase. Any pure-minded bloom would fold up, wither and die overnight.

Jamie stripped the bed speedily.

Kitty was ready. At least, she said she was. Well, thought Jamie, perhaps it wouldn't have been too clever to go to the town hall to ask for parish relief looking well-dressed. She was far from that. She wore an old beige calf-length dress that hung limply, and a knitted woollen grey cardigan that reached to well below her hips. It was darned in several places, and it's pockets sagged tiredly. There was something on her head. Jamie supposed it was a hat, but it could have passed for an ancient tea cosy. What with the shapeless dress, the cardigan that had had all the stuffing knocked out of it, and the thing she wore on her head, she probably looked like an old lady from behind, the kind of old lady one saw wandering about and talking to herself.

'You sure you're ready?' he asked.

'What d'you mean?'

'Never mind. I suppose it wouldn't have been wise to put your best clothes on.'

'These are me best,' said Kitty.

Jamie silently swore. Henry Mullins should have had a thousand burning arrows shot into him before he passed on.

'All right, monkey, come on. Got your shopping bag? Yes, I see you have, so after we've been to the town hall we'll go down the market and stock up your larder.'

'Well, our larder, really,' said Kitty.

'Ours?'

'Yes, I'm goin' to cook for you, like I said. I've got to do that, it's only right now you're lookin' after us and sittin' down with us for meals.'

'I'm not certain—'

'That man, he didn't 'ave any nice ways or manners, not like you 'ave,' said Kitty. 'When we went up to bed last night, Chloe remarked what nice manners you 'ad, and Alfie said you didn't spit fishbones out. Alfie likes people that don't spit their fishbones out, him bein' a boy that's got natural manners 'imself.'

'I'm pleased for him, but—'

'And you mustn't mind if I get a bit cross with you sometimes,' Kitty went on. 'I'm so used to bein' cross on account of him that's passed away that it comes over me remorseless, like. It came over me when you were gettin' off with Mrs Fitch, and anyway, just because we're poverty-struck it don't mean me and me sisters and Alfie don't go in for bein' respectable. We don't

107

want to keep an unrespectable 'ouse now he's gone, and d'you mind not callin' me monkey?'

'Finished?' said Jamie.

'Finished? I've 'ardly said anything.'

'All right, let's get going, old lady.'

Halfway up Larcom Street, Kitty said, 'What d'you call me old lady for?'

'You sounded like one, but don't worry, Kitty, it'll be a long time before you look like one. Women don't mind what they sound like as much as they mind what they look like.'

'I'm nearly a woman meself,' said Kitty. A woman turned into Larcom Street from the Walworth Road. 'Oh, here's Mrs Roper,' said Kitty, 'I bet she's goin' to have something to say to us.'

Up came Mrs Roper in a large straw hat, blouse, skirt and shawl. Her skirt was blowing in the gusting April wind.

'Well, if it ain't you, Kitty,' she said. 'Oh, yer poor dear, I couldn't 'ardly believe what I 'eard last night, that yer step-father fell down yer stairs an' died. I said to Mr Roper, I said you're 'ere one moment an' gorn the next, an' Mr Roper said let that be a lesson to yer, Mavis, not to fall down any stairs. Kitty, yer poor girl, if yer in need of anything, like a loaf of bread and some slices of cold mutton, you send young Alfie round.'

'It's ever so kind of—'

'Who's yer young man? Oh, is it yer lodger, name of Blair? I've 'eard about 'im, but never 'ad the pleasure of meetin' 'im. 'Ow'd yer do, Mr Blair, I'm Mrs Roper from down the end of the street. I can't tell yer 'ow sorry I am for Kitty and 'er sisters an' brother.'

'Miss Edwards is bearing up,' said Jamie.

'Who? Oh, yer mean Kitty.'

'Yes, her family name is Edwards, not Mullins,' said Jamie.

'That's right, so it is,' said Mrs Roper, 'but I never 'eard 'er called Miss Edwards before.'

'No, but it's very respectable,' said Jamie.

'Yes, I suppose it is,' said Mrs Roper.'

'And she's nearly a woman,' said Jamie, at which Kitty thought about giving him a kick, but decided it wasn't good manners. 'Well, we can't stop, Mrs Roper, we're on our way to the town hall to see if they'll pay Miss Edwards a pension on account of her step-father having been an employee of theirs. Glad to have met you.'

'Well, I must say it's kind of yer to be takin' Kitty, I'd 'ave been pleased to take 'er meself if I'd known she was goin' there, she needs someone to—'

Jamie and Kitty left her while she was still talking.

'You didn't have to tell her I was nearly a woman,' said Kitty, 'nor call me Miss Edwards. It sounded daft.'

'Did it?' said Jamie.

'Yes, it did,' said Kitty, and spent the next few minutes ticking him off for it. Then they entered the handsome town hall of Southwark.

'Not for dustmen, no,' said one of the town hall clerks, a short fat bloke in a black jacket and dark grey trousers. The jacket, done up, was having problems staying that way.

'Why not for dustmen?' asked Jamie.

'It's the rule,' said Fatty.

'Well, a rule like that isn't much help to Miss Edwards.'

'It's downright disgraceful,' said Kitty indignantly. 'Fancy not payin' a bit of a pension to me step-father's fam'ly that's been dependent on him. How would you like to be us?'

'Miss Edwards—'

'Yes,' said Jamie, 'how would you like to be four kids left without a mum or dad and not even a decent coat to their backs?'

'Excuse me,' said Kitty, 'but I'm not a kid, I'm as good as their mum now.'

'That's right, she is,' said Jamie to Fatty.

110

'You can pay some sort of pension to a dependent who's as good as a mum, can't you?'

'The rules don't allow us to,' said Fatty. 'Are you related to the family?'

'Course he is,' said Kitty. 'Well, he's as good as our dad.'

'Ah, is he the deceased's brother?' asked Fatty.

'No, he's our lodger,' said Kitty, 'and he's kindly lookin' after us.'

'Unfortunately,' said Fatty, 'we can't deal with him.'

'Here, don't you talk like that,' said Kitty, not a bit over-awed by stout officialdom and the handsome surroundings. 'I'll 'ave you know Mr Blair is a gent that's been in the war and won the Victoria Cross.'

'The Victoria Cross?' Fatty almost stood to attention.

'Well, he don't go around sayin' so, but he good as captured fifty Germans on his own,' said Kitty. Jamie, keeping his face straight, thought he might as well let her carry on. 'You ought to be ashamed, mister, sayin' you can't deal with one of the country's 'eroes. So how much you goin' to pay me on account of me step-father workin' himself to death for you? You wore his heart out, like Dr McManus said.'

'I don't think—'

'Could you make it a pound a week?' asked Kitty.

Fatty's *embonpoint,* having taken a fair beating from the Victoria Cross, visibly sagged, which was some relief to his jacket buttons.

'A pound a week?' he said hoarsely.

'She meant two pounds,' said Jamie.

'Two?' Fatty, hoarser, seemed to lose weight rapidly.

'It's reasonable,' said Jamie, 'there are four of them.'

Fatty struggled valiantly and made a recovery.

'With regret, I must inform you that Mr Mullins had no pension entitlement covering dependents.'

'What, when he worked himself down to 'is bones for the council?' said Kitty. 'It's criminal.'

Seeing the point was to tie Fatty up in knots so that he'd be glad to settle for an alternative, Jamie said, 'We'll have to talk to the Lord Mayor. Where is he? And we'd like your name.'

'Yes, you 'aven't been a bit 'elpful,' said Kitty, 'and I bet the Lord Mayor won't half cut up rough when he hears you've been tryin' to starve me brother and sisters to death, and me as well.'

'The Mayor is unavailable,' said Fatty.

112

'Course he's not,' said Kitty scornfully. 'How could he be? He wouldn't be the Lord Mayor if he was unavailable, he'd be in 'ospital or an infirmary.'

'I mean he's not at present in the town hall,' said Fatty. 'In any case, the rules concerning—'

'I'll go and get my bayonet if you keep talking about the rules,' said Jamie.

'I must warn you it's against the law to issue threats,' said Fatty.

'No, the law can't arrest anyone that's got the Victoria Cross,' said Kitty, and that made Fatty blink a bit.

'Now, which way is the Mayor's office?' asked Jamie.

'You can't do that, you can't go to his office,' said Fatty.

'Course we can, we've both got legs, yer know,' said Kitty. 'There, now look what you've made me do, mention me legs. That's not respectable.'

Fatty took on a helpless look.

'All right,' said Jamie, 'if you can't pay Miss Edwards a pension, you can arrange for her to have a weekly ticket that'll allow her to collect supplies from parish relief. She can collect from your supply place in Brandon Street. Weekly, she'll want six loaves, tea, sugar, tinned syrup, margarine, condensed milk, fruit cake—'

'Fruit cake?' Fatty wobbled. 'Parish relief

113

doesn't supply fruit cake.'

'What a disgrace,' said Kitty. 'Just because we're poor and starvin', mister, don't mean we don't like fruit cake. Everyone in Walworth likes fruit cake. You ask them.'

Fatty, fed-up, said, 'Could we talk sense?'

'Here, I 'eard that,' said Kitty, not given to bowing and scraping. 'I bet you wouldn't tell rich people they couldn't 'ave any fruit cake.'

Stout officialdom gave up.

'Very well, Miss Edwards, the rules allow me to recognize you've fallen on hard times. I'll make out a list of foodstuffs and give you a ticket. But you'll have to collect each weekly ticket here.'

'Now you're bein' 'elpful,' said Kitty. 'I'm sure I don't know why you had to make all this fuss. Mr Blair don't fuss, he just gets on with things. He 'elped me take all our curtains down last night and didn't fuss a bit. Well, now me step-father's passed on, poor man, we're gettin' the curtains washed. Are you sure you can't pay me a pension?'

'Sorry, we've no funds for that,' said Fatty, and made out the promised list of foodstuffs. He gave it to Kitty, with a ticket that would enable her to collect.

'That's kind of you, mister,' she said,

and parted on friendlier terms with him.

They made for East Street market. Housewives were out and about, doing their shopping in the strong breeze. A gust played havoc with the skirt of a young woman alighting from a tram. Jamie made an appropriate comment about the view, and Kitty ticked him off for looking.

Entering the market, he said, 'You'll be collecting a fair supply of groceries from parish relief, but you'll need to stock up with vegetables.'

'Yes, and we'll buy some pork chops for supper tonight,' said Kitty.

'Too expensive. Make do with mutton chops. Or you could try cooking your bird's nest.'

'What, me hat?' said Kitty.

'Yes, can you eat it? In a hotpot?'

'Think you're funny, don't you?' said Kitty, pushing her way to a vegetable stall. She asked the stallholder if he'd got any King Edward potatoes he didn't want. He looked her up and down, 'Oh, yes?' said Kitty. 'May I ask what you think you're lookin' at?'

'Search me,' said the stallholder. 'Is it Ascot week? No, can't be, we ain't 'ad the Derby yet, nor Steve Donoghue ridin' the winner. Could yer oblige me by statin' again what you wanted, only I dunno I 'eard it right first time.'

'I just asked if you'd got any King Edwards you didn't want,' said Kitty. 'If you 'ave, I don't mind carryin' some away for you.'

'It's yer lucky day, girlie,' said the stallholder, 'you can carry as many as yer like. I don't want any of 'em, I'm givin' them all away at seven pounds for fivepence. Would an 'undredweight suit yer ladyship?'

'No, I'll 'ave ten pounds for a tanner,' said Kitty.

'Eightpence,' said the stallholder. 'All right, sevenpence, what do I care about me starvin' kids?' He shovelled potatoes into his large brass weighing bowl and placed it on the scales. Down the bowl went, then rose again as he put two iron weights of five pounds each on the equalizing side of the scales. He chucked one more spud in, then tipped the lot into Kitty's shopping bag.

'What about them parsnips, leeks and onions?' she asked. 'I don't mind payin' 'alf-price for them.'

'I ain't chargin' any price for them, girlie, just tuppence a pound for the parsnips, an' tuppence-'a'penny for the leeks and onions. Can't say fairer.'

'That don't sound much of a bargain to me,' said Kitty. 'I've a good mind not to buy any.'

'That's it, break me kind 'eart,' said the stallholder.

'Oh, yer poor man,' said Kitty. 'All right two pounds of each, then, and one of them cabbages.'

'Honoured, yer ladyship.'

'No sauce,' said Kitty.

Jamie paid for the vegetables, and they went to the market butcher, where Kitty tried to buy five pork chops. Jamie said no.

'Here, whose money is it?' asked Kitty.

'Yours, but I'm in charge of it. I'll square up for my share of the goods. Buy mutton chops, they're a lot cheaper.'

'Ain't it a blessin' I've got you with me?' said Kitty. 'I don't have anyone else to advise me.'

Jamie took that with a pinch of salt. They bought other food, including a large packet of porridge oats for breakfasts and a jar of marmalade for breakfast toast. Jamie wanted to put food into the kids first thing each day. Then he insisted on the purchase of toothbrushes and toothpowder.

'You'll all end up toothless otherwise,' he said.

'It's nice you've got our good at 'eart,' said Kitty.

On their way home, they met another neighbour, one known to Jamie by sight and to Kitty by name. An Irishman, Sean Fitzpatrick was a permanently cheerful gent and almost as new to Larcom Street as Jamie was. He'd been lodging with the Murphy family, also Irish. They'd come over from Ireland two years ago to get away from the troubles and to live in friendly fashion with their English cockney neighbours. They'd taken Sean Fitzpatrick as a lodger two months ago.

Seeing Kitty, Mr Fitzpatrick's broad face creased into a smile and the light of old Ireland danced in his eyes. He lifted his bowler hat, disclosing curly black hair.

'Well, if it's not me darling Kitty herself,' he said. 'The top of the mornin' to yez, Kitty, and it's sorry I am to hear you've lost your step-father.'

'That's ever so kind of you, Mr Fitzpatrick,' said Kitty, 'but I don't know I'm your darlin' Kitty.'

'Sure yez are,' said Mr Fitzpatrick, 'didn't I drop me Irish heart into those brown eyes of yours the day me good friend Mrs Murphy introduced me to yez?'

'I bet,' said Kitty, who had no illusions about herself and her appearance, only a new feeling that she would love to have some new clothes and underwear so as to be more of a credit to her lodger. 'Honest, you don't half 'ave your share of Irish blarney, Mr Fitzpatrick.'

'Meself, is it?' Mr Fitzpatrick issued an infectious little chuckle. He was a personable gent and a favourite with some of the ladies of Larcom Street. 'Sure, it's pullin' me leg yez are, Kitty, since it's never me that's kissed the stone. It's me sincere self that's willin' to give yez any help now Mr Mullins has gone, God rest his soul.'

'Thanks ever so much,' said Kitty, 'but we've got our lodger, Mr Blair, lookin' after us. You know 'im, don't you?'

'In passing, so I do,' smiled Mr Fitzpatrick, and held out a hand to Jamie, who shook it firmly. They smiled at each other. 'Sure, it's pleased I am to make your acquaintance, and to count meself a friend and neighbour. Kitty's a fine girl, so she is, and one that can stand up to the divil himself.' He looked Jamie in the eye then, and Jamie knew he equated Henry Mullins with the devil.

'She'll survive,' he said, and Mr Fitzpatrick nodded cheerfully, said goodbye and went on his way.

'Crikey, them Irish,' said Kitty, as she and Jamie resumed their walk home, 'they've got blarney all right. Ain't they lovely with it? Mr Murphy's just the same. I don't know why some of them always want to blow other people up.'

'It's the devil in them,' said Jamie, 'and they've got reasons. But no patience.'

119

Chapter Six

Arriving back at the house, there was a note from Mrs Fitch on the kitchen table, in which she said that she and Mrs Reynolds had taken everything that needed washing, including clothes that Kitty and the kids had put out for laundering. She also said the clothes bought by Mrs Reynolds were in the parlour, and footwear as well. Which they were, with tuppence change out of the six bob. Kitty fell over herself. Mrs Reynolds had made some wise purchases and some excellent ones. To Kitty, they looked like new clothes.

'Crikey, undies as well,' she breathed in bliss, 'look. No, you're not to, it's not decent.'

Jamie left her to sort everything out while he made a pot of tea. They'd brought a can of milk in from the dairy. Kitty enjoyed a cup, said what a blessing he was, then took all the clothes and footwear upstairs. Jamie had half an hour before he needed to set off to his afternoon's work. Something was on his mind. He dug into his grey cells and came up with the realization that he was interested in

Henry Mullins's bedside vase. It simply didn't relate to the man. Let's see, he thought, Kitty had found that her step-father was flush. Nearly four pounds was very flush. Interesting. He went into the man's bedroom again. He picked up the elliptical vase with its narrow neck. It was made of thick glass and was weighty. He shook it. It made no sound. He peered into it. He could see nothing except darkness. How much was it worth? Not much. You could buy such vases any day down the market. He took it into the scullery. He found a cleaning rag, wrapped it around the vase and smashed the ornament. He opened up the rag. Amid the shattered glass was a neat roll of white fivers. He counted them. Ten. Fifty quid.

Jamie spoke ill of the dead then, but only to himself.

He went up to see Kitty. He knocked on the door of the room she shared with her sisters.

'No, you can't come in!' Kitty sounded alarmed. He rattled the door handle and heard a little shriek escape her. He guessed she was changing into something Mrs Reynolds had bought for her.

'Well, come down as soon as you can, Kitty. I've found some money and want to talk to you about it.'

'Money?'

'Yes. Fifty quid.'

'How much?'

'Ten five-pound notes in your step-father's room.'

'Oh, me sainted aunt!'

'I want to talk to you before I go off to work,' said Jamie.

Kitty came down to the kitchen in double-quick time. She was wearing a girl's calf-length dress of a deep mushroom colour, its skirt flounced. By comparison with her aged garments, it looked new. It was waisted and its well-fitting bodice provided Jamie with the discovery that seventeen-year-old Kitty had a figure, despite her step-father having kept her close to starvation. And her hair looked as if she'd actually given it a brushing.

'Mister,' she breathed, her dark eyes bright, 'did you really say fifty quid?'

'Is that you inside the dress, monkey?' asked Jamie.

'Yes, don't it look nice? I've never 'ad anything as new as this, nor as pretty. Mister, fifty quid?'

'Yes.' Jamie pointed. The ten white notes lay on the table. Kitty stared at them. She gulped. 'They were in that blue vase on your step-father's bedside table.'

'But—but how did yer know that?'

'I didn't. I simply thought it didn't fit

in his bedroom, and certainly not on his bedside table. No-one ever put a flower in it, did they?'

'Oh, he wouldn't let no-one go in his bedroom, nor touch anything, and who'd want to put a flower in any vase of 'is? I wouldn't, nor the kids.'

'Well, that saved anyone putting water in it,' said Jamie. 'I smashed it and up popped that fifty quid.'

'I'm faintin',' said Kitty, and sat down to take the weight off her weak knees. She stared again at the white fivers. 'Mister, is it ours?'

'Yes, it's yours, Kitty. Tell me, did you ever suspect he had that kind of money around?'

'As if I would,' said Kitty, eyes blinking. 'He was only a dustman, and if I asked 'im for anything, like to buy clothes for us, he'd ask me if I thought he was made of bleedin' money.'

'I don't suppose he went in for robbing banks, did he?'

'No, he just went in for bettin',' said Kitty. 'He always had money for that. He'd bet on the Derby and other big races. He used to sit sometimes lookin' at the *Sportin' Life.*'

'The sod,' said Jamie.

'I forgive you, mister, I could forgive you anything, findin' all that money for us.' Kitty's eyes were shining. 'I said it was the 'and of fate that brought you among us. It was writ that he'd fall down the stairs, which he wouldn't 'ave if you 'adn't been here.'

'Sometimes, Kitty, what comes out of your mouth gives me a headache.'

'Oh, I don't want to give you any 'eadache, mister, honest I don't. I'd feel ever so ungrateful if I did. Oh, 'elp, all them fivers, what're we goin' to do with them?'

Jamie had a sure feeling that a long shot had come up for Henry Mullins. A double, perhaps, or even a treble. The most he'd have staked would have been a pound. Dustmen and the like usually placed bob bets. But if Mullins had had a hunch or a tip, he might have staked a quid. Well, whatever he'd staked, he hadn't spent anything of his winnings on his step-children, the miserable swine.

'What you can do with the money, Kitty, is set yourself and the others up very nicely. You've got the clothes Mrs Reynolds bought this morning, and they'll do for everyday wear. But you'd all like new stuff for Sundays and Bank Holidays, as well as good shoes. There's bed linen too, you're short of that, and towels, probably. And other things, I expect, but make sure you save most of the money to help keep yourselves until you get a job.'

'Mister, could you take charge of it?' asked Kitty. 'I'd be scared to death 'aving to look after it meself. Would you do it for me and come shoppin' with us to 'elp us buy what's best for us?'

'Now look here, Kitty, you're seventeen and in that dress you look seventeen. You're up to the mark yourself when it comes to shopping for all of you. You haven't looked after Alfie and the twins all this time without turning yourself into a clever young mum.'

'But all that money, mister, I'd worry about it, honest I would,' said Kitty. 'And I'm not as old as you.'

'I'm not a grandfather yet,' said Jamie.

'No, course you're not,' said Kitty, 'but you're ever so much more worldly than I am—'

'I'm what?'

'Worldly.'

Jamie eyed her silently. Her dark brown eyes overflowed with innocence. That she was having him on he didn't doubt.

'Where'd you find that word?' he asked.

'In books,' said Kitty. 'You can read about worldly men in lots of books. People look up to them because they know about things, it's their worldly wisdom, like you've got. I bet you'd make a worldly-wise dad and be a nice one too.'

'Cut it out,' said Jamie, and shook his head at her.

'But you'll look after our money, won't you?' she said.

'All right, monkey.' He knew that had to be the best thing to do.

'And come shoppin' with us on Saturday?'

'This evening we'll make a list, and when we've made it we'll know if you'll need my help around the shops.'

'Oh, ain't it a blessin' we've got you and that you found all that money for us?' breathed Kitty blissfully. 'And d'you really like me in this frock?'

'Yes, very nice,' said Jamie. 'Listen, don't tell the kids about this money, or they'll spread the news that they've come into a fortune. It's not a fortune, it'll keep you and pay the rent for about six months.'

'Oh, I'll just tell 'em that you're providin', mister.'

'I'm not, so don't,' said Jamie. 'Just let them think you're making the original money last. My guess is that they won't ask questions.'

'Mister, you do good thinkin',' said Kitty, 'it shows you do 'ave worldly wisdom.'

'Well, I'm taking my worldly wisdom off to work now to help me knock down brick walls,' said Jamie.

'Yes, all right,' said Kitty, 'but mind you take care, we don't want any bricks fallin' on you, it would upset Chloe and Carrie.'

'Not as much as it would upset me,' said Jamie, and carried himself off to his work, taking Mrs Fitch's sandwiches with him. He had a gritty, dusty afternoon shovelling up rubble and loading it into a lorry, but it didn't do his muscles any harm. The council man in charge spoke to him when the part-time men knocked off at five o'clock.

'Like another job of work like this next week? We'll only need four of you, two each morning and two each afternoon until Friday. Pay will be a quid. You on?'

'I'm on, thanks,' said Jamie. 'Listen, gaffer, if you hear of anything permanent—?'

'I'll let yer know, mate.'

Reaching the house in Larcom Street, Jamie noted the blank look of the curtainless windows. Windows without curtains made a house seem lifeless from outside. Mrs Reynolds hurried up as he turned in at the railed gate.

'Mr Blair?'

'Hello.'

'I 'ope things 'ave been better today for Kitty and 'er brother an' sisters,' said Mrs Reynolds, an apron over her blouse and skirt.

'Well, the kids went off to school as if they were on their way to a Bank Holiday fairground.'

'What, 'appy as larks?' said Mrs Reynolds.

'Happy as larks,' said Jamie.

'Well, I can't say I'm not pleased for them.'

'By the way, many thanks for coming up with all those seconds,' said Jamie, 'they're just what Kitty and the kids needed.'

'It wasn't no trouble, Mr Blair, and seein' 'ow much you're doin' yerself for them gels and their brother, I wouldn't be able to 'old me 'ead up if I didn't do a bit meself, and Mrs Fitch feels the same. We've 'ad our coppers goin' today, boilin' the laundry, and we've been in to see Kitty and lent ' er blankets and sheets for a while.'

'She won't know how to thank you both.'

'Well, she's a deservin' gel when you think what she 'ad to put up with,' said Mrs Reynolds. Street kids stood off from this gateway dialogue, eyeing the participants in some awe. They knew what had happened in the house.

'Oh, it's in today's *South London Press* about Mr Mullins, about 'em bein' found dead from a fall at 'is 'ome.' The *South London Press* was the local paper. 'It said there's goin' to be an inquest.'

'Waste of time,' said Jamie, 'his heart gave out.'

'The law don't 'alf fuss,' said Mrs Reynolds.

'Yes, all over,' said Jamie, thinking of the very fussy police of Ulster, who had their eyes on his dotty parents.

'Well, I won't keep yer,' said Mrs Reynolds, 'except I don't mind sayin' Mrs Fitch and me think you're a young man doin' Christian good on behalf of them children. Bless yer, Mr Blair.' She took herself back home, next door.

Jamie pulled on the latchcord and let himself in. He heard Kitty and the kids in the kitchen. They all sounded lively. He went up to his room, took off his working jacket and shirt, and gave himself a good wash, getting rid of a film of dust. He cleaned his teeth and reflected on events. They all came down to the fact that for the moment he was committed to the welfare of Kitty and the others. He slipped on a jersey and went down to see how things were in the kitchen.

There they all were, in new clothes. Well, quality seconds. Clean frocks adorned

Chloe and Carrie, and clean jersey and shorts make Alfie look a presentable boy instead of a street urchin. But neither he nor the twins had done anything about their hair. Alfie plucked up a happy welcome.

' 'Ello, Dad,' he said.

'Who said that?' asked Jamie.

'Alfie,' said Chloe.

'We like yer for our dad, don't we, Chloe?' said Carrie.

'Now listen, kids—'

'Oh, you mustn't mind,' said Kitty, 'only we thought—well, I told them you're a worldly man that knows a lot more than we do, and that p'raps it wasn't respectful just to call you our big brother. I said it was ever so much more respectful to treat you like a dad.'

'Yes,' remarked Chloe, 'Kitty said remember the Ten Commandments and about 'ow thy father an' mother 'ave to be honoured, only not 'im that's passed away. Kitty said 'e wasn't no kind of dad.'

'Still, 'e did pass away peaceful,' said Carrie. 'Well, 'e nearly did, didn't 'e?'

'No, course 'e didn't,' said Chloe, 'I bet the stairs give 'im a real bashin'.'

'Let's get this straight,' said Jamie, not sure that the trap hadn't turned into quicksands, 'I'm nobody's dad, I'm not even married and I don't know the first thing about being a father.'

130

'Oh, we don't mind,' said Alfie.

'We don't want yer to get married,' said Chloe.

'You give us chocolate and yer sausages,' said Carrie.

'An' fish an' chips,' said Alfie.

'*He* never give us nothing,' said Chloe.

'Except wallops,' said Alfie.

'You ain't goin' to wallop us, are yer, please?' said Carrie.

Jamie looked at Kitty. She lowered her lashes. The monkey. She was working a flanker on him. She'd started by telling Dr McManus their kind lodger was going to look after them. That put her on course to her next target, a big brother. Now he was to be their dad. She'd ask him to grow whiskers next and smoke a clay pipe.

'What're you playing at, you Turk?' he asked.

'Me?' said Kitty. 'Oh, I've got the supper goin'. D'you mean the supper? I'm doin' the mutton chops with mashed potatoes and cabbage. We've got to 'ave cabbage, it's good for us, all greens are.'

'Ugh,' said Chloe.

'D'you like greens, Carrie?' asked Jamie.

'I don't mind a bit of greens, I don't like a lot,' said Carrie. She looked at Jamie, swallowed and said, 'You ain't goin' away to get married, are yer?'

'No, I'm going into the yard to knock

131

my head against the wall,' said Jamie, 'and I'm taking your big sister with me to stuff her into the dustbin.'

'But it's full of leavings,' protested Chloe.

'Good,' said Jamie.

'Oh, 'elp,' said Alfie.

'Don't take no notice,' said Kitty, 'he don't mean it, he's come home from work a bit tired, I expect, and what with that and 'aving to talk to the police yesterday, he's probably not feelin' well.'

'I dunno 'ow it's goin' to make 'im feel better knockin' 'is loaf of bread against the yard wall,' said Alfie.

'Tell your sister I'm watching her,' said Jamie.

'What yer watchin' 'er for?' asked Chloe.

'Artfulness,' said Jamie.

'Our Kitty ain't artful,' said Chloe, 'she just gets a bit cross with us sometimes, but she's nice really.'

'Mister, I don't know why you're goin' on like this,' said Kitty. 'I'm grievin' a bit at bein' called artful, I've never been called artful in all me life, except by 'im. Still, he called us all names. Oh, I collected the parish relief groceries this afternoon, we've got a whole larder of food now, and we'll 'ave a nice supper of the mutton chops. I told Chloe and Carrie and Alfie how 'elpful and kind you were round at the town hall with me this mornin', and how you got us on parish relief. I said no dad could 'ave been more 'elpful.'

'It's the dustbin for you, my girl,' said Jamie.

'Oh, you said that just like a real dad.'

Jamie couldn't help himself then. He laughed. The sound was infectious to Chloe and Carrie. Their smiles beamed. Alfie grinned. Jamie crossed to the door.

'Where yer goin'?' asked Chloe.

'Up to my room to give my ears a rest,' said Jamie.

'We'll call you when supper's ready,' said Kitty. 'Oh, there's a letter for you, it came with the afternoon post.' She took it from the mantelpiece and handed it to Alfie, who took it to Jamie. He looked at the envelope. It was his mother's handwriting.

Carrie whispered to Chloe.

'It's not a letter from 'er, is it?'

'Who?' asked Chloe, as Jamie left the kitchen.

'The lady 'e's goin' to marry.'

'Who said 'e's goin' to get married?' asked Chloe.

' 'E did, didn't 'e?'

'Carrie, you are soppy,' said Chloe, ' 'e's not goin' to get married, 'e's goin' to look after us and be our dad. Kitty said so,

133

when she told us it's best we call 'im dad and not mister.'

'Yes, but I only asked,' said Carrie. 'Is 'e really goin' to be our dad, Kitty?'

'Yes, course he is,' said Kitty, and smiled. 'We don't 'ave anyone else except 'im.'

Jamie read his mother's letter. She wrote to say she hoped he was in good health, that he'd got himself a good job and that he'd joined the Labour Party to help overcome capitalist oppression of the workers. His dad was still doing fiery work for the cause, she said, only more secretly on account of the Belfast police coming the old acid with everyone they found saying 'workers of the world unite' or 'up the IRA'. Actually, she confessed, she and his dad had given up supporting the IRA because they'd turned into chronic hooligans. They'd decided to support law and order instead, as you had to have some law and order. They were still thinking of going to Russia one day and joining the Bolsheviks, who'd done a brave job for the workers by doing away with all the rich people.

Now, she said, it's like this. We're pleased you're settled in Larcom Street, which me and your dad know quite well. Now there's a friend of mine, Rosemary

Allen, that's got herself into a little bit of trouble and is coming to London. Could Jamie look after her and get her into his lodgings, she was a nice girl who wouldn't harm no-one, only she didn't know anybody in London who'd be a friend to her, and she fancies what your dad and me told her about Larcom Street and what a fine boy you are, even if you were a bit wanting over that business with the German army. Your dad and me fondly hope you'll take Rosemary in, if your landlord could be obliging, and keep a friendly eye on her owing to her little troubles having got her down a bit. She has a job to go to, a Belfast friend has helped her get it, so she won't be a burden. She hopes you'll tell your neighbours she's a friend of yours so that there won't be any scandal about her lodging with you. She just wants a quiet life for a bit.

Mrs Blair closed by saying take care of yourself, you'll always be one of the workers as long as you get a job soon. With any luck, your dad might get to sink a capitalist ship before we go to Russia and meet Lenin.

With any luck, thought Jamie, they might get to bump heads and cure themselves of their pottiness. As to Rosemary Allen, whoever she is, before I give her any help

I'd like to find out if she's as potty as they are. Little troubles could relate to the Irish big troubles.

Only this morning the papers had reported another political assassination by the IRA.

Chapter Seven

Jamie had to give Kitty her due, her mutton chop supper couldn't be faulted. The meaty chops were sweet and tender, the mashed potatoes creamy with a lavish amount of margarine. There was a huge mound on each of the kids' plates and an acceptable amount of cabbage. They tucked in with undisguised delight. Kitty glanced covertly at Jamie as he began his meal, a little anxiety hovering in case it wasn't to his liking. However, it obviously was, and she smiled and commenced her own plateful.

The kids made their inevitable comments.

'Crikey,' said Alfie, 'we never ate like this before, Kitty.'

'I never saw all this on me plate ever,' said Chloe.

'That man that's passed away,' said Carrie, 'd'you think 'e'd belt us if he saw us eatin' all this?'

'Our new dad wouldn't let 'im, would yer, Dad?' said Alfie.

'Can anyone tell me who Alfie is talking about?' asked Jamie.

'Mister, it's you,' said Carrie shyly.

'I give up,' said Jamie. 'For the time being,' he added. 'Until I get your sister alone,' he further added.

Kitty, intoxicated by the arrival of wealth and a man to look after them, said, 'I'll 'ave to 'ave a chaperone.'

'Great thunderbolts,' said Jamie, 'who said that?'

'Kitty,' said Chloe.

'What's a chap'ron?' asked Carrie, eating her greens.

'Someone that a single girl has to 'ave with her when a gent wants to be alone with her,' said Kitty.

'That's in books too, is it?' said Jamie, releasing meat from the bone.

'Yes, course it is,' said Kitty. 'We all like you, I like you meself, but I don't know it's right to be alone with you. The neighbours might find out and think we're keepin' an unrespectable 'ouse. Still, I suppose Mrs Reynolds 'as told everyone you're bein' a dad to us, so it wouldn't be unrespectable then.'

'Read some more books,' said Jamie, 'they'll help you find out it's not unrespectable for precocious girls to get their bottoms smacked by any dad worth his salt.'

'What's precocious?' asked Alfie, enjoying his meal hugely.

'Its other name is Kitty,' said Jamie.

'You ain't really goin' to smack 'er

138

bottom, are yer?' said Chloe.

'I'm seriously thinking about it.'

'Crikey, she'll break yer leg,' said Alfie.

'Don't frighten me to death,' said Jamie. 'Listen, a friend of my mother's is coming to London, and I've been asked to find her lodgings.'

'A friend of your mum's?' said Kitty, who knew his parents were in Belfast.

'Yes. Are any of you going to take over your step-father's room?'

'Not me,' said Alfie, 'I ain't goin' in there.'

'Nor me,' said Chloe.

' 'E'll 'aunt it,' said Carrie.

'D'you want your mum's friend to 'ave it?' asked Kitty, looking at Jamie.

'Well, her rent as a lodger would be useful to you,' said Jamie.

'She could be our aunt,' said Chloe.

'More like our grandmuvver,' said Alfie.

'Oh, I'd like a grandma,' said Carrie.

'She'll only be lodging for a while,' said Jamie.

'All right, we don't mind,' said Kitty, 'and we couldn't say no to a friend of your mum's, specially if it's only for a while. What rent could we ask?'

'Five bob?' suggested Jamie.

'I bet we could do with that,' said Alfie. ' 'Ere, I could do errands for 'er at a penny a go.'

'Ain't it a blessin', Alfie, that we've got Mr Blair here?' said Kitty. 'I wouldn't know what to charge a lodger for rent.'

'Not much,' said Jamie.

'But I wouldn't,' said Kitty. He had finished his meal and only the chop bone remained on his plate. 'Was your supper all right?'

'A treat,' he said.

'That's good,' said Kitty.

'I'm goin' out after supper to meet some of me mates,' said Alfie.

'We're goin' out too, me an' Carrie,' said Chloe.

'Don't any of you stay out late,' said Kitty.

When supper was over and the washing-up done, out went Alfie and his twin sisters. Alfie put his head back round the kitchen door.

'See yer later, Dad,' he said, and vanished again.

'Now look here, Kitty,' said Jamie, 'what's the idea of putting them up to this "dad" lark?'

'Oh, it's just out of respect,' said Kitty, 'and they can't 'ardly remember their own dad. You don't mind actin' like a dad to us, do you?'

'It was only yesterday you lost your step-father,' said Jamie, 'but the things that have crept up on me since then make me feel it must have been a year ago. That includes you quoting to the kids the Commandment about honouring thy father and mother.'

'Oh, it only means good fathers and mothers,' said Kitty, who could never think of her own mother without remembering how often she smelled of drink. 'It don't mean those like my step-father.'

'What's that got to do with trying to make a dad of me at my age?'

'Oh, but you're lots older than us—'

'No, I'm not.'

'And we like you lookin' after us,' said Kitty, who knew that she and her brother and sisters would have a better chance of surviving as a family if their lodger took charge of them. She could manage quite a lot herself, but she knew they'd all feel more secure with a man about the house. A decent man, who'd help to see they didn't starve and deal with any authority in a bowler hat that might come knocking on the door. She had a feeling that authority would take Alfie and the twins away from her. Kitty was fiercely protective of her brother and sisters. She just had to hang on to Mr Blair. And she meant to, by hook or by crook. 'We won't be any bother, honest we won't,' she said.

For his part, Jamie knew he couldn't leave them until the situation satisfactorily resolved itself in some way.

'Well, I suppose I'll have to see you all settled into a decent kind of life before I start living my own again,' he said.

Kitty smiled.

He did his final four hours of work for the week on Saturday morning. At the end of it he received his wage of twenty-four bob, and was told where to report on Monday for another week of part-time labour.

Kitty was all ready to go out on the shopping expedition in the afternoon. Jamie tried to duck out. Kitty cornered him in his room and asked him how he expected her to manage on her own. This question, with its proprietary implications, floored Jamie for a moment. Then he said it might be a good idea to ask Mrs Fitch to accompany her and the kids. Kitty said not likely, Mrs Fitch would be curious about where all the money was coming from. It would be best if he came and if he paid for everything, because if she started producing the money herself, Alfie would soon ask about it. Chloe and Carrie were trusting and unsuspicious, she said, but Alfie was a bit sharp. We'd best make it look as if you're lending us the money until we can pay it back. If Alfie falls for that, Jamie had replied, he's not all that sharp. No, perhaps he's not, said Kitty, but he'll believe you. Believe me? he'd questioned. Yes, she said, when you tell him you're lending us. Leave me out, said Jamie, and I'll give you some of the money and you can say I lent it to you out of savings. Kitty started to get ratty then. Her eyes started to flash. That's not looking after us like you promised, she said.

'I wouldn't know how to spend the money properly,' she said, 'nor know what was best to buy and what to pay for it.'

Jamie gave in and went round the shops with the four of them. Kitty kept in close communication with him, asking his advice about everything, including what new clothes suited them all best, and reminding him how much she relied on his worldly wisdom. Jamie said she was overdoing that piece of flannel. Chloe and Carrie were in bliss about the buying spree, never once in any apparent curiosity concerning the available funds, but Alfie did ask where all the dibs were coming from. Kitty said their Christian lodger had been sent a lot of postal orders by his parents, that he'd cashed them and was lending them what they wanted until their ship came in. Alfie forgot his manners once and said it was taking a bleeding long time to come in, they'd been waiting for years for it already. Kitty boxed his ears for using disrespectful language in a shop in front of their kind lodger who was being as good as a dad to them.

In the bedding department of Hurlocks, near the Elephant and Castle, they bought a whole heap of sheets and blankets, these to be delivered. What they did have at home had come back smelling fresh and clean from Mrs Fitch and Mrs Reynolds, but they needed to make up numbers and to buy spares as well. Kitty left the choice of blankets to Jamie. That is, she asked him to make the choice for her, as she didn't have any experience in blanket-buying. Jamie said he'd been doing it all his life, of course, and Kitty said what a blessing.

They returned to Larcom Street laden to their chins with parcels. For Chloe and Carrie life had suddenly become rapturous, and Alfie wasn't sure if it was real. Thinking it was all due to Jamie, Chloe asked if she could give him a kiss. Jamie, resigned to the obvious, that he was temporarily committed to their welfare, said all right, Chloe, and Chloe gave him a smacker. So Carrie, of course, gave him another. Alfie asked to be excused, and Kitty said as they were all worn out from the shopping, she'd make a pot of tea. Jamie said he'd make it while they unpacked their things.

'No, you sit and 'ave a rest,' said Kitty, 'I'll make the tea.'

'Yes, he don't smell of drink,' said Chloe. 'Well, 'e didn't when I kissed 'im.' That was a reminder to her brother and sisters that their step-father smelled of drink most days.

'Yes, 'ave a rest,' said Alfie.

'Look, I'm not ninety,' said Jamie.

'Still, you'll be there before we will,' said Kitty.

She was at it again, thought Jamie, trying to make him feel old enough to be their dad.

'Hoppit,' he said. 'All of you take your parcels up to your rooms and unpack them. Put all the stuff tidily away, and comb your hair before you come down again.'

'Me?' said Carrie.

'All of you.'

'Comb our hair?' said Chloe.

'Yes, you're all developing mops again.'

' 'Ere, my 'air don't want combing,' said Alfie, whose mop needed a barber's scissors.

'We'd better do like he says, Alfie,' said Kitty.

'I suppose so,' said Alfie.

'What for?' asked Carrie.

'I'm in charge, that's what for,' said Jamie. 'I've been put in charge by your sister, so I'm taking charge. There's no reason why you can't look tidy and pretty each time you leave the house—'

'Me? Me look pretty?' said Alfie in horror.

'Clean and tidy,' said Jamie. 'Your neighbours are watching developments, and I don't want them thinking I'm doing a slipshod job with any of you. Your sister Kitty has got to stop going out with wrinkles in her stockings—'

'Here, excuse me,' said Kitty.

'And her hair not brushed. We ought to make something of Kitty at her age and send her out looking a credit to herself.' Jamie, stuck with responsibilities, had decided to lay down the law. 'Time she had a boy knocking on her door. We'll get those wrinkles out of her stockings and keep her hair from looking as if it's had an accident. The hair ribbons bought this afternoon will be used by one and all except Alfie, even if he does look as if he could use some at the moment. That's it, then, for the time being. Now take your parcels upstairs and when you come down again I want to see combed or brushed hair tied with ribbon, except yours, Alfie.'

'Crikey,' breathed Chloe, 'ain't 'e stern?'

'Never mind, up you all go,' said Kitty. She hustled them out, but had her own back as she followed. 'What a palaver,'

146

she said loudly, arms cradling parcels, 'I've never met anyone more bossy in all me life. Comb your 'air, do this, do that—you Alfie, now what've you done?'

Alfie had dropped his parcels.

Mrs Hilda Briggs, opening the scullery door of her house in Peckham, called to her husband Wally. He was in the yard, mending the lid of the coal bunker.

'Come in 'ere.'

Mr Briggs said, 'Yes, me love,' and came in from the yard. In the kitchen, she waved a copy of the *South London Press* at him.

'Why didn't you tell me me brother 'Enry went an' died? You read all through this paper yesterday an' didn't say a bleedin' word to me, me 'is own sister.'

Mr Briggs at forty-five was only half the size of his forty-two-year-old wife. She was large and aggressive, he was lean and watchful. He was in fact watchful of what he said on account of the fact that it was sometimes no sooner a word than a clout. He couldn't say she drank like her brother did—had—but she still had a face as red as Henry's. And the same kind of short fuse.

' 'Enry's dead?' he said, keeping his distance.

'That's what it says 'ere.' Again Mrs Briggs waved the newspaper at him.

147

'Gawd rest 'is soul, me love.'

'Never mind 'is soul. What about you not tellin' me an' the shock it's give me, findin' it out for meself?'

'On me oath, 'Ilda, I didn't see it. I know I went through the paper, but I didn't read all that was in it. I sympathize with yer from the bottom of me 'eart, 'Ilda.' Mr Briggs felt that was the right thing to say, even though he knew his wife and her brother had never got on. They'd chucked things at each other when they were kids, and had abused each other ever since. Mind, they'd had one or two friendly moments, one or two. ' 'As 'e really copped it, me love? What 'appened that it's in the paper?'

' 'E fell down the bleedin' stairs, didn't 'e?' said Mrs Briggs.

'Did 'e? Broke 'is neck, did 'e? Poor old 'Enry.'

'It don't say that.' Mrs Briggs felt she was due to show a bit of mournfulness, so she lifted a corner of her apron and dabbed her eyes and blew her nose. 'Me only brother, me only close relative, gorn to 'is grave an' me not knowin'.'

'What, they've 'ad the funeral?' said Mr Briggs.

' 'Ow do I know? It don't say. But what it does say is that there's goin' to be an inquest. That's upsettin', that is.'

Mrs Briggs blew her nose again on her apron.

'Well, 'e can't 'ave 'ad 'is funeral, me love, they wouldn't bury 'im an' then dig 'im up, they'd wait till after the inquest before they dropped 'im into 'is grave.'

'Don't give me no lip,' said Mrs Briggs, 'nor don't you talk about me only brother bein' dropped into 'is grave or I'll brain yer. Just put yer best suit on tomorrer afternoon, with a black tie.'

'Eh?' said Mr Briggs, at which Mrs Briggs rolled up the newspaper tightly and hit him with it.

'That's to shake up what brains you 'ave got,' she said. 'Tomorrow afternoon, we've got to go over there, ain't we? Trust that Kitty not to let me know me own brother met a sad end. What I want to know is what about 'is money?'

'What money?' asked Mr Briggs, and the rolled-up newspaper hit him again.

'You know what money,' said Mrs Briggs. 'Didn't I tell 'im where the safe was in the store, and didn't 'e give me twenty quid afterwards?'

'Did 'e?'

'Course 'e did. Out of 'is fondness for me. Listen, stand up straight when I'm talkin' to yer. That money, we ain't goin' to let them kids 'ave what's left of it. They ain't 'is relatives, I am. So we're goin' over

149

tomorrer, like I said, to speak our piece, so don't 'ide yerself be'ind my back when we get there.'

'Them kids'll be 'ard-up, 'Ilda—'

'Well, they ain't 'Enry's kids. More trouble than they were worth, that's what they were. I never did 'old with 'im marryin' their mother.'

'Good-lookin' woman, though,' said Mr Briggs.

'What took to drink, which a woman shouldn't,' said Mrs Briggs. ' 'Ere, are you answerin' me back?'

'I was only sayin'—'

'Well, don't say any more, just go an' finish mendin' that coal bunker or the rain'll get in. If you start bringin' wet coal into me kitchen I'll chop yer legs off.'

Mr Briggs gratefully escaped. He was always grateful whenever he escaped injury.

Sunday. There was going to be a roast dinner. Roast rib of beef, and in fact. Jamie had gone early to the market and come back with the joint. He'd put money into the pool from his wages to cover the cost of his share of the food so far. The rib of beef was an extra contribution. He felt he owed Kitty that. Kitty, overwhelmed, said he didn't have to do that because the family had the benefit of his protection and advice, which was worth a lot more

150

than money. Protection, what protection? Jamie put the question suspiciously. Well, fatherly protection, said Kitty. Cut it out, said Jamie, or I'll start breaking windows. Not ours, I hope, said Kitty, then told him she'd get the dinner all prepared in advance and put the joint in the oven so that they could all go to church.

Alfie turned a pale shade of grey. Chloe and Carrie goggled.

'Church?' they said.

'Yes,' said Kitty, 'we'll all put our new Sunday best on, and go with our Christian lodger to church. We 'aven't been for ages—'

'I ain't 'ardly been at all,' said Alfie.

'Well, we're all goin' this mornin',' said Kitty, 'we want the neighbours to see we're livin' respectable lives, which is what our kind lodger wants too, 'im bein' as good as a dad to us.'

'I'm going to read my newspaper,' said Jamie.

'Can't you read it this evenin'?' asked Carrie.

'Yes, that's it, this evenin',' said Kitty. 'Well, Mrs Fitch and Mrs Reynolds go to church, so do other neighbours, and I expect they'll be pleased to see you takin' us, Mr Blair. They'll tell everybody about 'ow respectable we are.' She was thinking of authority in bowler hats getting to hear.

151

'You can all go to church, but leave me out,' said Jamie.

'Let's all get on with the vegetables,' said Kitty, 'and then we'll put our best new frocks on, and Alfie can wear 'is new suit. You goin' to wear a suit, Mr Blair?'

'No, I'm going up to my room to give my ears a rest,' said Jamie.

But at ten to eleven, of course, he took them to church in their new Sunday best. The May morning was fine, and Kitty and the twins looked colourful. Alfie looked philosophical.

Kids in the street stared.

'Cor, look at old Mullins's lot.'

'Crikey, ain't they supposed to be wearin' black?'

' 'Ere, you Chloe, why ain't yer in mournin'?'

'Oh, 'elp,' breathed Kitty in sudden realization of a mortal error, 'we ain't even wearin' black armbands.'

Jamie, walking between the twins, said, 'Are you in mourning, Kitty? Are any of you?'

'Well, we're not actu'lly grievin',' said Kitty.

Alfie in straightforward fashion said he hadn't felt a bit grievous, and Carrie for once came up with a positive statement by saying she liked not getting walloped.

152

Chloe said she hadn't ever felt so happy.

'Well, good,' said Jamie, 'I like the lot of you for being honest.' It hadn't occurred to him at any time to suggest they should wear something black. He hadn't, in fact, thought about the matter at all. As far as he was concerned, this family of young people were free of a bullying and baleful drunkard. 'It's Sunday, kids, the sun's shining and there'll be a roast dinner today. Not a bad outlook, eh?'

Kitty, of course, with her mind set on making him their shield, said, 'I just don't know how we'd 'ave managed without you.'

Not much, you monkey, thought Jamie. She was talking now about doing Yorkshire pudding with the roast beef, in the warm air her words seemed to float into his ear. He realized then that this girl, as dark-eyed and black-haired as a gypsy, had a voice as beguiling as one. Some cockney girls could be shrill, usually because of wanting to be heard in the boisterous atmosphere of large families. He had heard Kitty shouting at Mullins, but she had never sounded shrill. Her angry yells had actually had a musical quality to them, and he wondered if her father had been Welsh. The name Edwards could be associated with the musical Welsh.

They turned into the bend housing the

vicarage and the parish church. People were crowding the church forecourt, saying hello to each other. The bell was ringing and the cockneys of Walworth were answering the call. Young ones were in their Sunday best. It had always amazed Jamie how the poorest families could somehow find Sunday best for their young ones, even if a close look revealed the cheapness of the garments.

Mrs Fitch was there with her little girl, talking to Mr and Mrs Reynolds. Their eyes opened wide as Jamie arrived in the forecourt with Kitty and the kids. The new frocks splashed the scene with bright colour, while Alfie's suit and tie were something to behold indeed. Mrs Fitch and Mrs Reynolds expressed pleasure and surprise. Mr Reynolds, a hard-working navvy, was heartier.

' 'Ow are yer, girlies, 'ow are yer, Alfie? Gawd love yer, Alfie, yer lookin' 'andsome, ain't yer? And what've yer done to yer fancy sisters, eh?'

'Oh, our lodger done it, Mr Reynolds,' said Alfie, ' 'e's made 'em all look fancy. I ain't fancy meself, I'm just wearin' a suit.'

'Well, yer lodger's done yer all swell,' grinned Mr Reynolds. 'Good on yer, Jamie, Kitty an' the twins is a right Sunday treat to me mince pies.'

'Kitty, don't you look a lovely grown-up girl now?' said Mrs Fitch.

'Oh, thanks ever so, Mrs Fitch,' said Kitty. 'We're all over our grievous shock now, and Mr Blair said 'e'd best take us to church this mornin' so we could give thanks that we didn't all fall down the stairs ourselves.'

Jamie coughed.

'And we all got toothbrushes now,' said Chloe, clean face bright and happy.

'Our lodger made us get them,' said Carrie.

'Yer lodger's a fine young man,' said Mrs Reynolds.

'Yes, but he's a lot older than us,' said Alfie.

'Yes, Kitty told us so,' said Carrie. ' 'E's like a new dad to us, she said.'

'Yes, he's been a real blessin',' said Kitty. The bell stopped ringing, and they all moved into the church.

St John's was a handsome church, and high Anglican. Chloe and Carrie were in awe most of the time. Alfie liked the hymns and sang them with gusto. Kitty did a lot of thinking. She thought about being free of her step-father and of all that money found by Mr Blair. She thought about her feelings, all of which were to do with relief and hope. She felt the only problem about being free was if some interfering bloke

155

from the council came round to see if the family was destitute. Interfering blokes from the council might decide to split them up and put them into separate homes. She hoped Mr Blair wouldn't let them do that, that he'd say he was looking after them. Then he'd be able to tell them to buzz off. She felt she'd have to make sure he didn't leave them, which he might just do if he met some young lady and wanted to marry her. She thought if that looked likely, then the best thing to do would be to have a talk with their lodger. About her step-father's fall down the stairs. Realizing exactly what she was thinking about, and at a moment when the vicar was leading everyone in prayer, she hastily prayed for forgiveness.

Alfie, finding things a bit obscure at this point, prayed for the family's ship to come home so that they'd be rich and he could buy himself a bike.

Chloe prayed that their lodger would see to it that they didn't go hungry any more.

Carrie prayed that Jesus wouldn't let their lodger get cross with Kitty, as it would make Kitty throw plates and saucepans about, like she had at their step-father sometimes, which had made him growl and roar and hand out wallops all round.

Kneeling on her hassock, Carrie turned her head to glance at their lodger. He met her eyes. Carrie turned a little pink. Jamie winked.

Kitty quite liked the sermon, given by the vicar, the Reverend Mr Edwards, much admired for his kindness and understanding. It was all about help thy neighbour. The vicar, who thought far more of his flock of resilient hard-up cockneys than he did of certain archbishops and politicians, knew that the greatest virtue of the people of Walworth lay in their willingness to help each other. Some might have thought, as he began his sermon, that he was going to preach to the converted. But he did no such thing, he did not exhort any of his congregation to help their neighbours. He knew there was no need to. What he did do was to stress the Christian nature of such acts and to make it quite clear that although poverty and hardship were abroad in Walworth, so was the spirit of Christianity.

'May God bless your many kindnesses to each other, and to others,' he said in conclusion, 'and may all who lack a Sunday roast today be favoured with one next week. Now, shall we sing the last hymn?'

The crowded church came to its feet,

and nodding old men were gently shaken awake.

'Oh, ain't the vicar a nice man?' whispered Carrie.

'I 'ope he 'as a roast dinner 'imself,' whispered Chloe.

Jamie smiled. In their outlook and their conversation the twins seemed a lot younger than their fourteen years. He felt that was due to the repression they had suffered at the hands of their step-father. But he also felt it wouldn't take them long to become as perky and sharp as most cockney girls now that Mullins had crashed his way out of their lives.

The last hymn was sung resoundingly. Afterwards, the vicar was at the open church doors to smile and nod at departing parishioners, and to say a few words to some of them. He spoke to Kitty, expressing regrets at her step-father's fatal accident.

'Yes, it was a grievous shock, vicar,' said Kitty, 'but we're bearin' up, and our lodger, Mr Blair, 'as been as kind and 'elpful as a real Christian gent.'

The smiling vicar shook Jamie's hand.

'They're endemic to Walworth, Mr Blair,' he said.

'What are?' asked Jamie.

'Good Samaritans,' said the vicar.

'Yes, and I expect he'll bring us to

158

church regular,' said Kitty.

'I hope so,' said the vicar.

Mrs Fitch appeared with her little girl and walked home with Jamie. Kitty, Alfie and the twins followed. Kitty heard Mrs Fitch laughing a lot. Here, she thought, I'll have to watch Mrs Fitch, we don't want her running off with Mr Blair, I've heard about married women running off with someone else's lodger. In fact, she'd once heard Mrs Warboys from across the street say that that was what most lodgers were for, for married women to run off with. I'm not having that, thought Kitty.

A neighbour's son, fifteen-year-old Herbert Joslin, caught up with Chloe and Carrie, and eyed their new Sunday best as if he was seeing things.

'What 'appened?' he asked.

'What d'yer mean, what 'appened?' asked Chloe. Herbert Joslin was nosy, and lippy as well.

'Where'd yer get yer fancy frocks an' clean faces from?'

'Cheek, mind yer own business,' said Chloe.

'I 'eard yer step-father's gorn,' said Herbert. 'Mind you, me dad says it wasn't a day too soon. 'E used to wallop yer, didn't 'e?'

'We don't talk about that,' said Chloe.

' 'E fell down the stairs, yer know,' said Carrie.

'Yes, we 'eard,' said Herbert. ' 'Ere, did 'e fall or was 'e pushed?'

'Oh, go away, you rotten lump,' said Chloe.

'Take you up the park this afternoon, if yer like,' said lippy Herbert.

'You'll be lucky,' said Chloe, and she and Carrie followed Kitty and Alfie into their house.

Kitty's roast beef was a triumph, and Jamie frankly marvelled at the kitchen accomplishments of a girl of seventeen. She'd made a thin batter pudding, which to Jamie was distinct from a thick Yorkshire pudding. Kitty said they were the same except for the difference in thickness, and that she'd done him a thin one in case he laid the law down again, like he had yesterday. Still, they all had to remember he was a good Samaritan, like the vicar had said. Jamie gave Carrie another wink. Carrie giggled.

Over the dinner, Chloe said she and Carrie were going up the park this afternoon.

'Girls get kissed in the park,' said Alfie.

'Well, Chloe and Carrie ain't goin' to be kissed anywhere,' said Kitty, 'they're too young.'

160

'I ain't kissed any girls meself,' said Alfie. ' 'Ave you, mister?'

'A few,' said Jamie, and the brown eyes all turned on him.

'Did yer like it?' asked Carrie.

'If a bloke doesn't like it,' said Jamie, 'he needs to see a doctor.'

'What, does it make yer ill, then, not likin' kissin' a girl?' asked Alfie.

'No, it just means you've got a problem,' said Jamie. He noted they were all eating with relish, putting food happily into stomachs that had suffered a paucity of rations. Their flesh-starved faces looked as if they were visibly changing for the better. For afters, there were pineapple chunks and hot custard. The kids all said Kitty had done swell, and Alfie was in such a good mood that he said he'd go up the park too.

'Take Kitty with you,' said Jamie. 'You might be able to find a boy for her in the park.'

'Here, what d'you think I am?' said Kitty indignantly. 'I can find a boy by meself when I need to and when I've got time to. Mind, I might 'ave more time now I don't 'ave certain worries risin' up in front of me every day.'

A walk in Ruskin Park suddenly appealed to her. It was a lovely afternoon and she'd got her new Sunday frock on, and there

161

might just be a good-looking young man around who'd fancy meeting her. 'Yes, I think I'll—' She stopped before she'd hardly started. If they all went out, herself included, their lodger would be left on his own. That wouldn't be very gracious, not when he was being such a help to them and she needed to make a father figure of him in the eyes of neighbours and council busybodies. Some busybody might easily say to another busybody, go round and see if those kids and their sister in Larcom Street have only got parish relief coming in. Go and see if they're destitute, we don't want their neighbours coming in and complaining that we're not doing anything for them, like taking them to institutions. Kitty could picture it all. So she just had to make sure that their lodger could say to any busybody or any bloke in a bowler hat that he was looking after them in a fatherly way. A good and kind fatherly way. Of course, if he'd been a bit older and sat around in his braces smoking a pipe, he'd have looked the part better. Still, he was old enough, really. 'No, I don't think I'll go out,' she said, 'I'll keep Mr Blair company.'

'No, that's not necessary,' said Jamie, 'I'm going to put my feet up and read my newspaper.'

'Oh, that'll suit you,' said Kitty, 'lots of dads do that on Sunday afternoons.'

'Only old dads that's a bit bald and 'ave got whiskers,' said Alfie.

'Don't be disrespectful,' said Kitty, 'Mr Blair's easily old enough to put 'is feet up, he don't 'ave to 'ave whiskers and be a bit bald. I'll bring you a cup of tea,' she said to their lodger.

'No, you go out,' said Jamie. 'You deserve an outing, and you need one. Never mind my old age, go and show your new Sunday dress off in the park.'

'But—'

'I insist,' said Jamie.

'Well, all right, if you're sure,' said Kitty. For the first time she was thinking how much she'd like to have a young man. It was something she couldn't ever have thought seriously about before. What girl could when she'd been kept in a state near to rags by a step-father who was as bad as Cinderella's step-mother? All a girl could seriously think about under those conditions was survival.

Yes, I'll do meself up and go to the park, she thought, now that our lodger's insisted.

Chapter Eight

Alfie and the twins had been gone twenty minutes, departing, Jamie had noticed, without bothering to comb their hair.

Kitty, upstairs, was just about ready to depart herself, and Jamie, in the kitchen, was about to take his newspaper up to his room and have a comfortable read on his bed. He'd get all the exercise he needed tomorrow, at his work. He'd have enjoyed going out himself frankly if he had had a young lady to meet, which he hadn't. Unemployment interspersed with part-time work now and again hardly put him in a position to be favoured by the opposite sex.

He answered a knock on the front door. On the step stood a large buxom woman and a bloke who was a bit of a lean and wiry job. However, he had a pleasant face. The woman had a red beefy one that put Jamie in mind of the choleric countenance of Henry Mullins.

'Hello,' he said, 'what can I do for you?'

'Good afternoon,' said Henry Mullins's sister, Mrs Hilda Briggs, 'might I hask 'oo you are?'

164

'My name's Blair,' said Jamie.

'Might I further hask what you're doin' in this 'ouse?'

'I'm lodging here.'

Mrs Briggs had first placed him as some bloke taking advantage of her brother's death to do things he ought not to do with that girl Kitty, although how any bloke could fancy her she couldn't think. Mind, as a lodger, he might still be taking advantage. Some blokes could fancy anything in drawers. Still, no point in getting on anyone's wrong side to begin with.

'Well, I'm Mrs 'Ilda Briggs, an' this is me 'usband, Mr Briggs. I'm Mr 'Enry Mullins's sister. Well, I was till 'e come to 'is sad end some days ago in this very 'ouse, as I understand it. Me an' Mr Briggs 'ave come to see the children that me unfortunate brother was step-father to.'

She'd put 'unfortunate' in the wrong place, thought Jamie. She should have said 'unfortunate children'.

'Kitty's just about to go out, Mrs Briggs. The younger ones are already out.'

'Oh, we'll see 'er, then, we won't keep 'er long,' said Mrs Briggs.

Kitty came down the stairs then. From the open doorway, Mrs Briggs stared at her. Kitty, reaching the passage, stopped as she saw the callers. She looked all of an attractive young lady in her daffodil yellow and a little round straw hat. Jamie made a note of the fact that her hair was well-brushed and tied neatly with a ribbon at the back of her neck. He smiled. Kitty was bothering with herself.

'Oh,' she said.

' 'Ello, Kitty,' said Mr Briggs kindly.

'I can't believe it,' said Mrs Briggs, 'I've never seen yer dolled up like this before. That's a new 'at an' frock.'

'Yes, the first I've 'ad since I don't know when,' said Kitty.

'Well, yer step-father's 'ad four of you to keep and was always an 'ard-workin' man earnin' poor wages,' said Mrs Briggs, highly suspicious of where the money had come from to buy the hat and frock. 'Me an' Mr Briggs'll come in an' talk to yer for a bit. I expect you need some comfortin' after the shock of me brother's death. I suppose it was the shock that made you forget to write an' let us know 'e'd gorn. Come in, Wally. We don't mind the kitchen, I don't suppose you've been able to make much of the parlour yet, Kitty.'

Kitty looked disgusted. Her step-father's sister hadn't ever been much of an aunt, and had only ever called about twice a year. She'd always dragged her down-trodden husband along with her. He'd

166

once slipped them a penny each behind her back. Kitty sometimes felt as sorry for him as she did for herself and her brother and sisters.

'If Kitty's goin' out, 'Ilda—'

'Oh, I'm sure she can spare us a bit of time.' Mrs Briggs let a smile appear. It made a few creases in her red face, but didn't improve her looks. 'We just want to talk to yer for five minutes, Kitty, we've got 'urt feelings about me brother, poor 'Enry, an' we'd like to know exactly what 'appened.'

'Well, Mr Blair can 'elp inform you,' said Kitty, 'he was here at the time, on the landin' with me and Mr Mullins.'

'Yer step-dad,' said Mrs Briggs. Kitty grimaced and took them into the kitchen. Jamie followed. He had a feeling about Mrs Briggs. The lady said he didn't have to be present. Kitty said she'd rather he was. 'Oh, all right,' said Mrs Briggs, and sat down at the table. 'Well, what 'appened, then?' she asked.

Kitty told her and was brief in the telling. Jamie confirmed her account.

' 'Is 'eart gave out, eh?' said Mr Briggs. ' 'Ighly fatal, that is, 'Ilda.'

Mrs Briggs looked again at Kitty. That frock, that hat, and her hair and face done up. Sign of someone in the money, all that was. And the lodger, he looked like a bloke

167

who had his feet under the table, she'd take a bet on that. And he'd got himself a little bit of what he fancied in Kitty. Who'd have thought the young ratbag would have turned herself into an eyeful? Who'd have thought she could have, unless she was flush?

'Well, Kitty,' she said, 'it was fatal all right. I saw it in the *South London Press*. It was grievous to me, losin' me only brother, an' I dare say it was grievous to you too, losin' yer step-dad. I see there's goin' to be an inquest, but that ain't goin' to bring 'im back to us, poor man. Mind, I never thought 'e'd be one to fall down the stairs, 'e 'ad very solid feet, as me 'usband knows.'

'Yes, solid all right, 'is feet were,' said Mr Briggs, knowing he was having to echo his wife.

'Still, 'e's gorn, it seems,' said Mrs Briggs, and took a handkerchief out of her handbag, a shoplifted repository. She dabbed her eyes. 'I'm sorry for yer, Kitty, and yer brother and sisters.'

Ugh, thought Kitty, what an old hypocrite.

'We'll be all right,' she said, 'we're gettin' parish relief, and Mr Blair's bein' a great 'elp.'

'Oh, I'm sure,' said Mrs Briggs, 'and I must say parish relief 'as made yer look well-off, ain't it, Wally?'

'Never seen yer lookin' better, Kitty,' said Mr Briggs.

'Now, if we could just 'ave a word in private with yer, Kitty?' said Mrs Briggs. 'Fam'ly, yer know,' she said to Jamie.

'Call me if you want me, Kitty,' he said, and left the kitchen to seat himself on the foot of the stairs.

'What d'you want to 'ave a word about?' asked Kitty.

'Well, yer know, dear, I'm me tragic brother's only relative,' said Mrs Briggs, 'so I suppose it's me duty to see to what 'e's left. I dare say I could let you 'ave all the furniture. Me an' Mr Briggs wouldn't dream of sellin' the stuff over yer head.'

'No, of course we wouldn't,' said Mr Briggs, shifting uncomfortably on his feet.

'Here,' said Kitty, 'the law wouldn't let you sell it, anyway, it would say Mr Mullins owed 'is step-children something.'

'Well, it's a question of blood relatives, dear,' said Mrs Briggs, 'and you and yer brother and sisters ain't blood relatives. That's what the law would say, wouldn't it, Wally?'

'Well, I—' Mr Briggs wasn't at all keen on what was going on.

'I'm talkin' to you,' said Mrs Briggs, 'so stop garglin'.'

'You carry on, Mrs Briggs,' said Kitty,

who had never been able to call the woman Aunt.

'I don't want yer to worry,' said Mrs Briggs, 'you can 'ave the furniture.'

'It's mostly fallin' to bits,' said Kitty.

'No, you got some nice stuff in this kitchen,' said Mrs Briggs, 'and you can 'ave it all. But where's 'is money, love?'

'Beg yer pardon?' said Kitty, on her guard immediately.

' 'Is money.'

'What money?' asked Kitty. 'He was only a dustman.'

' 'E 'ad a bit of money that come to 'im last year, dear, that rightly belongs to 'is only livin' relative, which is me, 'is only sister.'

'Well, we didn't see any of it,' said Kitty, eyes beginning to darken, 'nor much of 'is wages, either.'

' 'E always did what 'e could for all of yer, Kitty. 'E was a bit rough in 'is ways sometimes, but 'e 'ad a kind 'eart and was savin' 'is bit of money to make sure you didn't fall on 'ard times when the rainy days come along. But now 'e's gorn, me 'usband, yer Uncle Wally, says it's rightly mine. It put me in a bit of a flummox, but 'e says that's the law. And never you mind, I'll see you get a bit of it, enough to pay yer rent an' buy yer some food for a year.'

Kitty visibly quivered. The cost of a year's rent and food would be all of fifty quid, if not a bit more. So the ten fivers that Mr Blair had found could only be part of what this horrible woman was talking about. And a small part, probably.

'I don't know what you're talkin' about, Mrs Briggs.'

'Well, maybe yer don't love, yer step-dad was a bit close about what 'ad come to 'im by way of—what was it, Wally?'

'What?' said Mr Briggs. His wife, seated though she was, trod heavily on his foot. 'Oh, yes, a gift, that's what it was,' he said.

'From a bookmaker?' said Kitty. 'He used to bet on 'orses. Did 'e bet on a big winner?'

'Well,' said Mr Briggs, 'I don't re-collect—'

'That's it, dear,' said Mrs Briggs, ' 'ow did yer guess?'

'Because he made bets,' said Kitty.

'Of course, 'e didn't want people to know,' said Mrs Briggs, ' 'e'd 'ave 'ad everyone knockin' on 'is door to ask for a loan. Mind, 'e confided in me, us bein' close, and 'e said 'e was savin' it for the rainy days to see that 'is step-children didn't suffer. It'll be in 'is bedroom somewhere. 'Ave yer looked?'

'No, course I 'aven't,' said Kitty, 'I

didn't know there was anything to look for, did I? We just 'ad the money that was in his pockets.'

'Now don't fret,' said Mrs Briggs, 'me and yer Uncle Wally'll look, and give yer some of it when we've found it. We won't keep yer from goin' out any longer.'

'I'm not goin' out, not now I'm not,' said Kitty, 'you don't 'ave any right to go searchin' in this 'ouse.'

'I don't want to get cross with yer, love,' said Mrs Briggs, 'but I've got to stand on me rights as me brother's only relative. Still, let's see what yer Uncle Wally says, 'e knows about these things. You can speak up, Wally.'

'Best to get it over with, Kitty,' said Mr Briggs, and gave her a look. It was a look that tried to tell her he'd let her have half the money if he found it before the old dragon did.

Kitty opened the door and called to her lodger, whom she thought was upstairs. 'Mr Blair?'

He appeared sooner than she expected, entering the kitchen with the smile of a man who had no quarrel with anyone.

'Can I help?' he asked.

'Yes,' said Kitty. 'Mrs Briggs says her brother won a big bet on the 'orses and that he kept the money as savings, that it'll be in 'is bedroom. They want to search it, because Mrs Briggs says the money's hers on account that she's 'is only relative.'

'Oh, step-children are relatives as well,' said Jamie.

'Not blood relatives,' said Mrs Briggs.

'Blood relatives, yes, I see,' said Jamie, and kept as quiet about the fifty quid as Kitty had. 'Well, let them search, Kitty.'

'It's probably a lot of money, Mr Blair, because Mrs Briggs says she'll let me have enough of it to pay for food and the rent for a year.'

Jamie knew she was telling him that that must mean her step-father had had far more than the ten fivers when he died. From a bet on a horse race?

'Well, I suppose we'd better help in the search,' he said.

'Me an' Mr Briggs can manage, if yer don't mind,' said Mrs Briggs.

'That's up to Kitty,' said Jamie.

'Eh?' Slight aggression surfaced.

'Actually, you can't search at all without her permission,' said Jamie. 'She's the tenant, her landlord changed the name to hers in the rent book on Friday.'

'You seem to know a lot that ain't yer business,' said Mrs Briggs. 'Tell 'im, Wally.'

'Er, yes, well, me wife's got rights as 'er brother's next of kin, yer know,' said Mr Briggs.

173

'Well, the law will take that into account if there's money to share out,' said Jamie.

Mrs Briggs had a job not to get up and bash the interfering lodger. Her red face turned redder. But she controlled herself.

'I'm sure Kitty can understand me rights,' she said, 'I'm sure she won't mind if I do the sharin'-out an' that she don't want the law pokin' its nose in. While me an' Mr Briggs is 'ere, I'm sure Kitty'll let us do the search. Me brother's bound to 'ave put the money somewhere safe.'

'Somewhere where it couldn't be easily found?' suggested Jamie. Quite sure the woman would cause ructions if she didn't have her way, he said, 'All right, Kitty, let them search, and we'll help them.'

'I told yer, we can manage by ourselves,' said Mrs Briggs.

'No, we'll search as well, me and Mr Blair,' said Kitty, 'I've got rights too, I bet I 'ave.'

'Don't stand there with yer mouth open,' said Mrs Briggs to her husband, 'can't yer see they're sayin' they don't trust us? I never 'ad anyone say they don't trust me in all me life.'

'No, course you 'aven't, me love,' said Mr Briggs.

'There y'ar, that's good enough for yer, ain't it, Kitty?' said Mrs Briggs.

'We'll all search,' said Kitty firmly.

'That ain't unreasonable, me love,' said Mr Briggs, and received a look that plainly told him he could expect a clouting when his wife got him home.

'Come on, Mr Blair,' said Kitty. It was a real blessing now that she had him in the house. Without him, she knew her step-father's beefy sister would have made short work of her. As she and Jamie made for her step-father's bedroom, Mrs Briggs heaved herself rapidly to her feet like a baby elephant that had found itself sitting on a bed of long nails, and followed, pulling her husband along with her.

The bedroom was searched from wall to wall and top to bottom. The wardrobe was emptied and all clothes examined. Boots were delved into. The chest of drawers was minutely investigated. The bed was stripped, the pillows and mattress examined. The skirting-board was also examined, Mr Briggs down on his knees in the hope of finding a section that had been neatly cut out and now covered a hole in the plaster. Mrs Briggs was pugnaciously active, barging about the room in her determination to be the first to lay hands on the treasure trove.

'It must have been quite a bet,' said Jamie, 'if he made such a business of hiding the winnings.'

'Never you mind,' said Mrs Briggs,

purple now with effort and a growing frustration. 'Me brother was careful with money, and 'oo can blame 'im, knowin' there's always some shifty people about that can't keep their 'ands off someone else's property. Kitty, you sure no-one's been in this room an' searched it already?'

'Course I'm sure,' said Kitty, but suddenly wasn't sure. She looked at Jamie, who was running his hand down the underside of the marble-topped table containing a bowl and pitcher. Oh, me gawd, she thought, he'd been in here, and he'd found that fifty quid. But had it only been fifty quid? He'd said let Mr and Mrs Briggs search, and he'd said it almost casually, as if he knew they wouldn't find anything.

'It don't seem to be 'ere, me love,' said Mr Briggs, rising to his feet.

'It's got to be 'ere,' said Mrs Briggs, ' 'e wouldn't 'ave spent it. 'E was savin' it.' He'd been waiting, she knew, until he'd got those ungrateful kids off his hands. 'Well, we'd best 'ave a look in the parlour.'

'I didn't say you could,' declared Kitty.

'Oh, you been lookin' in there yerself, 'ave yer, dearie?' said Mrs Briggs.

'No, I 'aven't,' said Kitty.

'Come on, Wally,' said Mrs Briggs, and bruised her way out of the bedroom in a manner remindful of her brother. Mr Briggs followed, giving Kitty a sympathetic glance. Kitty went after the pair of them.

'You come too,' she said to Jamie over her shoulder, 'or don't you think it's worth botherin' about?'

'He won't have hidden it in the parlour,' said Jamie, going with her, 'you and the kids used it. What he wouldn't let you into was his bedroom.'

'I'm goin' to talk to you in a minute,' said Kitty.

In the parlour, Mrs Briggs had pounced on the split in the sagging sofa. Her hand was inside it, rummaging in the horsehair.

'It's in 'ere, it's got to be,' she panted.

Jamie let her get on with the useless rummaging without making any obvious comments. She was so obsessed that she turned the sofa upside-down with one flip of her large hands.

'Here, don't knock our furniture about,' said Kitty, 'it's all we've got.'

'It's all right, I'll buy yer a new sofa,' said Mrs Briggs, pulling at limp supporting webbing. All her efforts proved negative.

She and Mr Briggs as good as turned the parlour inside-out. Kitty and Jamie just watched.

'It's not in 'ere,' said Kitty, disgusted.

'Oh, yer know that, do yer, love?' said

Mrs Briggs sourly. 'You been through the 'ole bleedin' 'ouse, 'ave yer?'

'Why should I 'ave been?' said Kitty. 'I told you, I didn't know there was any money. I think you'd better go now you've turned the bedroom and this parlour upside-down.'

'Well, yes, there don't seem nothing 'ere,' said Mr Briggs.

'It's 'ere somewhere,' fumed Mrs Briggs.

'Don't come round again,' said Kitty. 'If there is any money and we find it, I'll let you know, but I'd be obliged if you'd go now.'

'I'll be back, don't you worry,' said Mrs Briggs. 'What was me brother's is now mine, and I ain't lettin' yer rob me of it. Might I hask where yer got the money from to doll yerself up like you'd suddenly come into riches?'

'There were some pounds and silver in your brother's pockets,' said Kitty. 'I told you that as well. The police said that what was in 'is pockets was mine, which it was, seein' all the slavin' I did for 'im and only gettin' belted for it.'

' 'Ere, don't you speak ill of a good man that's dead an' gorn,' said Mrs Briggs, 'it don't become yer. All right, we'll be off now, me an' Mr Briggs, but this ain't the last you've 'eard of us. Come on, you,' she said to her husband.

They left the house, Mrs Briggs barging her way through the open door, and Mr Briggs slipping through. He turned his head and gave Kitty the ghost of a smile. His lips framed words.

'Good on yer, gal.'

He was berated for his uselessness as he walked with his wife towards the Walworth Road.

'Bleedin' 'alf a man, that's all you are,' she said. 'You should've 'it that lodger for pokin' 'is nose in, but no, yer useless when it comes to givin' me a bit of 'elp.'

'Look, me love—'

' 'Old yer tongue. Gawd knows why you've got one, it don't do yer much good, nor me, either. That money's there all right. One thing, that Kitty ain't found it.'

' 'Ow'd yer know?' asked Mr Briggs.

'Well, 'er an' that lodger wouldn't 'ave cared where we searched if she 'ad, and nor would they 'ave watched us an' done all that searchin' themselves. She was after makin' sure that if we found it, well, she'd 'ave 'ad that interferin' lodger try an' take it off us. 'Enry always said she was a thievin' sort of minx, an' lazy at that. I know that money's still there. 'Enry couldn't flash it about, people would've talked, an' nor could 'e 'ave bunked off with it, not without the police

179

wonderin' why. 'E only ever did the one job, and 'e only did that on account of all the ruinous expenses of keepin' them kids.'

'Tell me another,' said Mr Briggs, but only to himself. 'Yes, I suppose the cops did 'ave their suspicions.'

'Course they did, with their nasty minds,' said Mrs Briggs, 'even if it was 'is one and only job. Up to their eyeballs in nasty-mindedness, they were, on account of not recoverin' the proceeds. Them kids 'eld 'Enry back all right, 'e couldn't leave 'em without the neighbours goin' round to the police station an' complainin' about 'im. If 'e'd been able to get them in 'omes, 'e'd 'ave been free as air and taken 'is time to move somewhere better without no-one askin' questions. We've got to 'ave that money, you 'ear?'

'Course I 'ear, me love,' said Mr Briggs, watching a couple of girls in their Sunday frocks giggling together. He'd said to his wife in the early days of their marriage that he'd like some kids. She boxed his ears. That was the start of things to come, of finding out it wasn't wise to say anything she didn't like.

'We've been 'ard-up long enough,' said Mrs Briggs. 'What you earn as a post man wouldn't keep two cock sparrers in birdseed. If it wasn't for me doin' a reg'lar bit of shopliftin', I don't know where we'd be. In the work'ouse, probably.'

The bright warm day and the thought that Kitty had a chance to find that money now she knew it was somewhere in the house, gave Mr Briggs such a sprightly feeling that he said, 'Well, yer know, 'Ilda, I don't think yer'd come across many postmen an' their wives livin' in work'ouses. And yer don't 'ave to go round shops nickin' 'andbags an' goloshers, yer'll get nicked yerself one day.' Ruddy rosy prospect, that was, Hilda getting herself nicked and spending a few months in Holloway. Bleeding bliss, in fact.

'Watch that lip of yourn,' said Mrs Briggs, 'you know I don't 'old with 'usbands talkin' back. 'Ere, and what d'yer mean, goloshers? You can't get nothing for them.'

'You come 'ome with a pair once,' said Mr Briggs, 'an' they're still under the dresser.'

'Accidental, that was,' said Mrs Briggs, 'I picked 'em up in an accidental moment.' They halted at the Browning Street tram stop in the Walworth Road. 'Anyway, I'll get that money. I know someone that'll be a lot more 'elp than you was. I just remembered, we didn't look up the bleedin' chimney. Why didn't yer think of

181

that, you useless 'a'porth?'

'Tram's comin',' said Mr Briggs.

'Wait till I get you 'ome,' said Mrs Briggs.

Next time she comes back from shopping with what she ain't paid for, thought Mr Briggs, I think I'll pop round and lay some confidential information with the Peckham rozzers.

'I want to know,' said Kitty, 'was it only them ten fivers you found?'

'That's a suspicious question,' said Jamie.

'Well, I can't 'elp it, can I?' said Kitty. 'There's supposed to be a lot of money that me step-father hid somewhere in 'is bedroom.'

'And it's funny, is it, that I only found fifty quid of it?'

'Yes, funny peculiar,' said Kitty.

'Well, I'm sorry for you, Kitty, if you think that,' said Jamie.

'That woman's upset me.'

'So it seems, but don't take it out on me,' said Jamie.

'Look, I'm just askin', ain't I?' said Kitty.

'I'd say your step-father kept that fifty quid close at hand, ready to be put into his wallet at a fiver a time whenever he felt he was a bit short of beer money, and that if there was a lot more, he tucked it well away.'

'I suppose I've got to believe you,' said Kitty.

'You don't have to suppose anything, you either believe me or you don't.'

'Well, I want to believe, don't I?' said Kitty. 'Only you don't 'ave a regular job, you're 'ard-up, and you can't say you couldn't do with a windfall. I wouldn't blame you for bein' tempted and for 'elping yourself—' She stopped, not liking the expression on Jamie's face or the glint in his eye.

'Helping myself to what doesn't belong to me?' he said.

'I'm only sayin',' complained Kitty, 'you don't 'ave to get cross with me.'

'You'll know it if I do.'

'All right, hit me, then, go on,' she said.

'Listen, you infant,' said Jamie, 'I've never been an angel, but I've never helped myself to other people's money. It's a mug's game in the end. Now, have you thought about the fact that Mrs Briggs seems to know just what a tidy sum your step-father had? And have you thought about what's obvious, that a large sum of money couldn't have come from a dustman's winning bet? Even that fifty quid would have been a hell of a lot.

Did she say your step-father won it from a bookie?'

'No, not until I mentioned it,' said Kitty.

'Then if there's a lot more besides the fifty, it all came from somewhere else,' said Jamie.

'Oh, me gawd,' breathed Kitty, 'd'you mean it might be ill-gotten?'

'Yes, I do mean that,' said Jamie. 'Did your step-father keep his bedroom door locked whenever he was out of the house?'

'Yes, always. He said he'd murder anyone who mucked about in 'is room.'

'Kitty, are you saying you couldn't get in to make his bed for him?'

'He always did it 'imself, and when he wanted his sheets put in the wash, he'd take them off 'imself. He'd chuck them at me.'

'So the money really is in his room, if Mrs Briggs was right about him saving it. You'll have to have another look, Kitty, but if you find it and it's ill-gotten, you'll have to think hard about what to do with it.'

'Oh, 'elp,' said Kitty, 'I 'ope he didn't do someone in for it. But I ain't goin' to grub around his room by meself, specially seein' I don't have any fancy for 'andling money that's not honest.'

'Well, I've a feeling about it,' said Jamie,

'but I may be wrong, and it might be legitimate gains. If it is, it belongs to you and your brother and sisters as much as it does to Mrs Briggs.'

'I'm all over upset feelings,' said Kitty, 'and I don't want to go into that room again today. Perhaps you could 'elp me look tomorrow, and perhaps we could 'ave a cup of tea now. I'll give you some biscuits with it.'

'Will you?' said Jamie, still thinking about things.

'Yes, just to show there's no 'ard feelings,' said Kitty. 'What a blessin' you were here this afternoon, it was like 'aving a real dad standin' up for me.'

'I'm not a real dad, I'm—'

'And I'll do a nice tea later, when Alfie and the twins get back from the park,' said Kitty. 'Imagine that man dead and gone, and all of us being able to 'ave a nice Sunday tea.'

'I hope Mr Briggs gets one,' said Jamie.

'She'll give him a good 'iding first,' said Kitty.

Chapter Nine

The following morning Jamie and Kitty each received a summons to attend the inquest on Mr Henry Mullins at the Southwark Coroner's court on Wednesday. Kitty said what a palaver when he passed away sort of peaceful. Still, we know what to say, don't we? Well, said Jamie, I know and you know that he wasn't pushed. Yes, I mentioned that first off, said Kitty, I mentioned that was best. Not best, said Jamie, true. Yes, said Kitty, I know that, don't I? I said I wouldn't say you pushed him.

'Leave off,' said Jamie.

He went out at a quarter-to-ten. Kitty, who had some Monday washing to do, wanted to know where he was going. To find something out, said Jamie. What something? I'll tell you after I've found it out, he said. She then wanted to know when he was going to help her search her step-father's bedroom again. He suggested the evening as he was going straight to his new job of work after finishing what he wanted to do this morning.

Out he went and, with her brother and

sisters at school, Kitty felt the house go all quiet. She hadn't minded that previously, it had always been a relief to have her step-father out of the way. The kids would come in for their midday school break and she'd do what she could to give them something to eat. Regularly of an afternoon, she'd go down the market and see what she could buy cheaply with the little amount of money her step-father allowed her. Later, when the kids were home from school, they'd all be hoping he'd be in a good temper when he arrived home himself.

Kitty couldn't bring herself to feel in the least sorry that he'd passed away. The relief that they were all free of him was still with her. Usually, the quietness of the house had had a kind of nervousness about it, as if the place knew it was going to explode into ugly noise the moment her step-father entered it. It was a different quietness today. A sort of brooding one, and she wished their lodger hadn't gone out. She missed having him to talk to. He'd been down in the kitchen a lot since that fateful day.

She got on with the Monday washing. There wasn't very much because of all the laundry Mrs Fitch and Mrs Reynolds had kindly done for her last week. There were a few things for herself and the kids, and shirts for Mr Blair. She'd offered to do them, she didn't know how he'd managed doing his things for himself in the handbasin of the upstairs lav. He hadn't been able to afford taking them to the laundry in the Walworth Road, and he used an iron which he heated on his gas ring. It was only right she should do his washing for him when he'd been such a help.

She jumped when, just after ten-thirty, someone opened the front door by pulling on the latchcord. For one horrid moment, Kitty thought it might be that awful woman, Mrs Briggs. Yesterday afternoon was still on her mind, and so, in an uneasy way, was that money. She'd asked Mr Blair this morning if he thought they could still make use of the fifty pounds. Yes, he'd said, use it and don't worry about it.

'Who's there?' she called.

'It's only me, Kitty.'

Kitty breathed with relief. It was Mrs Fitch.

'Oh, come through, Mrs Fitch,' she called.

Mrs Fitch entered the kitchen, which smelled of steaming suds. The scullery copper was going.

'I just thought I'd pop in and see 'ow you were, Kitty.'

'Oh, we're all quite 'appy, Mrs Fitch.'

'That's good,' said Mrs Fitch, no more inclined to feel sorry for Henry Mullins than any of the neighbours were. 'I'm doin' my own wash, but took a minute off to come and see you.'

'Oh, would yer like a cup of tea?' asked Kitty. 'We could both take five minutes off.'

'What a good idea,' smiled Mrs Fitch. 'My little girl's next door, playin' with a friend.'

Kitty put the kettle on. She was wearing the frock Mrs Reynolds had bought down the market. She hoped it looked nice on her, because Mrs Fitch was managing to still look pretty, even with her apron on.

'I was feelin' like a bit of company, Mrs Fitch.'

'I know that feelin' myself,' said Mrs Fitch. 'How's Mr Blair?'

'Oh, he always seems in the pink,' said Kitty. 'He's got more afternoon work this week, and he's gone out this mornin'.'

'Does he have a young lady?' asked Mrs Fitch.

'I—' Kitty, about to say she hoped not, said instead, 'I don't think so.'

'If I was twenty and single, I'd quite fancy 'im,' smiled Mrs Fitch.

Oh, me gawd, thought Kitty, I really will have to watch her, and any other woman who makes eyes at him. Me and Alfie and the twins just can't afford to let him be collared, we need him to be like a dad to us.

'Yes, I suppose he's a bit good-lookin',' she said.

'And fancy-free,' said Mrs Fitch, smiling again.

'Oh, he don't think of 'imself like that, not while he don't have a regular job,' said Kitty.

'That's near to tragic,' said Mrs Fitch, 'a nice man like 'im havin' no real job. Is there anything I can help you with, Kitty?'

'Oh, we're managin' fine, Mrs Fitch,' said Kitty. She had stopped her kind neighbour providing sandwiches because she was able to look after the wants of Alfie and the twins herself, what with the parish relief supplies and everything.

'I must say you all looked very nice at church yesterday,' said Mrs Fitch.

'Well, we found quite a bit of money in our step-father's pockets after he'd passed on,' said Kitty.

'It helped you buy Sunday best? I'm pleased for you.' Mrs Fitch hoped that what they'd found would last them a while. 'If anyone from the council comes round, they'll be able to see you're managin' fine.' Authority might well place them in homes if they were officially classed as destitute and all under age. Especially if there were no parents.

'Yes, and Mr Blair will speak up for us, I'm sure,' said Kitty.

'Yes, 'aving got to know him, I think he would,' said Mrs Fitch, 'and tell him not to say he's unemployed.'

'Well, he's only partial unemployed at the moment,' said Kitty, 'and we don't want any busybodies thinkin' he can't look after us. There, I can 'ear the kettle boilin'. I'll make the tea.'

Jamie rode back from the City on a tram. He was on his way to his new week's work in a street off the Old Kent Road. Afternoons again. He'd had a successful morning, if successful was the right word. He'd gone to the offices of the *Daily Mail*, and they'd been very helpful. In a room in which the ceiling looked yellow with age and tobacco smoke, a homely bloke with whiskers had consulted reference files. That led to appropriate back numbers of the newspaper and to the information that Jamie was after. Unsolved cases of robbery in the London area. There weren't many. In most cases, the police could recognize whose handiwork was responsible. Burglars generally had their own individual ways of carrying out a job. The flatties arrived at their door all too soon.

'You again, Sykes?'

'It's a fair cop, guv.'

'Why'd you keep doing it?'

'Search me, guv.'

There were only two unsolved cases during the last three years. One concerned a polished and highly professional job in Hatton Garden resulting in the theft of jewels worth as much as five thousand pounds, a fortune, and the other the theft of a day's takings from a Peckham store. The safe had been cracked wide open by a long jemmy tougher than the safe door. Nearly a thousand pounds had gone missing. The jewel robbery had taken place two and a half years ago, and the Peckham store had been burgled just over a year ago. The former case had proved too professional for the police so far, and there had been no identifying clues about the latter. Well, thought Jamie, if Henry Mullins had done a burgling job, that was the one. Which meant that the fifty quid found in the vase were 'ill-gotten' in Kitty's words. Let's forget those fivers, he thought, and let Kitty and the kids make use of them. But where was the rest of the money, allowing perhaps for some that Mullins had spent? On the other hand, why bother? If it was found, Kitty would only have to hand it over to the police, and the police would descend on the house. The Peckham store would have absorbed the loss by now.

Hairy Jack Spratt, real name Percival Spratt, was as bald as a duck's egg. Having spent most of his forty years in clink, he was going straight now. Well, up to a point. He carried out awkward jobs for certain acquaintances who couldn't be bothered with the inconvenience of handling out a bit of bodily harm themselves. Hairy Jack usually took a mate with him, One-Eyed Duffy, real name Fred Duffy. He had two good eyes, actually, but as a boy he'd worn spectacles with one black lens to correct a cast in his left optic. It took a few years, the correction, and those few years earned him his nickname.

A tram brought him and Hairy Jack from Peckham to the Manor Place stop in the Walworth Road, where they alighted. They crossed the road and began a walk to Larcom Street.

' 'Ow much did yer say she'll give us?' asked One-Eyed Duffy, who looked like a dressed-up barrel on short legs.

'I didn't say,' said Hairy Jack, as lean as a beanpole.

'Thought you didn't.'

'I said it'll earn us a few.'

'So yer did,' said One-Eyed Duffy, 'so 'ow much is a few?'

'Five per cent.'

'I 'ate per cent.'

'Per cent is fair earnings.'

'I still 'ate 'em.'

'Yer retarded, yer daft bugger,' said Hairy Jack.

'Never been ill in me life,' said One-Eyed Duffy. 'Let's fix our earnings. Fifty smackers each, what d'yer say?'

'Want yer leg broke, do yer? She knows what should be there, and she'll call up Mush 'Oskins to sort us out if we 'elp ourselves to what ain't been agreed.'

'I 'ate Mush 'Oskins,' said One-Eyed Duffy, ' 'e's a bleedin' gorilla.'

' 'E's twice our size, I grant yer,' said Hairy Jack. They turned into Larcom Street. 'And you ain't a tich except for yer short legs. What 'appened to 'em?'

'Wha'd'yer mean, what 'appened to 'em?'

'Well, they ain't proportionate to the rest of yer,' said Hairy Jack. 'I admire yer chest, I wish I 'ad one like it meself, and yer loaf's passable, but yer legs look as if they've been cut orf at yer knees.'

'That ain't funny, 'Airy, that's 'ighly personal.'

'Yer shouldn't take it personal, One-Eye, it's just that you've been physic'lly victimized by an accident of nature—'ere, gorblimey, she's come along 'erself.'

Mrs Briggs was waiting for them outside the church.

'Bit late, ain't yer?' she said.

'Us?' said Hairy Jack.

'I told yer not later than two o'clock, and it's nearly 'alf-past,' said Mrs Briggs, brawny in a blouse and skirt, and a large hat on her head. 'I told yer to give yerselves enough time before the kids come 'ome from school. Now yer'll 'ave to get a move on. This way.' She led them around the bend to where the terraced houses on either side of the street looked compact and homely.

'What made yer turn up yerself, 'Ilda?' asked Hairy Jack.

'Me in'eritance,' said Mrs Briggs. She was carrying an umbrella as well as her handbag. The umbrella was new. She'd popped into a shop on her way to a tram stop in Peckham, and come out equipped to shelter herself from a shower. She hadn't paid for the article, of course.

'I 'ope it don't mean you don't trust us,' said One-Eyed Duffy.

'Course I trust yer,' said Mrs Briggs, 'I just 'ad a feelin' I ought to come an' protect me in'eritance. 'Ere we are.' She opened the gate and advanced to the door. She pulled on the latchcord and the door opened. She stepped into the passage, her hired helpers at her back. ' 'Ello, Kitty,

195

you there, dearie?' she called.

Kitty wasn't there. She was at the town hall asking, as she'd been told to, for a ticket that would enable her to collect this week's parish relief supplies. Authority was making a delaying business of it. Authority was paid not to do things in a hurry.

Mrs Briggs called again. The response was silence.

'No answer was the stern reply,' said Hairy Jack, grinning.

'Shut the street door,' said Mrs Briggs.

'Right y'are, 'Ilda,' said One-Eyed Duffy, and closed it.

'Now get on with it,' said Mrs Briggs. 'Do me dear departed brother's bedroom first. It's this way.'

Her bruisers would see to it that the search wasn't interrupted.

Kitty knew something was wrong as soon as she opened the door. The house was sort of vibrating, and the inner doors were all open. She rushed through to the kitchen and put down her two shopping bags that were laden with parish relief supplies. The time was twenty to four, and the vibrations were coming from upstairs. A crash shattered them. It sounded as if a bed had been pitched over on to its side. Kitty was sure she knew who was up there.

Mrs Briggs and her henpecked husband. The old cow.

Kitty dashed into her step-father's bedroom. It looked as if an earthquake had hit it. The bed frame was bare and on its side, the brass knobs off the hollow bedposts. The mattress was ripped open. The chest of drawers was on its back, the drawers all out. The wardrobe had been stripped again and pulled free of the wall. Two pillows, ripped and with feathers spilling, had been thrown into a corner. Lino had been rolled back from one wall, and the roll, trodden on, showed ruinous cracks.

The parlour was in no better shape, the old sofa looking as if it had burst apart. Up the stairs Kitty ran. The door of the lodgers's room was open, and noise seemed to balloon out. In went Kitty to confront the old cow, and saw there were two men with her, one stringy, the other short and thickset. They both wore old bowler hats, jerseys, jackets and trousers, the traditional togs of bruisers. The stringy character was down on his knees in the hearth, using the kitchen rolling-pin to poke about up the chimney. Soot was falling. The thickset man was kneeling on the mattress from the overturned bed and just about to slice it open with a knife.

' 'Ello, dearie,' said Mrs Briggs, 'I told yer I'd be back.'

Kitty didn't answer. Her eyes dark with fury, she ran at the man on the mattress and kicked him. The sharp toe of her right shoe struck him in his barrel-like chest. His chest sang like the plucked string of a violin, and hurtful pain creased his unshaven features. His mouth fell open, and Kitty delivered another kick, this time at his right hand. Nor did she miss. One-Eyed Duffy emitted the strangled roar of a man diabolically offended, and the knife dropped from his numbed fingers. From the hearth, Hairy Jack, head turned, looked on in aggrieved astonishment.

'Ruddy fanackapan, 'oo's she?' he asked.

'I'll see to 'er,' said Mrs Briggs, and wrapped a beefy arm around Kitty from behind. She dragged her aside. 'Now what d'yer go kickin' me friend for, love? You sit down nice an' quiet over there, then I won't ask me friends to paste yer.'

'Let go!' Kitty turned inside the large arm and knocked the old cow's hat off. The hatpin was dragged from its moorings, and the hat fell to the floor.

'Yer young bitch,' said Mrs Briggs, 'yer goin' to get a real pastin' now.'

'I don't think so,' said Jamie from the open door. Mrs Briggs wheeled round like a startled carthorse.

' 'Ere, where'd you come from?' she asked, mottled with indignation that his interfering hooter, which should have been at work with him, was poking itself again into her private business. 'Why ain't you at yer job?'

'Early finish,' said Jamie. Actually, the ball and chain machine had broken down, and at three-fifteen the part-time men had been laid off for the day. 'What's going on? No, don't tell me, I can see. I suppose you realize I'm renting this room, do you?'

Hairy Jack and One-Eyed Duffy were both on their feet. Hairy Jack looked sooty and One-Eyed Duffy looked cross.

' 'Oo's this clever cove, 'Ilda?' asked Hairy Jack.

'He ain't nobody,' said Mrs Briggs.

'I 'ate nobodies,' said One-Eyed Duffy, 'they always think they're somebody. And nor ain't I too partial to alley cats like that one there. She bleedin' kicked me. Twice.'

'And you'll get some more if you don't push off,' said Kitty. 'Did you see what they've done downstairs, Mr Blair?'

'I saw,' said Jamie. 'It's trespass, damage and assault.'

'It's me in'eritance,' said Mrs Briggs, 'see to 'im, boys.'

'Pleasure,' said Hairy Jack.

'Likewise,' said One-Eyed Duffy, and rushed at Jamie like a projected barrel. Jamie stopped him by sticking out a

199

straight right arm and a balled fist. One-Eyed Duffy's face ran into it. His head jerked back and his rusty-looking bowler flew off. He fell on his back.

'Crikey,' breathed Kitty, and stared at Jamie with new eyes.

Hairy Jack, leaping obstacles, went for Jamie with a swinging poker plucked from the fireside. Jamie ducked and the scything iron poker struck the door frame.

'Ruddy 'ell, where's 'e gorn?' shouted Hairy Jack, and found out then. Jamie belted him in his belly-button. His lean body folded up and collapsed on top of One-Eyed Duffy.

'Oh, yer bleedin' useless gits!' yelled Mrs Briggs. Hairy Jack rolled about and sucked in air, his bowler hat off, his bald head shining. Mrs Briggs glared at Jamie. 'I'll 'ave the law on yer!' she shouted. 'I'll 'ave yer for doin' grievous bodily 'arm.'

Kitty, in awe and delight, breathed, 'Oh, you did 'em like Jack Dempsey, Mr Blair.'

'I did a little boxing in the army, Kitty,' said Jamie.

'Crikey, heroic,' said Kitty.

'Oh, you ungrateful little bitch,' said Mrs Briggs, ' 'ow can yer stand there not carin' that old friends of yer step-dad's 'ave been nearly done to death?'

'They're all right, worse luck,' said Kitty.

'Yer right, I ain't dead yet,' said One-Eyed Duffy, and came up like an india rubber ball. His arms rushed forward to take Jamie in a bear-hug. Jamie hit him again, in the jaw. It staggered him and put him on his back a second time. 'Bleedin' Fanny Adams,' he gasped.

'Oh, you ruddy 'ooligan!' shouted Mrs Briggs at Jamie, her red face purple.

'I 'ate 'im,' groaned One-Eyed Duffy.

'Likewise,' breathed Hairy Jack, sitting up and nursing his stomach.

'Come on, get up,' said Mrs Briggs, 'we're goin' for the coppers. They'll sort 'im out.'

'Eh?' said Hairy Jack.

'Yes, what's that you said, 'Ilda?' asked One-Eyed Duffy, alarmed as well as hurt.

'Grievous bodily 'arm, that's what it is,' said Mrs Briggs, 'and interfering with me rightful search for me in'eritance. Let's get the law on 'im and 'er too.'

Hairy Jack, getting up, said, 'Listen, 'Ilda, I got a fractured stomach that's 'urting me all over, I ain't in no condition to walk round to a police station.'

One-Eyed Duffy came to his feet and gingerly felt his injured jaw.

'Police stations is bad for me 'ealth,' he said, 'specially in me present condition.'

'We'll save you the bother,' said Jamie. 'Kitty, you go for the police, while I stay here and keep an eye on all three of 'em. Tell the sergeant you've suffered trespass and damage.'

Kitty, quite sure he didn't mean it, nevertheless said, 'Yes, all right, Mr Blair, I'll go.'

' 'Ere, 'old on,' said Mrs Briggs, 'there ain't no cause for that, dearie. There's been blows struck that ain't been friendly, but I'm a forgivin' person, like me departed brother 'Enry was, and I ain't goin' to 'arbour no 'ard feelings. All I want is to find me rightful in'eritance.'

'What, tear the house apart, you mean?' said Kitty.

'I'll make good, love, don't you worry.'

'Excuse me, I'm sure,' said Kitty, 'but 'ow many winnin' bets did your brother have?'

'What's that?' Mrs Briggs didn't like the question.

'Well, all this money you're after, it must 'ave come from a lot of wins,' said Kitty.

'Yes, 'e knew 'ow to pick a good 'orse,' said Mrs Briggs.

'I wouldn't like to think there was money in this 'ouse that wasn't come by honest,' said Kitty.

'That ain't nice,' said Hairy Jack, 'it's castin' aspersions.'

'I can't 'ardly believe I 'eard it,' said One-Eyed Duffy.

202

'You Kitty,' said Mrs Briggs, looking shocked, ' 'ow can yer say something like that about yer step-dad? 'E 'ad 'is faults, like we all 'ave, but 'e was as honest as the day is long.'

'He was rotten 'orrible,' said Kitty.

'Oh, yer little 'eathen,' said Mrs Briggs, 'I suppose you was glad 'e fell down the stairs.'

Kitty, eyes on fire, said, 'It was what he earned for 'imself.'

'I'll 'ave a fatal turn, I will,' said Mrs Briggs.

'I've nearly had one meself,' said Kitty, 'at the way you sneaked into this 'ouse and smashed most of it to pieces. You—oh, that's the kids home from school.'

Downstairs, noise rolled about in the passage as Alfie and the twins scrummaged their way in.

'Alfie, I'll 'it you!' yelled Chloe.

'What for? I ain't done nothing—crikey, Chloe, a bomb's 'it the parlour—look!'

'I'll go down for a minute,' said Kitty.

'I'll stay here,' said Jamie.

Kitty went down to talk to her brother and sisters in the kitchen, telling them not to worry about the parlour and their step-father's bedroom being in a mess. She and Mr Blair were going to sort it out, Mr Blair having come in early from his work. Mrs Briggs was upstairs, she said. She told

Chloe to make a pot of tea for themselves and to have some bread and jam with it. Then she went back up to the lodger's room, to find that Jamie had been laying down the law. Mrs Briggs and her friends, he said, were to put everything to rights before they left the house. Further, they were to take note of the fact that there was one ruined mattress and a sofa that would cost a lot to repair.

'What mattress?' said Hairy Jack.

'What sofa?' asked One-Eyed Duffy.

' 'Ardly touched 'em,' said Hairy Jack.

'Yes, an' what about my rights, what about them?' demanded Mrs Briggs.

'Blow your rights, you don't 'ave any in this 'ouse,' said Kitty. 'You owe me for a new mattress and repairs to the sofa. Mr Blair, 'ow much d'you think that would be?'

'Four quid to cover everything,' said Jamie.

'Some 'opes you got,' said Mrs Briggs.

'A word in your ear, missus,' said Jamie, and took the bristling woman into Alfie's bedroom. He delivered a whole string of words into her ear. She didn't like most of them. In fact, she could have done without any of them, and she looked as if her dearest wish was to clout Jamie with a sledge hammer. 'The point is,' he said finally, 'if this money *is* the proceeds of that burglary and you know as much about it as you seem to, the police might see you as an accessory—'

'A what?'

'An accomplice.'

'Oh, yer bleedin', interferin' 'ow d'yer do, you ought to be 'ung up by yer feet, takin' me brother's name in vain, an' mine as well!'

'Think about it,' said Jamie, and went back into his own room with her.

' 'Ere, did 'e 'it yer, 'Ilda?' asked Hairy Jack.

'Only you ain't lookin' too good,' said One-Eyed Duffy.

'I'm shocked to me core,' said Mrs Briggs, having trouble with her breathing. 'Me brother 'Enry that's dead an' gorn 'as been insulted an' so 'ave I.'

'I ain't in favour of that,' said Hairy Jack, spitting on his hands.

'I'm takin' umbrage meself,' said One-Eyed Duffy, and buttoned up his jacket.

'I'm leavin',' said Mrs Briggs.

'Not till you've all tidied the place up,' said Jamie.

'Rush 'im, One-Eye,' said Hairy Jack, 'you know tidying-up ain't our kind of work.' They rushed Jamie together. Kitty stuck out a quick foot. One-Eyed Duffy fell over it. Hairy Jack kept going, then wished he hadn't. Jamie deposited him on top of his friend again.

'Oh, yer bugger!' bawled Mrs Briggs.

'Stop shoutin',' said Kitty, 'there's innocent kids downstairs. Go on, all of you do what Mr Blair said, tidy the place up, or he'll knock all your 'eads off. Go on, just do it, and then push off.'

They did it, Mrs Briggs vibrating with rage, Kitty and Jamie keeping a check on their endeavours, and the kids staying put in the kitchen.

'What's 'appening?' whispered Carrie, a spot of jam marking the front of her blouse.

' 'Ow do I know?' said Chloe.

'It's that Mrs Briggs, I betcher,' said Alfie. 'I betcher she was the one that's messed all the furniture up. I ain't never been 'appy about 'er.'

'Well, it's a blessin' we've got our lodger 'ere,' said Chloe.

'Kitty said 'e's our dad now, didn't she?' questioned Carrie.

'Yes, something like that,' said Chloe.

'But 'e goes all funny when it's mentioned,' said Carrie.

' 'E give me a look when I called 'im Dad,' said Alfie. 'Can I 'ave anuvver slice of bread an' jam, Chloe?'

'It'll spoil yer supper,' said Chloe.

'Course it wouldn't,' said Alfie, 'I could

eat an 'undred slices of bread an' jam wivout it spoilin' me supper.'

'No, but it would blow you up, I bet,' said Chloe.

'Crikey,' said Carrie, 'fancy bits of Alfie flyin' about all over the kitchen.'

'And Kitty 'aving to stick 'im together again,' said Chloe, and the twins giggled as one.

'That ain't funny,' said Alfie, sitting on his dignity.

Chapter Ten

Everything was back in place, but Mrs Briggs was still being forced to cough up for the ruined mattress and for repairs to the sofa. Kitty settled for three pounds, which Mrs Briggs said was all she had and that it was criminal to take it from her. Jamie still insisted she handed it over, and she did.

'Me, an 'ard-workin' woman all me life,' she said, 'and yer cleanin' me out. You ain't 'eard the last of this. 'Ere,' she said in a whisper to Jamie, 'what yer goin' to do with the money if it turns up?'

'Hand it over to the police,' said Jamie.

'Then yer off yer bleedin' rocker,' said Mrs Briggs.

'Goodbye,' said Kitty, and her step-father's sister left. Hairy Jack and One-Eyed Duffy left with her, and she assaulted their ears all the way to the tram stop.

At the stop, Hairy Jack said, 'Turn it up, 'Ilda, yer killin' me fractured stomach.'

'And yer 'urting me 'ead,' said One-Eyed Duffy. 'On top of which, yer started us off in the wrong place.'

'What d'yer mean?'

' 'Enry wouldn't 'ave used 'is bedroom. 'E'd 'ave known that if the coppers got on to 'im, that's the first place they'd 'ave searched. It's in the perishin' kitchen somewhere.'

'Those kids 'ave been in that kitchen day in day out ever since 'Enry married that mother of theirs,' said Mrs Briggs.

'Course they 'ave, 'Ilda,' said Hairy Jack, 'which is why One-Eye 'as 'ad a flash of lightning. 'Oo's goin' to look for them dibs in a place lived in by the kids every day of the week? What d'yer think of One-Eye now, eh?'

'Well, 'e's the first man I ever met that's got brains,' said Mrs Briggs. 'The pair of you'll 'ave to break in one night and go over that kitchen. But leave it tidy, you 'ear me? We don't want Kitty or 'er bleedin' lodger findin' it's been turned over. Not yet, mind, I'll let yer know. 'Ere's our tram.'

When they reached Peckham, they went their separate ways. To console herself for a cruel afternoon, Mrs Briggs popped into Peckham's best store and came out with some elastic that she'd paid for and a gent's expensive leather wallet that she hadn't. When Mr Briggs arrived home from a late turn of duty, his wife regaled him with a detailed account of the uselessness of men and showed him proof of her talents as

209

a woman. The proof lay in the umbrella and the wallet. Mr Briggs said she didn't need to have done that, it was safer to be useless than too clever.

She clouted him.

Ruddy elephants, thought Mr Briggs, I'll have to seriously consider shopping me dear old Dutch. That'll be the day, Wally mate! While she's in jug, you could knock on Mrs Peake's door, she being a nice but lonely widow woman that you deliver regular letters to. She might like some sociable calls from her cheerful postman, which is you, Wally. Well, it will be if you can help the coppers land Hilda in Holloway. You only need to make up your mind. You're right, Wally, I'll think about it.

Kitty and the kids sat at supper, Jamie with them. The meal was a bit late, owing to Mrs Briggs and the two men treating the house like something the council's sanitary inspector had said needed to be pulled down and rebuilt. Sanitary inspectors could say that sort of thing and mean it. Landlords didn't like it. They'd offer to strip the house of its ancient wallpaper, massacre the bugs and have another look at the drains. Yes, you do that, Mr Guzzlebag, the sanitary inspector would say, and while you're about it, knock the whole works down. It's condemned. Some sanitary inspectors were on the side of the workers.

One thing, the local sanitary inspector wouldn't condemn any house in Larcom Street. The terraced dwellings were prime examples of solid Victorian construction, and any mice that got in received short shrift from the cat population. Kitty thanked the Lord that despite the way her step-father had neglected everything, they didn't have bedbugs or mice. She'd have died if their lodger had been eaten alive by bugs or had his belongings chewed by mice.

She thought of something as everyone tucked into fried sausages and mash.

'You didn't actually say why it was you finished work early, Mr Blair.'

'The demolishing machine packed up,' said Jamie, 'and we were laid off for the rest of the day. Just hope it'll be in walloping good form tomorrow.'

'What's a demolishin' machine?' asked Carrie.

'It's a huge iron ball on an iron chain,' said Jamie, 'and it wallops into brick walls. Down go the walls.'

'Crikey, like Jericho,' said Chloe.

'We 'ad Jericho in our Scripture lessons, didn't we, Chloe?' said Carrie.

'We 'ad 'em too in our class,' said Alfie.

'The walls all fell down.' He looked at Kitty. 'Like *he* did.'

'Just forget it,' said Kitty, but she knew, of course, that the kids still had a strange sense of freedom on their minds, and they were all old enough to think about the happening in a way that much younger kids wouldn't.

After supper, Jamie gave Alfie and the twins a penny each. In delight, they all went off to buy toffee-apples at a shop in King and Queen Street, which was often open up to eight o'clock. So were many Walworth shops.

'Why'd you do that?' asked Kitty. 'You know you can't afford it.'

'Can't I?'

'Oh, sorry.' Kitty went a little pink. 'I don't like people not mindin' their own business, and I've just done it meself.'

'Don't worry,' said Jamie, but gave himself a kick, not for handing out pennies he couldn't afford, but for handing them out just like a dad. Gestures like that drew him deeper into the trap.

'Perhaps you could talk to me now about that money,' said Kitty.

'I can tell you where I think it came from, if it's here,' said Jamie, and recounted details of his visit to the *Daily Mail*.

Kitty, open-mouthed, sat heavily down. 'You're jokin',' she said. 'I mean, I thought if it was a lot Mrs Briggs was after, it couldn't 'ave been from a bet, but I never thought it could really 'ave been burgled.'

'Ill-gotten, you said.'

'I know. Oh, me gawd, mister, 'ave we got burgled money in this 'ouse?'

'Mrs Briggs thinks we have, but it doesn't seem like it,' said Jamie. 'I can't think your step-father would have stacked it away in any room but his own, and that's been thoroughly searched twice. Including the chimney yesterday.'

'Yes, all that soot in there and the parlour,' said Kitty, and managed a smile. 'Still, they 'ad to clear it up themselves. I'm not goin' out again without puttin' the latchcord back through the letter-box. Did you tell Mrs Briggs what you've just told me?'

'I thought it might sober the old buzzard up, and I'd say from the way she looked and from the way her buxom bosom sagged—'

'Here, d'you mind?' said Kitty.

'No, I don't mind. It as good as flopped—'

'Don't be vulgar,' said Kitty. 'Nor common, either.'

'I wouldn't call a sagging bosom common,' said Jamie. 'It's a sad sight in a way, although I was pleased to see it.'

'You're gettin' worse,' said Kitty, who had the firm bosom of a young lady. 'You'll tell me it fell out in a minute.'

'No, I won't. It didn't. But it told me Mrs Briggs knew it was burgled proceeds. So you can let it rest, Kitty.'

'Me?'

'What's the point of looking for it? If you find it, you'll only have to hand it over to the police.'

'Crikey, no, I don't want ill-gotten gains,' said Kitty. She thought about it, then said, 'Couldn't we keep a bit of it, like we've already kept the fifty quid?'

'You could, if you wanted to,' said Jamie.

'No, I mean us.'

'Pardon?' said Jamie, and Kitty fidgeted with her hands.

'Well, we're ever so grateful, me and Alfie and the twins, that you're sort of one of us now.'

'I'm your lodger, sort of keeping an eye on you.'

'Yes, I said we're ever so grateful you bein' like a dad to us—'

'If you say that again, I'll begin to believe it.' And then I'll be done for, thought Jamie.

'Oh, we wouldn't mind,' said Kitty. 'What I mean is that if we did find the money, I wouldn't keep a bit of it unless you took charge of it. I couldn't handle money like you, you're older and you've got all that—all that—'

'You're not going to say worldly wisdom again, are you?'

'Oh, don't you like 'aving worldly widsom?' asked Kitty. 'Here, where you goin'?'

'Into the scullery, to knock my head on the wall,' said Jamie, but poured himself a glass of cold water instead.

'I don't know why you get cross when I mention you're older and wiser than me,' said Kitty. 'Mister, shall we keep a bit of the money if we do find it?'

'Shut up,' said Jamie.

'Well, bless me, that ain't nice,' said Kitty. 'Still,' she said with a perceptible sigh, 'some dads do get a bit irritable with young people, and I don't suppose you can blame them. Now where you goin'?'

'Out. I'm taking my headache for a walk.'

'Oh, fresh air's good for 'eadaches,' said Kitty, 'and I've got the ironing to do. I'll make a nice pot of tea when you come back, and try and find you a Daisy Powder.'

'Suffering cats,' said Jamie, and was laughing to himself as he went out.

He and Kitty attended the inquest at

the Southwark Coroner's Court the next day, arriving at fifteen minutes to ten, as requested. The proceedings opened at ten, and Jamie hoped they'd be over in time for him to get to his work by one. The coroner asked for the police evidence first, and the CID man, Sergeant Watkins, took the stand. Kitty, sitting with Jamie, showed no nerves as she listened. It was all a lot of fuss about nothing as far as she was concerned.

Sergeant Watkins recounted how the police were summoned to the house by Miss Kitty Edwards, step-daughter of the deceased, and how the body was discovered lying in the passage. He further recounted the details given to him by Miss Edwards and Mr Jamie Blair, the lodger, concerning the relevant events. He then, he said, asked them to show him exactly what happened. This they did and he described the actions they went through with his assistance. He could not dispute either their reproduction of the struggle between Miss Edwards and her step-father, with Mr Blair attempting to intercede, or their explanations, but he had suggested something other than the deceased's lost grip on Miss Edwards might have contributed to the subsequent fall down the stairs. Both Miss Edwards and Mr Blair were quite sure there was no other contributory factor.

'Thank you, Sergeant Watkins,' said the coroner. 'Is there anything else?'

'Well, sir,' said Sergeant Watkins, 'it was diagnosed that the deceased died of a heart attack, but we're not sure if he fell because of this or if it was brought on by the fall. If the latter, and if there was a contributory factor—well, there was a bruise on his left cheek—'

'Thank you again, Sergeant Watkins,' said the coroner, 'but supposition must rest for the moment.'

Dr McManus, giving his evidence, detailed the cause of death, cardiac arrest.

'That, in more common terms, is heart failure?' said the coroner.

'Quite so,' said Dr McManus.

'As a result of the fall?'

'Not at all,' said Dr McManus. 'Cardiac arrest took place before he fell.'

'You are certain?'

Dr McManus pointed out that the deceased's eyes were wide open when he examined him, which meant that his eyelids had ceased to function before he hit the floor. The conclusion that Mr Mullins had died before he actually fell was confirmed by Mr Blair's statement that at the moment when he lost his grip on his step-daughter, his colour receded and his eyes rolled to become wide open. Since he was known to suffer the occasional murmur and was in a physical struggle with his step-daughter at the time, the combination would have been enough to cause a fatal attack.

'We haven't yet had Mr Blair's statement, of course,' said the coroner, 'but I think I shall ask you now, Dr McManus, if the statement was made before or after you diagnosed heart failure?'

'It was made to Sergeant Watkins before I arrived,' said Dr McManus, 'and subsequently mentioned to me by Mr Blair.'

'I think Sergeant Watkins should have included that in his notes,' said the coroner. 'Thank you, Dr McManus. Might we now hear Miss Kitty Edwards?'

Kitty, wearing a second-hand dress and a passable hat, and looking nicely presentable rather than out of order, took the stand without any sign of nervousness. Her only sign of mourning was in the hat. It was black and Mrs Fitch had kindly lent it.

After the coroner had expressed his sympathy, Kitty gave her evidence quite clearly. She knew exactly what she was going to say, and it was more or less a repeat of what she had twice said to the police, except that she refrained from showing any of the indignation she'd exhibited then. The coroner, however, wanted a little more than a statement of the events. He wanted to know what her exact relationship with her step-father was. Jamie suspected the coroner might be thinking of what Sergeant Watkins had implied, that one could reasonably ask did Mullins fall or was he pushed? Or struck? Sergeant Watkins had mentioned a bruise on his cheek.

Kitty thought for a moment, then said, 'Well, sir, he 'ad his faults and I suppose I had mine.'

'Does that mean the relationship was not a happy one?' asked the coroner.

'To be honest,' said Kitty, 'there was room for improvement.'

'Would you say, then, that his treatment of you, your sisters and your brother left something to be desired?'

'I don't want to speak ill of the dead,' said Kitty.

'Of course not,' said the coroner, 'but we've heard from Sergeant Watkins that you stated he was violent towards you on the occasion in question, so would you like to answer up, Miss Edwards?'

'If you want me to,' said Kitty. 'Is it enough to say again there was room for improvement?'

'Perhaps that is enough,' said the coroner. 'Were there other occasions when Mr Blair, your lodger, interceded on your behalf?'

'Oh, round our way,' said Kitty, 'people wouldn't call it intercedin'. They'd call it interferin', but only in a good cause, mind. Mr Blair didn't go in for interferin', but he knew our step-father wasn't—well, he wasn't very lovin'—and he brought us chocolate once. He didn't interfere at all, not until that evenin' when he spoke in a stern way to my step-father and asked 'im to let me go. Then it all 'appened.'

'What did?' asked the coroner.

'I pulled meself free and my step-father lost his balance and fell down the stairs.'

'Mr Blair neither touched you nor your step-father?'

'No, he just asked him to let me go,' said Kitty.

'Thank you, Miss Edwards. Might we hear from Mr Blair next?'

Jamie took his turn. Sunlight, entering the coroner's court, gilded tiny risen specks of dust. Invited to proceed, Jamie emulated Kitty in repeating the salient details he had given to Sergeant Watkins. Kitty, from her bench seat, eyed him with interest. She hoped he wouldn't get flustered. Well, as if he would. He'd been one too many for Mrs Briggs and those two men.

The coroner asked Jamie what his mood was at the time.

'Not very pleasant,' said Jamie.

'You were angry, in fact?'

'Mr Mullins was bullying and cuffing his step-daughter. Yes, I was angry about it.'

'So you interceded?'

'I pointed out to Mr Mullins that the reasonable thing to do would be to let go of the girl.'

'What was his reaction to that?'

'He told me to shut my trap.'

'Did he hit you, Mr Blair, or attempt to hit you?'

'No. He was dragging at Miss Edwards.'

Bless me soul, thought Kitty, listen to him calling me Miss Edwards. It makes me sound posh.

'I must ask you, Mr Blair,' said the coroner, 'did you hit the deceased or strike him in any way to cause the bruise on his cheek?'

Jamie was able to answer that quite truthfully.

'I did not,' he said.

'You mentioned to Sergeant Watkins and subsequently to Dr McManus that you saw Mr Mullins lose colour and his eyes turn glassy at the moment when he lost his grip on Miss Edwards.'

'I did mention that, yes.'

'I see,' said the coroner. 'I'm simply a little concerned about the implication that Mr Mullins might have been hit or struck. Can you declare that Miss Edwards, naturally angry herself at her step-father's treatment of her, did not hit him or strike him?'

'I assure you she did not, sir.'

'Thank you, Mr Blair,' said the coroner, and recalled Sergeant Watkins. 'Sergeant Watkins, why did you feel there might have been a contributory factor other than that of a lost balance?'

'I had to consider the natural anger, sir, and what it might have led to,' said Sergeant Watkins.

'A blow?'

'Exactly,' said Sergeant Watkins, 'a blow that could have caused the heart attack. I had that bruise on my mind.'

'Dr McManus?' said the coroner.

'Superficial,' said Dr McManus, 'and I did advise Sergeant Watkins that a blow would have caused a more significant contusion.'

'Thank you, Dr McManus,' said the coroner. 'Thank you, Sergeant Watkins.'

The verdict was subsequently given. Death by natural causes, brought about by a fit of uncontrollable temper.

Kitty left the court with her dark brown eyes swimming with sunshine.

'What a palaver,' she said, 'but we stood up to them, didn't we?'

'We had to,' said Jamie. 'Sergeant Watkins obviously felt there was more to it than you twisting free of your step-father.'

'Oh, blow him,' said Kitty.

'In his mind's eye he could easily picture me clouting your step-father.'

'The rotten rozzer,' said Kitty, as they waited for a tram.

'It's part of police procedure to examine every angle, Kitty.'

'There, didn't I tell you it was best to say you never touched me step-father?' said Kitty. 'I told you I'd never say anything about you puttin' a hand on 'is chest.'

'You said you wouldn't say I pushed him.'

'And I didn't,' said Kitty, 'and I wouldn't, not even if they set lions and tigers on me, not when you're all we've got.'

It's ruddy blackmail, thought Jamie.

'Tram coming,' he said, 'and I'm going to chuck you under it.'

'Here, what for?' demanded Kitty.

'Because you're a young monkey.'

Kitty smiled. When they were on the tram, she said she'd see about getting the new mattress.

'Mattress?' said Jamie.

'I'll go down the market and ask at the second-hand clothes stall. They'll know where I can get a mattress nearly new for just a few bob. I mean, we're goin' to need it when your mum's friend arrives.'

'I'd forgotten her,' said Jamie. What was

223

the woman's name? Rosemary Allen, yes. His mother had said she was coming to London, but hadn't said exactly when. 'Yes, a mattress, of course,' he said.

'And her bit of rent,' said Kitty. 'That'll add to our savings, won't it?'

'Your savings,' said Jamie.

'Yes, all right, you're the boss.'

'Will you cut that out?'

'Don't get cross, not on a tram,' said Kitty, 'the conductor'll throw us off. Mr Joslin, who lives near us, got thrown off a tram once.'

'What for?' asked Jamie.

'Well, he was fightin' with a man and 'is trousers fell down. Conductors always throw men off a tram if their trousers fall down. Did yer know that?'

'It seems a bit unfair to me,' said Jamie, 'landing a bloke in the road without his trousers.'

'It's to keep the peace,' said Kitty. 'Oh, am I relieved we've got that inquest out of the way. When we get 'ome, I'll do something nice for you to eat before you go off to work.'

'I'm going straight on to the job,' said Jamie, 'I haven't got time to even get off the tram, let alone come home with you.'

'Oh, that's a shame, you won't 'ave had anything to eat,' said Kitty.

'I'll find something.'

'Mind you do,' said Kitty, 'or you'll 'ave a grumblin' stomach all afternoon. Still, I'll do a nice supper, I might try me 'and at a roly-poly jam puddin' for afters.'

'By the way,' said Jamie, 'thanks for the laundry you left on my bed yesterday. The shirts were ironed to perfection. Thanks, Kitty, thanks very much.'

Kitty did a little kind of gulp. Her step-father had never ever thanked her for anything.

'Oh, that's all right,' she said.

'You'll make some decent bloke a treasure of a wife some day,' said Jamie.

'D'you think so? Honest? I'd like a decent bloke for me 'usband—oh, and you could give me away, couldn't you?'

'I'm sorry I spoke,' said Jamie.

But Kitty saw a little grin on his face. She smiled.

Chapter Eleven

Mrs Fitch popped in on Thursday morning, wanting to know all about the inquest. Kitty and Jamie gave her details, and she said good, that's all over now. They didn't tell her anything about the implication that a blow might have been struck. She said Kitty and her brother and sisters could enjoy a better life now. That is, if Kitty could get a job and still have parish relief, and if Mr Blair still kept an eye on them. Jamie said he was a fixture at the moment, at which Mrs Fitch smiled and invited him to Sunday tea. Her husband wanted to meet him sociably, she said.

Kitty didn't think much of that and said so after Mrs Fitch had gone.

'What a sauce,' she said.

'Very nice of her, I thought,' said Jamie.

'I bet it's not her 'usband that wants to be sociable with you,' said Kitty, 'I bet it's her. It's not decent, her a married woman with a little girl. You ought to be ashamed, sayin' yes to her. You're supposed to 'ave Sunday teas with us. I don't know what Chloe and Carrie are goin' to say, their new dad 'aving Sunday tea with a married woman.'

'And her husband and little girl,' said Jamie.

'Yes, but I bet that after tea she'll get you in 'er parlour on your own,' said Kitty. 'I don't know what *that'll* do to our respectability, our lodger bein' sociable with Mrs Fitch in 'er parlour. I won't be able to look our neighbours in the face.'

'Well, I wouldn't want that,' said Jamie.

'We couldn't be respectable before, not while that man kept us all lookin' ragged and unrespectable,' said Kitty, 'but now we've got you lookin' after us, we've got a position to keep up.'

'You've got what?' said Jamie, whose determination not to sink inextricably into the trap was hopelessly failing him every day.

'Yes, Alfie and the twins don't want to grow up not decent,' said Kitty, 'and I don't want people pointin' at me and sayin' look at that young lady, she' got a lodger that's socializin' with a married woman. Married women run off with lodgers, you know. Me and Alfie and the twins wouldn't get over the shame of it if Mrs Fitch run off with you.'

'And what would it do to my respectability if Mr Fitch ran off with you?' asked Jamie.

'Eh?'

'Yes, what?'

227

'Oh, you daft thing, that's barmy,' said Kitty.

'It might happen while I was in his parlour with Mrs Fitch.'

'That's not funny,' said Kitty.

'What are you giggling about, then?'

'You bein' daft, that's what. Well, I just 'ope that when your mother's friend comes to lodge here she can keep an eye on you, just like your mum would, and see you don't make us ashamed of you. Can we really charge 'er five bob rent?'

'Easily,' said Jamie. 'Thanks for getting the mattress.'

'Yes, Alfie 'elped me carry it 'ome, and it only cost three and six. 'Ave we still got lots of money?'

'Loads,' said Jamie.

'What a blessin',' said Kitty, but was still a bit peeved about him accepting Mrs Fitch's invitation to Sunday tea. He'd be taking her out next, when Mr Fitch's back was turned.

However, the following day she decided to be extra nice to him and let him see she didn't want to be a problem to him. She asked him if he liked fish. Jamie said yes. So Kitty said well, as it's Friday I'll buy some really nice fish for our supper. Not bloaters, she said.

'Yes, spare me bloaters,' said Jamie.

'They're cheap but bony,' said Kitty. 'Skate's nice, don't you think, mister?'

'Look, nothing too expensive, Kitty.'

'Oh, skate's not expensive. I'll fry it with mash and tinned peas. Peas are nice with fish.'

'Go ahead,' said Jamie, and out Kitty went to the market, leaving him to think about the fact that unless the council had more demolition jobs to carry out, he'd be workless again next week. He'd been calling in regularly at the Walworth labour exchange, but always there were fifty men ready to go after every job offered. The cockneys generally didn't think much of the post-war world, especially those who, like himself, were ex-Servicemen. If he were reduced to just dole money again, he wasn't going to be much of a help to three girls and a boy who'd only have parish relief when their money ran out. And that money was almost certainly part of ill-gotten gains. Never mind that, he thought, let them have it.

He decided to go and see one or two building contractors. It might be hopeless, but you had to fight that thought. There was always a chance that one building worker had had a hodful of bricks drop on his head and been put out of action at just the right moment.

Someone knocked on the front door

then. He went down and opened the door. 'Hello, hope I've come to the right address,' said a young lady of remarkable good looks. A little brown velvet hat sat on her chestnut hair. Friendliness showed in her hazel eyes and in her smile. Her fine mouth was parted, revealing that the smile had reached her moist white teeth. Her pearl-buttoned blouse, of a delicate oyster shade, enhanced the pouting contours of her bosom, and the hem of her dark brown skirt reached to the tops of her laced calf-length boots. Jamie thought her about twenty-one and pretty self-possessed in her air.

'It's the right address if you're looking for the Edwards family,' he said.

'I'm not,' she said.

'For me, then? I'm Jamie Blair.'

'Well, that's just fine,' she said. 'I'm Rosemary Allen, friend of your parents.'

'Come in,' said Jamie, and picked up a laden suitcase that stood on the doorstep beside her. She entered and looked around. 'I've been expecting you,' he said, 'but wasn't sure when you'd arrive.'

'I came off the ferry from Belfast yesterday evening and took the night train to London,' she said. 'Am I taking advantage of your good nature, landing myself on you? Your mother said you'd got too much of it.'

'Too much of what?'

'Good nature.' She gave him a long look. She seemed to like what she saw, for her smile came again. Jamie at twenty-four was a personable young man, if toughened mentally and physically by his years in France and Flanders. The fact that Kitty was digging holes in his mental toughness was something that was giving him headaches.

'It's the first time I've heard I'm good-natured,' he said. 'Come on, I'll show you the room Kitty Edwards says you can have.'

'Kitty Edwards?'

'You could call her my landlady,' said Jamie with a smile. He carried her suitcase into the downstairs bedroom, formerly the closely guarded bedroom of Henry Mullins. Rosemary Allen followed him in. 'This do you?' he asked.

She looked around again.

'I shan't complain about this,' she said. Jamie had helped Kitty give it a thorough going-over with broom, duster and polish. 'I thought the best you'd be able to do for me would be something poky. Your mother said there were poky lodging rooms all over Walworth.'

'Slightly out of her mind, as usual,' said Jamie. 'Will it suit you?'

'Very much,' said Rosemary.

'That's the good news, then. The bad news, I'm afraid, is that it's not for free. It's for rent.'

'Why, of course,' said Rosemary, taking in every aspect of the room. 'How much?'

'Six bob,' said Jamie, adding an extra shilling to the amount he and Kitty had agreed on. Rosemary Allen's clothes and looks didn't come from being hard-up. Not rich, though. Good middle class. An extra bob would be welcome to Kitty.

'Six shillings?' said Rosemary. 'Well, I'm happy with that. I've a job waiting for me in the City, as a typist, and I start on Monday. I could have looked for lodgings without bothering you, but I don't know good old London town all that well, and I don't mind telling you that as I'm a friend of your parents, I felt I could find a friend in you. London's big and awesome to someone born outside it.'

'I thought you'd be an Ulsterwoman,' said Jamie.

Rosemary laughed. It was an infectious sound.

'Do I talk like one?' she asked.

'Not a bit,' said Jamie, 'but I thought you would.'

'I was born in Chester,' she said.

'Look, unpack your things,' said Jamie, 'while I make you a cup of tea. D'you fancy a cup?'

'Thanks,' said Rosemary, 'thanks very much. What do we call each other?'

'I'm Jamie.'

'I like it. I'm Rosemary.'

'You're on, Rosemary, I'll shout when the tea's ready. I've got the run of the kitchen.'

He put the kettle on. There was one thing he had to do, and that was to find out why the lady had done a bunk from Belfast to take up lodgings in Walworth. If it was anything to do with the Irish troubles, then he'd have to put his foot down. He didn't want her bringing the North and South problems into this house. Kitty had enough of her own.

'Lovely,' said Rosemary, sitting at the kitchen table with him and sipping hot tea. 'I say, what kind of family is it you're lodging with here?'

'A hard-up one,' said Jamie.

'Is that typical of their crockery?' she asked, nodding at the dresser on which cups hung and plates and saucers stood. Everything looked odd, nothing matched.

'Yes, that's typical,' said Jamie, and gave her a little potted history of Kitty and the kids. Rosemary listened with interest. Then with spasms of disgust. The dramatic end of Jamie's account brightened her up considerably, however.

'The old bugger fell down the stairs and conked out?' she said. 'You've made my day. Did you hit him hard?'

'Who said I hit him?' asked Jamie.

'I'd have taken a chopper to him and finished him off without knocking him down the stairs,' said Rosemary.

'Who said he was knocked down the stairs?'

'Natural assumption,' said Rosemary.

'He died of a heart attack,' said Jamie.

'So you said.'

'So did the coroner's court.'

'Good for the coroner's court. Good for you, Jamie.'

'He simply fell down the stairs.'

'Best thing I've ever heard,' said Rosemary.

'Don't get excited,' said Jamie, 'don't make a meal of it and don't make assumptions.'

'I'm an understanding girl,' said Rosemary. 'Where are the amenities?'

'Upstairs on the landing, or at the end of the yard.'

'I favour upstairs,' said Rosemary, finished her tea, and up to the landing amenities she went. When she came down again, she said, 'There's no towel.'

'You take your own in this house,' said Jamie, 'Kitty can't afford guest towels.'

'I'll treat her,' said Rosemary, sitting

down again. Jamie refilled her cup from the pot. 'She's seventeen, you said?'

'I did.'

'And she's having to look after her brother and her twin sisters?'

'And doing a good job. She got to the point where she hardly cared while her step-father was alive. They all looked like ragamuffins. Since he went she's done wonders.'

'I've an idea you've been helping,' said Rosemary, 'and that's why you've got the run of their kitchen. What, you may ask, can I contribute?'

'I'm not asking,' said Jamie.

'I'm willing to be some help.'

'You'll be sorry if you do, they'll make you their mother and start calling you Mum. They occasionally call me Dad.'

Rosemary pealed with laughter.

'You're a father figure, Jamie?' she said.

'I'm out of work.'

'Still? Your mother told me months ago you were unemployed. Is that still the case?'

'Yes, apart from some part-time work now and again. I've got a half-day's work this afternoon. When that's been done, I'm on the dole again. But never mind that, I've got something else on my mind. What have you been doing in Belfast that's made you leave in a hurry?'

'Oh, nothing you need worry about,' said Rosemary.

'Believe me, Miss Rosemary Allen, I'm not going to worry, I'm going to have you tell me and then, if necessary, pack you off to where you were born. Chester. Out with it.'

'Hello, what have we here?' smiled Rosemary. 'Holy Inquisition?'

'Unholy, more like,' said Jamie. 'Let's have it. Was it anything to do with the ruddy great divide between Catholics and Protestants?'

The Catholic IRA leaders wanted a free and united country. Sir Edward Carson, leader of Ulster's Protestants, wanted an independent Ulster, though as part of the United Kingdom. The British government had been forced to grant this. The IRA yelled with rage, and continued to commit mayhem, ignoring the fact that Ireland and Ulster had never been united. Jamie was fed-up with both of them.

Rosemary laughed again.

'You think I'm an idiot?' she said.

'You are if you get yourself involved with the IRA, whether you're for or against them,' said Jamie.

'I don't go in for politics, especially Irish politics,' said Rosemary. 'My troubles are more personal. Do you want to know about them?'

'I do,' said Jamie.

'Bless the man,' murmured Rosemary, 'he wants to be a father figure to me too. Well, all right, Jamie, I'll tell you.' She had gone to Belfast three years ago, when she was eighteen, to stay with an uncle and aunt, and enjoy a summer holiday. Her uncle was from Chester too, but had taken up a post with the Belfast branch of his company, manufacturers of leather goods. She enjoyed herself so much, finding the countryside lovely, that she took up a job there herself, doing the accounts and the typing for a Mrs Lindsay, who owned a fashion house in the best part of Belfast. Mr Lindsay was actually the brains behind the business, and unfortunately, Rosemary fell in love with him, so much so that she began an affair with him. Extremely infatuated, she dressed herself like a fashion plate to please him and excite him, and spent any amount of money on herself and her appearance. Even more unfortunately, Mrs Lindsay found out everything.

'What does everything mean?' asked Jamie.

'Oh, dear, the affair itself,' said Rosemary, 'and the rest.'

'The rest?'

'Dresses and coats not paid for, and certain cash receipts that I didn't enter

237

in the bank pay-in book,' said Rosemary. 'I don't think I want to get as infatuated as that again. Mrs Lindsay was going to prosecute me. I'd got to know your parents by then.'

'My cock-eyed parents?' said Jamie.

'But very lovable,' said Rosemary. 'Not only did they take me in and hide me, but they put it about that I'd crossed the Irish Sea to good old England. They wrote to you while I waited for the coast to be clear. I had to wait until yesterday.'

'Wait a moment,' said Jamie, 'why didn't you go home to your parents?'

'Unfortunately again, my parents knew all about my bad luck—'

'What bad luck?'

'I hope you're not a policeman,' said Rosemary, 'you're beginning to sound like one. Well, it was bad luck, getting found out and having Mrs Lindsay write to my parents. My father was furious, and my mother wrote to say I was never to darken their door again. I'd got your mother to post a letter to them for me, telling them I needed to come home. After all that, your mother wrote to you. She told me you were a kind boy, even if she was sad that you hadn't joined the Labour Party.'

'I don't know what I've done to deserve parents slightly out of their minds and now a mad, bad, young friend of theirs. Well, listen, you heathen, behave yourself while you're lodging here, or if Mrs Lindsay turns up on this doorstep, I'll hand you over to her.'

'I get some good marks, don't I, for confessing everything?' said Rosemary.

'Is that suitcase of yours full of lifted goods?' asked Jamie.

'My Belfast glad rags? No, Mrs Lindsay managed to grab them all back. I'll spend my time here redeeming myself, although I'm praying that a typing job in the City won't be too boring. Jamie, thanks so much for finding me a room here, I'd like us to become friends. I'll go and finish unpacking.'

When Kitty came back from shopping, Jamie was washing up cups and saucers.

'Who's been?' she asked. 'It wasn't Mrs Fitch again, was it?'

'No, it was my mother's friend, Rosemary Allen. She's arrived, Kitty, and she's making herself at home in her room.'

'Oh, I'd better go and meet 'er,' said Kitty, and knocked on the bedroom door.

'Come in,' called Rosemary. Kitty went in, Rosemary said hello, Kitty said hello, and then marched straight back to the kitchen.

'Here,' she said, 'you told me it was a

239

friend of your mum's that was comin' to lodge.'

'So I did, and she is,' said Jamie.

'But I thought she'd be like someone's aunt and as old as your mum.'

'Not everyone is as old as my mum,' said Jamie.

'Well, that person ought to be,' said Kitty. 'How can any grown-up man's mother 'ave a friend that's not as old as she is?'

'Bit of a puzzle, I suppose.'

'We don't want 'er livin' here,' said Kitty, who could see only too well what might happen.

'What difference does it make that she's young?' asked Jamie.

'Well, she's tarty,' said Kitty.

'No, she's not.'

'She can easy find other lodgings.'

'I've already told her she can have the room, seeing you agreed,' said Jamie.

'I 'adn't had a look at her then,' said Kitty, 'so now you can tell her she can't 'ave it.'

'You don't mean that.'

'Yes, I do.'

'No, you don't. You agreed and you have to stick by that, Kitty. I've agreed to help you and the kids as much as I can, and I'm sticking by that.'

'Yes, but you might go off,' said Kitty.

240

'Go off? I'm not a lump of old cheese.'

'I mean—'

'Stop mucking about,' said Jamie.

'Well, I like that,' said Kitty, 'I'm not the one that's goin' to sit with a married woman in her parlour, I'm respectable and don't go in for muckin' about. Oh, all right, let that person stay, then, I don't want you flyin' off the handle. It'll uspet Chloe and Carrie.'

'Well, we can't have that, can we?' said Jamie. 'By the way, I told that person that the rent's six bob. She's quite happy to pay it.'

'Crikey, six bob?' said Kitty.

'That rent and mine will pay most of the house rent for you.'

'Oh, I'd best put up with her, then,' said Kitty.

'Come and have a few words with her,' said Jamie.

'I suppose I must,' said Kitty, and went back to the bedroom, this time with Jamie. Rosemary was hanging clothes in the wardrobe. Jamie made the introductions.

'Kitty, this is Miss Rosemary Allen, my mother's friend. Rosemary, this is Miss Kitty Edwards, our landlady.'

'Pleased to meet you,' smiled Rosemary. 'You must be the youngest landlady ever.'

'Yes, it 'appened by the hand of fate,' said Kitty. 'My step-father—'

'I heard,' said Rosemary, 'Jamie told me about it.'

'Oh, do you two know each other, then?' asked Kitty, quick with suspicion.

'We've only just met,' said Jamie.

'We simply knew of each other, through his parents,' said Rosemary.

'Well, I 'ope the room suits you,' said Kitty.

'It's fine,' said Rosemary, eyeing the girl in curiosity. She looked all right. Quite attractive, in fact, although she could have made a lot more of herself with better clothes and better-dressed hair. But her eyes couldn't be bettered, they were a marvellous deep brown. 'I shan't be any trouble, I know you've got enough already. Jamie said you're coping like a girl wonder. If I can be of help anytime, just ask. Oh, do I pay the rent in advance?'

'Yes,' said Jamie, 'and you start today.'

'I'll start right now,' said Rosemary. She opened her handbag, took out her purse, found three florins and handed them to Kitty with the brightest of smiles. I don't trust her, thought Kitty, there's too many smiles, and they're all for his benefit, not mine, I bet. She's fast, that's what she is, and I don't want her staying here for long.

'I'll get a rent book for you.'

'Oh, don't worry about things like that,' said Rosemary.

'It's no bother, and they only cost a penny,' said Kitty. 'We'll leave you to settle in—oh, we don't allow rowdiness in this street, by the way.'

Jamie coughed. Rosemary looked enquiring.

'Rowdiness?' she said.

'Yes, like havin' noisy friends in,' said Kitty. 'Of course, we won't mind if you want to entertain your young man, as long as—well, I'm tryin' to bring my brother and sisters up respectable.'

'That counts in Walworth,' said Jamie with a straight face.

'I'm pleased to hear it,' said Rosemary, 'but I shan't be entertaining any young man.' She smiled again at Kitty. 'I don't have one.'

Oh, blow you, then, thought Kitty, no wonder you're making eyes at Mr Blair, and calling him Jamie when you've only just met him.

'Well, I 'ope you'll be comfortable,' she said, and went back to the kitchen. Her temper wasn't improved by Jamie staying to chat to the person for ten minutes. When he appeared, she said, 'As the landlady, I've got to tell you I don't 'old with you bein' alone with her in her bedroom.'

'Don't fret,' said Jamie, 'she's not a married woman.'

'All the same,' said Kitty, 'I'll 'ave to forbid it.'

'Would you mind saying that again?'

'No, I don't mind,' said Kitty, 'I've got to forbid it.'

'I'm hearing things,' said Jamie, and went up to his room.

Oh, lor', thought Kitty, I've done it again and made him cross. Impulsively, she ran up to his room. The door was open, and he was brushing his hair in front of the washstand mirror.

'Look, you're not cross, are you?' she said.

'No, I'm just having a fit,' he said.

'Oh, 'ave you got an empty stomach?' asked Kitty in concern. 'Empty stomachs can give anyone a fit, Mrs Reynolds said so once. Shall I get you something to eat?'

'Not yet,' said Jamie, 'it's only half-eleven. I want to remind you, by the way, that I'm adding to the money I'm holding for you. I'm putting in what I think I should to cover all the food you're giving me.'

'Oh, you don't need to do that,' said Kitty, 'how could I charge you for food when you're sort of part of the fam'ly and bein' so kind and 'elpful all the time? I've got some nice skate for all of us tonight, and I'll do lots of mash, creamy mash, and make sure I fill you up. We'd all get upset if you kept 'aving fits on account of not gettin' enough to eat. Chloe said only this mornin' that you're ever so nice to her and Carrie when you're eating supper with us, which shows food does you good.'

'You surprise me,' said Jamie.

'No, honest, food is good for most people unless they're too fat,' said Kitty. 'We used to feel faint sometimes from not 'aving enough, but it didn't give us fits.'

'Who said I'm having a fit from being hungry?' asked Jamie.

'Well, I thought it could be that,' said Kitty. 'What was it, then?'

What a monkey, thought Jamie. God alone knew what went on behind those brown eyes of hers. She was having him on at the moment, that was for sure. But he couldn't help liking her funny little ways and her tendency at times to talk like a little old lady.

'Never mind,' he smiled.

'Just as long as you're not cross,' said Kitty.

She fried him egg and bacon before he went to his work, and for the kids too when they came in for their midday break. That had them in rapture. Alfie said it was like eating like lords. Chloe said like ladies too. Carrie asked if lords and ladies always had eggs and bacon at this time of the day.

Chloe said she didn't know as she'd never met any lords and ladies. Carrie asked Jamie if he had. Jamie said no, but he'd met some monkeys in his time.

'Oh, do monkeys have eggs an' bacon?' asked Carrie.

'No, course not,' said Alfie, 'just monkey nuts.'

'I only asked,' said Carrie.

'I'd faint if you didn't,' said Chloe.

They all said goodbye to Jamie when he left for his work. He had another attack of weakmindedness. He gave the three kids a penny each again. Carrie was so overcome she asked if she could give him a kiss. Jamie's first inclination was to duck that one, but then he thought about the fact that those twin girls had probably been starved of any gestures of affection.

'Help yourself, Carrie,' he said, and Carrie jumped up and gave him a smacker on his cheek as he bent down. Kitty smiled. Chloe, still sitting, gave Jamie a shy look. He delivered a kiss on her nose. 'So long, kids,' he said, and left. He looked in on Rosemary. She was sitting on the edge of the bed, a pencil in her hand making a note in her diary.

'Hello,' she said, 'off to work?'

'The last of it for the time being, probably,' said Jamie. 'Settled in all right?'

'Fine,' she said.

'Well, behave yourself,' he said, and off he went to walk the distance to the Old Kent Road. It was good exercise and gave him time to reflect on his problems. He couldn't go on like this. He was a skilled man and given the opportunity could have built a house by himself. It might be worth enquiring at Australia House to see if there were prospects in Australia. He could take Kitty and the kids with him.

He was in Rodney Road and he almost stopped dead as he realized what he had said to himself.

Take them with him?

Well, why not? Someone had to give them some kind of a future. Alfie had the adaptability of most Walworth boys. Give him an objective and he'd go for it. He'd do well in Australia. And the twins would blossom. And Kitty would be the last one to fail.

One thing about Walworth, it always gave the impression that it was putting up a cheerful fight against poverty. It was in the nature of its cockneys to look at things optimistically. But since the end of the war, Walworth had had very little to offer its people. Some factories had closed down, and others were on part-time shifts. The unemployed might say there's always tomorrow, mate, but they knew and Jamie knew that tomorrow was going to be a long time coming. Depression was world-wide. All the same, a number of Australia's immigrants were making a go of things. He'd give it some serious thought.

The kids had gone back to school. Rosemary knocked and put her head into the kitchen.

'Just thought I'd let you know I'm going out to see the sights of London,' she said to Kitty.

'Oh, you can go out whenever you like,' said Kitty, 'you don't 'ave to tell me, Miss Allen.'

Rosemary smiled.

'Just thought I'd let you know. Oh, and shall I call you Kitty? That seems friendly, don't you think? You can call me Rosemary. Goodbye, I'll be back later.'

'Yes, don't get run over,' said Kitty. She'd better make an effort with the new lodger, she thought, or the other lodger might get cross again. Still, making an effort didn't mean she couldn't do some secret discouragement.

A boy brought a note from Dr McManus during the afternoon. It told Kitty the funeral was to be on Monday, and that the expenses were being met by the council.

Oh, I'll have to go, thought Kitty, but I bet the kids won't want to.

Mrs Reynolds popped in just after three o'clock.

'You there, Kitty?'

Kitty came out to the passage.

' 'Ello, Mrs Reynolds.'

Mrs Reynolds gave the girl a kind and motherly smile.

'My, yer lookin' so much better all the time, Kitty, and Alfie and the twins too. I never saw such a nice change in anyone, you're a compliment to yerself an' Mr Blair that's lookin' after all of you like a real Christian.'

'Yes, he's nearly as Christian as a kind dad,' said Kitty, 'and doin' all he can to see we're respectable. He's ever so respectable 'imself.' She thought she'd better say that just in case Mrs Reynolds might start to wonder if there was any mucking about going on.

'I never knew a more upright young man,' said Mrs Reynolds, 'and everyone's 'oping 'is luck will change and that 'e'll get a job. Are you 'aving an 'ard time makin' ends meet, Kitty?'

'Oh, we've got enough to last us a bit, Mrs Reynolds. It's what we found that our step-father 'ad left to us in 'is pockets.'

'Well, I 'ope the sun starts shinin' for you soon, Kitty. Look, 'ave you seen the local?' Mrs Reynolds had a copy of the *South London Press* in her hand. 'It's the one that's come out today and it's got a report of the inquest. I popped in just to tell you I didn't like that police sergeant sayin' a blow might've been struck. It's all right not speakin' ill of the dead, although that comes a bit 'ard with some dead, but speakin' ill of the livin' by makin' aspersions, I don't 'old with that an' never will.'

Kitty, who hadn't given a thought to the inquest being reported, gave it quick thought now and said, 'Yes, you can't believe the aspersions some people can make, but Mr Blair took it in a manful way and didn't get a bit upset. The coroner was very admirin' of him, and he gave me a kind look too.'

'I don't know what that police sergeant could of been thinkin' about,' said Mrs Reynolds. 'It says in the paper that Mr Blair admitted 'e was angry with yer step-father, Kitty, but who wouldn't of been, I ask? I can't honestly say I'm sorry Mr Mullins 'ad that fatal attack, I can't 'ide me feelings. D'you want to read the report, Kitty? I'll leave the paper an' you can let me 'ave it back later.'

'Yes, all right, thanks, Mrs Reynolds.'

'Well, you're a brave gel, Kitty, and me old man said last night that 'e wishes yer good luck.'

Kitty read the report in the kitchen.

It was quite interesting, really, and it didn't say a lot about Sergeant Watkins mentioning a blow might have been struck in anger. It just said it, that was all. Blessed copper, she thought, I suppose he felt he was being clever.

It was the first time she had ever had her name in a paper. Miss Kitty Edwards, that was what it said. And Mr Jamie Blair. Imagine that, both their names in a paper.

That man's name was there too. Mr Henry Mullins. Kitty wondered if he liked being dead and having to face up to stern questions from St Peter, who was bound to ask him about his rotten temper and that money.

Suppose it was in his bedroom, hidden away so that no-one could find it except himself? That person, Miss Allen, had the bedroom now. Suppose she accidentally found it? Blow it, thought Kitty, we don't want her here longer than a week.

Chapter Twelve

'Crikey O'Reilly,' said Alfie over the fried skate supper, 'we're eatin' like lords again.'

'And ladies, you forgetful boy,' said Chloe, 'me and Carrie and Kitty can't eat like lords when we're ladies.'

'Course you're not,' said Alfie, 'you don't wear 'ats with fevvers or skirts down to yer feet.'

'We're young ladies,' said Carrie, 'ain't we, mister?'

'Well, you've all got clean faces,' said Jamie, 'and you don't look so much now as if you've been having trouble getting through a hedge bottom first.' Carrie giggled. 'Yes, I think we can say you're all young ladies, and that Kitty'll soon be old enough to wear hats with feathers.'

'An' skirts down to 'er plates of meat?' suggested Alfie.

'With an umbrella,' said Jamie.

'Here, excuse me, I'm not that old,' said Kitty.

'Bless yer, me child,' said Alfie. ' 'Ere, mister, Kitty says we've got a new lodger. She said a female person that's a friend of yer mum.'

252

'That's right,' said Jamie, enjoying the meaty wing of skate with creamy-looking mash and tinned peas. 'I believe she's out at the moment.'

'Yes, I told you, she went out this afternoon to see the sights,' said Kitty.

'What for?' asked Carrie.

'Carrie, what d'yer mean, "what for"?' asked Chloe.

'Well, we've got sights round 'ere,' said Carrie, 'specially old 'Ooray Abie and old 'Umpback Fanny in Brandon Street.'

'Carrie, you silly, not them kind of sights,' said Chloe.

'And Mrs Fanny Postle don't 'ave a humpback, Carrie,' said Kitty, 'she's just got shoulders bowed with age. The street kids shouldn't call 'er Humpback Fanny, it's not kind.'

'I was only sayin',' said Carrie.

'Makes a change from only askin',' said Alfie. 'Mister, is yer mum's friend nice-lookin'? I mean, would I fancy 'er?'

'Listen to 'im at 'is age,' said Chloe.

'Yes, I think you'd fancy her, Alfie,' said Jamie.

'He'll want 'is brains testin' if he does,' said Kitty.

'Is she ugly, then?' asked Carrie.

'Sort of,' said Kitty. 'Still, it's not her fault.'

'Oh, poor woman,' said Chloe, and

glanced at Jamie. 'Kitty, mister's laughin'.'

'Yes, he's puttin' some good food into 'is stomach,' said Kitty, 'he gets a fit when his stomach's empty. Is your skate all right, Mr Blair?'

'Best I've ever tasted,' said Jamie.

'Oh, that's good, you won't 'ave a fit now,' said Chloe.

'I 'ad a fit once,' said Alfie.

'Well, don't tell the whole street,' said Chloe, 'or ev'rybody'll want one.'

'What sort of fit was it?' asked Carrie.

'It was when I was under old Ma Earnshaw's fruit stall in the market,' said Alfie, 'tryin' to get some specked apples, and I 'ad a fit in case she copped me.'

'That boy's gettin' dafter ev'ry day,' said Chloe.

'Kitty, mister's laughin' again,' whispered Carrie.

'Yes, he's 'appy when he's eatin' good food,' said Kitty.

'Do you know where Australia is, kids?' asked Jamie.

'Yes, it's underneath us,' said Chloe.

'D'you know what it's like?'

'Yes, it's got a barren reef or something,' said Carrie, 'and rabbits. But I wouldn't like to go there, you 'ave to walk upside-down.'

'Cor,' said Alfie, tunnelling skate into himself, 'fancy Mrs Fitch 'aving to walk upside-down, I wouldn't 'alf like to be there. I fancy Mrs Fitch, specially upside-down.'

'What an 'orrible boy,' said Chloe, 'do we 'ave to 'ave him all the time for our brother?'

'Alfie, kindly don't talk about Mrs Fitch walkin' about upside-down,' said Kitty, 'it's not decent.'

'Well, they 'ave to do it in Australia,' said Alfie, 'it's upside-down itself, and if Mrs Fitch just 'appened to go there, she wouldn't be able to 'elp 'erself.'

'Nor would you,' said Chloe.

'Still, I suppose people get used to it,' said Carrie.

'And there's a lot of sunshine about,' said Jamie.

'I think I could fancy Australia,' said Alfie.

'Who wants jam roly-poly?' asked Kitty.

'Oh, jam roly-poly's better than walkin' upside-down,' said Carrie.

The warm evening drew the kids out after supper. Jamie, however, first made them help him with the washing-up to give Kitty a rest. Alfie tried to dodge it, Jamie told him it wasn't proper to, and Alfie, propelled by that into a mood of good family behaviour, did his stint.

When the kids had gone out, Kitty

255

showed Jamie the inquest report in the local paper. Jamie read it, said it was a pretty faithful account and that he couldn't quarrel with it.

'But that bit about Sergeant Watkins sayin' a blow might have been struck in anger, I don't think much of that,' said Kitty. 'It could cast a shadow over your good name.'

'It could what?' said Jamie.

'Well, it could,' said Kitty. 'I was cross when Mrs Reynolds told me about it, but I didn't show it. She said it was casting aspersions, that she didn't 'old with that sort of thing. It's rotten that it's in the paper now for people to read. Never mind, I'll always stand by you, Mr Blair, wild 'orses wouldn't drag anything out of me that shouldn't be said.'

'That record's beginning to wear out,' said Jamie.

'No, I mean it, honest,' said Kitty. 'Oh, Carrie and Chloe were ever so touched you gave them a kiss today, they only ever got wollops before.'

'You'll get one in a moment,' said Jamie.

'A kiss?' said Kitty, startled.

'A wallop.'

'Well, I think that might be best,' said Kitty. 'I don't mind a wallop if I've made you cross, but it wouldn't look right, you givin' me kisses at my age. Well, you know what the neighbours might think.'

'I know what I think,' said Jamie, 'that I'd be better off if I vanished in a puff of smoke.'

'I won't tell Alfie and the twins you said that, Mr Blair, they'd be ever so upset.'

The front door opened then, by a pull on the latchcord, and Rosemary entered the house. She came straight through to the kitchen and knocked.

'Anyone home?'

'Come in,' said Kitty, and Rosemary showed herself. She looked so attractive in a stylish dress and hat that Kitty made a face.

'Hello, you two,' said Rosemary, smiling.

'How were the sights of London?' asked Jamie.

'Thrilling,' said Rosemary. 'Is anyone putting the kettle on? I'm dying for a cup of hot sweet tea. That is, if I'm not interrupting anything. I think I deserve one, I've found you a job, Jamie.'

'What?' said Jamie.

'Well, I remembered a friend of my father's who's the managing director of a building contractors. He works in their head office in the City, so I went to see him this afternoon. I told him you were a war hero, that you were an expert builder—well, your father said you were—and that you once saved my life. They're building a number of houses in Streatham, and you're to report to their site office at eight o'clock on Monday morning. It's in—let's see.' Rosemary delved into her handbag and brought out a slip of paper. 'Yes, Kirkstall Road, Streatham, wherever that is. You're to see the site manager, Mr Robbins. It's all on this piece of paper. Here.' She gave it to him.

'Is this on the level?' asked Jamie.

'Of course,' said Rosemary. 'You've no idea how upset your mother is that you're still out of work. I think she feels it's a blot on the family honour, since your father's been employed all his married life. Their friendship was valuable to me, so I thought the least I could do was to go the City this afternoon and see my father's old friend. Are you pleased with me, Jamie?'

'I'm your friend for life,' said Jamie. Kitty saw the look on his face, like that of a man who's just been saved from being eaten by lions. She may have been young, but she knew what prolonged unemployment could do to a man's pride. She couldn't help feeling glad for the lodger who'd been a tower of strength to her and the kids, but nor could she help feeling that with a job he'd be more independent. With only bits of work coming his way, he was sort of tied to the house, to his lodgings. He couldn't afford to go anywhere else. But he could once he started this job. Streatham was miles away, and he'd probably look for lodgings in Brixton. Oh, blow, just when she'd got things working ever so well. Alfie and the twins were fond of him now and would really be upset if he went. Bother it, she might have to remind him about her step-father; the bit about did he fall or was he pushed.

'Well, who's going to put the kettle on?' asked Rosemary.

'I'll do it,' said Kitty.

'Thanks,' said Rosemary, 'I'll just go and freshen up.' She went to her room.

Kitty, filling the kettle from the sink tap in the scullery, felt that that female person was going to make herself at home in the kitchen as much as Jamie had. But Jamie had been invited to, the female person hadn't. Putting the kettle on the gas, Kitty said, 'I suppose you'll go and live in Brixton now.'

Jamie, still in a state of disbelief, said, 'Pardon?'

'Well, I don't suppose you'll stay here when your job's in Streatham.'

'Who said?' asked Jamie.

'Streatham's miles away,' said Kitty.

'Half an hour's tram ride, that's all,' said Jamie. 'Look, I can't leave you and the kids, Kitty. You've got to have someone around while things are as they are. I know you've some money, but it won't last for ever. You need to get a job yourself, and so do the twins when they leave school next year. That'll secure a future for all of you.'

'Oh, you're goin' to stay?' asked Kitty, wide-eyed.

'Yes, of course I am.'

'Thanks ever so much,' said Kitty, wondering why she felt a little bit tearful.

Mr Briggs arrived home from his late shift at twenty past eight. Mrs Briggs was waiting for him.

'You can sit down to yer supper,' she said when he'd taken off his postman's cap and jacket and given his braces a twang. She put his meal on the kitchen table for him. It was meat rissoles, fried potatoes and greens. She'd had her own supper.

'I 'ad rissoles last night,' said Mr Briggs, careful to make a statement of it and not a complaint.

'Well, I'm glad you're thankful,' said Mrs Briggs, 'not ev'ry 'usband's as lucky as you. Now listen, see this copy of the *South London Press?*'

'I see it, me love,' said Mr Briggs. She had thrust it under his nose, interfering with his knife and fork.

'Well, it's got a report on the inquest of me departed brother in it,' said Mrs Briggs, looking as if she'd got over the pain of being done out of her investment by Clever Clogs, alias Kitty's nosy lodger. 'And d'yer know what it says?'

'Well, no, 'Ilda, I ain't seen it yet, 'ave I?'

'Don't give me no lip. It says a police sergeant said a blow might've been struck in anger.'

'Eh?' said Mr Briggs, a forkful of rissole coming to a stop halfway to his mouth.

'Look at me when I'm talkin' to yer, then yer'll 'ear me. At the inquest, a police sergeant said a blow might've been struck. That lodger of Kitty's it seems 'e was right on the spot when me poor brother fell down the stairs. The inquest said 'e died of 'eart failure, but I can see it all now, 'e died from bein' knocked down them stairs, not fallin' down them.'

'Give over, me love—'

'Give over me foot,' said Mrs Briggs. 'That Kitty and 'er lodger both 'it 'Enry.'

Mr Briggs felt heartburn coming on, and a headache as well.

' 'Ilda, yer shouldn't talk like that, it ain't fair to Kitty.'

'I'm goin' to give up on you one day, Wally Briggs,' said his chronic trouble-and-strife. 'I'm goin' to cart you off somewhere

261

quiet an' medical, where they can 'ave a look at yer brains, to see if you've got any. Didn't Kitty an' that interferin' lodger of 'ers rob me of me rightful in'eritance?'

'I wouldn't say that, 'Ilda, when it's more like criminal loot than an in'eritance,' said Mr Briggs, getting ready to duck. He hoped his nose wouldn't finish up in the rissoles.

'What's up with you?' said Mrs Briggs. 'You keep soundin' lately as if yer answerin' me back. I 'ope you ain't. I don't want you upsettin' me when I've been upset enough by that schemin' Kitty and 'er crafty lodger. I'll give 'im something to remember me by, and 'er as well. She'll be sorry. She told us that 'er step-father deserved all she give 'im, didn't she?'

'Eh?' said Mr Briggs, who'd gone right off his supper.

'Mind, I didn't take it in at the time, bein' in such an upset state,' said Mrs Briggs.

'I didn't take it in, either,' said Mr Briggs, 'I didn't 'ear 'er say it.'

'Yes, you did. And she said it was what me poor brother earned for 'isself.'

'No, that must've been when you went there on Monday with them two 'alf-baked old lags I ain't too keen on,' said Mr Briggs.

'Don't you talk about my friends like

262

that or I'll knock yer silly 'ead orf,' said Mrs Briggs. 'It don't matter when Kitty said it, you was there and 'eard 'er. We both 'eard 'er.'

'I ask yer, me love, I ask yer,' said Mr Briggs, ' 'ow could I 'ave been there on Monday when I was at work?'

'She said it on Sunday,' said Mrs Briggs.

'On me life, 'Ilda, she didn't,' said Mr Briggs.

Mrs Briggs gave him a clout, and he wished he'd remembered to duck.

'Answerin' back's bad enough,' said Mrs Briggs, 'contradictin' me's worse. You 'eard Kitty on Sunday, we both 'eard 'er, an' we both 'eard 'er lodger back 'er up. "That's right," 'e said.'

'I'm 'earing things,' said Mr Briggs.

'What's that?'

'Now look, me love—'

'We're goin' to the Walworth police station to do what's our duty, Wally Briggs.'

'That we ain't,' said Mr Briggs, but only to himself. 'Now that ain't right, 'Ilda,' he complained, 'I can't see young Kitty sayin' things like that—she's a good girl.'

'You'll do as yer told, you 'ear me?' said Mrs Briggs.

' 'Ilda, I ain't after upsettin' yer,' said Mr Briggs, 'but if we start tellin' the Walworth police things like that about

Kitty an' Mr Blair, don't you realize they could end up swinging for it?'

'Course they won't, yer brainless 'alf-wit,' said Mrs Briggs, 'it'll only be manslaughter. That's what blows struck in anger mean, manslaughter.'

'They'll get prison,' said Mr Briggs.

'Only a year or two,' said Mrs Briggs, 'which'll be what they deserve. Then we'll 'ave the kids 'ere for a bit so's we can search that 'ouse from top to bottom. That money's there, I know it is. You on late shift again tomorrer?'

'Yes, but—'

'I don't want no buts. Anyway, tomorrer's no good, it's me special monthly shoppin' day.' Mr Briggs knew just what that meant. That she'd take advantage of crowded shops and stores and come home with goods she'd lifted. Give her her due, the old cow was a dab hand at it and she'd been getting away with it for years. He had an idea she'd got a little nest egg stowed away somewhere, as well as a suitcase. But he knew where the suitcase was. Under the bed. There were always some things in it waiting to be sold. 'What about next week, what's yer shift then?'

'Early,' he said. 'Six till three.'

'All right, then,' said Mrs Briggs, 'we'll go to the Walworth police station on Monday afternoon, we'll go as soon as yer get 'ome, you 'ear me?'

'Course I 'ear yer, me love, don't I always listen respectful to yer?' said Mr Briggs.

'We'll do our duty,' said Mrs Briggs.

'I'll do mine all right, 'Ilda me pet,' said Mr Briggs.

He did it the following morning, leaving early for his late shift to give himself time to call in at the Peckham police station. There he told the desk sergeant that he had a private matter of the law to discuss with one of the CID blokes.

In an interview room, a detective-sergeant and a detective-constable introduced themselves.

'Pleased to meet yer,' said Mr Briggs, and was invited to seat himself. He did so. 'Gents, you ain't goin' to believe this,' he said.

'Givin' yourself up, are you, Mr Briggs?' said Sergeant Thomas. 'What for?'

'Now don't be like that,' said Mr Briggs, 'I'm speakin' of a matter that's 'ighly delicate, and I don't feel too good about it. But it's got to be done. I've told her she shouldn't do it till I'm blue in me face, but she still does it.'

'Does what?' said Sergeant Thomas.

'And who's she?' asked the detective-constable.

'First off, gents,' said Mr Briggs, looking surprisingly smart in his postman's uniform, 'I'd like yer promise that I'm to be treated confidential. I can't afford for me name to be mentioned, I'll get both me legs broken if it is.'

'Mr Briggs, you intendin' to lay information?' asked Sergeant Thomas.

'As long as I ain't mentioned,' said Mr Briggs.

'Information that might lead to an arrest is always treated confidentially,' said Sergeant Thomas.

'No names, no pack drill?' said Mr Briggs.

'I can take it, can I, that you're an innocent party yourself, sir?'

'Yes, and I'm honest as well,' said Mr Briggs. 'I'm a postman.'

'Good enough, Mr Briggs.'

'All right, I'll trust yer. You can understand me position bein' a bit awkward when I tell yer the information concerns me own wife.' Mr Briggs did his best to shake his head in a sad way. 'And I ain't comfortable about it, either.'

'Did you say your wife?' asked the detective-constable.

'Tragic,' said Mr Briggs.

'Unusual,' said Sergeant Thomas. 'Like to proceed, sir? Detective-Constable Jones will be takin' notes.'

'That don't sound confidential,' said Mr Briggs.

'It will be,' said Sergeant Thomas.

'Well, 'ere goes, then,' said Mr Briggs. 'Mind, it's only recent that I've realized what she's been up to, though I did sometimes think to meself that she was comin' up reg'lar with fancy goods considerin' I only got a postman's wage. Still, I 'ave to 'and it all over except for a few bob. I did say to 'er once, I said you don't need another new 'andbag, 'Ilda, you bought one last month. I lost that, she said, someone pinched it off me. Then there was things like new blouses an' skirts, which made me ask 'er once where they was all comin' from, was it out of her 'ouse-keeping? Course it was, she said. I'm a simple bloke, gents, that's a fact I am, so I didn't argue. Well, she don't like argufyin'. Anyway, the other day she come 'ome with a new umbrella. She don't need any new umbrella, we already got two. So I said what's that, I said. Ask no questions, she said, and you'll 'ear no lies. Then a day or so later, up she come with another new 'andbag, another one, would yer believe. Only this time time I copped 'er puttin' it in a suitcase she keeps under our bed. Well, I 'ad to speak up then, so I did. I told 'er she'd nicked it in some store, that she was to take it back along with any other things she 'ad in the case. That upset 'er. She gets upset quick, and she ain't a small woman. She fetched me a wallop that nigh took me 'ead off. So I said, after I got up, that she was actin' very unreasonable an' that she'd got to turn over a new leaf. You're a postman's wife, I told 'er, and it ain't right for any postman's wife to lift things from shops that she ain't paid for. Go an' post some letters, she said, an' mind yer own business. Be it on yer own 'ead, 'Ilda, I said.'

'Your wife is Mrs Hilda Briggs, sir?' said Detective-Constable Jones.

'That's 'er,' said Mr Briggs, sighing. 'I tell yer straight, if I can't learn 'er a change of ways, the law will 'ave to. I dare say you gents might think I ain't much of an 'usband, shoppin' me own wife, but she's got to be learnt a lesson. I ain't 'aving no more of 'er takin' ways, it's 'urting me and it's painful as well. And it's 'urting me more to 'ave to tell yer she's goin' out to the shops today, and it's a pound to a penny she'll come back with more fancy goods that she ain't paid for. She'll be 'ome by four at the latest, she always 'as a pot of tea then. I'll be workin', I'm on late shift today, which is me only consolation. Well, you can understand I don't want to be there if you gents decide to knock on 'er door as soon as she gets back.'

'Mr Briggs, how long has your wife been doin' this?' asked Sergeant Thomas.

'Years, I should think,' said Mr Briggs, 'but as I already told yer, it's only recent that the penny's dropped.'

'Do you know if she sells these goods?' asked Sergeant Thomas.

'Well, though I ain't never seen 'er make a transaction, I've got a sad feelin' it's what she's always been doin',' said Mr Briggs. 'I've wondered frequent why she's got more money in 'er purse than I'd expect.'

'Has she ever given any money to you, sir?' asked Detective-Constable Jones.

'That she ain't. She'd 'ave known I'd've asked questions, wouldn't I?'

'So you had none of any possible proceeds, Mr Briggs?'

'Never 'ad a penny from 'er, except the few bob she gives me from me wages,' said Mr Briggs. 'I tell yer, this is a sad day for me, but it 'ad to be done. She's got to be learnt. Now you've got me address and me wife's monicker, and I leave it to you to do what I suppose you must.'

'Yes, we must, Mr Briggs,' said Sergeant Thomas, 'and we'll first apply for a search warrant. I think you said it's pretty certain she'll get back home this afternoon with more items that have probably been stolen.'

'I'd say dead certain.'

'Right,' said Sergeant Thomas. 'Thanks for your help, Mr Briggs.'

'Confidential, of course,' said Mr Briggs.

'Confidential, sir,' said Constable Jones.

'Thanks again,' said Sergeant Thomas.

'Don't thank me,' said Mr Briggs, 'try an' feel sorry for me. Shoppin' me own wife, who'd 'ave thought I'd do it?'

When he left the police station, his walk was jaunty. Well, Hilda, he thought, if that don't stop you landing young Kitty and her decent lodger in the dock, my name ain't Walter Harold Briggs, which it is.

He still had some time to spare, so he went out of his way to knock on the door of a house in Commercial Way. Mrs Lily Peake presented herself, a comely forty-year-old widow whose two daughters were away in service.

'Oh, 'ello, Wally,' she said, 'what brings you to me abode in yer 'andsome cap? A parcel? I could do with a parcel.'

Mr Briggs, having no parcels, gave her a cheerful and admiring grin instead.

'I was just passin' on me way to the sortin' depot, Lily me love, so I thought I'd see 'ow you were lookin'.'

Mrs Peake was looking very inviting on account of having a proud bosom, a tight bodice, a fine head of auburn hair and a saucy smile.

'Callin' me "Lily love", are yer, Wally?

You sure you should, seein' you're a postman and a married bloke?'

'It's been me pleasure to deliver yer letters personal to yer, Lily, and to exchange some friendly words with yer quite frequent.'

'Which 'as been pleasin', Wally, pleasin',' said the comely widow, 'but you've never stepped in for a cup of tea.'

'Regulations, yer know, Lily, regulations,' said Mr Briggs.

'And yer wife, the one I've seen yer out with, and you lookin' like she just fell on yer,' said Mrs Peake.

Mr Briggs grinned again. Away from his better and bigger half, he was a different man.

'Occasionally, Lily, she's fell on me, I grant yer.'

'Must be like bein' under a bus,' said Lily. 'Like to step in now for a cup, would yer, ducky?' She was fond of her cheerful postman.

'Well, it so 'appens I do 'ave ten minutes.'

'Then in yer come, and don't mind the neighbours,' said Lily. Mr Briggs stepped in and she took him through to the kitchen, which he thought bright and airy and nicely kept. She made the tea in quick time, and they sat down at the table to enjoy it.

'What's on yer mind, Wally?' she asked.

'I was thinkin', Lily, I might be an unmarried bloke for a while.'

' 'Ello, 'ello, postin' 'er off to Land's End, are yer, Wally?'

'I'm not in a position to give yer details yet, Lily, except it won't be Lands End. Anyway, you bein' a widow and a fine-lookin' one as well, and me bein' in an unmarried state for a while, would yer care to do a few music 'all shows with me?'

'Your kind invite, Wally, is accepted,' said Lily. 'Anything else, ducky?'

'Well, I ain't a young man any more,' said Mr Briggs, 'but nor ain't I past me prime. I mention that in passin', yer know, Lily.'

'Might I mention in passin' meself that a little bit of what you fancy does yer good?' said Lily.

'Might I ask if you're offerin', Lily?'

'Bless yer, love, course I am.'

Well, thought Mr Briggs, when he was on his way to his depot a few minutes later, I ain't all that happy about shopping the old haybag, but I'm happy about what's been offered by Lily.

A little bit of what I fancy might get to be a lot, Lily being a cheerful and warm-hearted woman, and Hilda, with any luck, enjoying six months in Holloway.

Mrs Briggs could hardly believe what hit her at ten to four that afternoon. First, just as she got her doorkey out, two men appeared and surrounded her on her own doorstep. Well, that was what it felt like. Then they told her they were coppers. Since coppers weren't her favourite kind of people, she told them to sod off. They said they'd like to have a word with her. She had a thought then, that they'd come about her brother, having found out she was his sister. So she let them into the house. But then they took the liberty of asking to examine the contents of her shopping bag and to enquire after the new handbag that was dangling from her arm. What followed was horrible, especially as her regular handbag was in her shopping bag with a blouse, a box of handkerchieves, a brooch and a little bottle of expensive scent, none of which were wrapped. She was asked where she bought them. Naturally, she told them to mind their own bleeding business. She wasn't a woman who took kindly to interference, especially from coppers.

If that wasn't bad enough, they produced a search warrant they said entitled them to poke their noses in everywhere. She said she'd never heard of such a diabolical liberty, but they did a search all the same, and found a number of things in her suitcase under the bed and some clothes in her wardrobe that they regarded as highly suspicious. Of course, she stood on her rights, she said that as they were interfering buggers she was going to chuck both of them out of her house, one at a time or both together.

They ignored that and kept asking her questions that were the nosiest she'd ever heard and implied she wasn't an honest woman. Naturally, she raised the roof. Then they said they were going to arrest her on suspicion of habitual shoplifting, and warned her that anything she said might be taken down and used in evidence against her. Come along quiet, madam, they said.

Mrs Briggs was well and truly worked up by then. Who wouldn't have been? She said she wasn't going along anywhere, especially not with coppers. She set about them, in the bedroom. They sought to restrain her. She hit Detective-Constable Jones with the bedside chair and sent him flying. He crashed to the floor.

'Gawd help you, lady,' he gasped, 'that's aggravated assault and grievous bodily harm.'

She responded to that by kicking him and giving Detective-Sergeant Thomas a swipe at the same time. He put an armlock on her and held her while Detective-Constable Jones perforce had to dash off and summon up a Black Maria. It was in the Black Maria that Mrs Briggs was taken to the police station, along with any amount of evidence. What she said on the way was highly inflammatory and couldn't have been put down in the notebook without it catching fire.

At six o'clock, a uniformed policeman called at the GPO sorting depot to advise Mr Briggs that his wife had been arrested and was at the police station. The superintendent, feeling for Mr Briggs at this shock, allowed him to go to the station where, in the interview room, he came face to face with poor old Hilda. The CID men were there, and also a woman constable. Mrs Briggs said thank the Lord you've come, Wally. Mr Briggs asked what it was all about. Detective-Sergeant Thomas informed him what had taken place. Gawd, said Mr Briggs, what a daft woman you've been, Hilda. Mrs Briggs tried to get at him and knock his head off. The police-woman intervened and had her uniformed bosom flattened by a beefy hand. She was fairly slim there, however, so it didn't make a lot of difference to her shape, but it counted as assault. This reminded Detective-Sergeant Thomas to advise Mr Briggs that his wife was also to be charged with assaulting police officers. Mr Briggs said that was the most upsetting thing he'd ever heard, that he was the first postman whose wife had been had up on a charge of assault. Mrs Briggs bawled she was the first woman whose husband was as useless as a wet paper bag.

Mr Briggs said calm down, love, you'll get a fair trial, it's the law of the land, a fair trial, and it'll give you a chance to prove your innocence, and I don't suppose, in regard to the assault, that you meant to knock any police officers about. It's me lucky day, he thought, assault as well, that'll put a couple of extra months on her sentence.

With Mrs Briggs nearly foaming at the mouth, Detective-Sergeant Thomas asked Mr Briggs if he wanted to stand as witness to her character. Mr Briggs said he'd better not as he might say something accidental, and as her husband he wouldn't be able to forgive himself for anything accidental. Best ask some of the neighbours, he said. He asked his wife then if he could fetch her anything.

'Yes, she wants a few things,' said the woman constable, 'I'll come to your house with you, Mr Briggs, and you can let me have them.'

There, said Mr Briggs, don't you worry,

Hilda, you'll be all right, you'll be looked after and I'll call in now and again. Detective-Sergeant Thomas advised him his wife would be remanded in Holloway. Mr Briggs said Holloway was nearly in foreign parts, but he'd see what he could do about getting there to cheer his wife up.

Mrs Briggs demanded the right to get at her husband, so that she could brain him. Mr Briggs said he'd better go, and he went, the policewoman accompanying him.

The superintendent had said he needn't go back to work on account of the shock, so Mr Briggs went round to see widow Lily in the evening. He took her out to the music hall at the Camberwell Palace, and she took him back home afterwards, and he had a little bit of what he fancied. She fancied it too, which made it nice, really.

Mr Briggs, all in all, had a lovely Saturday. Mrs Briggs had one that was close to purgatory.

Chapter Thirteen

Over Sunday morning's breakfast of porridge and toast, Carrie asked a question of Kitty.

'Is mister goin' to take us to church again?'

'I expect so,' said Kitty.

'Did I say I would?' asked Jamie.

'Well, you sort of said you might.'

'Did I sort of say that?'

'Yes, in a way,' said Kitty, feeling pleased again that he wasn't going to find lodgings in Brixton.

'I sort of said it in a kind of way, did I?' asked Jamie with a little grin.

'Mister's askin' questions now,' said Chloe.

'Betcher 'e caught it from Carrie,' said Alfie. 'I caught measles from 'er once. It's an 'ard life for a bloke when 'is own sister gives 'im her measles. Mister, do we 'ave to go to church? Only I told Billy Paget I'd go down the market with 'im and see if we could nick some bananas, the ones the stall'olders don't want. I fancy a banana, I ain't 'ad one since I nicked one last year. Mind, it was nearly black, but not bad inside.'

'Mister don't want you nickin' bananas on a Sunday,' said Chloe.

'What d'yer mean?' said Alfie. 'Ev'ryone nicks bananas.' He thought about that. 'Well, not on Sundays, I s'pose.'

'Mister, are you takin' us to church?' asked Carrie.

'Well,' said Jamie, 'as I seem to have sort of said in a kind of way that I might, then I will.'

'Oh, we like goin' with yer,' said Carrie.

'Corblimey, fancy likin' goin' to church,' said Alfie, 'yer elastic must be pinchin' yer.'

'Alfie, d'you want a clip round the ear?' said Kitty. 'Elastic's private.'

'It ain't as private as bloomers,' said Alfie.

'Right, come 'ere, you,' said Kitty, and jumped up. Alfie left his chair at speed. Out he ran, Kitty after him. Up the stairs he galloped, Kitty on his heels. From the landing a yell sounded. Kitty had caught him.

Wallop.

'Oh, 'elp,' said Carrie.

'Poor Alfie,' said Chloe.

'Mister's smilin',' whispered Carrie.

'Alfie's not,' said Chloe, 'he's 'urting.'

Down Alfie came. He bounded into the kitchen.

'Cor, Kitty ain't 'alf got the rats,' he said, 'I been walloped all over.'

Kitty came back in a more dignified way than Alfie. She sort of swam in graciously, just like a mum satisfied she'd done her duty.

'Let that be a lesson to you, my lad,' she said.

' 'Ere, someone's ate my toast,' said Alfie.

'It's on the floor,' said Jamie. 'You knocked it off your plate when you jumped up.'

Alfie retrieved it, blew on it and sat down and ate it.

Footsteps sounded and Rosemary looked in on them through the open kitchen door. She wore a smart green costume with a white blouse. She'd been out all day yesterday, seeing more sights.

'Hello,' she said, 'did I hear ructions?'

'Only Alfie being walloped,' said Jamie, 'there's no crisis, not since he found his toast.'

'Spoke out of turn, did you, Alfie?' smiled Rosemary.

'Yes, 'e said elastic,' Chloe informed the new lodger.

'An' Kitty walloped 'im,' said Carrie.

'Oh, dear,' said Rosemary.

'Would yer like a cup of tea?' asked Chloe, with natural Walworth hospitality.

'Love one,' said Rosemary, and Kitty gave Chloe a look. Rosemary pulled up a chair from the wall and sat down next to Alfie. Chloe got up and fetched a cup and saucer from the dresser. Kitty took the cosy off the teapot and poured.

'Milk, Miss Allen?' she said.

'Thanks.'

'Sugar, Miss Allen?'

'Thanks, I like my tea sweet,' said Rosemary.

'Did yer 'ave a nice day up West yesterday?' asked Chloe.

'Lovely,' smiled Rosemary, and glanced at Jamie. 'But I could have done with a little company.'

Oh, thought Kitty, I've got to watch this one all right, she's after him already.

Jamie, aware that he was in debt to Rosemary, said, 'I'll stand in whenever you're in need, except that I'm not the Prince of Wales.'

'And I'm not a Grand Duchess,' said Rosemary. 'You'll do very nicely, Jamie.'

Oh, the rotten hussy, thought Kitty, she's pinching him from under all our noses. I'll have a nervous breakdown.

'We're goin' to church this mornin',' said Carrie.

'Well, good for you,' said Rosemary.

'We're all goin',' said Chloe, 'mister's takin' us.'

'Well, good for mister,' said Rosemary. 'But what about your Sunday dinner, who'll look after that?'

'I shall prepare it,' said Kitty haughtily, 'and see to it when we get back.'

'I'll look after it,' said Rosemary, 'I'm not a bad cook, actually. What have you got?'

'Shoulder of mutton, ain't it, Kitty?' said Carrie.

'I'll be happy to prepare it and look after it,' said Rosemary.

'That'll give you a break, Kitty,' said Jamie.

'I don't require a break, I like to attend to all me responsibilities,' said Kitty.

'Well, I'll just keep an eye on it for you while you're at church,' said Rosemary.

'She can 'ave some with us, can't she, Kitty?' said Alfie, and Kitty could have walloped him all over again, because she simply couldn't say no.

'We'll lay a place for you, Miss Allen,' she said.

'Lovely. I'm Rosemary, by the way.'

Delilah, that's what you are, thought Kitty.

'After breakfast,' said Jamie, 'let's have hair combed and brushed, kids, and your Sunday best on.'

'I combed me 'air yesterday,' said Alfie.

'I brushed mine last night,' said Chloe.

'So did I,' said Carrie.

'Well, that's fine,' said Jamie, 'but catch up with the process by doing it again after breakfast.'

Some while after breakfast, Kitty had a quiet word with Alfie in his bedroom. First she said she was sorry she had to wallop him. She didn't like doing it, she said, she'd promised herself there'd be no more walloping now that that man had passed away, but she didn't want Mr Blair to think they weren't respectable, seeing it was obvious he'd been nicely brought up himself. He wouldn't want to be their new dad if there was language and rude words flying about. Alfie said that it was all right, the walloping hadn't hurt him.

'It was supposed to,' said Kitty.

'Oh, yer don't wallop like *he* did,' said Alfie.

Kitty said *he* was a past master at it, of course. Then she mentioned there was always a stall down the Sunday market that sold rabbits and white mice as pets. Alfie said he knew it. Kitty gave him a threepenny bit and asked if he'd go and buy one of the white mice after church. Alfie asked what for?

'Well, Mrs Baker's little girl's been a bit unwell just lately,' said Kitty, 'so I thought we'd buy her a white mouse to cheer 'er up. Only don't say anything, it's a secret. Put it in a cardboard box in your wardrobe until tomorrow. That's when I'll be able to pop round and see Mrs Baker.'

'All right,' said Alfie, and Kitty gave him a sisterly hug.

Rosemary appeared when they were all about to leave the house.

'Enjoy the service,' she said.

'Watch the shoulder of mutton,' said Jamie.

'It's a promise,' said Rosemary. 'And this afternoon, Jamie?'

'Mr Blair don't 'appen to be available this afternoon,' said Kitty, 'he's been invited next door for Sunday tea.'

'My, my, there's a girl next door?' smiled Rosemary.

'No, a married fam'ly,' said Kitty.

'How unusual,' said Rosemary, and laughed.

I don't like her, thought Kitty, she's a forward cat and a bit too smart.

Outside the church, neighbours greeted the new domestic group that had miraculously developed following the accidental demise of Henry Mullins. Chloe and Carrie felt blissful about the neighbours saying hello to them and smiling at them. Alfie felt he was being patted kindly on the head, which didn't do a bloke much good in the eyes of his mates. But he noticed that their new dad—well, he was as good as their new dad—took everything in his stride, and that grown-up girls gave him the eye. Kitty wasn't half putting it on, though, she kept saying how'd-you-do to people in a kind of posh way. I suppose a bloke could blame respectability for that, he thought.

After church, which his sisters seemed to enjoy, being girls, Alfie went off to the market, looked at the stall selling white mice, picked one out, a lively running-about specimen, and bought it. He'd first pinched a cardboard box from under another stall, and he put the mouse in that, with a piece of cheese he'd brought with him. Back home, he gave Kitty a wink and took the box up to his room, placing it in his old wardrobe.

Rosemary enjoyed her dinner, and in return was as tactful as she could be with Kitty, having realized she wasn't exactly popular with her. She wondered if the girl was in love with Jamie. By the time the meal came to an end, she decided no, she wasn't. Her attitude towards him wasn't that of a girl in love. It was something more subtle. Love wasn't a bit subtle. It hit you and floored you. Young Kitty wanted Jamie as the guardian of herself and her brother and sisters. She was after a fatherly figure and had cast Jamie in the mould because he was at hand, living in the house, and obviously a different kettle of fish from the man who'd been the step-father. It was easy to understand the girl's motives. In this day and age, when victory in the Great War had been an economic defeat for the victors as well as the losers, a family of four parentless young people needed a lifeboat if they weren't to sink. A father figure equalled a lifeboat.

It was very convenient to be lodging here, in the cockney heart of South London, with the heart of London itself only just across the river. Not that the Irish troubles were at a distance. Factions of the IRA were as active in London as in Dublin and Belfast, and their agents came and went in elusive fashion. Jamie's mother, Mrs Blair, had said that before the IRA turned into hooligans they'd just been poor suffering workers. It had been a disappointment to her and Mr Blair, she had said more than once, that Jamie had never struck a blow for the workers' cause. He hadn't even joined the Labour Party. Not that he wasn't a fine boy, it was just that he couldn't see there'd always be trouble in the world while it was ruled by capitalists and not the workers. He was going to be a bit of a stick-in-the-mud.

Rosemary thought he was far from that.

He wasn't any kind of a boy, either. It hadn't been difficult to find him a job, to use her influence on his behalf. Mrs Blair would be happy about that, at least.

It was gone half past three. Alfie, Chloe and Carrie were out, they'd gone to Ruskin Park again. Having Sunday best clothes meant the twins could hold their own with other young girls. Alfie had gone to make sure his sisters, to whom he was very attached, didn't get accosted. Jamie had queried 'accosted'. Alfie said he'd seen it or read it somewhere, and it had sounded as if it wouldn't do Chloe and Carrie much good. So he meant to save them from it. Chloe said what a burden it was having a brother who was as daft as a brush, and Carrie said yes, he could do with a bit of improving, couldn't he? It made no difference to Alfie, he accompanied them in the role of protector, and was ready to conk the hooter of any accosters in the shape of hooligans from places like Brandon Street. Chloe said in an aside to Carrie that they'd lose Alfie if they could, and Carrie asked if they could afford to, as she wasn't keen on being accosted, whatever it meant. Chloe said well, we could try it, we might like it. Anyway, off they went, with their brother. Halfway up the street, a kid called after them.

'Oi, did yer step-dad fall or was 'e pushed?'

Alfie didn't quite understand what the kid meant, but he was sure he didn't like it, so he went for him. He didn't spoil his Sunday best by grabbing him and rolling about over the pavement with him. He just plonked a fist in the kid's left optic. This flabbergasted the kid and didn't do his mince pie much good, either. Off home he went and told his dad what had happened, and his dad said, 'Serve yer right, yer young perisher.' 'But what about me eye, Dad, look what he done to it.' 'Lucky he didn't flatten yer hooter,' said his dad. Walworth dads had sound instincts.

Rosemary was in her room, writing a letter. If Mrs Lindsay of Belfast had laid charges against her, then that young lady was a fugitive from justice, thought Jamie. She had a slightly provocative air, not out of keeping with a woman who had enticed someone else's husband into her bed. But she also had a warm, outgoing personality, and he hoped the police wouldn't catch up with her, particularly as she'd gone out of her way to find a job for him.

Entering the kitchen, he found Kitty standing on a chair, trying to reach something on the top shelf of the larder.

'Can I help?' he asked.

'There's empty jamjars up 'ere,' said Kitty, 'I remembered pushin' them to the back of the shelf to keep them for a rainy day.' Empty jamjars could be sold to grocers for a penny each. 'I thought I'd give them to Alfie and the twins for pocket money.' Up she went on tiptoe to reach farther in. The chair rocked and she fell. Jamie caught her just in time to save her a cruel drop on to the fender and hearth, the larder being a built-in job in the recess to the left of the kitchen range. Her involuntary gasp was cut short as he caught her, and she found herself in strong arms and against his warm chest. Sensations quite foreign took hold of her, and so did sudden breathlessness. She lifted her head and looked up at him, her face flushed. The deep brown of her eyes turned to the familiar burnt sienna. He sensed confusion.

Releasing her, he said, 'Don't do that again, don't reach like that when you're standing on a chair.'

'But I can't get to the top shelf without standin' on a chair,' said Kitty faintly.

'Well, call me,' said Jamie, 'and if I'm not here, call a policeman or borrow someone's step-ladder. The kids can't afford to have you break a leg.'

Kitty, drawing breath, said lightly, 'It's daft, a larder 'aving a shelf I can't reach.

I bet it was built by a carpenter seven or eight feet tall.' She had a point. The larder reached to the ceiling. 'How tall are you?'

'Oh, about as tall as a piece of string, Kitty.'

'Now 'ow can anyone be as tall as a piece of string?'

'You only have to be the same length,' smiled Jamie.

'Pull me other leg,' said Kitty.

Jamie had a sudden thought. He stood on the chair himself. The shelf and its space opened up to his eyes. He saw half a dozen jamjars, but nothing else. He handed the jars down to Kitty and took another look at the shelf. The larder had no back to it. It was fixed to the wall, a wall of bare smooth plaster. Well, thought Jamie, Mullins might have considered this top shelf, he might have fashioned a hole in the plaster and removed a couple of bricks, but he hadn't. He'd have had to get the kids out of the house for an hour or so, and done a replastering job. And the new plaster would have shown up against the faded whiteness of the old.

'H'm,' he said.

'What're you lookin' for?' asked Kitty.

'The proceeds, Kitty.'

'Oh, see what you mean,' she said. 'But it's not there?'

'No, it's not here,' said Jamie, and stepped down from the chair.

'Well, never mind,' said Kitty, 'it don't matter so much now you've got a proper job. I mean, if we 'ad found it, it would've only been fair for you to 'ave some of it, but you don't need it now—oh, I've just remembered, Dr McManus sent a note round on Friday, sayin' the funeral's tomorrow. I'd best go, but I'm not goin' to ask Alfie and the twins to. I'd better buy a few flowers to put on his grave, with a note. I was thinkin' of writin' something like, "Here lies poor 'Enry Mullins who's gone to 'is reward, we hope 'is soul's at rest now, we hope he's with the Lord." D'you think something like that would be all right, mister? We don't want to keep thinkin' badly of him now he's passed away.'

The forgiving nature of the girl touched Jamie.

'No, it doesn't do much for any of us, Kitty, hanging on to unpleasant memories,' he said. 'Write the note in bold black. Use a J nib. Those lines are as good an epitaph as your step-father could have hoped for.'

'Would they put something like that on a gravestone?' asked Kitty.

'You could certainly put that on your step-father's gravestone,' said Jamie. 'Now I'm off to Sunday tea with the Fitches.'

Kitty's beguiling eyes darkened.

'Enjoy yourself, I'm sure,' she said stiffly.

When he'd gone, the kitchen seemed depressingly empty. She even felt like crying. She never did. Not even her stepfather had made her cry. He'd made her kick and yell, but she'd have sold her soul rather than have him see her cry.

What's happening to me, that's what I'd like to know. What's happening?

At four-thirty, Rosemary decided to go out. With Jamie out next door, the house was boring, her room more so. She had a letter to post, anyway, and then she'd go on to the West End and enjoy a film at the new picture palace in Leicester Square. Picture palaces opened on Sunday evenings.

Out she went, the heels of her smart shoes tapping the pavement. Mr Sean Fitzpatrick, emerging from the Murphy house, saw her walking up the street towards the Walworth Road, her light summer costume close-fitting, her little hat bobbing to her sprightly gait. There was an engaging swing to her hips.

Ah, be Jasus, young Kitty's new lodger, he thought, and it's me meself that's willing to give her the benefit of an introduction to Sean Fitzpatrick. That's a lady with a fondness for pleasure, I'd say. Didn't she give me a look and a smile when I passed her yesterday? That she did.

And Mr Fitzpatrick, a highly personable Irish gent near to forty, lengthened his stride in typically self-confident fashion. All work and no play brought nothing to a man's day.

It was not Rosemary's intention to finish up in the picture palace with an Irishman she'd seen but not been introduced to. Nevertheless, she did. Mr Fitzpatrick proved irresistible to a young woman who found older men entertaining. Nor was it her intention to be kissed in a taxi on her way back to Walworth. But she was. Mr Fitzpatrick was not only irresistible, he had an Irish flair for knowing which young ladies liked to be kissed and which would yell for help.

Prior to all this, Alfie, Chloe and Carrie returned from Ruskin Park in time to sit down for tea at six. Alfie said he didn't know if there'd been any accosting as Chloe sent him back to the park gates to look for her hankie which she said she must have dropped there.

'I couldn't find it, yer know,' he said, 'and nor couldn't I find Chloe an' Carrie after. They wasn't where I'd left them. I didn't find them for ages, not till me feet was nearly all wore out, then they come up with two boys and 'ad the sauce to ask me where I'd been all the time. Blow me, don't some sisters make a bloke want to spit?'

'Don't you do any spittin', my lad, it's common,' said Kitty. 'Who were these boys?'

'I dunno who they were,' said Alfie, while the twins kept their heads down, 'but they both told me to push off again.'

'You girls,' said Kitty, 'you're too young to let yourselves get picked up in a park.'

'We wasn't picked up,' said Chloe, 'we just 'appened to meet them. That Alfie, disappearin' the way he did and leavin' me an' Carrie alone.'

'Where's your Sunday 'ankie?' asked Kitty.

'In me elastic. I forgot it was there, I thought I'd lost it. It wasn't our fault our daft brother couldn't find us.'

'Alfie,' said Kitty, 'next time you go up the park with your sisters, you see you don't lose them again, you 'ear?'

'Yes, all right,' said Alfie, 'and I'll make sure Chloe's 'ankie don't drop out of 'er elastic so that I 'ave to go an' look for it again.'

'It didn't drop out this afternoon, I just forgot it was there, I just said so.' Chloe wrinkled her nose at her brother.

'Kitty, ain't mister comin' down to 'ave tea with us?' asked Carrie.

'He's 'aving tea next door, you know he is,' said Kitty.

'Oh, yes, I forgot,' said Carrie, and looked disappointed.

Alfie remembered something.

' 'Ere, Kitty, young Johnny 'Obday called after us when we went out,' he said. ' 'E called, did our step-dad fall or was 'e pushed. I dunno what 'e meant, but I give 'im one in 'is mince pie to take 'ome with 'im.'

Kitty stiffened. She hadn't missed the fact that one or two people had given her and Mr Blair funny looks outside the church this morning. She supposed the report of the inquest had got around.

'Never mind kids like that Johnny 'Obday,' she said, 'don't take any notice of them. They're little 'ooligans. Don't repeat what they say, and best not to tell our new dad. He's got his mind on his new job that he's startin' tomorrow, and we don't want to worry 'im about little 'ooligans.'

'That Miss Allen calls 'im Jamie,' said Chloe in a questioning way.

'Could we call 'im Jamie?' asked Carrie.

'No, we got to try an' get used to callin' 'im Dad,' said Alfie.

'It makes 'im give us looks,' said Chloe.

'Yes, 'e don't give us looks when we call 'im mister,' said Carrie.

'Still, they ain't scowlin' looks, not like those 'e used to give us,' said Alfie.

'But you can't call 'im Jamie, it wouldn't be respectful at 'is age,' said Kitty, and thought again about how strange she'd felt when he'd caught her and held her. It hadn't been uncomfortable or embarrassing or anything like that. But it had made her lose her breath.

She went for a walk with her sisters after tea. It was a lovely evening, and Walworth actually looked sort of soft in the light. Sort of balmy. They passed some loitering boys.

' Ello, 'oo yer lookin' for, girlies?' asked one.

'Our cat's mother,' said Chloe.

'Chloe, we don't 'ave a cat,' said Carrie.

' 'E don't know that,' said Chloe, and Carrie giggled.

' 'Ere, ain't yer all dolled up fancy?' called a second boy.

'Kitty, ain't it nice, 'aving Sunday best to wear?' said Carrie.

'Lovely,' said Kitty.

'It's funny we got more money now than when 'e was alive,' said Chloe.

'Yes, but funny nice,' said Carrie.

Kitty walked in a thinking mood.

When they got back, Rosemary was still out and so was Jamie. With summer twilight softening the grey of Walworth's rooftops, Kitty wondered what was keeping Jamie. He wasn't really in Mrs Fitch's parlour, flirting with her, was he?

She made cocoa for the kids, and a cold mutton sandwich for each of them. Then she went upstairs. She looked into Alfie's wardrobe. The white mouse was still in the cardboard box. Alfie had made little holes in the lid to make sure it could breathe. There wasn't much left of the lump of cheese.

Jamie came in just before ten. The kids were in bed, Kitty was up. He put his head into the kitchen and said hello to her.

'Thank goodness,' she said, 'we thought you'd fell down a hole.'

'Not today,' said Jamie.

'I suppose you've been in Mrs Fitch's parlour all this time,' said Kitty.

Jamie entered the kitchen and sat down opposite her.

'Yes, bit of a struggle to get away,' he said. 'And what've you been up to?'

'Me?'

'You look as if you've been up to something. You're a little flushed.'

'Me? Well, I suppose I've been worryin' a bit.'

'What about?' asked Jamie.

'Yes, you might well ask,' Kitty said. 'Of course, I know it's none of my business, but I can't 'elp worryin' about you gettin' yourself talked about. I mean, all this socializin' with Mrs Fitch in her parlour.'

'What about Mr Fitch?' asked Jamie.

'I'm sure I don't know where Mr Fitch was, I wasn't there,' said Kitty. 'I've just been sittin' here worryin' about your good name.'

'All right, I'd better own up,' said Jamie, and went on to tell her he'd enjoyed a Sunday tea of shrimps and winkles with Mr and Mrs Fitch and their little girl Betty. He'd have enjoyed it even more if little Betty hadn't kept chucking her winkle shells at him. Kitty told him to give over, that little Betty didn't do things like that. Jamie replied that she was learning. After tea, Mr Fitch took the girl on to his lap and read to her from a story book, while he and Mrs Fitch retired to the parlour. Mrs Fitch looked very bosomy in a low-cut evening gown.

'She what?' gasped Kitty.

'She looked bosomy. She was low-cut,' said Jamie.

'Oh, I can't believe me ears,' said Kitty, 'I never ever 'eard Mrs Fitch 'ad any evenin' gown,' I never ever 'eard anybody in Walworth 'aving one, specially low-cut.

It ain't decent, not on a married woman.'

'Still, it was very nice,' said Jamie.

'Nice? Nice?' Kitty fumed. 'A married woman showin' half 'er bosom?'

'Only in her parlour,' said Jamie, 'not on a tram or down the market.'

'Oh, I'll 'it you in a minute!' cried Kitty. Her hair seemed to spring loose in her outrage. 'Sittin' in her parlour with her and lookin' at her bosom, I never 'eard anything more indecent. You don't sit and look at—' She stopped, and flushed pink.

'We sat on the sofa and I looked at her aspidistra mostly,' said Jamie. Kitty wanted to chuck cups and saucers at him. He said he and Mrs Fitch talked about the weather, but it didn't seem too interesting to her, and she asked if he liked her gown. He asked if there oughtn't to be more of it. She said no, of course not, it was what society ladies wore to balls, where it was fashionable for them to show half their bosoms.

'Oh, I'll scream in a minute,' gasped Kitty. 'To think me and Alfie and the twins 'ave been 'aving a respectable Sunday evenin' while you've been talkin' to Mrs Fitch about ladies' bosoms. You ought to be ashamed.'

'Well, I did feel slightly nervous,' said Jamie, 'and as it turned out, I had good cause to.' He went on to say he did his best to keep things very respectable, seeing it was Sunday, but Mrs Fitch said never mind about Sunday, act as if it's Saturday night. But he had to remember he'd taken on the responsibility of helping Kitty and the kids to live decent lives, and he didn't want to let them down by doing any Saturday night stuff with Mrs Fitch. He said he was thinking of all of them while he was trying to keep Mrs Fitch off, but after an hour of struggle she overcame him. He begged her to remember he was his mother's only son, but Mrs Fitch said blow that for a lark. Then everything went blank. Afterwards, Mr Fitch came in and asked him if he'd like a glass of Watney's ale.

Kitty, utterly steamed up, threw a cracked teacup at him. It smashed itself to pieces on the wall behind him.

'Oh, you ain't decent!'

'But I'm still in one piece,' said Jamie. Kitty gave him a furious look. She saw a grin. 'Oh, yer beast! It's been all lies!'

'Well, I didn't want to disappoint you by telling you we all sat in the parlour and had a long chat about you and the kids, and your step-father,' said Jamie. 'You wanted something a lot more juicy than that, didn't you, Kitty?'

'No, I didn't,' said Kitty. Jamie winked.

She saw it all then, and shrieked with laughter. 'Oh, you daft man!'

'Let's have a cup of tea, shall we?' suggested Jamie.

'Oh, would you like one?'

'Shall I make it?'

'No, I will,' said Kitty, feeling a lot happier.

301

Chapter Fourteen

A piercing scream travelled through the house just after midnight and attacked Kitty's ears. Another followed, then a series. Jamie woke up, flung the bedclothes aside and leapt off the sheet in his pyjamas. Kitty stayed where she was, with Chloe and Carrie.

Down the stairs ran Jamie, the bannister rail guiding him in the darkness. The door of Rosemary's bedroom opened and she burst into the passage in her nightdress. The nightdress made a rushing contact with Jamie's pyjamas. She gasped.

'Rosemary?'

'There's something in my bed, something horrible!'

Kitty, having decided to make a calm if belated appearance, showed herself at the top of the stairs, a lighted candle and holder in her hand.

'What's goin' on down there? It's like Bedlam.'

'It's the screaming fits,' gasped Rosemary, lightly-covered breasts seeking sanctuary against Jamie's chest. 'There's something ghastly in my bed.'

Kitty descended the stairs in calm and dignified style, her candle flame illuminating the scene.

'Excuse me, I'm sure, but we don't 'ave ghastly things in beds in this 'ouse. I hope you 'avn't brought East End fleas in with you. We've never had a single flea in here all our lives.'

'Well, something's in my bed and it's not fleas,' said Rosemary, releasing herself.

Upstairs, Chloe and Carrie had their heads under the bedclothes. In his own room, Alfie was still sleeping peacefully. It took a lot to wake Alfie.

Kitty stared at Rosemary. Her nightdress was black, and vaguely visible in places was the white of her body.

'Well, I don't know what to say to you, Miss Allen.' Kitty had a coat over her own nightdress, which was respectable white flannel. 'Except you ought to 'ave put something on before comin' out of your room.'

'Let's have the candle, Kitty,' said Jamie. He took it from her, went into Rosemary's bedroom, turned the gas up and applied the flame to the mantle. The room swam with soft light. Rosemary's bedclothes were halfway off. Kitty inspected the partly uncovered bottom sheet.

'I can't see anything,' she said. 'It must be fleas. They're not easy to see, specially if they're 'opping about. You must've brought them in with you, Miss Allen.'

'I'll scream again if you keep talking about fleas,' said Rosemary.

Jamie looked at the bed, then swept sheet and blankets fully down. A white mouse, startled at being uncovered, sat up. Its nose twitched, then it began to clean its whiskers.

'Oh, my God,' said Rosemary, 'a bloody mouse.'

'Well, would you believe it,' said Kitty, ' 'ow did that get there?'

'Yes,' said Jamie, eyeing her with interest, 'how did it?'

'You little devil.' Kitty addressed the mouse accusingly. 'I'll give you something, gettin' into someone's bed. Alfie bought it in the market this morning as a present for a little girl down the street who's not been well. He was keepin' it in a cardboard box to give to 'er tomorrow. It must've chewed its way out.' She picked the mouse up. 'Blessed cheek you've got,' she told it.

'It came down the stairs, walked into my bedroom and climbed into my bed?' said Rosemary caustically.

'I suppose it likes a bed,' said Kitty.

'Well, it's not having mine,' said Rosemary, 'not unless it's willing to pay the rent. Are there any of its brown cousins around?'

'No, not many,' said Kitty. 'Well, hardly any to speak of. Just one or two. And all you 'ave to do is to feel around with your feet each time you get into bed. They do seem to like beds round 'ere, I suppose they feel a bed's cosier than a hole under the floor. But they won't harm you, Miss Allen. Not like rats. Me late step-father woke up just in time one night, otherwise he'd 'ave had his foot gnawed off.'

'Wait a minute,' said Rosemary, 'I can cope with mice, but not with rats.'

'There are no rats,' said Jamie.

'Just now and again you might see one, that's all,' said Kitty.

'If I do, I'll set fire to the place,' said Rosemary, who had put a jacket on over her nightdress.

'The landlord won't like that,' said Kitty.

'He'll have to lump it,' said Rosemary. 'All right, nightmare over, I hope.'

They left her. Jamie took Kitty into the kitchen and placed the candle on the table. She was still holding the mouse.

'You monkey,' he said, 'when did you put that thing into Rosemary's bed?'

'Me?' said Kitty, thinking his striped pyjamas sort of manly. 'I 'ope you're not makin' aggravatin' accusations.'

'What was the idea?'

'Idea?'

305

'Yes.'

'What idea?'

'Don't come it, miss,' said Jamie.

'Me?'

'The next time there's a mouse in her bed, I'm going to smack your bottom.'

'Well, I don't think much of that,' said Kitty, 'it's downright shameful. No decent bloke would do a thing like that to an 'elpless girl.'

'Come here, helpless,' said Jamie. Kitty yelped and darted around the table. Jamie went after her. Kitty dashed from the kitchen into the darkness, turned in the passage and ran for her life up the stairs. On the landing she stopped. He wasn't following her. Then she clapped a hand to her mouth.

The mouse.

She'd let go of it.

Oh, me gawd.

Still, it couldn't be helped. They'd find it in the morning.

And she could put it in one of Rosemary's pockets next time.

The building site at Streatham was extensive. A number of double-fronted houses were going up. John Robbins, the site manager, was a brisk and energetic man. Having listened to Jamie detailing what he was capable of, he gave him the job of fitting doors and window frames. The shells of several houses were up, and three were roofed. Window frames and doors were now required to be fitted.

'It's two pounds five a week wage, less sevenpence for this new-fangled Government stamp. You'll draw it Fridays. How's that?'

'Fine,' said Jamie.

'Can't say you look like a carpenter or joiner, though.'

'What do I look like?'

'Police inspector,' said Mr Robbins, 'except that your feet aren't flat. Right, report to your foreman, Josh Simmonds. That's him over there, in the brown Derby.'

Josh Simmonds turned out to be a typical foreman. He wanted maximum effort and no lip. He inspected Jamie's progress halfway through the morning.

'Call that fittin' a frame?' he said.

'What else?'

'Like it, do yer?'

'You bet I like it,' said Jamie.

'It's the bleedin' wrong way round.'

'I beg to differ,' said Jamie.

'Stop talkin' like a ponce. It's the bleedin' wrong way round.'

'So's the house, then,' said Jamie.

Josh Simmonds rubbed his moustache.

'All right, only testin' yer,' he said. 'On

the other 'and, I don't like yer lip.'

'No lip, Mister Foreman,' said Jamie, 'just standing up for my work.'

'Same thing,' said the foreman. 'I do all the standin' up for work done by my gang, and if I can't stand up it means the guv'nor's landed me with a dud. That makes me cross. I'm a proud bloke.'

'So am I,' said Jamie.

'Sod me,' said the foreman, going on his way, 'who found 'im?'

Jamie discovered that some of the brickies were Irish. Irish, not Ulstermen. There were a lot of them in the building industry, and there'd been a generous number of them in the Army, many of whom had actually come over from torn and troubled Ireland to fight for the country they saw as the enemy. And they'd fought and died for it.

They were naturally good brickies, and could shoulder a hod as heavy as a ton weight. By the end of his first day, Jamie was on matey terms with them and the rest of the men. From the day he'd left school he'd favoured work in the building industry rather than at a desk. He went home satisfied with his day's labours, and nor was he less than happy that he at last had a job at a decent wage of forty-five bob, less sevenpence for a stamp.

Turning into Larcom Street from the

Walworth Road, the first people he saw were young ones, and none other than Alfie, Chloe and Carrie. They were standing outside the vicarage. When he was halfway towards them, they came running. He couldn't help smiling. Come to that, he couldn't help being touched, either.

'Oh, yer back from yer new job,' said Alfie.

' 'Ello, mister,' said Carrie shyly.

'Kitty's doin' a nice supper,' said Chloe.

'We've been lookin' out for yer,' said Alfie.

'Are yer pleased?' asked Carrie.

'About a nice supper?' said Jamie, as they fell into step with him.

'Was it about supper, Chloe?' asked Carrie.

'No, ask 'im if he's pleased we've been waitin' for 'im,' said Chloe.

'Are yer, mister?' asked Carrie.

'Tickled pink,' said Jamie. Well, what else could he say?

Chloe ran on ahead to tell Kitty that mister was on his way and that he was tickled pink. And he didn't look as if he was all wore out, like Carrie had said he might be.

'That's good,' said Kitty.

'What yer doin' that for?' asked Chloe.

'Doin' what?'

'Lookin' in the mirror,' said Chloe. There was an old spotty mirror, unframed, on the mantelpiece, and Kitty had taken a quick look at herself.

'I was just thinkin' we could do with a nice new mirror,' she said, as Alfie and Carrie came in. Jamie called from the foot of the stairs.

'Evening, Miss Edwards, just going up for a wash and a change.'

'Yes, all right, Mr Blair, I can serve supper soon as you come down,' called Kitty.

'Bless you, Miss Edwards,' said Jamie and went up.

'What's 'e call yer Miss Edwards for?' asked Alfie.

'It's right for a young lady my age,' said Kitty, knowing, of course, that Jamie was having her on.

' 'E calls yer monkey sometimes,' said Chloe.

'Yes, but 'e just blessed 'er,' said Carrie.

'That old Mullins never blessed anyone,' said Alfie, and had an improper moment. ' 'E just said things like "get out of the bleedin' way".'

'Alfie, I'll box your ears for you if you keep usin' language,' said Kitty, and thought about her step-father's funeral at Southwark Cemetery. There'd hardly been anyone there, just a vicar, the undertakers, a man from the council and herself. There'd been a service in the cemetery church, and then the burial. The vicar had let her put a bunch of flowers on the coffin, together with the note on a plain postcard. The vicar had read it. It was in bold black ink.

Here lies poor Henry Mullins who's gone to his reward,

We hope his soul's at rest now, we hope he's with the Lord.

It was signed from Kitty, Chloe, Carrie and Alfie.

The vicar had almost smiled. Almost. Kitty had watched the coffin being lowered into the deep grave, thinking about the man who had never wanted her and Alfie and the twins. She couldn't hate him any more. But she could feel sorry for him, and suddenly she had done. Poor man. Fancy not wanting Chloe and Carrie even. When the coffin had come to rest and a handful of earth had been scattered over it, she had left, and all the way home she had not looked as if she'd been to a funeral. Well, her step-father was in his grave and gone for ever, and she was looking into the future, not the past. The first thing she had done when she arrived home was to brush and comb her hair until it shone.

Jamie came down in a jersey and trousers, a white paper bag in his hand.

The table was set for supper, the kids were seated and Kitty was at the gas oven in the scullery, waiting to dish up.

'Well, hello again,' he said, 'and as it's the end of my first day's work and the foreman hasn't said I'm useless, it's up to me to be cheerful and to overlook all those who haven't brushed their hair today.' Kitty appeared at the open door to the scullery. 'Hello, here's mother,' he said.

'Yes, good evenin', Mr Blair,' said Kitty, 'if you'd kindly sit down I'll serve the supper.'

'I could eat a horse,' said Jamie, and sat down.

'What, an 'ole 'orse?' said Alfie.

'Saddle as well,' said Jamie, putting the paper bag on the table. There was something in it, that was obvious, and the kids stared at it.

'What's that, mister?' asked Carrie.

'Just a paper bag,' said Jamie.

'Yes, but what's in it?' asked Carrie.

'That's nosy, that is,' said Alfie.

'I only asked,' said Carrie, and Kitty began bringing in laden plates. Because of the funeral, she hadn't done the weekly washing today, she had left it until tomorrow. But she had found time to cook a sausage-and-onion pudding, cheap and nourishing, with creamy mash and cabbage. The kids looked rapturous as they tucked in, and Jamie thought what a change there was in them, all due to the fact that Kitty had the means to feed them and the willingness to see to their appearance. And she took more care of herself every day. As for her sausage-and-onion pudding, it was as good as a masterpiece.

'Was it all right, your first day at your new job?' she asked.

'Fine,' said Jamie. 'The foreman was a bit saucy, but we came to an understanding.'

'I bet he wondered what hit 'im,' said Kitty. 'Was it a long tram ride all the way to Streatham?'

'I didn't notice,' said Jamie, 'I sat next to a chatty old lady and she gave me all her family history.'

'What a treat,' said Kitty. 'Here, excuse me, but what's that paper bag doin' on the table?'

'I can't see it doin' anyfink,' said Alfie, 'it's just sittin' there.'

'Who put it there, and what's in it?' asked Kitty sternly.

'Mister put it there, but 'e didn't tell us what's in it,' said Chloe.

'I don't know it's right puttin' bags on the table at meal times,' said Kitty. 'Still, as it's his first time home from 'is new job, I won't say anything.'

'But you just 'ave,' said Carrie.

'I'm overlookin' it,' said Kitty.

'Mister,' said Chloe, 'we can't find the white mouse that got out last night an' made Miss Allen scream.'

'What a funny woman,' said Alfie, 'fancy screamin' over a white mouse.'

'It can't be found?' said Jamie.

'Well, Kitty said this mornin' that she'd look for it,' said Chloe, 'but when we come 'ome from school she said she 'adn't found it.'

'Me an' Chloe 'aven't 'ad a look at it yet,' said Carrie, 'we didn't know Alfie 'ad bought it yesterday for that little girl that's not been well.'

'I can promise ructions if it turns up in Rosemary's bed again,' said Jamie, glancing at Kitty.

'What're you lookin' at me for?' asked Kitty.

'Just a thought I had.'

There was a vanilla blancmange for afters, and it gave the kids another rapturous chapter. When the meal was over, Jamie said come on, three cheers for the cook. The cheers were given boisterously.

'What a lot of fuss,' said Kitty.

Jamie said they could get rid of the bag now. He emptied it of its contents. There were three tuppenny bars of milk chocolate and a large sixpenny bar. Alfie, Chloe and Carrie each received a tuppenny bar, and Kitty received the sixpenny bar. The kids were overwhelmed, and Kitty blinked. Jamie said he was standing a treat to celebrate his new job. Kitty didn't think it was quite like that. The circumstances being what they were, she thought it was much more like a nice dad bringing chocolate home for his children. Not her, though. She couldn't include herself among children. Not at her age. He'd brought her home an enormous bar because—

Because of what?

Oh, what's coming over me? I don't know what to say to meself.

Right at this moment, Detective-Sergeant Thomas, with Detective-Constable Jones in tow, was having a word with Mr Briggs in his house.

'It's your wife, Mr Briggs.'

'Poor old 'Ilda,' said Mr Briggs mournfully, 'but you 'ad a sample of the trouble she can be to 'erself. I ain't up to learnin' 'er the error of 'er ways.'

'She'll be up before the magistrates on Friday, sir,' said Sergeant Thomas. 'Aside from that, I have to tell you she insisted on layin' an accusation concernin' an incident that led to the death of her brother, Mr Henry Mullins of Walworth. We checked

315

details of the inquest. She said you could confirm her story.'

'What story?' asked Mr Briggs.

'Well, Mr Briggs, she declared that her late brother's eldest step-daughter, one Kitty Edwards, together with the lodger, one Jamie Blair, were responsible for the death.'

'Gawd, now she's gone off her chump,' said Mr Briggs. 'I ain't surprised. The shock of bein' arrested, that's what done it. An' what does that make me feel like on top of what I already feel like? I ask yer, when a bloke 'as to decide to shop 'is own wife an' then 'ears that it's sent 'er bleedin' barmy, what's it make 'im feel like?'

'She's an irate lady at the moment, we grant you that,' said Detective-Constable Jones, 'but I wouldn't say she's gone mentally deficient.'

'She's just shoutin' a lot,' said the sergeant.

'Poor old lady,' said Mr Briggs. 'What did she say about Kitty exactly?'

Detective-Constable Jones produced a notebook and consulted it.

'She alleged that in the presence of you and 'erself, Miss Kitty Edwards said, "My step-father deserved all I gave him." And that she also said direct to your wife, "It was what your brother earned for himself." Which was referin' to his death. It's further recorded, sir, that Mr Blair said, "That's right." As alleged.'

'Barmy,' said Mr Briggs.

'Your wife certainly isn't in the best of tempers,' said Sergeant Thomas, 'but barmy?'

'Sounds like it,' said Mr Briggs, due to take his weekly washing round to Lily this evening. She'd promised to do it for him.

'You were present with your wife in the house of her late brother last Sunday week, Mr Briggs?'

'I was.'

'Can you confirm the statements alleged to have been made by Miss Edwards and Mr Blair?'

'I can confirm I didn't 'ear them, I can confirm they wasn't said.'

'Mrs Briggs is very positive.'

'Well, gents, all I can say is I've been sorry for 'er an' sorry for meself since forcin' meself to lay information with yer,' said Mr Briggs, 'but I'm even sorrier for 'er now.'

'The statement, if true, suggests that your wife's late brother might not have fallen down the stairs. It suggests he might have been knocked down them. Your wife declared that's what happened.'

'Barmy,' said Mr Briggs again. 'I ask yer, gents, is a young girl goin' to as good as admit that's what she did, or what the lodger did? And is the lodger goin' to back 'er up? If that makes sense to you, it don't to me. It's—let's see—yes, it's what you'd call self-incrimination. Now, seein' they didn't say what poor old 'Ilda says they did, and I was with 'er all the time, and seein' they'd 'ave been off their own chumps if they did, I've got to repeat me trouble-an'-strife 'as gone barmy.'

'Could you say, then, what your wife's motive might have been in makin' these allegations?' asked Sergeant Thomas.

'I can make a guess,' said Mr Briggs. 'She didn't like 'er brother marryin' the kids' widowed mother, an' she didn't like the kids, either. An' she didn't like 'im bein' saddled with the kids when their mother died. Funny, that, in a gloomy sort of way, yer know. She fell off a pleasure boat, and 'e fell down the stairs, and it was fatal for both of them.'

'She drowned?' said Sergeant Thomas.

'Drunk as a lord, she was,' said Mr Briggs. 'Poor woman. Look, I ain't goin' to beat about the bush, me old Dutch is a troublesome female, and I dare say you've cottoned on to that yerselves by now. She's been copped fair an' square, she knows it, an' she's lashin' out at someone she ain't very fond of, young Kitty. You can tell 'er straight, I ain't too pleased with 'er.'

'I don't think I'll risk that,' said Sergeant

Thomas. 'All right, Mr Briggs, sorry to have troubled you, but it had to be done.'

'No 'ard feelings, gents,' said Mr Briggs, and saw them out. Later, he took his washing round to his friendly widow and had a nice cup of tea and a loving chat with her. He also gave her a box of chocolates and with it the suggestion that he was going to see if he stood a chance of getting a divorce. Widow Lily said you're not, are you, Wally? That I am, he said. And if I got it, Lily, would you have me? You bet I would, said Widow Lily, and was so taken with the idea and the box of chocolates that she treated him to a little more of what they both fancied.

Sergeant Thomas thought he'd better follow procedure and let his colleagues in the Walworth force know of the allegations, even if Mr Briggs had said they were balmy.

Rosemary's job took her out of the house at nine every morning. Jamie said that was a lazy time. Rosemary said nine-thirty was a City time for starting. Most days she didn't get back to her lodgings until well into the evening, for she found an eating place in Fleet Street where she could have supper. Her lodgings were boring, anyway,

Jamie providing the only light relief. On the other hand, the house in Larcom Street was a very suitable refuge from the arm of the law, and the Irish charmer, Mr Fiztpatrick, was only a few doors away. He met her at the Fleet Street tavern one evening, had supper with her, entertained her, and then took her for an excursion around London in one of the remaining hansom cabs. He exercised his blarney, she exercised a natural female talent for holding him off. Up to a point.

On another evening, Friday, it was Jamie who took her out, to a music hall performance at the Camberwell Palace. He'd just received his first week's welcome wage of two pounds four shillings and fivepence net.

Kitty didn't like him taking Rosemary out one bit, and Carrie wasn't too sure about it, either.

'Why's mister gone out with Miss Allen?' she asked.

'Oh, just because she's a poor and needy woman,' said Kitty, hiding her temper.

'She don't look poor an' needy,' said Chloe, 'she looks posh an' talks posh.'

'Oh, she's poor and needy in a different way, like some women are when they don't have much in the way of looks,' said Kitty. 'Mr Blair's just takin' pity on her.'

'If 'e took pity on me, he could take me out,' said Chloe.

'He's too old to take either of you out,' said Kitty.

'Oh, blow,' said Chloe. Alfie was out with some of his mates, so the twins walked to St John's Institute to see if they could look in on the local troop of Boy Scouts. The Scouts used the Institute on Friday evenings. Chloe and Carrie, much more self-confident now that they weren't poverty-stricken, thought there might be a chance of finding a Scout each. With girlish ambitions having been given a chance to blossom, they both felt they'd like to have boys to go up the park with on these summer Sundays.

At twilight, Kitty went out to the gate to call Alfie and the twins in. They weren't visible. A neighbour's mongrel dog trotted over and wagged its tail at her.

'And what do you want, Tuppence?' she asked.

A kid going by said, 'Well, 'e don't want more fleas, 'e's lousy wiv 'em already. I ain't got none meself,' he added, and went on in a proud flealess state.

'Like a biscuit, Tuppence, would you?' invited Kitty, and the dog wagged its tail again. 'Sit,' said Kitty, and it sat, wagging its tongue now that its tail was out of action. Kitty disappeared. She reappeared, with two biscuits, and showed them to the mongrel. 'Come on, come an' get them,' she said. Joyfully, Tuppence followed her through the passage and into Rosemary's bedroom. Kitty turned back the bedclothes and showed the biscuits again. 'Up 'ere, Tuppence,' she said, and the dog leapt on to the bed. She thrust a biscuit deep into the bed, and Tuppence burrowed after it, tail wagging rapturously. It foraged, found the biscuit and ate it. 'And here's your afters,' said Kitty, and thrust the second biscuit farther in. The dog disappeared. Kitty held the bedclothes down and trapped it for long seconds. Then she released it. 'Come on,' she said, and out she went, Tuppence following her into the street. 'Off you go now,' she said, but the dog sat on the edge of the kerb, watching her hopefully. The twins materialized. They were talking to two Scouts. She called them. They came running, their faces alight, and she thought, they're going to be really pretty soon. They asked if they could go out on Sunday with the two Scouts they'd just met. When Kitty asked about those other boys from the park Chloe replied very positively that the Scouts were much nicer. And Carrie said she thought the posh boys had pimples. She wasn't sure, mind, she just thought so. She asked Chloe for confirmation, and Chloe said no, they didn't have pimples, but they did have Adam's apples that jumped about when they talked and made them look soppy. Yes, that's it, said Carrie, I remember now, it was like pimples.

'All right,' said Kitty, 'I don't mind Scouts, as long as they keep to good deeds. I don't want Alfie to come back and say he saw them kissing you.'

'Oh, he won't see us,' said Chloe, 'we'll go behind trees.'

'Yes,' said Carrie, 'that's where boys kiss girls in the park, behind trees.'

Kitty said that they were not going behind any trees with any boys.

'Oh, blow,' said Chloe.

At which point Alfie came in, and Kitty made their cocoa.

Jamie returned with Rosemary at eleven o'clock. He said good night to her at the door to her room. Rosemary said lovely evening and gave him a kiss. Her bosom warmed his chest for a couple of seconds.

Kitty was still up and seething. Her eyes were that dark sienna brown, and fire was lurking. Jamie, entering the kitchen, said, 'Still up?'

'I 'appen to be sittin' here, so I suppose I'm still up,' she said.

'Too late for a cup of tea, I suppose?' ventured Jamie.

'Excuse me, but I don't make tea when it's past midnight,' said Kitty.

'It's five past eleven.'

'Well, that's as good as nearly past midnight, ain't it?' fumed Kitty.

'Just an hour's difference, that's all.'

'Might I ask where you've been with that fast person?'

'Camberwell Palace,' said Jamie. 'Then we had fish and chips, a sit-down session, and a—'

'Fish an' chips?' Kitty's lurking fire flamed. 'Oh, so I don't give you enough to eat of an evenin', don't I? Oh, what a shame, you goin' out all 'ungry and starvin' on account of me not feedin' you decent.'

'Hello, hello,' said Jamie, 'who's lit the fire?'

'No-one,' said Kitty. 'Can't you see straight? We don't light the fire in summer. Oh, I can't believe you 'ad to go and eat fish an' chips when you 'ad date puddin' for afters at supper. I never felt so insulted.'

'That was a beautiful date pudding, Kitty, and a fine meaty chop,' said Jamie. 'It beats me, how a seventeen-year-old girl who's never had much in her larder can cook as well as you do. Which reminds me, housekeeping. Since you're treating me like one of the family, I'll have to pay my fair whack now that I'm one of the workers. I'll give you a pound a week.'

'What? 'Ow much?' Kitty was flabbergasted.

'Not enough?'

'What, a whole pound?' Kitty, who hadn't thought about being given housekeeping money, just something for his share of food, didn't know if she was on her head or her heels. 'But it doesn't cost even 'alf as much for what you eat at breakfast and supper. A pound a week is nearly three bob a day, and it would only cost a bob more for all of us to eat nearly like lords. Well, we've still got all that money you're keepin' for us.'

'Kitty, you're not rich,' said Jamie. 'Look, you feed me, you do my washing and ironing, and you've got the rent and other expenses to think of. I'll let you have the rent for my room on top of the pound, of course. You're a fine girl, Kitty, and you're doing wonders for the kids.'

Much to her confusion, Kitty had a lump in her throat. A pound a week? It was just like what a dad gave to a mum for housekeeping.

Or like what a husband gave to his wife each week.

She swallowed.

'Oh, did you say you'd like a cup of

tea? I don't mind the time, I'll make one for both of us.'

'That's my girl,' said Jamie, who could drink tea at any time of the day.

Filling the kettle, Kitty said, 'I'm sorry I was cross with yer.'

'Don't mention it.'

'Mind, I still can't understand why your mum's friend isn't as old as she is,' said Kitty.

'Yes, bit of a puzzle, I suppose,' said Jamie with a smile.

'Still, it's not her fault,' said Kitty.

The day hadn't been a bad one for Jamie. He'd drawn his first week's wages, passed muster with his slightly cantankerous foreman and spent an enjoyable evening with Rosemary, a young lady with a fresh personality who was naturally entertaining. He liked her sense of humour, her well-dressed appearance and her attractiveness. And he liked the fact that she had put herself out to get a job for him. Kitty wasn't too keen on her, but she had no need to worry. He wasn't going to leave her and the kids until they were on their feet. It might take six months, but at twenty-four he could afford that amount of time.

Rosemary didn't complain about her day, either. Her work might not be the kind she wanted to do all her life, but it was a necessary commitment. Her evening out with Jamie had been enjoyable, and Sean Fitzpatrick was a fixture in her present background. She liked to have men around.

It was Mrs Briggs who'd had a bad day. The magistrates sentenced her to six months. As it was the first time she'd been up before the beaks, she might have received only fourteen days if the police hadn't been able to easily prove she'd been shoplifting for quite some time, and if she hadn't been found guilty of resisting arrest, common assault and bodily harm. Detective-Constable Jones was still wearing a bandage. That useless, brainless husband of hers didn't even appear until just before sentence was passed. And when it was passed, the rageful and highly offended lady set about reducing the court to matchwood. It took two policewomen and three policemen to get her down to the cells, where Mr Briggs was given the privilege of saying goodbye to her for six months. But he cut the farewell short, for Mrs Briggs did her best to get at him and tear his legs off. He escaped only in the nick of time.

Poor old Hilda, he thought. He hoped they'd take the right kind of care of her in Holloway, or she'd pull the roof off.

Chapter Fifteen

What a cheek, thought Kitty the next morning. As it was Saturday, the kids were having a lie-in, and she and Jamie were breakfasting on tea and toast before he went off to do a half-day's work. She couldn't help being nice to him, she still felt giddy about the pound he'd given her for housekeeping as well as four shillings for his rent instead of three-and-six. But then that fast thing, Rosemary Allen, came into the kitchen without even knocking and said she'd love a cup of tea if there was one going. She didn't want anything else, she said, as she rarely ate breakfast.

Kitty thought about telling her to push off, but she couldn't, and the aggravating person sat down and began to talk about the music hall turns she and Jamie had seen last night. Kitty gave her a cup of tea, the person helped herself to sugar, said thanks a lot and went on talking. However, a little quiver animated Kitty when the chatty lodger put a hand to the side of her left thigh and rubbed it. She did it again a minute later. Then, just as she was finishing her cup of tea, Kitty saw her pull the skirt of her costume up on one side. She was sitting opposite Jamie, so he missed out on her exposed leg. Kitty didn't. She saw Rosemary rub a little pink patch on the side of her thigh just above her stocking. Kitty experienced a spasm of fiendish glee.

Jamie was on his way minutes later, and Rosemary returned to her room. When she left, she told Kitty she wouldn't be back until late. She was meeting a friend after she finished her work at midday, she said. She meant Sean Fitzpatrick. The audacious Irish rogue was a definite entertainment to a woman missing the attentions of her Belfast lover.

Apart from feeling she had to watch what that fast person got up to with Jamie, Kitty couldn't help thinking that nice things were happening. She wondered if it wouldn't be a good idea, when she next went to church, to ask God to make sure things stayed like this. She further wondered if she ought to ask forgiveness for letting the dog Tuppence get into that person's bed.

Oh, lor'.

She went in quick search of an item she knew was somewhere in the kitchen or scullery. It hadn't been used for years, it hadn't needed to be, thank goodness. She found it on the scullery shelf among lots of odds and ends. A little cardboard drum of Keating's flea powder. With the kids not yet out of bed, she entered Rosemary's room, carrying a long feather duster as well as the flea powder. She smothered the duster with powder. Without turning the bedclothes down, she thrust the long feather duster in between the sheets and moved it from side to side. She knew Rosemary didn't throw the bedclothes back when she got up. She just turned a corner down and slipped out. Kitty had seen the bed before it was made. With luck, the fleas wouldn't have escaped, except those that had transferred themselves to Rosemary. They wouldn't have wanted to escape, not from a warm bed, where they'd be happy to wait for her every night. Not many people in Walworth didn't know about the habits of fleas.

Kitty finished by dusting the inside of Rosemary's nightdress, then refolded it and put it back between the pillows. She didn't want fleas all over the house. Imagine if Jamie picked them up.

Oh, me gawd, he'd leave.

Mr Murphy had some private words with Mr Fitzpatrick before he went to his work in a Walworth coal yard. The conversation took place in Mr Fitzpatrick's room, while the lodger was still in bed and the door was closed. Mr Murphy said he'd be obliged, so he would, if Mr Fitzpatrick would kindly get rid of a certain contraption he'd brought into the house yesterday. Mr Fitzpatrick said bejabers, is it you, John Murphy, that's giving orders to meself? It's me that's standing here and saying so, said Mr Murphy. Mr Fitzpatrick said he'd do Mr Murphy the favour of not hearing that. Mr Murphy said he didn't regard that as a favour, and begged to remind Mr Fitzpatrick that he'd taken him in as a lodger only on the strict understanding there was to be no hanky-panky. There was Mrs Murphy to consider and Mr Murphy's Bible oath that for her sake and the sake of the children he'd respect their English friends and neighbours. This was their home now, and he'd be greatly obliged if Mr Fitzpatrick would join them in respecting the people they lived among. The contraption, he said, indicated that Mr Fitzpatrick intended to show a painful lack of respect. From his bed, Mr Fitzpatrick said Mr Murphy was showing a painful lack of respect for his own people, but he could rest happy in being assured the contraption wasn't for his friends and neighbours. Whoever it's for, our friends and neighbours won't like it, said Mr Murphy. Nor will I, so drop it in the river, Mr Fitzpatrick, or I'll have to

331

break both your arms, don't you see? That's unfriendly, Mr Murphy, said Mr Fitzpatrick, and harmful to you yourself, so it is. Harmful, is it, said Mr Murphy, and to me and Mrs Murphy and our little ones? It could be, Mr Murphy, it could be, said Mr Fitzpatrick. Mr Murphy said the old game, is it? But I'm ready for that, Mr Fitzpatrick, and can match a threat with a promise. So get rid of it, that contraption. Sure, you're a pitiful Irishman, Mr Murphy, in having respect for the English, said Mr Fitzpatrick. I'm a family man, Mr Fitzpatrick, that's the way of it, said Mr Murphy, and kindly don't forget it. He left then, and for once Mr Fitzpatrick was far from cheerful.

He met Rosemary in a tavern near Charing Cross. He was carrying a brown leather bag identical to a doctor's bag.

'What's that?' asked Rosemary, as he sat down beside her.

'Sure, it's a surprise, me darling,' he smiled.

'Who for?' asked Rosemary, surreptitiously rubbing an itching rib.

'Well now, there's Mrs Murphy and Maureen Murphy and Billy Murphy.'

'And how many more?' asked Rosemary, liking his never-failing air of good fellowship.

'A few more, a few more,' said Mr

Fitzpatrick, 'but it's only Mrs Murphy, Maureen and Billy with birthdays next month, and I'd not be the warm-hearted man I am if I didn't show appreciation of same. In this bag are birthday presents carefully selected and bought by me meself this morning out of me generous pocket.'

'Your pocket is very generous,' said Rosemary. 'Most men have to work to fill theirs. Why don't you have to?'

'Ah, sure, didn't I come into a little bequest from me late Aunt Mary, and hasn't that bequest spared me toiling and sweating for a year?' said Mr Fitzpatrick.

'Well, bless your late Aunt Mary,' said Rosemary. 'By the way, I'm hungry.'

'That's a happy coincidence, so am I,' said Mr Fitzpatrick, and set about ordering drinks and food. Rosemary acknowledged he was a man most women would like simply for his open-handedness. Over the meal he returned to the subject of the birthday presents, the point being that Mrs Murphy's brood had a collective inquisitiveness that directed their noses into everything in the house. They also had foraging fingers. Might Rosemary do him the favour of keeping the bag in her lodgings until the right time arrived?

'Can't you lock it up somewhere in your room?' asked Rosemary.

'Sure I could, me darling, if I had a

cupboard that could be locked.'

'You're Irish,' said Rosemary, an itch irritating her stomach now.

'That I am, and wouldn't I let the Holy Inquisition itself burn me before I denied it?'

'That's not the point,' said Rosemary. 'The point is, what's actually in that bag?'

'God save me soul,' said Mr Fitzpatrick, 'where's your trust in a gintleman devoted to yez?'

'I don't trust any Irishman,' said Rosemary.

'Be jasus, test me, then,' said Mr Fitzpatrick. Picking up the bag from beside his chair, he placed it on her lap. She put her knife and fork down and accepted the challenge. She sprang the clip and opened the bag. Inside was a blue and white striped carrier bag with the name of a West End store on it. She lifted it out, opened it and saw three items neatly wrapped in blue and white striped paper. She unwrapped one. It was a bottle of Yardley's lavender water.

'That's fair,' she said, and wrapped it up again. She put it back, closed the bag and returned it to Mr Fitzpatrick, who placed it beside his chair again.

'It's a sweet girl you are,' he said, 'and a sensible one.' His smile was teasing and under the table his hand touched and caressed her knees. 'There's a hotel I know in Kensington,' he said.

'Well, keep it to yourself,' said Rosemary, enjoying her relationship with him and with Jamie, but not yet sure which of them she might be willing to have as a temporary lover.

'We'll go there for tea,' said Mr Fitzpatrick, 'and a theatre this evening, so we will. I'll leave my bag in the parcels office of Charing Cross Station.'

He did that later, Rosemary going with him to the station. He handed the bag in, received a ticket, and then took Rosemary to Selfridge's, much to her pleasure, although she was suffering an increasingly itchy state.

'Have you done your Saturday shopping?' asked Jamie, when he and Carrie were doing the washing up after the midday meal.

'Me?' said Carrie.

'Do you do Saturday shopping, then?' asked Jamie.

'Me?' said Carrie.

'She's not old enough,' said Chloe from the kitchen, 'and she don't 'ave any shoppin' money.'

'I don't 'ave no money at all,' said Carrie.

'We're waitin' till our ship comes 'ome,' said Alfie.

'Then we'll all go shoppin', won't we mister?' said Carrie.

'Well, you will, Carrie, I'm sure,' said Jamie. 'I was actually asking Kitty about today's shopping.'

'I'm doin' it this afternoon,' said Kitty.

'I'll take you,' said Jamie in another feeble-minded moment.

'Oh, 'elp,' said Kitty, and felt warm with pleasure.

'What d'yer want 'elp for?' asked Alfie, about to go out and knock up some of his mates.

'I mean I'm honoured, I'm sure,' said Kitty.

Alfie still couldn't make sense of it.

'Yes, but why'd yer need 'elp?' he asked.

'Well, it's swoony,' said Chloe.

'What is?' asked Alfie.

'Bein' honoured,' said Chloe.

'Kitty don't look swoony,' said Alfie.

'No, but you'd soon know she was if she stood up,' said Chloe, 'because she'd fall over.'

'Cor, what a lemon,' said Alfie, 'I never 'eard anyfink more daft. I'm goin' out now.'

'Well, you be careful you don't get honoured by some girl,' said Chloe, 'or you'll fall over yerself, in the street.'

'Crikey, I fancy bein' honoured by Mrs Fitch,' said Alfie, 'I don't mind fallin' over for 'er.' And out he went in hope.

Kitty answered a knock on the door a minute later. Two boys were on the step.

' 'Ello,' said one, 'is Carrie in?'

Kitty looked them over before answering. Their jerseys and shorts had seen better days, but their faces were clean, their socks pulled up and their manner respectful. Kitty was setting great store by respectfulness these days. It went with respectability.

'You both askin' for Carrie?' she said.

'No, I'd like to see Chloe meself,' said the second boy.

'Where you from?' asked Kitty.

'Brownin' Street. I'm Billy Rogers and he's Danny Morris. We're in the Scouts.'

'Oh, you're the ones, are you?' said Kitty. 'Aren't you goin' up the park with Chloe and Carrie tomorrow?'

'Yes, but we thought we ought to see if they're comin',' said Billy.

Kitty smiled. They were both about sixteen, and neither had pimples. Chloe and Carrie weren't keen on pimply boys. Not that they'd ever had much chance to exercise their likes and dislikes. Boys had never taken much notice of them in their old and tatty garments, which made them look sort of dilapidated. But that was all over now. The twins looked nice these days. She called.

'Chloe? Carrie? Two young gents 'ave come visitin'. They're Scouts.'

In the kitchen, Chloe said, 'Oh, crikey, it's them, Carrie.'

'Who's them?' asked Jamie.

'Billy an' Danny,' said Chloe, 'we met them yesterday evenin'.'

'Oh, crikey,' breathed Carrie, 'I never 'ad visitors before.'

'Well, you've got some now,' said Jamie, 'go and present yourselves.'

The girls went, and Kitty left them to it. Danny said hello, like to come and help us do a good deed? Chloe asked what good deed, she and Carrie were shocking busy and they hadn't got time to do any good deeds if it meant larking about. Billy said you look nice, Chloe. I'm not Chloe, said Carrie, that's Chloe. You look nice Carrie, said Danny. I'm honoured, said Carrie. Oh, help, she said, but she didn't fall over.

The good deed referred to was to do shopping for two old ladies of King and Queen Street. Chloe said oh, she and Carrie would help with that. So off they went, eyes a melting brown in the sunshine of early June.

Jamie and Kitty were ready to go to the market five minutes later, Kitty thinking, of course, that it was just like a mum and dad about to do the shopping together.

But then came another knock on the front door. Jamie answered it this time.

'Afternoon, Mr Blair,' said Detective-Sergeant Watkins of the Rodney Road police station. His Inspector had seen details of a report emanating from the police in Peckham. Without being actively interested, he'd said you'd better call in sometime, Watkins.

Sergeant Watkins had a uniformed constable with him.

'Hello,' said Jamie, 'what can I do for you this time?'

'Is Miss Edwards at home, sir?'

'She is.'

'Can we talk to both of you for five minutes?'

'Come in,' said Jamie.

Kitty wasn't as welcoming as that herself. What a blessed inconvenient lot, the police, calling just as she was going out with Jamie. If they'd come to mess up her afternoon, she'd have something to say to them.

Sergeant Watkins apologized for his call, but thought Saturday afternoon might find both Miss Edwards and Mr Blair at home. Well, yes, we are, said Kitty, but were just going out. Sergeant Watkins said he wouldn't keep them long. The point was, something had come up. It was only hearsay, but he'd just like to get things clear again. Could Miss Edwards remember what she said to her late step-father's sister, Mrs Hilda Briggs, when the lady was here with Mr Briggs last Sunday week?

'What a question,' said Kitty. 'I said lots of things. They was here ages.'

'Well, can you remember what you said to Mrs Briggs about your step-father's death, Miss Edwards?'

'We talked about it,' said Kitty, 'and I told her how it 'appened.'

'I must ask you, did you tell her that your step-father deserved what you gave him, and that he earned it for himself?'

'You can't speak ill of the dead,' said Kitty, 'even if the dead didn't live good lives. And how could I 'ave said that, anyway, when it wasn't true? I didn't give 'im a punch, if that's what you mean.'

'Mr Blair, you were present, I believe?' said Sergeant Watkins.

'I was,' said Jamie.

'And heard all that Miss Edwards said to her step-father's sister?'

'Yes.'

'I'll get ratty in a minute,' said Kitty. 'All the questions before, then the inquest, and now more questions. I bet it's not legal.'

'It's just a clearing-up process, Miss

340

Edwards. Mr Blair, regardin' the statement Miss Edwards was said to have made—'

'She didn't,' said Jamie.

'Quite sure?'

'Positive.'

'I wonder, would you be very patient with me and show me again what took place at the top of the stairs?' said Sergeant Watkins. 'I have an idea that we can clear the matter up once and for all.'

'It had better be a good idea,' said Kitty, 'or I'll get a nervous ailment from all the 'eadaches you're givin' me.'

On the landing, she and Jamie took up the now familiar positions, while Sergeant Watkins put himself in the dead man's shoes, and the uniformed constable looked on.

'This is right, as we are, Mr Blair?' said Sergeant Watkins.

'It's right,' said Jamie.

'Good. Give me your arm, Miss Edwards, the one your step-father was dragging on.' Kitty put out her left arm. She had Jamie on her right, and Sergeant Watkins was facing them on the top stair. The CID man noted the positions, his own included. 'Do you recall the bruise?' he asked.

'Course we do,' said Kitty.

'Which Dr McManus described as superficial,' said Jamie.

341

'To be frank, I always felt it could have been made by a glancing blow. It was on his right cheek. Are you right-handed, Mr Blair?'

'Yes.'

'Well, if you had been angry enough to aim a blow, it would have struck his left cheek or glanced it. And as Miss Edwards had her right hand free, the same would have applied. Thanks very much.' Sergeant Watkins allowed a slight smile to surface. 'Report negative.'

'That's a comfort to Miss Edwards,' said Jamie, 'it'll save her getting a nervous ailment.'

'Glad to have helped,' said Sergeant Watkins.

'Yes, and lucky for you you did,' said Kitty, 'because when I get a nervous ailment I go round to police stations and chuck bricks at their windows.'

'Hard on the windows, miss,' said the constable, and departed with the CID sergeant. 'What d'you think now, sarge?'

'From what I've heard, I think Henry Mullins could've done his kids a favour by fallin' down the stairs a lot sooner than he did,' said Sergeant Watkins. 'And I put it to you, Tosh, I might have helped him on his way if I'd been there and if I hadn't sworn to uphold the law.'

'Still got suspicions, have you?'

'Not of murder, no. But there he was, standing on the top stair, bawlin' at those two and maulin' his step-daughter. Who wouldn't have hit him without actually thinkin' of doing him in?'

'Manslaughter, then?'

'Yes, that's what I'm thinking, but I haven't got the heart to keep on at Kitty Edwards without any real proof. Now if Mullins was bawlin' at the lodger at the critical moment, and had his face turned towards him, and the lodger had aimed a blow with his left fist—'

'Turn it up, sarge.'

'You're right, Tosh, it's all ifs and buts at the moment.'

'Listen, Kitty, did you say that at any time to Mrs Briggs?' asked Jamie.

'What, that he deserved what I give 'im? No, course I didn't, and you said yourself I didn't.'

'I wasn't present all the time,' said Jamie, 'not on the Sunday or the Monday. You know what's happened, don't you? Mrs Briggs has informed the police that that was what you said.'

'Oh, the old cow,' breathed Kitty. 'Well, that sergeant knows now I didn't say it.'

'He knows you said you didn't and that I said you didn't.'

'Well, that's good enough, specially as

it's true,' said Kitty. 'Mind, I did say me step-father earned 'imself his heart attack, but I didn't say it was what I gave 'im. Anyway, that Sergeant Watkins was satisfied you couldn't have hit that Mullins man.'

'Nor you,' said Jamie.

'Me? I didn't touch 'im.'

'I'm not going to say you did.'

'No, that's me,' said Kitty indignantly, 'it's me that's not goin' to say you touched 'im.'

'Yes, little monkey weren't you, when you thought that up?'

Kitty stared at him. She swallowed. Oh, that hand of fate, it was writing her doom. He was thinking about that, about what it meant, and he'd never have any respect for her. But she'd had to keep him with her and the kids, he'd been their only chance of surviving together and not being split up, of not becoming destitute. But he wasn't ever going to like that what she'd said to him had really been a threat. Oh, she could sink into the floor.

'I wouldn't ever—honest, I wouldn't ever 'ave—'

'I know you wouldn't.'

'I didn't realize what I was sayin' at the time.'

'Look me in the eye,' said Jamie.

She tried to, but her attempt failed. She

thought of something.

'Oh, I remember now,' she said, 'the shock of it all gave me a nervous ailment, a chronic one.'

'Hello,' said Jamie, 'we're goin' to work that one to death too, are we?'

'Girls my age 'ave nervous ailments when they don't know what they're sayin'. Of course, I won't 'ave them by the time I'm eighteen, they go away when a girl's of a marryin' age.'

'Thank God for that,' said Jamie.

'Yes, I'll be thankful meself,' said Kitty. 'Are we still goin' to the market?'

Jamie said yes, which pleased her, and he walked with her to the market by way of Brandon Street, where urchins and street kids abounded, shawled women gossiped on doorsteps, and crochety old ladies in granny bonnets told each other that kids these days ought to be done away with. One kid eyed Kitty speculatively.

'Carry yer shoppin' bag for a penny, young missus?' he called.

'Not today,' said Kitty. 'Here,' she said to Jamie, 'did you hear that? Him thinkin' me a young missus, would you believe.'

'And me your old man, I suppose,' said Jamie.

'Oh, you're not that old,' said Kitty.

'Sure?'

'Well, I never ever meant you was

345

ancient,' said Kitty.

'When do you get to be eighteen?' asked Jamie.

'September.'

'Good,' said Jamie. 'While we're in the market we'll look for a sound upstanding bloke of about nineteen with prospects. Fancy that?'

'Yes, we'll invite 'im for supper,' said Kitty, 'and take 'im to meet the vicar in the mornin'. Rapturous, I don't think.' They entered the crowded market and Kitty made for a fruit and veg stall run by a well-known character called Ma Earnshaw. She was stout and hearty in her calico apron and cloth cap; she greeted Kitty cheerfully.

' 'Ello, love, I 'eard about Mullins, and 'is inquest. I can't say it grieved me, except I felt for 'ow it left yer. But my, 'ere you are an' lookin' a treat. 'Oo's yer young gent, might I ask?'

'Oh, he's our lodger,' said Kitty.

'Pleased to meet yer, mister,' said Ma Earnshaw.

'Yes, he's Mr Blair,' said Kitty, much as if the name signified a gent of some importance. 'He's been a kind 'elp to us in our hour of trial, and is fond of Alfie and the twins. Could I 'ave four pounds of garden peas, four pounds of new potatoes, two pounds of carrots and three pounds of cookin' apples, please?'

'That yer can, Kitty,' said Ma Earnshaw, and began to weigh up. ' 'As Mullins left yer well off, ducky?'

'Oh, we've got enough to manage on for a bit,' said Kitty, 'and we've got another lodger to 'elp with the rent.' The one with fleas, she thought. Oh, lor', I bet Jamie would kill me if he knew. 'But it was Mr Blair who was kind enough to 'elp me do the shoppin'. I just couldn't manage without 'im.'

Not much, thought Jamie, and was smiling as he took charge of the shopping bag and let Ma Earnshaw tip each purchase in from the scale. Kitty paid in a proud kind of way. Ma Earnshaw noted her bright look.

'Good luck to yer, Kitty,' she said, 'I'm that pleasured to see yer lookin' lovely after yer hour of trial.'

'Oh, thanks, how kind,' said Kitty, who'd never been called lovely before. Going on her way with Jamie, she said, 'Did you hear that?'

Jamie, moving with her through the market crowds, said, 'It calls for a new hat and some Sunday stockings.'

'Oh, can we afford that?' asked Kitty.

'Just this once,' said Jamie.

'Oh, bless yer, Mr Blair—here, where you goin'?'

Jamie was heading for the pavement and a shop. Kitty followed, and they squeezed through between two stalls. The shop sold second-hand furniture. There was a tapestry-upholstered sofa in the window amid a display of other items. It was priced at one pound.

'We'll buy that,' said Jamie.

We will? We? Kitty felt a funny little flutter.

'But it's a pound,' she said.

'Your old sofa's ruined,' said Jamie.

'Yes, but—'

'It'll make your parlour look more respectable,' said Jamie.

'Oh, 'elp, yes, we'd best buy it, then,' said Kitty, and they went in and bought it, paying an extra shilling to have it delivered. Then Kitty completed her shopping, after which she bought a new hat from a shop in the Walworth Road. Jamie said how about one with feathers? Not at my age, said Kitty, and was highly pleasured when he approved her choice of a cross between a tam-o'-shanter and a beret in golden-brown velvet. She also bought a pair of flesh-coloured imitation silk stockings. 'Oh, ain't you been kind and gen'rous to me?' she said, as they made their way back to Larcom Street along the Walworth Road.

'Not me, Kitty, it's your nest egg.'

'Yes, but you've got charge of it—oh, d'you still think the rest of it could be somewhere in the 'ouse?'

'I still think there's no point in bothering with it,' said Jamie.

'But if we did find it and 'anded it over, we might get a reward,' said Kitty.

'Yes, you might,' said Jamie.

'No, I mean us,' said Kitty, 'it would only be right, you 'aving half.'

'Well, if we all get hard-up and down to rags,' said Jamie, 'we'll think about it.'

'Yes, all right,' said Kitty. 'Oh, I never met anyone with more worldly wisdom than you, Mr Blair.'

Jamie laughed.

Chloe and Carrie were out all afternoon with Billy and Danny, first helping with the good deed and then sitting in Browning Gardens with them, next to Browning Hall. The boys brought them home just before six, having treated them to toffee-apples which they'd enjoyed in the Gardens.

'Call for yer tomorrow,' said Billy.

'To take you up the park, Chloe,' said Danny.

'I'm Carrie, you soppy thing, you know I am.'

'Only jokin',' said Danny, and gave her a kiss. So Billy gave Chloe one. The girls quivered on the doorstep.

'Cheek,' said Chloe.

'Blessed sauce,' said Carrie, quite pink.

'I liked it,' said Danny. 'Did you like it, Billy?'

'Rapture,' said Billy.

'Oh, we're not supposed to be kissed, are we, Chloe?' said Carrie.

'Don't you do it in the park tomorrow, you Billy,' said Chloe.

'No, all right, on the tram,' said Billy, and he and Danny departed like Scouts who'd done more than one good deed this afternoon.

'Oh, what's Kitty goin' to say when we tell 'er we've been kissed?' asked Carrie.

'Best if we don't tell 'er,' said Chloe, 'we don't want to upset 'er.'

'Yes, she might not let us go up the park tomorrow,' said Carrie. She pulled on the latchcord and they went in, brown eyes meltingly innocent.

Rosemary was going mad. She and Mr Fitzpatrick had returned to Charing Cross Station to pick up his bag before going to the theatre, since the parcels office would be shut when they left the theatre. By this time her condition was what Mrs Reynolds would have called sufferingly chronic. She was itching in places undreamed-of. Mr Fitzpatrick produced his ticket and the bag relevant to the ticket was handed over to him. It wasn't the bag Rosemary had seen him deposit. It was identical to it. And the ticket, of course, wasn't the one Rosemary had seen him receive.

In any case, she was concerned now only with the dire necessity of getting back to her lodgings. She informed Mr Fitzpatrick that she was feeling ill, that she needed a taxi immediately. Mr Fitzpatrick expressed deep sympathy and a gentleman's wish to accompany her. No. Rosemary was adamant. She needed to be alone, to scratch and to rub. She did not tell him so, she said she was too ill to stand anyone's company. Certainly, she looked as flushed as a young lady suffering a fever. Mr Fitzpatrick saw her into a taxi outside the station and told her he would look in on her later that evening to see how she was. He'd bring the bag then, he said.

'Yerself, me darling, you look in on a doctor on the way now,' he said.

'Damn a doctor,' breathed Rosemary, and when the taxi was on its way over Waterloo Bridge, she pulled her skirt and slip up to her hips. Above her stockings and below the dainty lace of her drawers, large spots of pink patterned her bare thighs. And she saw the cause then. She saw a flea. It was nestling just at the top of her left stocking. She wanted to scream. In a spasm of almost hysterical disgust she brushed it off.

It took quite kindly to the cab floor before beginning to hop and investigate.

Chapter Sixteen

There was a shocking scene when Rosemary returned that evening. Alfie was next door, actually consorting with Mrs Fitch, his heart-throb. Well, perhaps not consorting with her, but cleaning and polishing all the family footwear for tuppence. Chloe and Carrie were out with girl friends. Kitty was in the kitchen, baking a cake. It was her first attempt at baking a cake, and she was following a recipe with a hope and a prayer. Jamie was in the parlour. The second-hand sofa had been delivered. He'd done some re-arranging of the furniture, and was about to carry the old sofa into the yard and break it up for winter firewood.

Rosemary rushed in and hurled herself into her room like a mad thing. Jamie heard her. She was noisy in her rush through the passage. And she sounded even noisier in her room. There were even strangled little yells. Jamie investigated. The door of her room was half-open and he looked in.

Rosemary already had her costume and blouse off. He blinked. Who wouldn't have? The attractive young woman from Chester looked startlingly bewitching in a figure-hugging white basque, colourful French knickers and black stockings. Not that she was in poised immobility, waiting to be admired. She equated at this moment with a jerking marionette as she wrestled like a madwoman with the hooks and eyes of her basque.

'Good God,' said Jamie.

'Well, don't just stand there,' she gasped, 'do something!'

'I rather think—'

'Do something! Unhook my basque—oh, my God!' Rosemary jerked and thrust her hand down inside the top of her right stocking, rubbing madly at her flesh. 'I've picked up an army of fleas, they've been eating me alive—Jamie, for God's sake, do something!'

'It's a woman's work,' said Jamie, and Kitty appeared then, in her apron and with her hands floury.

'What's 'appening? Oh, how disgustin', I never saw such an unrespectable sight—go away, Mr Blair. Miss Allen, put some clothes on.'

'Damn my clothes,' panted Rosemary, 'I'm all over bloody fleas and they're eating me alive—fill a bath for me!'

'Fleas? Fleas? In this 'ouse?' Kitty struck an appalled note. 'Mr Blair, come out, shut the door or they'll be everywhere.' She literally pushed Jamie out and came out herself. She pulled the door to with a bang. Rosemary screamed. 'Now look what you've done, Mr Blair, bringin' a woman here that's got fleas. I thought the other day she was 'aving a suspicious scratch.'

'Rubbish,' said Jamie. From the bedroom came a yell.

'Oh, the poor woman,' said Kitty, 'she'll 'ave to go round to the sanitary inspector and be deloused, won't she?'

'Shut up, you monkey,' said Jamie. 'I'll take her to the public baths, they're still open.'

'Take her?' Kitty struck another appalled note. 'But you'll catch them yourself, they'll jump off her on to you. She'll 'ave to go by herself while I dust all over 'er room with flea powder, if I can find some.'

'I'll take her.' Jamie knocked on the door. 'Rosemary, put something on, a coat or something, and I'll take you to the public baths in Manor Place. Don't waste time, let's get there before they shut.'

'I'll be raving mad by the time I arrive,' yelled Rosemary. But she came out only seconds later, wearing a spring coat, her face flushed, and carrying a skirt and jumper over her arm. Her eyes looked feverish.

'Shut the door,' said Kitty, and pulled it to herself.

Rosemary rushed out of the house, Jamie going after her.

Kitty closed the front door, pulled the latchcord in, went back to the kitchen and took all her clothes off. Carrying the little drum of effective flea powder, she went naked into Rosemary's bedroom, shutting the door behind her. The first thing she did was to inspect the bed. Between the sheets she found several limp and expiring fleas. She put them in the washstand basin. Then she re-dusted the sheets and shook powder all over the room. Oh, help, I'll have to ask for forgiveness at church tomorrow, she thought. Still, Jamie won't be in any hurry to take that person out again. Oh, suppose he comes back from the baths with fleas himself? He'll smash the house up.

She put that awful thought aside and gathered up Rosemary's stockings and underwear. She rushed them to the scullery, put them in the copper and placed the wooden lid on the copper. She found a paper carrier bag, went back to the bedroom and stuffed Rosemary's blouse and costume into the bag. She put that in the copper too. Then she inspected her body. No fleas. That was something.

She dressed herself, but only after giving her hands and arms a good wash.

The public baths were about to close to customers. Attendants were letting active customers know they were to be out in ten minutes. Rosemary, just out of the water, was drying herself on the huge if coarse towel. Silent wails of anguish indicated her disgust at the pink patches evident all over her body. Dried, she put on the jumper and skirt, nothing else, and slipped into her shoes. She shook her spring coat vigorously above the bath. Then she left the cubicle. She found Jamie in the waiting area.

'Better?' he said.

'They're all drowned, I hope,' she said.

'Fleas don't drown, the little buggers,' said Jamie, as they emerged into Manor Place, 'they swim about. But they won't be able to prevent themselves being sucked down the plughole.'

'Then they're on their way,' said Rosemary. Bareheaded, she swept back her damp hair. Her jumper moved to the healthy dancing motions of her unconfined breasts. 'God, what a day I've had, bitten all over. Is there a decent pub around here?'

'That's not the kind of question you should ask in Walworth,' said Jamie. 'All its pubs are noted for good beer and clean sawdust. Well, fairly clean. And rousing song.'

'Good, let's try one,' said Rosemary, 'I

feel like getting drunk. Well, I certainly feel like drowning my sorrows.'

'I don't think you're dressed for a pub,' said Jamie.

Rosemary, who had absolutely nothing on under her jumper and skirt, said, 'I'll agree I'm not dressed for the theatre or for the Pope, but I'm dressed for a pub, and I don't want to go back to that room yet, not until your funny young landlady has exorcized any fleas I left behind.' They turned into the Walworth Road, towards East Street and a selection of pubs. A young man and his lady friend glanced at Rosemary. The young man blinked and his lady friend's mouth dropped open. Jamie grinned. Carrying Rosemary's coat, he shook it out.

'I think you'd better put this on,' he said.

'It's too hot,' said Rosemary, 'and I'm too itchy.'

'You'll cool down. And you need covering up, or you'll stop the traffic.'

Rosemary managed a smile.

'See your point,' she said.

'I've seen yours. Two of them.' Jamie helped her on with her coat, but she didn't button it up. He took her into the saloon bar of the pub on the corner of Penrose Street. It wasn't as crowded as the public bar, where cockneys flush with weekend money had their wives with them. Jamie found an unoccupied table and Rosemary asked for a whisky.

'Whisky?'

'Just to begin with,' she said, 'and the next round is my treat.'

She followed the whisky with a Guinness. Jamie drank old ale. They chatted. From the public bar came the sound of songs, music hall songs, all rendered with cockney exuberence. Rosemary kept off the subject of her erstwhile lover and his wife, and favoured Jamie instead with details of her job in the City office of an exports company, mostly concerning her immediate boss, the manager, and his slave-driving habits, which included threats to take her to Brighton for a weekend if he could get his wife to go and visit her mother. She asked Jamie if he was under threats like that in his new job. Jamie said no, that she was the lucky one, that his foreman's wife hadn't approached him yet and that, in any case, he'd heard she preferred Southend.

Rosemary had two more Guinnesses. Jamie had two more old ales. He paid each time and Rosemary said just let me know how much I owe you. She was a lively companion, and the drink helped her to forget the horror of the fleas and her itches. They didn't leave until closing time. Rosemary tucked her arm through his on the way back to Larcom Street.

'Your funny young landlady,' she said, 'is she sweet on you?'

'Hardly,' said Jamie. 'She sees me more as a dad than a Romeo.'

'Well, good old Dad,' said Rosemary, 'you can Romeo with me now and again.'

'Let me know if it's serious.'

Kitty, of course, was furious that they'd stayed out so long, but kept her feelings to herself while she explained to Rosemary that she'd dusted her bed and all over her room, that she was going to boil her underwear in the copper tomorrow, but that the costume would have to be taken to the dry cleaners. Of course, she said, when you take it, tell them about the fleas, as they won't want them all over their laundry. Rosemary, mellow now, said what a kind girl she was. Kitty said Mr Fitzpatrick had called and put a bag in her room. Oh, yes, thanks, said Rosemary, and murmured her way to bed. Kitty confronted Jamie.

'She's been drinkin'.'

'She's had a Guinness or two to drown her woes,' said Jamie. 'Well, good night, Kitty, thanks for doing a soldier's job on her room. I meant to ask her how she picked the fleas up in her City job, but forgot.'

'Dear me, did you really?' said Kitty,

heavily sarcastic. 'I can't 'ardly tell you how surprised I am at 'aving you come in the worse for drink, and her too. I've seen some of that, and I 'ope it's not goin' to get a habit.'

'Bless you, no,' said Jamie. 'Good night.'

'Wait a minute,' said Kitty, 'I 'aven't finished tellin' you off yet.'

'Well, have another go in the morning,' said Jamie, and went up.

Oh, that person, thought Kitty, she's getting her drunken hands on him. He never said anything about her being a woman who drinks. Just wait till the morning, I'll tell her I don't want drinking women in this house, and I'll tell Jamie that the first time he's arrested for being drunk and disorderly, he'll have to go. Oh, lor' no, I can't tell him that, I'll have to protect him from her. I'll put more fleas in her bed and that'll send her back where she came from. Mind, if Mr Fitzpatrick fancies her, let's hope he kidnaps her.

Jamie, sound asleep, was gently shaken until he awoke. He peered at what looked like a misty blur beside his bed.

'What—'

'Shush,' whispered Rosemary, 'just move up and make room for me. I can't sleep downstairs tonight, not in that room. It smells of flea powder.'

361

Jamie sat up. Hell's bells, she was naked. He wasn't an insensible bloke, nor an innocent one. He'd known obliging young war widows in France and Flanders. But somehow he didn't fancy taking what the obliging Rosemary was offering. The circumstances weren't right. He quite disliked the thought of having her in his bed with Kitty and the twins close by. No, it couldn't be done, not in this house.

'Not now, Rosemary.' He smiled to himself. 'I've got a headache.'

She laughed softly, and lifted the bedclothes. Jamie slipped from the bed and opened the door. Then he picked her up, her body warm and glimmering, and carried her carefully over the landing and down the stairs, eyes used to the darkness. He spilled her on to her bed.

'Well, I'm damned,' said Rosemary.

'It's my young landlady and the twins, you see,' whispered Jamie, 'they wouldn't like it. Kitty runs a respectable house.'

'I'm laughing my head off,' she murmured.

'Hope you're not angry.'

'Not a bit. In a way, I like you for it.'

'Sleep tight,' said Jamie, and went silently back to his bed.

There wasn't a sound from Rosemary's

room in the morning. She was dead to the world. Jamie came down in advance of the kids at a little before nine. Kitty was waiting for him.

'Now about last night—'

'You look bright and well-brushed, Kitty. Have you got your Sunday stockings on?'

'Never you mind,' said Kitty, 'I want to say something before the kids come down. Supposin' they'd woken up last night and 'eard the drunken goings-on?'

'Pardon?' said Jamie.

'You and that person, comin' in like you did, with all that drink inside you,' said Kitty.

Since neither he nor Rosemary had been reeling about, Jamie said, 'Have you been seeing things?'

'It's not nice,' said Kitty. 'Mind, I'm not blamin' you, I'm sure you was led to the drink by her, you've been a sober and respectable man ever since you started to lodge 'ere, which I've been grateful for, seein' we've seen a lot of drinkin' in our time and been on the worst end of it. Didn't your mum tell you that Miss Allen was an 'abitual drunk?'

'I can't recall she ever mentioned it.'

'Well, she should 'ave,' said Kitty, 'then we'd 'ave known.'

'I think the fleas did it,' said Jamie.

'Well, I've never 'eard of a few fleas

363

drivin' a woman to drink,' said Kitty. 'There's poor people round in places like Brandon Street that get driven to drink by troubles and woes, but they wouldn't let a few fleas pour gin into them. I wasn't driven to drink by my hour of trial, I've got more self-respect than that, I 'ope. You'll 'ave to tell that drunk person we don't want her comin' in like that from a pub again, nor draggin' you to the pub with her. If the neighbours ask about it, I'll say that out of your good 'eart you went and brought her back from the pub, that you were only staggerin' about because she was leanin' on you. I don't want you to get a bad name, Mr Blair, not when you've been like a dad to us, and Chloe and Carrie 'ave made friends with two nice respectable Scouts.'

'Any more?' asked Jamie.

'No, I've said what ought to be said, I don't like goin' on about things, and I can't be a lot cross with you when you're a nice man really, and I'm sure you didn't mean to spend the whole evenin' in the pub with a drunken woman. I just 'ope those fleas of hers have all gone to their doom now and don't finish up on Chloe and Carrie. Here, where you goin'?'

'Just to the scullery copper,' said Jamie.

'What for?'

'Just to put my head in it and boil it,' said Jamie.

'Oh, would yer like to do some toast under the grill while you're out there?' asked Kitty. 'There's a plate of sliced bread by the gas stove. Mr Blair? Now what're you doin'?'

'Expiring,' said Jamie.

'Mr Blair, it's not funny, you know.'

'Don't I know it,' said Jamie.

Oh, bless me, thought Kitty, it's just like having a husband, with me having to tell him off and him being funny, except we don't go to bed together. Kitty had thoughts then that she'd never had before. She turned all rosy.

Over breakfast, Chloe said, 'Kitty, we don't 'ave to 'ave Alfie come up the park with us, do we?'

'I ain't goin' up the park with no-one,' said Alfie, 'I'm goin' to do Mrs Fitch's indoors winders. She give me tuppence for doin' all their boots an' shoes, and a cuddle as well.'

'A what?' said Jamie.

'Well, a sort of pat on me loaf,' said Alfie, 'which was like a cuddle, only Mr Fitch was there. Cor, she ain't 'alf a lovely gel.'

'You Alfie, she's a wife and mother,' said Kitty.

'Yes, but that ain't 'er fault,' said Alfie,

365

'it's what life done to 'er when she wasn't looking. I bet if she 'ad been lookin', she'd 'ave waited for me to grow up. She said to me yesterday, she said, "Ain't you gettin' to be a fine figure of a man, Alfie?"'

'That boy,' said Chloe, 'is 'e all there?'

'She asked after you, mister,' said Alfie to Jamie. 'I told 'er you was in good 'ealth, and she said Mr Fitch was pleased to 'ave got to know yer.'

'Tell me, Alfie, does Mr Fitch mind that you fancy Mrs Fitch?' asked Jamie.

'Well, I ain't told 'im yet,' said Alfie, 'I'll wait till I'm as big as 'e is.'

'Kitty, is Alfie right in the 'ead?' asked Carrie.

'He don't always sound as if he is,' said Kitty, 'but he's part of the fam'ly, so we'll 'ave to put up with it.'

'Would you like an outing to the park this afternoon, Kitty?' asked Jamie.

'Me?' she said.

'Then we'll be able to keep an eye on what those two Scouts get up to with Chloe and Carrie.'

'Oh, yes,' said Kitty, 'I'll be glad to come with you.'

'But, Kitty,' said Carrie, 'Scouts only do good deeds, don't they, Chloe?'

'Yes, they did lots of good deeds yesterday,' said Chloe.

Carrie turned pink.

Rosemary was up midway through the morning. She was going out for the day, she said, to meet an old friend from Chester in Regent's Park. Jamie asked how her fleas were. Rosemary shuddered and said she wanted to get away from any that might have survived Kitty's onslaught of flea powder. She left the house in a hurry, having placed Mr Fitzpatrick's bag in her wardrobe.

Jamie somehow found himself inveigled into taking Kitty and the kids to church again. During the service, when she felt the atmosphere was holy enough, Kitty silently asked forgiveness for getting fleas into Rosemary's bed and for making Jamie think she'd tell on him when there wasn't really anything to tell.

In the afternoon, Jamie actually did take her to the park, on a tram, and she strolled around with him in the June sunshine. With her Sunday best she was wearing her new hat and Sunday stockings. She liked Ruskin Park, she said, you didn't get common people there. Jamie said he was fairly common himself. Kitty said of course he wasn't, he didn't talk common or act common. She said she wouldn't have come to the park with him if he'd been common. I know you took to a bit of drink last night, she said, but I'm sure it won't happen again.

They came across the twins in company with Billy and Danny, and the two Scouts looked as respectable as Kitty could have wished. She thought Chloe and Carrie looked sweet. She knew how much they were enjoying themselves, and what bliss it was to have Sunday frocks. They owed it all to the hand of fate that had brought Jamie into their lives.

She felt just a little shy about being in company with him, but he didn't seem to notice, which was a relief to her. She didn't want to be thought soppy at her age.

It was a lovely day, and no-one in the park seemed worried by the fact that there'd been more fighting in Dublin on account of some of the Irish still wanting to get their hands on Ulster, and that a member of Parliament had nearly been shot dead by a suspected IRA gunman in Kensington yesterday.

'That's a chestnut tree over there,' said Billy.

'It's growin' conkers,' said Danny.

'Let's go and have a look,' said Billy. 'Come on, girls.'

'Not likely,' said Chloe

'You'll kiss us,' said Carrie.

'And we're not old enough to be kissed,' said Chloe.

'Well, let's just see if the conkers are comin' on,' said Danny.

368

'Oh, we don't mind that, do we, Chloe?' said Carrie.

'No, we don't mind that,' said Chloe.

The four of them disappeared behind the large tree, so no-one knew if the girls were kissed or not. Of course, Chloe and Carrie knew, but they weren't going to let on.

The old have secrets they've never told Mother,
The young have secrets they tell to each other.

There was a letter for Jamie from his mother the next morning. It arrived by the early post and he read it on his way to Streatham. She said she was glad he was still in good health, and that she herself was as well as could be expected considering she'd lived all her life under the strain of capitalism. I don't know what gets into the workers of the world, she said, they never get united. And the poor Irish, they don't get united, either. She said she was pleased to have heard from him about Rosemary getting safely there, and what a good friend she'd been to get him a job. I hope it's not brutal capitalists you're working for, though, she said. If it is, try and do a bit of secretive sabotage, like your father. She said she was sorry to hear about the tragedy that happened to the family he was living with, but he was to remember things like that didn't take place in Russia these days, as Lenin didn't allow any suffering. Perhaps we'll all go there one day soon, she said, and then you could find a nice Russian Bolshevik girl to marry. Bolshevik girls are very caring. Me and your father are still doing our bit for the cause and we never despair, even if some people over here don't like us singing the 'Red Flag' or 'up the workers'. Look after Rosemary now she's lodging with you, she's had some awkward financial troubles and been a silly girl. Your dad sends his regards.

Funny old girl, thought Jamie, can't help being fond of her. Lucky she's too potty to be taken too seriously.

Mrs Briggs had never felt more disgusted or more put upon. It was criminal, locking her up in Holloway with dishonest female hooligans. She'd got to get her own back on somebody, and she knew who that somebody was. That young bitch Kitty. Having come to the conclusion that she'd been shopped, she decided it had to be Kitty. Her useless husband had been allowed to come and see her on Sunday, and he'd told her the police weren't going to do anything in regard to what she'd told them about

370

Kitty. He'd had to tell them in all honesty that Kitty hadn't said them things. 'Hilda,' he'd said, 'you oughtn't to have made things up about her.' She went for him then and managed to give him a couple of clouts before she was pulled off him. As for that Kitty, well, poor Henry must have let slip to her that his sister sometimes forgot to pay for things when she went shopping. He was probably one over the eight at the time. But Kitty had remembered what he'd said, and had spitefully told the police.

I'll get me own back, thought Mrs Briggs, and she asked if Detective-Sergeant Thomas of Peckham could be brought to see her, as she had something to tell him.

'Want to confess you did some poor old shopkeeper in, do yer, missus?' said a wardress.

'Me? I ain't even 'armed a fly in all me life. You just get 'im to come 'ere or I'll break yer legs.'

'You do that and you'll get another six months, all in solitary.'

'I want to talk to 'im about a robbery.'

'Course you do, missus, but just do your time for this lot first.'

'I got a right to see a policeman.'

'Later, I'm busy at the moment.'

371

Rosemary was busy too, in her City job, and just as busy playing off Mr Fitzpatrick against Jamie. Jamie recognized the type. A butterfly, a female with wings. She'd end up getting them burnt. Her kind forgot that men didn't have wings. He could imagine she had helped herself to a good life at her Belfast employer's expense without worrying about it at all. Naughty girl, though. She'd helped herself to her employer's husband as well.

He took her out again one evening, to see *Show Boat* at the Drury Lane theatre. It left him short until pay-day, as the seats were three-and-six each. But she thoroughly enjoyed the musical, and when they got back to the house in Larcom Street, she invited kisses from him on the doorstep. It was nearly eleven, and the street was a patchwork of alternating light and shadow, the street lamps providing the light. Jamie felt that if Kitty was still up, the doorstep was the only place where kisses could be given without offending her. So he applied himself. Rosemary, after all, was a very kissable young woman. Her response was a healthy one. She wound her arms around him and pulled him close to her, very close. With her back against the door she began to vibrate with pleasure.

'Like me?' she murmured between kisses.

'I'm not complaining,' said Jamie but had no intention of taking her seriously.

'Mmm, it's a nice change from work.'

Her lips ate his and against her back the door trembled. Half a minute later it opened, and Rosemary, suddenly deprived of its support, fell backwards into the lamplit passage.

'Oh, I don't believe it,' breathed Kitty in outrage, 'she's drunk again, and showin' her legs this time. No wonder I heard the door makin' funny noises, I suppose she was usin' it to help 'erself stand up. Get her up in case some neighbours come along.'

Jamie extended a hand, Rosemary took it and hauled herself to her feet.

'Drunk, who's drunk?' she asked.

Kitty, closing the door, said, 'Takin' to drink at your age, it's a disgrace. I hope *you* 'aven't had a drop too much,' she said to Jamie.

'Give you my word,' he said.

'Couldn't you 'ave stopped her pourin' gin into 'erself?' demanded Kitty.

'She must have done it behind my back,' said Jamie.

'Hold on,' said Rosemary, 'who's drunk what, and when?'

'It don't matter what you drank, it's how

373

much,' said Kitty. 'I don't like a lodger comin' in at this time of night and not bein' able to stand up straight. I'm only too thankful both of you didn't fall over, it might 'ave woken the twins.'

'I'm not drunk,' smiled Rosemary.

'A likely story when your hat's all crooked and your legs were up in the air,' said Kitty in haughty style. 'I just don't know what to do about you, Miss Allen, first all that noise in the middle of the night when you got into bed with a mouse, then bringin' fleas to your room and now not bein' able to stand up straight, it's not givin' our house and 'ome much of a reputation.'

'Believe me, Kitty, knowing about all the hard luck you've had, the last thing I'd want to do is give you new worries,' said Rosemary. 'Neither Jamie nor I have been drinking, I'm afraid I simply tripped over your doorstep. D'you mind if I go to bed now, I'm played out. Thanks for a lovely evening, Jamie, we'll do it again some time. Good night, Kitty.'

She disappeared into her room. Jamie accompanied Kitty to the kitchen.

'Of course,' she said, 'it's not my business if you're courtin' that person, but I can't 'elp bein' surprised that you're doin' it with someone who's got fleas and likes a drop too much.'

'The fleas were accidental,' said Jamie, 'and she's not yet taken to drink. And I'm not courting her, I'm feeling my way.'

'Feelin' your way?' gasped Kitty, shocked to her core.

'Now, Kitty, stop thinking thoughts like that. How about a cup of tea?'

'D'you mean you're thinkin' about courtin' 'er?' asked Kitty.

'It's not serious,' said Jamie.

'Oh, I'll make some tea, then.' Kitty filled the kettle. 'Was it nice at the theatre?'

'Magic,' said Jamie.

'I've never been to a theatre meself.'

'Nor the kids, I suppose?'

'No, we've never been, any of us.'

'All right, I'll take all of you to the Camberwell Palace on Saturday evening.'

'Oh, will yer really?'

'I might as well do a fatherly job once in a while, or you'll give me the sack,' said Jamie.

'Oh, Chloe and Carrie will fall over themselves,' said Kitty in bliss.

'We don't want too much of that,' said Jamie, 'keep them off the drink, Kitty.'

Kitty laughed. Jamie smiled.

Units of the IRA were being troublesome in London, but he didn't think they'd use the Camberwell Palace as a target for a bomb.

Chapter Seventeen

'How's the new man coming along?' asked Mr Robbins, the site manager.

'So-so,' said Josh Simmonds, foreman of the carpenters and joiners.

'What's that mean?'

'Passable, guv'nor, passable.'

'He's good, is he?'

'I've seen worse,' said Josh Simmonds.

'Haven't we all. Keep an eye on him. An encouraging eye. And have a word with Ted Marshall.' Ted Marshall was the foreman of the brickies and masons. 'There's trouble brewing up with our Irish hands. They're getting things dropped on their heads.'

'Bound to,' said Josh Simmonds. 'The others think they're all in the bleedin' IRA.'

'Well, you're a mate of Ted Marshall's. Tell him to quieten things down, or our Irish hands might make the whole site look like an Irish stew that's boiled over.'

'Can't have that, guv'nor.'

'We can't. It'll make our Mr Murgatroyd think he's losing money.' Irish Mr Murgatroyd was the owner of the company,

376

and he expected a consistent return for the wages he paid.

' 'E won't like that, guv'nor,' said Josh Simmonds.

'Nor will I. I've got a wife and four kids.'

General Sir Henry Wilson, a distinguished soldier of the Great War, and now a member of Parliament for North Down in the newly-created Northern Ireland, had made several speeches about the Irish troubles that had rendered him extremely unpopular with his countrymen in the South. He was an Irishman himself, but very much attached to the United Kingdom. It has to be said he was as critical of the policies of the British government as he was of Irish extremists.

The IRA extremists were gunning for him.

Of course, Jamie's mother would have seen him as one more capitalist. All people with titles were capitalists to her, and the kind who ought to be done away with.

'Now what's all this about?' asked Detective-Sergeant Thomas on Friday afternoon. He was in an interview room at Holloway Prison for women, with Detective-Constable Jones in support. Mrs Briggs had been so aggressively insistent on talking to the police, that the interview had finally been arranged.

'Listen, sonny,' said Mrs Briggs from the other side of the table, 'I 'ope you ain't like that useless old man of mine, I 'ope you wasn't deprived of brains at birth, like 'e was. From what 'e told me, you don't seem to 'ave taken a blind bit of notice concernin' what I told yer about me brother's step-daughter Kitty an' that lodger of 'ers.'

'Give over, missus,' said Sergeant Thomas, 'we interviewed Mr Briggs as was officially incumbent on us.'

' 'Ere, talk English,' said Mrs Briggs, 'you ain't a bleedin' Eskimo, are yer?'

'No, I'm a Peckham man,' said Sergeant Thomas. 'When we interviewed your husband he couldn't confirm your statement. He insisted that Miss Edwards didn't say what you said she did. We notified the Walworth police, and left them to interview Miss Edwards and her lodger. She denied using such words, and her lodger was certain she didn't.'

'Well, she would, wouldn't she, and so would 'e,' said Mrs Briggs. 'They did it all right, they done me poor brother in. An' why, you'll ask.'

'You should be talkin' to the Walworth CID, not me,' said Sergeant Thomas, 'but all right, I will ask. I'll ask what their motive was.'

'I'll tell yer,' said Mrs Briggs. 'Me late brother, 'Enry Mullins, rest 'is soul, done the Peckham job.'

'Eh?' said Sergeant Thomas.

'What Peckham job?' asked Detective-Constable Jones.

'The day's takings at that Peckham store about a year ago,' said Mrs Briggs.

'Ruddy hell,' said Sergeant Thomas.

' 'E was desp'rate,' said Mrs Briggs, ' 'e 'ad those four step-kids to look after an' the cost was beggaring 'im. 'E wouldn't 'ave done it otherwise, 'e may 'ave 'ad 'is faults, but 'e was as honest as I am. Like I said, I never did no shopliftin', I just forgot to pay for a few things now and again. Mind, 'Enry didn't tell me about the job till just before 'e got done in. I remember tellin' 'im to do what was right, an' give 'isself up, but 'e said no, 'e was savin' the proceeds for a rainy day. Wasn't it about a thousand quid?'

'It was,' said Sergeant Thomas.

'Well, there y'ar, then,' said Mrs Briggs, 'now yer know why 'e got done in. Me brother was bound to 'ave told that eldest step-daughter of 'is that 'e'd got a nice bit of money set aside so's 'e could provide for 'er and the others when rainy days arrived.'

379

Sergeant Thomas doubted that very much. He'd heard enough about Henry Mullins to suspect that the last thing he'd have done would have been to tell any of his step-kids that he'd got a thousand quid stacked away.

'Are you alleging, Mrs Briggs, that Miss Kitty Edwards contrived the death of her step-father in order to get her hands on the proceeds of the robbery?'

'Stands to reason, don't it?' said Mrs Briggs aggressively. 'With the 'elp of 'er lodger, and goin' fifty-fifty with 'im, I shouldn't wonder. What some people get up to can make honest people spit, specially if they get away with it. Look at me, locked up in 'ere with common female criminals just for forgettin' to pay for a few odds and ends. And 'oo told on me, eh? I can make a good guess.'

'Mrs Briggs, your brother died of an 'eart attack,' said Detective-Constable Jones.

'Well, 'oo wouldn't 'ave after bein' attacked by two bleedin' 'ooligans? I bet 'e didn't fall down no stairs, I bet that Kitty and 'er lodger set about 'im.'

'There was no evidence of that,' said Detective-Sergeant Thomas.

'Crafty, that's what they were,' said Mrs Briggs. 'But the money's evidence, ain't it? They've got it all right. I went and asked them about it, but all I got was abuse.

380

Me, me late brother's sister, gettin' abused for tellin' them to 'and it all over to the police.'

Lying old haybag, thought both policemen.

'Did they indicate in any way that they'd found the money?' asked Sergeant Thomas.

'Well, they kept smirkin', as I remember. Mind you,' said Mrs Briggs, 'I suppose on account of 'Enry actu'lly passin' away through an 'eart attack, you can only get that step-daughter an' the lodger for manslaughter, but I ain't goin' to be vengeful and ask for more. 'Ere, when you get yer 'ands on the money, I'll be expectin' a reward for givin' yer all this 'elpful information, as well as 'aving five months knocked off me sentence. You can believe me, me brother 'Enry done the job. And I wouldn't mind bettin' Kitty and 'er lodger twisted 'is arms an' tortured 'im a bit to make 'im tell them where 'e'd 'id it.'

'You're flyin' a bit high, missus,' said Sergeant Thomas, 'there was no evidence that your brother had been tortured.'

'You can't tell what some people might get up to for a thousand quid,' said Mrs Briggs. She thought about saying that Kitty had told her she knew the money was somewhere in the house, but then she thought her useless husband might not back her up. I'll talk to the bugger when he next visits, she decided.

'Well, we'll have to pass all this on to Walworth,' said Sergeant Thomas.

When the two coppers left, Mrs Briggs felt she'd planted the right kind of seed. The CID men felt she was a nasty piece of work. All the same, they'd have to contact Walworth.

'What an old cow,' said Detective-Constable Jones.

'No wonder her old man turned her in,' said Sergeant Thomas, 'I hope he's livin' the life of O'Riley now.'

Mr Briggs had already gone to see a solicitor whose mail he delivered, and the solicitor had said no postman could expect to put up with a wife of established ill-repute. Yes, and what about her shoplifting habits as well? Mr Briggs put the question seriously.

Widow Lily was so pleased he was filing for divorce that she cooked him and herself a lovely supper of stewed rabbit and later treated him to some very affectionate lovey-dovey stuff. She existed on a part-time morning job and postal orders her daughters regularly sent her out of their wages. The prospect of having a postman husband, one as cheerful as Wally Briggs, made her fuss over him in a way that had him wondering where all the floating stars were coming from.

Off to the Camberwell Palace on Saturday evening went Kitty and the kids in company with Jamie. Kitty and the kids were in their Sunday best. Kitty had said it was the kind of auspicious occasion that called for their Sunday best. Jamie said their usual day wear would do as long as everyone had combed and brushed hair, and clean faces. Kitty said no, they'd got to dress nice for the theatre. Chloe said, when Jamie was up in his room, that she didn't think Kitty ought to tell him off so much. Kitty went into shock, then repudiated the charge. I wouldn't do a thing like that, it wouldn't be respectful of his age, I just tell him sometimes about things, but I don't tell him off, it wouldn't be right. Well, said Chloe, it's just that we don't want you to turn into a nagging woman. Kitty went into shock again, a worse one. She thought about it and realized that the way she'd been behaving with Jamie was all to do with getting him to be what they wanted him to be, their fatherly protector, whose presence and help would keep authority from splitting them up. Only this week, when she'd called at the town hall to collect the weekly parish relief ticket, she'd been asked what their situation was, and she'd said that it was inspiring. *Inspiring?* Yes, Mr Blair's looking after us like a real Christian gent and taking us to Sunday church as well, he wants my brother and sisters to be well-behaved and all of us to be respectable, which is very inspiring to us. Who's paying your rent? Authority was inquisitive. Mr Blair is, she said. Also, we've got another lodger to help with the rent, and now we're on regular parish relief we don't go hungry. Mr Blair is sort of fostering our stomachs. H'm, said authority, we'll send someone round to take a look at your circumstances. Excuse me, said Kitty, but our circumstances don't need looking at, they're clean and respectable. Well, we'll see, said authority, we'll see.

But oh, help, Chloe saying they didn't want her to turn into a nagging woman was awful. Jamie had taken to having a chat with Rosemary in her room in the evenings, and Kitty had had to speak to him about it, saying it could easy get the house a bad name. That wasn't nagging, was it? Oh, me gawd, suppose he himself thought it was? Kitty went all hot.

However, they did all wear their Sunday best to the theatre, and her insistence was rewarded when Jamie said they all looked good enough to eat, except Alfie. Alfie said thank goodness for that.

Jamie treated them to shilling seats in

the circle. Kitty and the kids were thrilled and awe-struck. The theatre looked ever so plush, and they felt ever so posh. Up in the sixpenny gallery seats, the people were noisy, sounding a bit common to Kitty. She was sensitive these days about making sure she and the kids didn't get to be common themselves. Being cockneys was all right, but not common. Common was being loud and using language, being near to hooliganism. Kitty was sure Jamie had never been a hooligan.

It was a variety performance this evening, which was as good as a music hall show. Kitty and the kids were fascinated and enthralled. Real live people on the stage, doing comic turns or singing well-known songs or doing a rendering of 'The Bells', which was awfully sad and gripping. During the interval they ate apples. Kitty had brought five in a bag. Teeth crunched into them and munched them.

'They ain't 'alf nice,' said Alfie.

'Ma Earnshaw let me 'ave them a bit cheap,' said Kitty.

'I thought so,' said Jamie, 'mine's got pips in it.'

'Oh, it 'asn't, 'as it?' said Kitty. 'I specially asked for—oh, what d'you mean, it's got pips in it? All apples 'ave pips.'

'Well, blow me,' said Jamie, 'did you hear that, Carrie?'

'Yes, we didn't know that before, did we?' said Carrie. 'Mister, ain't it lovely, bein' in a theatre? I'm goin' to tell Danny tomorrow that we went.'

'That's it,' said Jamie, 'then you can charge him a penny for the privilege of taking you to the park and talking to you.'

Carrie giggled. From the gallery came yells, and an apple core was chucked down into the stall seats.

'Noisy lot, they didn't ought to be let out of an evenin',' said Chloe.

'Tell yer what,' said Alfie, 'give me all yer apple cores and I'll do some chuckin' up.'

'You Alfie, don't you talk like that,' said Kitty, 'I'll 'ave all the cores back in this bag, if you don't mind.'

'Oh, all right,' said Alfie. 'I suppose that's more proper, don't you, mister?'

'It'll save you getting a thick ear,' said Jamie.

The second half began.

Mrs Reynolds, having a gossip with Mrs Fitch on the latter's doorstep in the evening sunshine, said, 'That man's been walkin' up an' down the street I don't know 'ow long. I 'appened to spot 'im from me parlour winder quite a bit ago.'

The man was well-dressed in a light

grey suit and dark grey Homburg hat, and at this moment he was approaching the two housewives. He stopped at the gate of Kitty's house and smiled at them.

'Excuse me,' he said, lifting his hat, 'would either of you ladies know if Miss Rosemary Allen lives here?'

'Yes, she's a lodger,' said Mrs Fitch.

The man, tall, handsome and forty-ish, smiled again.

'I've been hoping to have a word with her,' he said. 'I've knocked a couple of times, but there doesn't seem to be anyone in the house.'

'Well, they're all out at the Camberwell Palace,' said Mrs Fitch. 'Well, except Miss Allen, that is. I don't know where she could be.'

'She's 'ere,' said Mrs Reynolds. 'That's 'er, comin' down the street with a neighbourin' lodger, Mr Fitzpatrick.'

Rosemary, spotting the little group and recognizing the man, said to Mr Fitzpatrick, 'I can't invite you in, I know that man by the gate, he's an old friend of mine. Walk on to your own lodgings and don't say anything to embarrass me.'

'Right, me darling—'

'Particularly don't say anything like that.'

'That I won't,' said Mr Fitzpatrick cheerfully, not in the least jealous. He knew scores of women intimately in Ireland, Ulster and England, and he did not intend to stay in Walworth much longer. 'Goodbye to yez, Miss Allen,' he said when they reached the gate. He smiled at Mrs Fitch and Mrs Reynolds, gave the waiting gentleman a friendly nod, and went on to his lodgings.

'Hello,' said Rosemary to the waiting gentleman.

'Hello,' he said.

'Come in,' said Rosemary, but spared a moment to say a few words to the housewives. 'Isn't it a lovely evening? Excuse me while I renew acquaintance with a friend of mine.' She pulled on the latchcord and entered the house. The well-dressed gentleman followed her in and the door closed.

' 'E's a smart gent, I'll say that much,' murmured Mrs Reynolds.

'She's smart herself,' said Mrs Fitch.

'Well, there's them that's smart and them that's a credit to theirselves,' said Mrs Reynolds. 'Mind, it ain't for me to cast aspersions, but Kitty's lady lodger ain't in the same class as 'er gentleman lodger, Mr Blair.'

'I think Jamie can handle her,' smiled Mrs Fitch.

' 'E needs to,' said Mrs Reynolds, 'when she's out one day with 'im and with Mr

Fitzpatrick the next.'

'Well, she's single and fancy-free,' said Mrs Fitch.

'I 'ad a cousin once who was fancy-free,' said Mrs Reynolds. 'It was when I was a girl. Alma, that was 'er name. If she 'ad one feller, she 'ad twenty, and all at the same time. Still, she finally made up 'er mind that one of them for good was better than bein' left on the shelf by all twenty. But would yer believe, come the mornin' of the weddin' and there she was tellin' 'er mum she was marryin' the wrong one. "Well, that's a shame, that is," said 'er mum, "but the banns 'ave been read and you're goin' to the altar at twelve, me gel." So she went to the altar, and what d'yer think 'appened? Two months later she run orf with a young tram conductor, only two days after she'd met 'im on a number 18 tram comin' from the Elephant an' Castle. It don't do to get too fancy-free, it makes girls that disobedient to the laws of marriage, so I 'ope Mr Blair don't take up too serious with that Miss Allen, specially now she's invited that new gent into the 'ouse and no-one there to see what she gets up to with 'im.'

Two things happened an hour later, only five minutes after the gentleman had gone. Rosemary, wrapping a negligee around her well-shaped body, felt something touch her bare foot. She looked down, just as Alfie, Chloe and Carrie, back from the theatre, came pouring into the house. Return of those kids coincided with the return of that bloody white mouse. It was nibbling at her foot. An involuntary scream escaped her. The door was flung open and Jamie looked in.

'For God's sake, now what?' he asked.

'That damned white mouse, for God's sake!' hissed Rosemary.

'What?' Kitty looked in. She could hardly believe her eyes. Oh, that fast cat, wearing a negligee that didn't leave anything to the imagination. 'Well, excuse me, I'm sure, Miss Allen, but d'you mind not bein' nearly undressed so frequent? It's turnin' this house into one of them low common places.' The mouse whisked past her feet then and she saw it run into the passage. 'Here, what've you been doin' with that white mouse? We've been lookin' for it for ages.' She called. 'Alfie, come and get the mouse—you hear me, Alfie?'

Alfie darted from the kitchen.

'Mouse? Where is it?' he asked.

'In the passage,' said Kitty. Alfie spotted Rosemary then. He blinked.

'Crikey,' he breathed, his mouth falling open. 'Ruddy lovaduck,' he said, 'me eyesight's 'urting.'

'You Alfie,' cried Kitty, 'get that mouse!'

Alfie stopped goggling and went after the elusive creature.

Rosemary, recovering, said, 'I was just going to bed.' Jamie noticed a brown leather bag on the floor of the open wardrobe and a rather untidy heap of clothes and underwear on a chair. And the bed itself looked as if Rosemary had already been in it. 'Look,' said Rosemary, 'I don't like mice popping up all over the place. Is that white one being given the run of the house? I thought it was for a little girl who'd been unwell.'

'It got lost,' said Jamie, 'and it seems to have invited itself back to your bed.'

'Don't be funny,' said Rosemary.

'Mr Blair, d'you mind comin' out of here?' said Kitty. 'It's not decent, standin' there with Miss Allen undressed like she is. It's bad enough Alfie sufferin' a shock.'

'I ain't sufferin',' said Alfie, reappearing. 'Miss Allen, d'you want the mouse back? I've got it. Crikey, don't yer look—'ere, who's pushin' me?'

'I am,' said Kitty, and bundled him out. 'Go to the kitchen.' Alfie went. 'We'll say good night, Miss Allen, if you don't mind.'

'Yes, good night,' said Rosemary, and closed the door.

'That fast person ought to 'ave her

bottom smacked,' said Kitty on her way to the kitchen.

'Shall I do it?' asked Jamie.

Kitty's look of disgust told him what she thought of that suggestion.

When the kids had had their cocoa and gone to bed, she said, 'I couldn't hardly believe what I was seein.' No wonder Alfie nearly lost 'is eyesight, and no wonder you look embarrassed.'

'I can't say—'

'Mind you,' said Kitty, 'bein' embarrassed shows you've got gentlemanly feelings, so I won't say any more about it, specially as you've given all of us a lovely evenin' at the music hall. Thanks ever so much. All the same, you mustn't throw your wages about too reckless, you ought to—' She stopped and made a face. 'Oh, I'm doin' it again.'

'Doing what again?' asked Jamie, smiling.

'Tellin' you off. Have I been doin' a lot of that?'

'Only now and again,' said Jamie.

'Oh, lor',' said Kitty, 'I'll have to be more respectful.'

'You won't be half as much fun,' said Jamie.

'You're pullin' me leg,' said Kitty.

'Not much. Good night, Kitty.'

'Thanks ever so much again for takin' us all out,' she said.

Jamie had arranged to meet an old army comrade on Sunday. Leaving the house at ten in the morning he met Mrs Reynolds coming back from an early trip to the market.

'Well, good mornin', Mr Blair,' she said, her Sunday hat adorned with clusters of wax fruit.

'Same to you, Mrs Reynolds,' said Jamie.

'I must say Kitty and 'er little fam'ly look more of a credit to theirselves ev'ry day,' she said. 'It just shows what a bit of lovin' care can do, and don't you worry, Mr Blair, if one or two people give yer looks.' One or two people had been inclined to hand out looks on account of what had been said at the inquest, but Mrs Reynolds, Mrs Fitch and other neighbours had let them know they didn't think much of that unChristian attitude, which was downright uncalled-for.

'You're a good soul, Mrs Reynolds,' said Jamie.

'Well, yer a gent, Mr Blair, that you are,' said the good soul. 'Is the other lodger bein' an 'elp to Kitty?'

'Her rent's a great help,' said Jamie.

'Mind, she likes 'aving friends, don't she?' said Mrs Reynolds. 'There was that smart gentleman that called on 'er last night.'

393

'Last night?' said Jamie.

'Yes, while you was all at the Camberwell Palace. She invited 'im in, she said 'e was an old friend. Very distinguished, 'e looked.'

'I didn't meet him myself,' said Jamie, thinking of Rosemary in her negligee and her rumpled bed. 'He'd gone by the time we got back.'

'Oh, well, she's single and fancy-free,' said Mrs Reynolds who, like most Walworth ladies, liked to know exactly what was going on in the neighbourhood.

'Yes, she gets around,' said Jamie, 'and I must get on. 'So long, missus.'

He thought about Rosemary on his way to the tram stop in the Walworth Road. A naughty girl when she was in Belfast. And being naughty now she was living here, was she? With a distinguished-looking man? In her bed? Very naughty. And what about that large brown leather bag? She hadn't had it with her when she arrived, just a suitcase. Where had it come from, and what was in it? She'd got into trouble in Belfast. She'd given an explanation. Had it been true? Truth wasn't easy to come by in Ulster or Ireland these days. It might be a good idea to sneak a look at the contents of that bag.

Kitty and the kids missed having Jamie

around, and Kitty worried again in case his absence somehow meant he'd go off for good. Rosemary slept late, and then she went out too. Kitty hoped it was to meet Mr Fitzpatrick, because Mr Fitzpatrick was the kind of bold cheerful Irishman who wouldn't think twice, probably, about carrying her off to a fate worse than death. Kitty hoped, in a moment of Christian pity, that a fate worse than death wasn't actually as bad as breaking a leg. Of course, everyone knew a fate worse than death was pretty awful, and shocking as well, and that young ladies who suffered it didn't half kick and scream. Still, if that Rosemary Allen suffered it at the hands of Mr Fitzpatrick, smelling-salts might help her to recover, if she had some with her.

All that led Kitty to wonder what it would be like if Jamie went off his head over her telling him off and made *her* suffer a fate worse than death. I mean, she thought, if he was alone with me and got the rats with me, he could easy drag me up to his room and have his shocking way with me. I wouldn't dare to scream in case the neighbours came rushing in, I wouldn't want them witnessing his shocking behaviour, because they might send for the police, and I know I wouldn't want him sent to prison. Oh, lor', I'd have to suffer it. I'd best start carrying some smelling-salts about with me.

Chloe and Carrie went to Ruskin Park with their Scouts in the afternoon, and Alfie joined his mates. Mrs Fitch popped in, found Kitty alone and invited her next door. Kitty had Sunday tea with them and decided Mr and Mrs Fitch were really nice company. Mrs Fitch happily let slip that she was going to have another baby. Kitty thought that the best news ever. It meant Mrs Fitch wouldn't dream now of running off with Jamie.

Jamie was back just before eight that evening. He knocked on the kitchen door.

'Who's that?' called Chloe.

'Only me,' he said, and put his head in.

'Oh, you don't need to knock,' said Kitty.

'Yes, what did yer knock for?' asked Carrie.

'Well, I heard you giggling, Carrie,' said Jamie, 'and thought you and Chloe might be privately entertaining Billy and Danny.'

'Crikey, what a thought,' said Alfie. They were all having a Sunday supper of cold meat, left-over roast potatoes and pickle.

'Excuse me,' said Kitty, 'but I 'ope at

my age, which is nearly eighteen, that I wouldn't allow me young sisters to do private entertainin' in the kitchen with boys.'

'Oh, we wouldn't mind doin' it with Danny and Billy,' said the forthright Chloe. 'We'd do it ever so private, honest, Kitty.'

'Yes, an' we wouldn't 'ave to go be'ind trees, would we?' said the ingenuous Carrie.

'What's that she said?' asked Alfie.

'Yes, what was that you said, Carrie?' asked Kitty.

'Well,' said Jamie, sitting down with them, 'I suppose getting kissed behind trees in a park isn't as private as getting kissed in a kitchen.'

'You Carrie,' said Kitty, ' 'ave you and Chloe let them boys drag you behind trees and kiss you this afternoon?'

'Oh, 'elp,' breathed Carrie, going pink.

'You Chloe?' said Kitty.

'Me?' said Chloe, looking sweet and innocent, thought Jamie. 'Me?'

'Yes, you, my girl,' said Kitty, putting on a disapproving adult look. She had to let Jamie see she wasn't irresponsible in her role as Mum.

'I didn't say anything,' said Chloe.

'Cor lovaduck,' said Alfie, 'I think me twin sisters 'ave been accosted this afternoon, don't you, mister?'

'You girls,' said Kitty, 'don't you know it's downright unrespectable lettin' boys kiss you behind trees in a park?'

'Oh, 'elp,' said Carrie again, and gave Jamie an appealing look.

'Mind you, Kitty,' he said musingly, 'it's more private behind trees than in the open. When I was a boy I always kissed girls in private. What parents don't see they don't grieve about, and what they don't grieve about they don't wallop you for.'

'Cor bless me cotton socks,' said Alfie, 'if I get to kiss Mrs Fitch, I'll do it in private, when Mr Fitch ain't there. Well, 'e's bigger than me.'

'I can't hardly believe what I'm hearin',' said Kitty, 'all this talk about private kissin' and you not grown up yet, Alfie, nor you two girls, either. Who started it?'

All brown eyes turned on Jamie.

'H'm,' said Jamie. Chloe smiled. Carrie giggled, just a little. Alfie grinned. Kitty looked accusingly at her lodger.

'I'll 'ave to talk to you, Mr Blair,' she said.

'What, about kissin'?' asked Alfie.

'You'll get your ears boxed in a minute, my lad,' said Kitty.

'Any tea going?' asked Jamie.

'Oh, would you like some?' asked Kitty. 'I was just goin' to put the kettle on.'

'I'll do it,' said Jamie, 'you finish your supper.' He got up and filled the kettle.

Carrie whispered, 'Mister's ever so much nicer than that man was, ain't 'e?'

'Listen,' said Jamie from the scullery, 'if it's a fine Sunday next week, would you all like a tram ride to Purley and to go on the Downs? And to take a picnic?'

There was a breathless silence. Kitty swallowed. Carrie gulped. Chloe's eyes went blissful. Alfie blinked. No-one had ever taken them out into the country. None of them could remember a family outing, except once to Peckham Rye when their real dad had been alive. And that was when Alfie had only been three.

'Mister?' said Chloe.

'Well, what d'you think, is it a good idea or not?' asked Jamie, the kettle on the gas.

'Mister, you're ever so kind,' said Chloe.

Jamie glanced at them. They all looked as if he'd offered them a pot of gold instead of just a tuppenny tram ride to Purley. Not for the first time he felt touched. Ruddy bananas, he thought, I'm not only right in the trap, I'm doing my best to shut off the only exit. I'm not lodging with them any more, I'm living with them. Next thing, they'll take it that I'm a permanency, and that won't be their fault, it'll be my own. I'll have to start keeping to my room again. The most sensible thing I can do now is to cancel any outing next Sunday.

'All right,' he said, 'it's a good idea, then? Tram ride and picnic?'

'Oh, I wish it was next Sunday tomorrer,' said Carrie.

Kitty was too emotional to say a word. A family outing to Purley and the Downs? With Jamie taking them, just as if he really was their dad? Theirs, of course. Not hers. If she knew anything for certain among all her confusions, it was that she didn't want him for her dad.

And she was sure that if he ever got mad at her and she suffered a fate worse than death, she'd hardly mind at all.

Oh, me soul, what's happening to me?

At his work on Monday morning, Jamie was thinking again about Rosemary. The fact was that if she was a close friend of his parents, she might be as potty as they were. His mum had said she and his dad had given up supporting the IRA. But where did Rosemary's sympathies lie after her several years in Ulster? She had the kind of character that belonged to people who liked to get involved in events and causes. She might be a butterfly as far as men were concerned, but she was a bit of a mystery outside of that. She'd been out all

400

day yesterday, apparently. With whom?

' 'Ello, 'ello, fallin' asleep on the job, are yer, Blair?' His foreman, Josh Simmonds, had arrived behind him.

'No, just doing some eye calculations.' Jamie was regarding a door frame.

'You look as if yer standin' about to me. By the way, the guv'nor wants to see yer in the site office in fifteen minutes. Not before, not after, in fifteen minutes precise and exact. Got that?'

'Got it, Mister Foreman.'

Josh Simmonds grinned as he walked away. Something's tickling him, thought Jamie. And if it's tickling him a lot, it's at my expense. Am I getting the sack?

He resumed his work. Kitty entered his mind. There was a girl for living a vigourous life. There were no mysteries about Kitty. She was like an open book in what she was prepared to do to keep her little family together. Give her three good years, years of having enough to feed and clothe them all, and she'd turn herself into a beauty, the twins into charmers and Alfie into fearless sturdiness. All she needed was just enough money and a feeling of security.

'Hello there,' said Mr Robbins, the site manager, 'I wanted to talk to you, Blair.'

'Seriously?' said Jamie.

'Well, I don't tell jokes. It's like this. We're having trouble on this site.'

'So I've noticed. Some of the men are hustling the Irish brickies.'

'Can't blame 'em, I suppose,' said Mr Robbins. 'To some of us, all the Irish belong to the IRA. So we're transferring ours to Eastbourne and bringing in a home-grown gang of brickies.'

'Eastbourne?' said Jamie.

'Yes, we're building a terraced row of three-storeyed dwellings suitable for boarding-houses.'

'Can anyone afford to take them on these days?' asked Jamie. 'Can anyone afford a holiday?'

'Families that go to Eastbourne can. It's Margate and Southend that are feeling the pinch. The boss man has gone into all the pros and cons, and the Eastbourne Council have sold the land to him for peanuts. Further, George Parkins will be back on this site next Monday.'

'Who's George Parkins?' asked Jamie.

'The man whose job you're doing at the moment,' said Mr Robbins. 'Don't worry, we're not giving you notice. What we're doing is offering you a job at Eastbourne, which should last a good nine months. After that, we'll probably bring you back to London. We need some good skilled men at Eastbourne. You're not married, so how about it? We'll find you accommodation, and would like you to travel down next Monday, give you Tuesday to get yourself settled in, and have you start work on Wednesday. It'll be hard graft, the contract's got a time limit, so we'll up your wages to fifty bob. Fair?'

'Very fair,' said Jamie, 'but tricky.'

'Is it? Why?'

'I've got some unusual commitments.'

Mr Robbins rubbed his chin.

'It's a woman, is it?' he said. A slight smile showed. 'They're most of 'em unusual. Well, I'll give you a couple of days to decide.'

'My job here finishes, in any case, at the end of this week?' said Jamie.

'With George Parkins coming back, after breaking his leg, I'm afraid it does. That's why we're offering you Eastbourne.'

'I'll need the two days to think it over.'

'Fair,' said Mr Robbins. 'Let me know by not later than Thursday morning.'

Jamie thought he'd do some serious thinking during his midday break. Speaking to one of the men just after the hooter sounded, he received some unexpected information that sent him down to Brixton, to a cafe run by a fat, bald and jolly bloke, Tom Robinson. A snack in Tom's place was always a simple repast, but one that was cooked to perfection. And good value. A fried egg and bacon, with two slices of bread and marge, plus a cup of tea, cost sevenpence. Two fried sausages with tomatoes, plus the identical extras, also cost sevenpence. A poached egg on toast with a cup of tea cost sixpence. There were similar bargains to be had. Jamie, with two or three other men from the site, had patronized the cafe several times.

Today he ordered bacon and egg, and Tom's daughter Ivy came up with it in quick time, the bacon with just a slight touch of crispness to it, and the egg with a deep golden yoke. Jamie enjoyed it, then managed to have a word with Tom.

'I've just heard about Ivy's wedding,' he said.

'Well, good on yer, matey,' said Tom, 'I 'eard about it six months ago and not much else since. What I didn't 'ear about was that she was goin' off to bleedin' Barnet to live.'

'Now, Dad, I 'eard that,' said Ivy, rolling sausages about and letting them gently sizzle. 'Barnet ain't bleedin'.'

'From 'ere it is,' said Tom. 'Mind, to be fair, matey, she didn't know 'erself till a week ago, when 'er fiance come up with the news that 'is firm was movin' 'im there from Camberwell. Blow to me 'eart, that was, seein' she was goin' to stay on 'ere with the fryin'-pan for a bit. I dunno as I'll ever get anyone else to do the fry-ups as good as me Ivy. I 'ad some lippy tart come an' try 'er 'and on Saturday, but I tell yer, matey, what come out of me old reliable fryin'-pan didn't look like what went into it. It cost me five eggs, four sausages an' five rashers before me groaning 'eart turned to stone and I chucked 'er out.'

'I know a girl who's a natural,' said Jamie.

'Natural what?' asked Tom.

'Cook,' said Jamie.

' 'Ope yer mean it,' said Tom, 'I ain't young enough to appreciate what else females are natural at.'

'Not much,' said Ivy, handing a plate of sausages and tomatoes to a customer.

'Not in me cafe I'm not,' said Tom. 'Look, matey, I'll give yer girl a go. I got a couple tryin' their luck on Friday. Can yer girl come before then? Ivy'll show 'er the ropes, and I'd like to see 'ow she performs, but I 'ope it ain't goin' to cost me more bacon and eggs.'

'I'll get her to come tomorrow morning,' said Jamie. 'Her name's Kitty Edwards.'

'Ain't one of them school leavers, is she?' asked Tom.

'No, she's nearly eighteen.'

'Promisin',' said Tom, 'promisin'. Send 'er along, matey. Tell 'er the hours, nine-till-five-thirty, an' that she don't get a break till two. Twelve till two is me busiest time, yer see. And it's 'alf-days Wednesdays. Four bob a day includin' Wednesdays. Twenty-four bob a week. Mind, she'd better be good.'

'She's better than good,' said Jamie.

Chapter Eighteen

'The point is,' said Detective-Sergeant Watkins, as he turned into Larcom Street in company with a colleague, Detective-Constable Hurst, 'it'll be better to interview her before Blair, the lodger, gets back from his work. Together, they're a team. Divided, well, who knows, eh?'

'Still got suspicions, have you, sarge?' said Hurst.

'Fresh suspicions, me lad.'

'Ill-treated step-daughter conspires with lodger to do her step-father in?'

'If Mullins had a tidy amount of oof stacked away somewhere, why not?' said Sergeant Watkins. 'I'd call that a cast-iron motive.'

'And if the house is floatin' in quids,' said Hurst, 'I'd call it a cast-iron case.'

'Not cast-iron,' said Sergeant Watkins, 'but highly promisin'. Here we are.'

He knocked on the door of Kitty's house.

She opened it. Recognizing Sergeant Watkins, she made a face. For his part, the CID man thought what a nice-looking young lady she'd become. Nicely dressed too, and not a bit like the scarecrow of a girl who came to the station to report the death of her step-father.

'Oh, not you lot again,' said Kitty. 'Me brother and sisters will be 'ome from school in five minutes.'

'Mind if we come in?' said Sergeant Watkins. 'This is Detective-Constable Hurst. We have to talk to you, Miss Edwards.'

'Well, 'ard luck,' said Kitty, 'I've got to make a pot of tea and do some bread and jam for me brother and sisters. And then I've got to start preparin' supper.'

'We've got a search warrant, miss,' said Constable Hurst.

'A what?' said Kitty, staggered.

'A search warrant.' Hurst produced it. 'It entitles us to enter and search the house.'

'I 'ope you're not all goin' daft round at the station,' said Kitty. 'Search for what, might I ask?'

'We're investigatin' allegations that your late step-father carried out a robbery at a Peckham store last year,' said Sergeant Watkins.

Kitty might have let herself down then if her instincts hadn't put her immediately on her guard. Kitty had sharp instincts where survival and self-defence were concerned. They told her that on no account was she to admit she knew of the robbery or

408

the money. They also told her she had to keep things going until Jamie came in. Then they could stand together against the questions.

'A robbery?' she said. 'You're jokin'.'

'May we come in, miss?' asked Hurst.

'Well, I don't see I can keep you out if you've got a search warrant,' said Kitty, but without moving aside. 'I've never 'ad anyone come round here with a search warrant all me life, and I don't think me step-father did, either. I don't want the neighbours to know or they'll be givin' us looks, and Alfie and the twins are too young to be able to stand up to looks, so would you mind not wavin' that warrant about? Oh, 'elp, there goes Mrs Birch and she's seen me.' Kitty lifted a hand to the passing neighbour, and showed the most natural smile she could summon up. 'All right, she's gone by now. Look, I wasn't askin' you to show the warrant because I didn't believe you. It's just that it don't make sense to me. My step-father robbin' a store you said, and 'im only a dustcart driver that wouldn't 'ave the brains too? That's daft all right.'

'The allegations come from a believable source, Miss Edwards,' said Sergeant Watkins, who'd been to see Mrs Briggs himself. While admitting she was an old cow, she had sounded believable.

'Oh, the horse's mouth, I suppose,' said Kitty, playing for time. 'One of me step-father's partners in crime, I'm sure. Well, come in, then, don't keep standin' there. Excuse me if I sound ratty, but I am ratty.' The CID men stepped in, at which point Alfie, Chloe and Carrie came through the gate, all a little ruffled from an exuberant run home to tea and bread and jam. They stared at the two policemen. 'It's all right,' said Kitty, 'I've just got to talk to these gents in the parlour for a bit. You go through to the kitchen and I'll be with you soon as I can. Chloe can put the kettle on.'

'Yes, all right,' said Chloe, and she went through to the kitchen with Alfie and Carrie. Kitty took the CID men into the parlour, which looked a lot better now that the old sofa had been chopped up by Jamie and the second-hand one installed.

'Miss Edwards,' said Sergeant Watkins, 'we'd like—'

'Oh, you'll 'ave to hold on for a bit while I go and see to me fam'ly,' said Kitty. 'I won't be long. You can sit down, if you like.' Off she went to the kitchen, using up more time.

' 'Ere, Kitty, what're they after, them gents?' asked Alfie.

'Oh, they've just come about us and the house,' said Kitty, 'and about how we're

410

managin'. I think the council asked them to call. But don't worry, they won't be sendin' us to any home. Chloe, you make the tea, and you do some bread and jam, Carrie. And see that Alfie don't eat all the jam and the jar as well. When you've had what you want, you can all go out till supper.'

'Oh, 'ow excitin', I'm sure,' said Chloe.

'Chloe, can't we go and meet mister a bit later?' enquired Carrie.

'Bless me,' said Chloe, 'I wondered if you'd ask.'

Carrie giggled. Kitty returned to the parlour. The CID men were still on their feet, their hats off.

'All right,' said Kitty, 'I'm ready now.'

'We're obliged,' said Sergeant Watkins. 'First, we'd like—'

'Oh, just a tick,' said Kitty, 'I'd be grateful if you didn't start searchin' until me brother and sisters 'ave gone out. They're goin' out as soon as they've had a cup of tea and some bread and jam. Is that all right? Only they'll feel uncomfortable if you go searchin' while they're here.'

'Understood, Miss Edwards,' said Sergeant Watkins, 'and we'd like to ask you a few questions first, anyway.'

'Honest, the questions you've asked already,' said Kitty.

'Well, they've all helped to establish how

411

your step-father died, miss.'

'I thought the inquest did that,' said Kitty. 'I don't know why there had to be an inquest if it didn't mean anything.'

'It meant something, don't worry about that,' said Sergeant Watkins. 'The robbery is something else. Miss Edwards, would you mind tellin' me if you knew anything about it, anything at all?'

'Well, I'm blessed,' said Kitty, 'you don't think that man did the robbery and then came 'ome and told me all about it, do you? He never told me anything, except what he'd do to me if I didn't make something out of nothing. He never 'ad a decent conversation with me all the time he was our step-father. Anyway, I don't believe he did any robbery. I'd 'ave known if he did, and so would the kids. Well, I mean, he'd 'ave had money, wouldn't he? He'd 'ave had his pockets stuffed with it.'

'It amounted to a lot of money, would you think, miss?' asked Hurst.

'How do I know?' said Kitty.

Sergeant Watkins said, 'I have to inform you, Miss Edwards, that your step-father's sister, Mrs Hilda Briggs, assured us that he definitely carried out the robbery.'

'Some sister, I don't think,' said Kitty, determination keeping her defences shored up. She had a peculiar feeling that these

412

policemen were after something more than establishing her step-father's guilt. 'Fancy sayin' that sort of thing about her own brother, and 'im in his grave too. That's really speakin' ill of the dead, that is. If I'd been the police, I'd 'ave told her she ought to be ashamed of 'erself. Anyway, how did she know? She hardly 'ad anything to do with her brother, she only saw him about once a year, twice at the most, and I can tell you they weren't sort of bosom relatives. He didn't think much of her, and she didn't think much of him. You sure she didn't make the story up?'

'She might have done, but it didn't seem so to me when I interviewed her,' said Sergeant Watkins, and Kitty put her nose in the air in a gesture of disdain. It caused Detective-Constable Hurst a problem in keeping his face straight. Kitty felt certain of one thing, that that old bag Mrs Briggs wouldn't have mentioned she'd come here in search of the money. The police would have taken a stern view of that. 'Miss Edwards, are you positive you knew nothing of the robbery?'

'Yes, course I'm positive,' said Kitty, 'and I'm sure as well.'

'You had no suspicions of any kind?'

'Look, why should I 'ave had? If I'd thought he was a burglar, I'd say so, seein' you're askin'. But he just drove a dustcart.'

'There's no suggestion he did other jobs, miss,' said Constable Hurst.

'Oh, he didn't nick the Crown Jewels, then?' said Kitty.

'No, just the day's takings from a Peckham store,' said Sergeant Watkins.'

'How much was it?' asked Kitty.

'Close to a thousand pounds in notes.'

'A thousand pounds?' said Kitty. 'Don't make me laugh, I'll fall over. My step-father makin' off with all that much and bringing it 'ome here, is that what you're sayin' he did?'

'It's what Mrs Briggs alleges he did, Miss Edwards. She further alleges you knew about it.'

'I'll get 'ysterical in a minute,' said Kitty. 'I wish I 'ad known, I'd 'ave wanted to know why he wasn't spendin' some of it on us.'

'Some of the proceeds of a breakin' and enterin' job?' said Constable Hurst.

'Come off it,' said Kitty, wishing she had Jamie standing with her. 'Me and me brother and sisters were as good as down and out, and most days we were close to starvation. Would we 'ave cared where the money came from? You might, because you don't look as if you've ever starved or only 'ad rags to wear.'

'You're not wearin' rags now, miss,' said Sergeant Watkins.

'Well, bless me heart, ain't I really?' said Kitty. 'I should think I'm not, nor the kids. We've been usin' the money that was in me step-father's pockets, with a bit that was on the mantelpiece in 'is room. Over five pounds,' she said, exaggerating a little. 'It was all 'is wordly goods. And now we've got two lodgers and two lots of rent. Then we've got parish relief and a pound a week from Mr Blair for givin' him breakfast, supper and Sunday dinner, and doin' his washin' and ironing. Imagine that step-father of ours 'aving that much money in 'is pockets and on 'is mantelpiece when he died and not givin' us even tuppence of it to buy food with that day. I know he's gone to 'is grave now, but I can't 'elp sayin' he wasn't much of a man. There's dads round here that would pawn their souls to keep their children from goin' hungry.'

'Well, miss, you seem a lot better off now that your step-father's gone,' said Hurst.

'Well, young Alfie don't get 'is head knocked off—here, excuse me, just what d'you mean by that?'

'It could be said that your step-father's death was to your advantage,' observed Sergeant Watkins.

Kitty saw at once what that meant, and

she knew then she had been right in her feelings.

'I wish you 'adn't said that, mister, it's disgraceful and not even decent.'

'I don't want to upset you—'

'That's a laugh,' said Kitty, 'you've just done it.'

'Sorry, Miss Edwards, but considerin' all the ill-treatment you and your brother and sisters had to put up with, you must have felt at times that you'd be better off without your step-father.'

'Now you've really upset me,' said Kitty, temper fighting to unleash itself.

'Have I?' Sergeant Watkins was actually in admiration of her. 'Why?'

'I'm not simple, yer know, I can see what you're after. You're after makin' me admit I knew about the robbery and the money, and that I could get my 'ands on it if my step-father died.'

'Well, did you have thoughts like that, miss?' asked Constable Hurst.

'Don't be daft,' said Kitty.

'What's daft about it?'

'Use yer loaf,' said Kitty, eyes darkening to burnt sienna. 'If I'd known there was as much money as nearly a thousand quid in the house, I'd 'ave looked for it every time he was out drivin' his dustcart, wouldn't I? So would both of you if you'd been in our condition. You saw what I looked like when I came to your station to fetch you to the house. I know meself what I looked like, a scarecrow. Mister, if there's money in a house and four scarecrows livin' there, they'd 'ave all been lookin' for it every minute of every day.'

'I see,' said Constable Hurst. The girl had made a point, a good point, and he knew it. And he knew that Sergeant Watkins knew it.

'All the same, Miss Edwards, there's the fact that you seem considerably better off now,' said Sergeant Watkins, 'and we have to examine the possibility that it's due to other reasons than those you've mentioned.'

'Here, if you keep makin' aspersions like that, I'll 'ave the law on you,' fumed Kitty.

'Miss Edwards, we'll have to carry out a search.'

'Who's stoppin' you?' asked Kitty. 'I just want you to wait until me brother and sisters are out of the house.'

Alfie and the twins were taking their time, which Kitty didn't mind at all. She heard Alfie's voice and then laughter from Chloe. And then Carrie was faintly heard.

'I was only askin', wasn't I?'

'If you could hurry them up, miss?' said Constable Hurst. Time seemed to be flying.

417

'Well, I'll do me best,' said Kitty. The CID man accompanied her to the kitchen. She knew why. To see that she dealt only with the kids and not with anything illegal, like shifting wads of money from a dresser drawer, perhaps, and hiding it under the yard dustbin. Chloe, Carrie and Alfie were still sitting around the table, and looking as if they were entertaining each other. Kitty couldn't help feeling what a lot they deserved from life. Because of their step-father they could easily have turned into sneaky, crafty young miseries, bad-tempered and cheating. But they hadn't. Kitty thought that perhaps they all took after their natural dad. He had died when she was nine, and although her memories of him weren't all that clear, she did remember he'd been a laughing and hearty man. Her mother, well, she never liked to think about her mother. As for Alfie, Chloe and Carrie, there was a lovely change in their appearance and their activities. No more unhappy scampering to get out of their step-father's way, no more flinching from threatened blows, no more sad and hungry looks, just three young people finding life could be fun. And the change had been so quick really, beginning from the time when Jamie had sent Alfie out for fish and chips that evening. 'Come on,' she said. 'I want you all to go out now.'

'Yes, I've got to see about when I can clean Mrs Fitch's indoors winders again,' said Alfie, and jumped up. ' 'Ello, mister,' he said to Detective-Constable Hurst on his way out of the kitchen.

'Hello,' said Hurst. Carrie sidled shyly by him, but Chloe gave him a smile.

'We're managin' ever so well, mister,' she said, 'we ain't so poor now.'

'That's good,' said Hurst, and Chloe followed her sister.

'Well, you can start your search now,' said Kitty.

'We'd like you to come round with us, miss,' said Hurst.

'I'm goin' to, don't worry,' she said. 'I mean, if you're goin' to turn everything inside-out and upside-down, someone will 'ave to tidy it all up again, and it's not goin' to be me.' Sergeant Watkins joined them. 'I'm the landlady 'ere, you know, and I've got a duty to keep the house lookin' respectable, which it won't be if you don't put things back where you find them. I don't mind bein' 'elpful to policemen, even if you 'ave upset me, but I'm not goin' to be a skivvy.'

'We'll tidy up as we go,' said Sergeant Watkins. A professional though he was, with a professional's inclination to cop crooks and villains, this was one occasion when he was beginning to feel he wouldn't mind if his suspicions fell on stony ground. It was only his professionalism that made him discount his feelings. The search had to be made. He shook himself. 'We'll start with the bedrooms, Mike,' he said. A bedroom was always the most likely place. And he had Kitty's bedroom in mind, as well as the bedroom of her lodger, Blair. 'Will you come up with us, Miss Edwards?'

'I've just said I'm goin' to,' remarked Kitty. 'To make sure you put everything back in place. Mind, if you left me down 'ere, I could put the money in the coal bunker in the yard, couldn't I, if it was in the kitchen, say. Honest, Sergeant Watkins, it's a wonder I don't get really ratty with you.'

'I appreciate your feelings, Miss Edwards.'

Kitty climbed the stairs and they followed. She took them into the bedroom she shared with her sisters and let them go to work. She carried on a challenging conversation with them, while saying nothing about the fact that the house had already been turned over by Mrs Briggs and her two old lags. She told the CID men things like they weren't to rummage about in drawers because she and her sisters kept personal things there. She'd turn them out herself, she said. In this and other little ways she made the search time-consuming.

She was waiting in hope for Jamie. She thought about what he meant to her and her brother and sisters. She thought about what she wanted. She knew what she didn't want, and that was policemen and men in bowler hats knocking on the door.

She wanted something a lot better than that.

Noticing her face was a little flushed, Constable Hurst wondered if it was the flush of guilt. His search became keener.

Jamie turned into Larcom Street at twenty five to six. He'd had a quick tram ride from Streatham.

'Look, there 'e is,' said Chloe. She and Carrie were outside the vicarage. They'd had a little trouble with cheeky boys who wanted to get off with them. It was a new thing, boys wanting to get off with them, and ever such a pleasure, of course. If Carrie was a little hesitant about telling any boy to push off, Chloe wasn't. She was selective and positive. Being selective meant that only Billy and Danny could take them up the park. All other boys had to be told to push off.

Healthy girls now and much cleaner —Kitty had bought an old but still

serviceable tin bath down the market—
Chloe and Carrie ran to meet Jamie.
Jamie, who had to make a decision
about whether to go to Eastbourne or
not, experienced an uncomfortable little
pang.

'Hello, kids,' he said.

' 'Ello, mister,' said Carrie.

'We've been waitin' to meet yer,' said
Chloe.

'Good for you,' said Jamie, 'and nice for
me. But let's see, who's that with a loose
hair ribbon?'

'Chloe,' said Carrie.

'Well, I suppose it can't be helped at
this time of the day,' said Jamie. 'How's
the mum?'

'Oh, yer mean Kitty,' said Chloe, and
laughed.

'There's two men with 'er,' said Carrie.

'What men?' asked Jamie.

'She said they'd come about us, to see
'ow we're managin',' offered Chloe.

'Are they from the council?'

'Yes, I think so,' said Carrie, 'I think
that's what Kitty said.'

'Well, I'll have to take a look at them,'
said Jamie.

'Oh, I expect Kitty'll like you doin' that,'
said Chloe. 'She told us the other day it
was nice 'aving a good man around the
'ouse.'

'She didn't mean me, did she?'

'Yes, course she did,' said Chloe.

I'm facing a hell of a problem, thought Jamie. The point is, do I consider my own future first, or theirs? If Kitty lands the job with Tom Robinson, that'll take some care of her outgoings, especially if she can get another lodger after I've gone. I've a decent job myself now, enough to rent a small house and keep a wife who won't go mad every time she enters a shop. First find a wife, of course. Certainly, I fancy one.

Now let's see who these two men are.

When he walked in, Carrie and Chloe following, the CID men had just entered Rosemary's room, formerly the fortress of Henry Mullins. Seeing them there, Jamie immediately thought they were policemen who'd come to nail Rosemary for embezzlement and theft. Then he recognized Sergeant Watkins. That might still mean Rosemary was the target, but somehow he didn't think so.

'Hello, what's going on?' he asked, and Kitty drew a breath and gave him a grateful look. Her hidden worries faded away now that he was here.

'What're they doin' in Miss Allen's room?' asked Chloe.

'Chloe, you and Carrie go out again, just for a little while,' said Kitty.

'Yes, just for a while,' said Jamie. 'Buy yourselves some toffee-apples.' He gave them a penny each. Brown eyes swam with pleasure, and they went off happily then. Sharper cockney girls of fourteen would have had highly suspicious thoughts about the two men. Not so the twins. They happily left Kitty and Jamie to deal with them, whoever they were.

'Good evening, Mr Blair,' said Sergeant Watkins.

'What's up this time?' asked Jamie.

'They've got a search warrant,' said Kitty, 'they've come to look for money which they said my step-father pinched from a Peckham store.'

'Not quite, Miss Edwards,' said Sergeant Watkins. 'For the record, we've come to investigate allegations that he did the job, and that the proceeds are somewhere in this house.'

'Yes, and what about what you alleged yourselves?' said Kitty. 'What about you sayin' that because of the money I might 'ave—'

'We'll do the talkin', Miss Edwards,' said Sergeant Watkins.

'Well, that's the way of it, miss,' said Constable Hurst. 'We do the talkin' and askin', and you give the answers.'

'Fat lot of chance I've got of givin' you enough answers,' said Kitty, finding new

424

resolution now that Jamie was standing with her. 'I suppose if you took away a hundred answers with you today, you'd still want another 'undred tomorrow.'

'Yes, you're putting Miss Edwards through it a bit, aren't you?' said Jamie. 'What the hell would she know about burglaries and proceeds?'

'It's like this, sir,' said Sergeant Watkins, and explained exactly why he and Detective-Constable Hurst were here. Jamie had to make a guess about what Kitty had said. Since she didn't look flustered or uneasy, he made a guess that she'd stood her ground in the most sensible way.

'That's a crazy piece of news,' he said. 'You're serious? You're saying Mrs Briggs made these allegations about her brother, and about Miss Edwards probably knowing the money was in the house?'

'That's correct, Mr Blair, and I can't say it's all that crazy. We might have birds of a feather in Mrs Briggs and her brother. Mrs Briggs was sentenced last week to six months in prison for habitual shopliftin' and assault.'

'What?' gasped Kitty.

'The silly old woman,' said Jamie.

'She was quite definite, sir,' said Sergeant Watkins. 'She assured me her brother told her he'd done the job, and that the proceeds are in this house. Accordingly, we've suggested to Miss Edwards that she knew about it.'

'Bloody marvellous,' said Jamie. 'It's all cockles and muscles. In short, codswallop.'

'On the other hand, sir,' said Sergeant Watkins, 'there's the fact that Miss Edwards and her brother and sisters are very much better off since the death of their step-father.'

'They're what? Look, sergeant, all they've got is twenty-four bob a week from me for my board and lodging, plus six bob a week from their other lodger, whose room you're in at the moment. The house rent has got to come out of that, leaving nineteen bob to feed and clothe all four of them. That's just the basics. You call that very much better off? They're not in the desperate state they were before their step-father died, that's true, but they're still up against it.'

'All the same, Mr Blair, they are better off and they've managed to get hold of good clothes. We've seen their wardrobes.'

'They managed, sergeant, to fit themselves out with some decent clothes from the money found on their step-father,' said Jamie. 'Saints alive, are you actually suggesting a motive?'

'A motive for what, sir?' asked Constable Hurst.

'For doing Mullins in,' said Jamie.

'Oh, me gawd,' breathed Kitty, 'I'm hearin' things.'

'It's our job, miss, to look into what could or couldn't be,' said Hurst.

'Whether we like it or don't like it,' said Sergeant Watkins stubbornly.

'Do some thinking,' said Jamie. 'First of all, remember that at the time in question everyone was in the house. Miss Edwards, her brother and sisters, and their step-father. And so was I. Now, if you're suggesting Miss Edwards's motive for getting rid of her step-father was to lay her hands on the proceeds of that robbery, you'll first have to prove she knew the money was in the house. Then, if you're going to suggest she persuaded me to help her, perhaps you'll explain why we set about it with her brother and sisters here. Now, supposing we did grab the chance to knock him down the stairs, how could we be certain it would kill him? I think you said more than once that it beat you how a man could kill himself falling down stairs. Further, suppose there'd been no heart attack? We'd have had to follow him down the stairs and beat him to death. We'd have done that with the boy and his twin sisters still around? And even if we had, we'd have needed a doctor to say that the fatal injuries were caused by the fall. It doesn't add up, sergeant, and it won't hold up, either. Would you like to do some fresh thinking?'

Oh, thought Kitty, am I glad he's here. He's made Sergeant Watkins look as if he's got stuck with a Chinese puzzle.

'You'd have made a good lawyer, Mr Blair,' said Sergeant Watkins. 'All right, I'll do some fresh thinking. But there's still that robbery and the proceeds, and the fact that Mrs Briggs swore the money was here somewhere. Miss Edwards, we'll have to complete our search.'

'Go on, then,' said Kitty, standing beside Jamie. His hand touched hers, he gave her fingers a reassuring squeeze. Oh, Lord, thought Kitty, I know now what's been happening to me.

They watched the CID men go to work. There was only this room and the kitchen to do now. The first thing Detective-Constable Hurst did was to open the wardrobe. Immediately the brown leather bag came to his eye. He picked it up and placed it on the bed.

'Who does this belong to?' he asked.

'Miss Allen, who's renting this room,' said Jamie.

'Do we open it, sarge?' asked Hurst.

'Yes,' said Sergeant Watkins, and Hurst attempted to spring the catch. But it was locked. He took a penknife out of his jacket pocket, opened up a blade and used the point of it to expertly free the lock. He pulled the bag open. There were three brown paper parcels inside. He lifted them out and placed them on the bed. Sergeant Watkins unwrapped all three to disclose a small alarm clock, sticks of dynamite, a detonator, a dry battery and some thin wire leads. 'Bloody hell,' he said.

Chapter Nineteen

Chloe and Carrie, talking to a street friend, saw their other lodger, Miss Allen, walking towards them and looking ever so posh in one of her light summer costumes and a little hat. Quite liking her, they went to meet her.

'Hello,' said Rosemary, 'isn't it your suppertime?'

'Yes, it is really,' said Chloe, 'but there's two men in the 'ouse.'

'They're talkin' to Kitty and Mr Blair,' said Carrie.

'Yes, and in your room,' said Chloe.

'In my room?' Rosemary came to a halt. Two men? Had the law caught up with her, then? She'd felt so safe in her Walworth lodgings. 'What kind of men?'

'Oh, from the council,' said Carrie.

'Yes, that's what Kitty told us,' said Carrie. 'She said they'd come to see if we were managin' all right.'

'Oh, council busybodies,' smiled Rosemary. 'Well, I'll stick up for you, Carrie, all of you. Leave it to me.' She went on to the house and entered by using the latchcord. She walked briskly through the passage and into her room. Jamie, Kitty and the two men were around her bed, and on the bed was the brown leather bag, open, and next to it items quite foreign to her. She stared at them. Kitty stared at her, and Jamie regarded her like a man who thought her a bad mistake on her parents' part. He thought, naturally, that she was in trouble because of a connection with the IRA, not because of any love affair, and he was furious with his mother for landing her on him. He had decided that the distinguished-looking man referred to by Mrs Reynolds was an agent of the IRA, and that the bag and its contents had passed from him to Rosemary. He had further decided the man was her lover.

Kitty said to Sergeant Watkins, 'This is Miss Allen.'

'For God's sake,' said Rosemary, 'what's that stuff on my bed?'

'I'd say they're the ingredients of a time bomb,' said Constable Hurst.

'A what?' Rosemary stared at the alarm clock.

'Miss Allen, we're police officers,' said Sergeant Watkins, 'and you'll have to explain why you're in possession of items capable, when fitted together, of causing an almighty explosion. I don't like it, miss, and nor does Detective-Constable Hurst here.'

'Well, I hate it,' said Rosemary, 'but don't look at me, that stuff isn't mine, nor the bag.'

'It was in the wardrobe,' said Hurst, 'with your clothes.'

Rosemary was galled to her trimmed eyebrows. Sean Fitzpatrick, the swine. He'd made a fool of her. Worse, he'd used her in a way typical of his kind. She didn't doubt now that his kind related to the IRA.

'That bag is not mine,' she insisted. Jamie was silent. He wished to say nothing that would push her deeper into the mire. She was far enough in as it was, up to her pretty neck. He could only hope she'd be able to dig herself out. 'Do you hear?' she said to Sergeant Watkins. 'It's not mine, and what was in it isn't mine, either.'

'I'm Detective-Sergeant Watkins, miss, and as things are it looks to me as if you're in serious trouble. This is a matter we'll have to refer to Scotland Yard. All right, you say the bag and its contents aren't yours. Right, then, let's hear how it came to be in your possession.'

'I was asked to look after it for a while,' said Rosemary, 'and when it was first shown to me it contained three birthday presents.'

'Come again, miss?' said Constable Hurst.

'It contained three birthday presents

when I first looked into it,' said Rosemary, feeling sick at the way Fitzpatrick's deceit had landed her on a bed of nails. And since she thought these CID men were here to arrest her on a charge that had originated in Belfast, she was doubly sick.

'Birthday presents?' said Sergeant Watkins, looking as if something was hurting his ears.

'Yes,' said Rosemary. Kitty glanced at Jamie. His expression was grim.

'Who owns this bag if you don't?' asked Sergeant Watkins.

'Mr Sean Fitzpatrick,' said Rosemary.

'And who's he?'

'Excuse me, sergeant,' said Kitty, 'Mr Fitzpatrick lodges a few doors down the street with Mr and Mrs Murphy. He brought that bag in one evenin' when Miss Allen was out.' That was the evening when her fast female lodger had come back to her room all flea-bitten and had gone out with Jamie and got drunk. Mr Fitzpatrick had knocked at the door and asked to see Miss Allen. Kitty said she was out. 'Ah well, me darling,' he had said, 'never mind, just let me leave this bag in her room.' Kitty said all right, and he carried it in and put it on the bed. 'That's 'ow it got in here, mister.'

Hell's bells, thought Jamie, is Rosemary an operative or an idiot?

'That's a fact, is it, Miss Edwards?' asked Sergeant Watkins.

'Course it is,' said Kitty.

'Is Mr Fitzpatrick Irish?'

'He's Irish,' said Rosemary bitterly. 'Look, let me give you all the facts.' She did so, recounting her meeting in the West End with Fitzpatrick, whom she'd become acquainted with, and all the details concerning the brown leather bag, including how he had deposited it in the parcels office at Charing Cross Station and collected it later, and how she had agreed to look after it for him for a while.

Jamie, relieved at being able to believe her, said, 'You simpleton.'

'All right, I'm an idiot,' said Rosemary. 'Sergeant Watkins, what made you look for the bag?'

'We're here in connection with another matter,' said Sergeant Watkins.

'A matter that required us to search the house,' said Constable Hurst.

'That's by the way,' said Sergeant Watkins, and Jamie appreciated that tactful touch. 'The point is, Miss Allen, we've only your word that the bag contained a bottle of Yardley's and two other store-wrapped presents. I hope you see that. It's a fact that you're in possession of explosives, and there's nothing more serious than that these days, except for murder.'

434

'Oh, come on, sergeant,' said Rosemary, feeling a lot better now that she knew he wasn't here to arrest her for the Belfast affair, 'how on earth could I have known the swine changed the contents?'

'Did he change them?' asked Sergeant Watkins. 'If you hadn't been taken ill, wouldn't you have gone to the theatre with him, as arranged, and wouldn't he have brought you back here and handed the bag to you then?'

'Oh, hell,' said Rosemary.

'Wait a minute, sergeant,' said Jamie, 'when he sent her off in the taxi, he could have given her the bag then, but he didn't.'

'I'll be frank,' said Rosemary, 'I didn't want to be bothered with it then.'

'He might still have persuaded you.'

'Miss Allen, where do you come from?' asked Sergeant Watkins.

'Chester,' said Rosemary.

'And what made you come here and take up lodgings which happen to be close to Mr Fitzpatrick's?'

'I was offered a job in the City,' said Rosemary. 'Look, I'd no idea Mr Fitzpatrick lodged in this street.'

'But you seem to have made a close acquaintance of him. How long have you been here?'

'Oh, just a few weeks,' said Rosemary.

435

'I'm single and I like to make acquaintances.'

Kitty wondered why she hadn't said she'd come from Belfast and that she was a friend of Jamie's mother. But since Jamie was keeping quiet, Kitty kept quiet too.

'I think you're still in trouble, Miss Allen,' said Sergeant Watkins, 'and I think Scotland Yard will want to interview you. You're not to leave your lodgings here, and you're not to leave London.'

Jamie, catching hold of a thought, said, 'Sergeant, isn't it possible that there might be another bag? One that might still be in the Charing Cross parcels office?'

'What's that, sir?' asked Constable Hurst.

'Well, I'd say, wouldn't you, that Fitzpatrick did a carefully planned job,' said Jamie. 'For some reason, and assuming Miss Allen isn't in the bomb-making business but merely wants her brains tested, he needed her to look after the bag for a while. He knew she'd want to know what was in it, so he bought three presents. She took a look and was satisfied, and he then deposited the bag at Charing Cross. Later he collected it. But it might not have been the same bag, especially if you agree he'd thought carefully about it. Identical, yes, but not the same.'

'Mr Blair, are you thinkin' what I'm

436

thinkin'?' asked Sergeant Watkins. 'That the bag he showed Miss Allen might still be at the parcels office, and that he deposited this one earlier? That when he collected, he handed in the ticket for this one?'

'Crikey, yes, he could 'ave been crafty enough, couldn't 'e?' said Kitty, feeling sort of proud of Jamie.

'Would Mr Fitzpatrick be back from his work now, would anyone know?' asked Constable Hurst.

'He doesn't go to work,' said Rosemary, 'he told me he came into a little money and doesn't need a job for the time being. He might be in his lodgings now, and he might not.'

'Well, he's on some kind of work,' said Sergeant Watkins. 'A nasty kind, I'd wager. Frank, go back to the station, report to Inspector Dodds, ask him to come here, and then take a uniformed man with you to the parcels office at Charing Cross. Get them to go through deposited items and see if they're still holding a bag like this one. If yes, take possession of it.'

'In the name of the law, of course,' said Hurst.

'Of course. And hurry it up.'

' 'Ere, why can't we go in for supper yet?' asked Alfie of his twin sisters.

'Because we can't,' said Chloe. 'Me and Carrie's just been, an' Kitty said to stay out a bit longer. She said she'll call us when she's ready.'

'I might as well go and 'ave supper with Mrs Fitch,' said Alfie.

'Why don't you, then?' asked Carrie.

' 'Cos she ain't invited me,' said Alfie. 'But I bet she would if she knew I was starvin'. I told yer a couple of times I fancied 'er—'

'You soppy bit of string,' said Chloe, ' 'ow can a boy your age fancy a married lady that's as old as Mrs Fitch? I bet she's as much as twenty-five.'

'That don't make no difference,' said Alfie. 'When you're a married lady that age, people might still fancy yer. That's if yer as pretty as Mrs Fitch. Cor, I fancy 'er something shockin'.'

'You ain't people,' said Chloe, 'you're only a kid.'

'Chloe, I'll 'ave to bash you in a minute,' said Alfie.

'I'll bash you back,' said Chloe, 'an' so will Carrie. And we'll kick you as well.'

'No, listen,' said Alfie, 'I can't 'elp meself, I do fancy Mrs Fitch, an' what I was goin' to tell yer is that I think she's beginnin' to fancy me.'

Chloe shrieked with laughter. Carrie giggled.

'Oh, Alfie,' she said.

'What's funny?' asked Alfie.

'Mrs Fitch fancyin' you,' said Chloe.

'Listen,' said Alfie, 'she nearly give me a cuddle when I left a few minutes ago.'

'Only nearly?' asked Carrie.

'Well, yes,' said Alfie, 'she couldn't give me a proper one because Mr Fitch 'ad just come in from 'is work. 'E ain't a bad bloke, yer know, but 'e's gettin' to be a bit of a nuisance at times. I mean, just when me an' Mrs Fitch are gettin' a bit romantic, 'e always comes in and interrupts. Still, she's goin' to 'ire me to clean 'er indoors winders again next Saturday. If she gets to be alone with me, I'll know she fancies me. She said to me an hour ago, she said "Yer a nice young man, Alfie, I 'ope you 'ave a nice future." So I said if she'd like me to take 'er up the park some time in me future, I'd be honoured. She said what a lovely idea.'

'Chloe,' said Carrie, 'd'you really think Alfie ain't all there?'

'Well, 'ow can 'e be, when 'e talks as barmy as 'e does?' said Chloe. 'Oh, look, there's another bloke goin' into our 'ouse.'

A sturdy man in a bowler hat, having come from the direction of Brandon Street, had turned in at their gate.

What followed a few minutes later mainly concerned the gregarious Mr Fitzpatrick. Detective-Inspector Dodds and Detective-Sergeant Watkins found he was in his lodgings and cornered him in his room. Mr Fitzpatrick, not the kind of Irishman to come quietly, made a bull-like attempt to burst through them. Inspector Dodds, solid as a rock, and Sergeant Watkins, sinewy with muscle, stopped him and downed him. Mr Fitzpatrick, not quite as cheerful or good-natured as usual, swore he'd see them in hell at very short notice. Inspector Dodds, who had brought handcuffs, did what was necessary with the help of his sergeant. Mr Fitzpatrick issued oaths so loud, violent and blasphemous that they shuddered into the ears of Mr and Mrs Murphy standing halfway up the stairs.

Further, if Mr Fitzpatrick thought Mr Murphy had treacherously informed on him, he soon discovered, when he was taken to Kitty's house and confronted with Rosemary and certain evidence, that the discovery of his bag in her wardrobe had been responsible for his arrest. He was questioned, of course, but refused to say anything except that hell was made for the English. Which made Rosemary say that his kind had turned Ireland into a hell for everybody.

Two uniformed constables arrived with

a Black Maria. Inspector Dodds had no intention of walking the Irishman to the station. Larcom Street was buzzing by this time, people out at their gates and kids crowding close to the Black Maria. Alfie, Chloe and Carrie were agape and goggling. Adults goggled too when Mr Fitzpatrick, handcuffed, was brought out of Kitty Edwards's house and forcibly bundled into the police vehicle. One uniformed man, together with the two CID men, kept Mr Fitzpatrick close company as the Black Maria was driven away.

Two more uniformed men arrived and completed the search of the house. Sergeant Watkins, in a temperate mood towards Kitty, had suggested that because it had to be done, it would be better, wouldn't it, to get it over with rather than descending on her again like a sack of potatoes from a police allotment. Kitty agreed. So did Jamie. Accordingly, the search was resumed and completed. It took in the scullery and the back yard lav, as well as the kitchen and Rosemary's room.

Nothing was found. Rosemary was curious, of course, and Jamie told her what it was all about—a robbery, said to have been carried out by Kitty's step-father. Rosemary said Kitty had had to put up with the kind of things that would try the patience of Christ himself. I'm going out, she said, and out she went, escaping a place that did not really suit her.

Detective-Constable Hurst and a uniformed man returned to Rodney Road police station from Charing Cross. Hurst was carrying a brown leather bag. In it were three birthday presents. The bag had been at the parcels office since Mr Fitzpatrick deposited it. It put Rosemary in the clear.

Chapter Twenty

The evening was well on. Jamie had kept naturally inquisitive neighbours at bay. More of them were swarming around Mrs Murphy, a few doors down, poor woman. Still, she had the kind of agreeable tongue that hardly ever tired out. Walworth women liked agreeable tongues, they were good for long and informative gossiping. There was nothing as pleasurable as an informative gossip, except perhaps a nice cup of tea. So Mrs Murphy, who liked Walworth and her neighbours, made a large pot.

Alfie, Chloe and Carrie, having been told by Kitty that the palaver had all been to do with Mr Fitzpatrick, who'd turned out to be a funny kind of Irish bloke—funny peculiar—felt they might now mention what was on their minds but not in their stomachs. Supper.

'Oh, I'm sorry, loveys,' said Kitty, 'I expect you're all starvin'.'

'Well, I don't feel full up,' said Carrie, 'not exactly I don't.' She glanced at Jamie. She saw him as one of the family now. 'D'you feel full up, mister?'

'Not exactly I don't,' said Jamie. 'Tell

you what, to save Mother cooking at this time of day, suppose we all have fish and chips? Or hot faggots and pease pudding?'

Alfie, Carrie and Chloe all voted loudly for fish and chips. Hot faggots and pease pudding were best in winter.

'I'll go,' said Alfie. 'Mister, did yer say Mother? Did yer mean Kitty? Mister, she ain't old enough to be our muvver, not like Mrs Fitch. Did I tell yer I think she's startin' to fancy me? She'd 'ave give me a cuddle this evening if Mr Fitch 'adn't come in.'

'That boy's gettin' barmier all the time,' said Chloe.

'Yes, can't 'e just go an' get the fish an' chips?' asked Carrie.

'I ain't been given no money,' said Alfie.

Jamie gave him enough and off he went, at a fast run.

Kitty said, 'Oh, with all the palaver, I forgot, there's a letter for you, Mr Blair.'

'What's she call 'im Mr Blair for?' whispered Carrie to Chloe. ' 'E's Jamie.'

'Yes, but 'e's more our dad than that man ever was,' whispered Chloe, 'and yer can't call 'im Jamie.'

'We could if 'e was our big brother,' said Carrie, 'and I was only askin' about Kitty callin' 'im Mr Blair.'

444

Jamie, seated at the table, was reading his letter, another one from his daft mum, except that she had important news to impart. She said she and his dad had actually met a Russian Bolshevik, he'd come to talk to the shipyard workers, only the bosses hadn't let him. He was going to see if could arrange for her and Jamie's dad to go to Moscow and see Comrade Lenin's working-class Utopia. Did Jamie want to go? Please to let her know quick. Also, he was to tell Rosemary the good news that Mrs Lindsay had dropped all charges against her. Mr Lindsay had persuaded her to. Mr Lindsay had been to London just recent, had accidentally bumped into Rosemary and found her sorry and penitent, and he'd persuaded his wife to forgive her. Wasn't that comradely of both of them? It just shows Mr Lenin's kind of comradeship is spreading all over, which is an object lesson to capitalists. Mind, tell Rosemary it's best not to come back to Belfast yet. You said in a letter that Rosemary had told you all about the Lindsays and the silly things she did, so you'll be as pleased as I am to pass the news on to her. Don't forget to let me know if you want to come to Moscow with us, as we have to sign all kinds of documents. We could all join the Bolshevik Party if you fancied it, and work for the good of the Russian peasants that's been oppressed for so long. Look after yourself now, your dad sends his usual regards.

'Is that from your mum?' asked Kitty, as Jamie folded the letter.

'Yes,' he said, 'the one a little barmy about politics.'

'Here, you shouldn't call yer own mum barmy,' said Kitty.

'All right, daft, then,' said Jamie.'

'That's not respectful,' said Kitty, then thought of how he had stood with her and how he had talked such sense to the police. She couldn't help thinking him a man who wasn't afraid of life or unpleasant people or the police, and that some young lady would get a lovely husband if she married him. Oh, lor', I hope she don't, whoever she is. 'Who'd like a nice cup of tea now I'm recovered from all the palaver?' she asked.

'Me,' said Chloe.

'Me too,' said Carrie.

'Me three,' said Jamie.

'No, I didn't say two,' said Carrie, 'it was tee-oh-oh.'

'Well, I said three-oh-oh.'

'You didn't,' said Carrie, 'did 'e, Chloe?'

'You don't always 'ave to ask,' said Chloe.

'Well, I don't always,' said Carrie, 'not

always, do I, mister?'

'No, not always,' said Jamie, and lightly ruffled her hair. That, he thought immediately, was the wrong thing to do. It had made Carrie smile with pleasure.

By the time Kitty had made a pot of tea, Alfie was back with the fish and chips, rock salmon having been his choice again. The kitchen, which had been suffering an inflicted atmosphere of sobriety, came to life in rapturous response to the aroma of the unwrapped fish and chips. Kitty and Jamie put aside the strain of a prolonged ordeal, and everyone sat down to the meal with healthy hunger. They drank hot tea with it.

'Oh, ain't fish an' chips lovely?' said Carrie.

'We've 'ad it twice since mister's been like a dad to us,' said Chloe.

'We never 'ad it all with *him*,' said Alfie.

'Well, 'e wasn't ever a proper dad to us,' said Chloe.

'We don't want to talk about that man,' said Kitty, not for the first time. Her nerves were a little on edge. It hadn't been exactly blissful, facing up to police suspicions that she might actually have conspired with Jamie to do her step-father in on account of some money that had remained invisible except for fifty pounds. She was sure she'd have eventually flown into a fury if Jamie hadn't arrived just when she most needed him. Oh, what a blessing that right from the start they hadn't said anything about him putting a hand on her step-father's chest to hold him off. That Sergeant Watkins really would have made a meal of it, with afters as well. Still, he'd been nice to her at the very end, just before he left. I promise you, it's all over, he'd said, except that the robbery is still an open case. But only the robbery.

Jamie, knowing he had to touch on another subject, said, 'By the way, I'm finishing at Streatham at the end of the week.'

'What?' said Kitty.

'Crikey, won't you 'ave no job again?' asked Alfie.

'I've been offered the same kind of work in Eastbourne,' said Jamie.

That did it. The brown eyes, all eight of them, turned his way and stared at him. Oh, my God, he thought, don't I get to have a future of my own?

'Eastbourne?' said Alfie.

'But, mister,' said Chloe, 'you can't get to Eastbourne on a tram.'

'Can't 'e go on a bus?' asked Carrie.

'No, course 'e can't, you silly,' said Chloe, 'Eastbourne's 'undreds of miles away.'

448

'Course it's not,' said Alfie, 'it's near Brighton, an' you can cycle to Brighton. Mind, it takes two days.'

Kitty swallowed.

'You're goin' to Eastbourne to work?' she said to Jamie.

'I've got to give it some thought,' he said. 'But listen, there's a cafe in Brixton, just by the market. It's run by a bloke called Tom Robinson. He serves eggs and bacon, and other snacks like that. His daughter does the frying. She's leaving to get married. He needs someone to take her place. It's twenty-four bob a week, Kitty, and I mentioned you. Well, you want a job, I know, and he's willing to take you on if you can do good fry-ups. I told him you'd be an asset.'

'What?' Kitty could concentrate on nothing except the fact that he was going to leave them. It was coming to an end, the feeling of security he gave them. 'What did you say?'

'You need a job. I think you could walk into this one, Kitty.'

'Which one?'

'At Tom Robinson's cafe by the Brixton market.'

Kitty, coming to a little, said thanks very much. Jamie said he'd arranged for her to go there tomorrow and show Tom how she could handle a frying-pan. Alfie,

Chloe and Carrie looked from one to the other of them and said nothing for the moment. Kitty said she'd be pleasured, of course, as she'd been dying all her life to fry bacon and eggs in a cafe in Brixton. Jamie said better than factory work, Kitty. Oh, do you think so, how kind of you, said Kitty. Acute depression began to sink beneath a rising tide of ragefulness. It'll help you, a wage of twenty-four bob a week, said Jamie. I can hardly wait, said Kitty, and I do hope it keeps fine for you in Eastbourne. Not much, I don't think, she said to herself, I hope you fall off the pier, if they've got a pier. I haven't quite made up my mind, said Jamie, but on the other hand I can't afford to be without a job again. Oh, no, that wouldn't do, would it, said Kitty, you've got to think about yourself, haven't you? We wouldn't want you out of work again, even if you had to go all the way to Japan or somewhere for it. We wouldn't mind a bit, would we?

'I would,' said Chloe, breaking her silence. 'Mister, ain't you goin' to come back again?'

'I haven't gone yet, Chloe,' said Jamie.

'Still, when you do go,' said Carrie, brown eyes a little sad, 'please could yer send us a picture postcard, mister?'

'Several, if I do go,' said Jamie. Oh, hell, he thought, I'm fighting a battle

450

here, not so much with them as myself. I've got to have a job, that's a number one consideration. If I could get a decent one anywhere in South London, I'd gladly stay with these kids. But two pounds ten a week in Eastbourne, that's a wage I can't easily turn down. 'Of course, Kitty, you'll need a new lodger to help with the rent still—'

'Oh, I expect a prosperous one will turn up,' said Kitty, 'and pay all our rent for us. Me and the twins can do dances for 'im in the parlour on Sundays, and he might start courtin' me. I'd like a prosperous 'usband, I wouldn't mind if 'e was a bit fat and bald as long as he 'ad a lot of prosperity.'

'Blow that,' said Alfie, 'I ain't goin' to let you marry someone a bit fat an' bald, Kitty.'

'Ugh,' said Chloe.

'Beggars can't be choosers,' said Kitty, steaming inside. 'I'll put a card in the newsagents, sayin' we've got a nice upstairs front for a prosperous lodger and that I do dances in the parlour on Sundays.'

'I ain't goin' to let you,' said Alfie, 'it just ain't proper, you doin' a knees-up for some bloke and showin' yer legs just to make 'im marry yer.'

'Kitty's got nice legs,' said Chloe.

'Specially in 'er new Sunday stockings,' said Carrie. She whispered to Chloe.

451

'Couldn't she do a dance for mister?'

The whisper was heard.

'I don't do dances for lodgers goin' to Eastbourne,' said Kitty.

'But 'e might not go to Eastbourne if you did lots of dances for 'im,' said Chloe.

'And in yer Sunday stockings,' said Carrie hopefully.

'Would yer like Kitty doin' a knees-up, mister?' asked Chloe.

'Well,' said Jamie, 'I—'

'Kindly don't answer that,' said Kitty. 'You've got to 'ave a job and you've got to go to Eastbourne.'

'Yes, he's got to 'ave a job,' said Alfie, 'it's only right. We'll miss yer, mister, and I'll see Kitty don't show 'er legs off to any fat an' bald blokes. 'Ere, Kitty, I wonder if I could go an' live with Mrs Fitch? Then you wouldn't 'ave to pay for any of me food. Did I tell yer I think she's startin' to fancy me? I could do a lot of work for 'er—'

'Stop talkin' daft,' said Kitty.

'Well, you stop talkin' about showin' yer legs to—'

'D'you want yer ears boxed?'

'Oh, 'elp,' said Carrie, 'Kitty's got the rats.'

'Cheer up,' said Jamie, 'it's not the end of the world.'

The brown eyes all turned on him again. Three pairs were a bit soulful. Kitty's were scornful. He ran a hand through his hair. He was a man with a headache.

'It's all right,' said Kitty, when the kids had gone up to bed, 'I didn't mean to get ratty. It was just a bit unexpected, that's all. Of course you can't turn the job down. But we'd like to 'ear from you now and again. Could you write just once in a while, so's we'll know how you're gettin' on?'

'Of course I'll write,' said Jamie.

'When d'you 'ave to go?'

'If I do go, it'll be next Monday.'

'Oh, blow that,' said Kitty, making a face.

'The firm's finding accommodation for me.'

'Somewhere posh, I expect,' said Kitty. 'Well, I mean, Eastbourne's posh, isn't it? Not like Walworth.'

'Walworth's all right, Kitty. A lot more than all right, in fact. It's got a heart-beat you can hear.'

'A bit worn out, though, I should think,' she said.

'Don't you believe it,' said Jamie. 'It's been having a hard time for years, but it's still standing up and so are its people.'

'Except the ones that get drunk,' said Kitty. 'Anyway, d'you think we've got rid of the police at last?'

'Yes, I do think so, Kitty.'

'Well, I hope so,' she said, knowing she'd hate it if they did come round again and he wasn't there to stand with her. 'That Mrs Briggs, I bet she had the shock of 'er life when the police went and charged her with shop-liftin'.'

'She probably set about them, since they charged her with assault as well,' said Jamie. 'Listen, I've a feeling that that money has to be here somewhere. Mrs Briggs was obviously certain about it. I'm going to take one more look at your step-father's room. There was a good reason for keeping you out of it.'

'But he always did,' said Kitty. 'D'you think it might 'ave been because he always had a fair bit of money in that vase, money that wasn't anything to do with the robbery?'

'Well, that's a point,' said Jamie, 'but I'll still take one more look.'

Kitty went with him. Rosemary was still out. Jamie looked around, trying to think what kind of hiding-place Mullins would have fashioned, one that would escape even the most exhaustive search. Had it been fashioned, or had it already existed? The hollow bedposts might have offered an answer, but they'd been investigated by the police and Mrs Briggs's old lags. 'Kitty, I suppose you never heard Mrs Briggs refer to any money the last time she saw your step-father?'

'Oh, they always talked in the parlour,' said Kitty. 'She'd come into the kitchen and say 'ello to us in a grudgin' way, then she'd go into the parlour with him. All I remember about the last time she saw 'im was that when she was leavin' I heard her at the front door. I heard 'er tell him off. She wasn't 'erself unless she was tellin' someone off.'

'What did she say?' asked Jamie, still looking around.

'She said, "Henry Mullins, you're up the bleedin' pole." He didn't 'alf laugh at that, and 'e didn't often laugh. He said something about she didn't know 'ow right she was and he laughed again, like it was the joke of the year. Mrs Briggs said—well, she said he was bloody barmy, and off she went.'

'What made her say that?' asked Jamie.

'Knowing her, I should think she called 'im barmy and up the pole because he still 'adn't got rid of us, and that we were costin' 'im money.'

'And he laughed his head off and said she didn't know how right she was when she told him he was up the pole?'

'Yes, I heard 'im, honest,' said Kitty.

Jamie did some new thinking. What

made Mullins say that? *You don't know how right you are.*

Up the pole? Up the pole?

Was there a pole? Had he seen one? A hollow pole? He searched his mind and emitted a low whistle.

'Kitty, my wee lass—'

'Who's a wee lass?' said Kitty, indignant. 'You callin' me a tich? I'm five feet five, I'll 'ave you know.'

'Och, aye, ye're a bonny lass, Kitty. Let's get back to the kitchen.'

'What for?' Kitty wasn't madly interested. She was utterly sick about him going to Eastbourne.

'Your kitchen curtains run on a brass pole,' said Jamie. 'Come on.'

'The pole's all right, the curtains don't amount to much,' said Kitty, but she followed him back to the kitchen. She watched as he climbed on to a chair. 'You said no-one should stand on chairs.'

'Well, catch me if I fall,' said Jamie.

She saw him lift the curtain pole from its rest and pull the other end free. He came down from the chair, the curtains flopping about. He unscrewed the brass head from one end of the hollow pole, then asked her to pass him the poker. She did so. He pushed it into the pole. It came to a stop about six inches in. He prodded. He felt something soft but resilient. He pictured a long sock full of pound notes and fivers.

It would have been the easiest thing in the world for Mullins to fill a sock and push it into the curtain pole while all the kids were out, and to ensure the filled sock was thick enough to stay put.

'The money's here, Kitty, in this curtain pole.'

'Show it to me, then,' she said, but without any great interest.

'It's stuck.' Jamie turned the pole upright. The curtains, on rings, slid to the bottom. Under the light, he peered. 'There,' he said, and let Kitty take a look. She glimpsed the bulging shape of a crammed sock a little way down inside the pole. 'We need a long pair of pliers to pull it out, Kitty.'

'Then what do we do?' Kitty was short on enthusiasm. There was too much depression floating heavily about. 'Tell the police?'

'Well, I think we're on fairly good terms now with Sergeant Watkins, but all the same if we go round and tell him we've found the money, he might suspect we knew where it was all the time, and that we're putting on an innocent act to finally clear ourselves. There'll be new questions.'

'I don't want any more questions,' said Kitty.

457

'Leave it, then,' said Jamie.

'Leave it?'

'We could get it out, and easily enough. But leave it, Kitty, and one day, if hard luck has caught up with you again and you're desperate, get in touch with me and I'll bring the right kind of pliers.'

'You mean I could use what's ill-gotten?' said Kitty.

'If you're desperate enough.'

'Wouldn't it be a bit criminal?'

'Useful, I'd say.'

'But not very respectable,' said Kitty. 'Still, perhaps the vicar wouldn't mind if I only borrowed a few pounds of it.'

'I'm sure he wouldn't.'

'I think I'll go to bed,' said Kitty.

When she was ready, she climbed quietly in beside her sleeping sisters. She put her head on the pillow, turned her face into it and wept just a few tears.

The following day, after the kids had gone to school, and Jamie and Rosemary had gone to their work, she took a tram to Brixton and introduced herself to the jovial Tom Robinson in his cafe by the market. She was not at her happiest, but she was still a girl of resolution and was able to put on a front that made Tom think her bright, cheerful and willing. He took to her at once, and more so when, with Ivy keeping a helpful eye on her, she began to produce perfect fry-ups at midday.

'Take 'er on, Dad,' said Ivy at a suitable moment.

'Well, I'm minded to, an' that's a fact,' said Tom.

'Take 'er on, I like 'er,' said Ivy, 'and give 'er some free eggs an' bacon with 'er wages.'

'Eh?'

'She's got a brother and two sisters to look after. And no parents.'

'Well,' said Tom, 'a nice cheerful girl like 'er, I ought to think about gettin' yer brother Eddie to come and marry 'er, but if that 'appened I dare say they'd go an' live in Barnet too.'

Kitty left soon after that. She had the job and was to start Wednesday week, when Ivy would spend her last three days in the cafe helping her to fully adjust to the work, to the conditions and to the peculiarities of certain regulars.

There it was, then, a job at twenty-four bob a week. But Kitty, of course, wasn't over the moon.

But Rosemary was. Jamie told her she no longer had criminal charges hanging over her. He said that he hoped the charges really had related to embezzlement and theft. Kindly don't put it like that, said Rosemary, it was all to do with the mad moments of a girl infatuated with her employer's husband. What else did Jamie think it could possibly be? The Irish troubles, he said. You took up with Fitzpatrick, and the guv'nor of the firm who gave me this job when you went to see him is also an Irishman. Murgatroyd. A coincidence, Jamie, believe me, said Rosemary.

So Jamie asked her the identity of the man who had called on her during the Saturday evening when he'd been at the Camberwell Palace with Kitty and the kids. Rosemary told him. Mr John Lindsay, she said. Jamie asked if she meant Mrs Lindsay's husband from Belfast. Well, yes, said Rosemary. You devious female, said Jamie. Rosemary smiled and said she couldn't help the fact that John had called on her. You could help the fact that you went to bed with him, said Jamie, and you could help the fact that you wrote to him giving this address. I'm damned sure Mrs Lindsay wouldn't have dropped those charges if she'd known you were still playing fast and loose. I'm leaving these lodgings, said Rosemary, I'm getting nowhere with you, but of course I'm up against dewy Brown-eyes, aren't I? Dewy Brown-eyes? Yes, your young landlady, smiled Rosemary. Don't talk rubbish, said Jamie, just behave yourself.

But she left that week. The following day General Sir Henry Wilson was assassinated on the doorstep of his London home by the IRA, and Jamie always wondered if Rosemary really was a butterfly or such a deadly agent for the IRA as to have shot Sir Henry Wilson herself.

That was Scotland Yard's problem. His own problem still concerned Kitty and the kids. Having decided he had to take the job at Eastbourne, he was committed to leaving them. He was relieved and pleased Kitty had secured the cafe job, but she had lost Rosemary as a lodger and the rent of six bob. Kitty would have no more than her wages and parish relief on which to exist with her little family. She'd received the news of his decision without complaint, but her face had been very straight.

'Look,' he said, over supper on Friday evening, 'I can't let go of certain responsibilities.'

'What do you mean?' asked Kitty.

'I dunno I could say that word meself,' said Alfie.

'I could,' said Chloe.

'So could I,' said Carrie.

'Women can say anyfing,' said Alfie, 'it beats me where it all comes from.'

'Listen, Kitty,' said Jamie, 'I can't duck what I owe you for looking after me so well. I propose to send you a ten-bob

461

postal order each week, it'll—'

'Excuse me, I'm sure, but you won't,' said Kitty firmly.

'Well, I'm not excusing you,' said Jamie.

'You'd better,' said Kitty, 'or I'll start chuckin' things.'

'I'll chuck them back,' said Jamie.

'If I get my temper up,' said Kitty, 'you won't get a chance to chuck anything back.'

'And if my temper goes to pot,' said Jamie, 'you'll find yourself over my knees.'

'Bloody cheek!' breathed Kitty.

'Oh, lor',' said Carrie.

'Oh, 'elp,' said Chloe.

'You just try puttin' me over your knees, you just try!' shouted Kitty.

'Stop shouting,' said Jamie.

'Yes, don't shout, Kitty,' said Chloe, uncomfortable.

Carrie thought about an Ethel M Dell book she'd read, and said, 'It's givin' you an 'eaving bosom, Kitty.'

Kitty, flushed, stiffened and sat up straight, but didn't dare look down at herself. She didn't need to. She could tell what temper was doing to her well-developed bosom.

'All over?' enquired Jamie.

'Oh, it's not, don't be personal,' gasped Kitty.

'Crikey, a bosom 'eaving all over,'

462

remarked Alfie. 'I dunno you should've said that, mister, it sounds worse than Kitty doin' a knees-up for a fat old bald bloke.'

'I meant, is the palaver all over?' said Jamie. 'It seems like it, so I'll have another go. The point being, Kitty, that I'd like you to keep my room free so that whenever I come to see all of you for a weekend, I'll be able to use it. I'll send the postal order each week, as I said—'

'It's charity, and we don't want charity, thanks very much,' said Kitty.

'It's not charity, it's a fair return for keeping my room for me.'

'Mister, will yer really come an' see us some weekends?' asked Carrie.

'I'll do yer room out each time, honest,' said Chloe.

'I'll clean yer inside winders,' said Alfie.

'Good, that's settled,' said Jamie. 'Now we can talk about the outing on Sunday, and the picnic.'

'You're not to send any postal orders,' said Kitty, 'I'll send them back if you do. I'll manage, I'll look after me fam'ly meself, if you don't mind, even if I 'ave to work me fingers to the bone. We'll still get parish relief, anyway, so we don't want any charitable postal orders—will you lot listen to me when I'm speakin'?'

Nobody was listening. The kids were all

talking to Jamie about the Sunday picnic.

That put Kitty into another temper, so when Sunday arrived she refused to go. She'd had a terrible week, all depressed one moment and all rageful the next. She knew she'd behaved badly, rowing with Jamie and upsetting the kids, but she simply couldn't help herself. No, she wasn't going on any picnic, thanks very much. But you've got to come, said Alfie. No, I haven't, she said, I've done the picnic for everyone, boiled eggs, cucumber sandwiches, rockcakes and apples, but I'm staying home. We can't go without you, said Jamie. Yes, you can, said Kitty, I'm going to spend the day doing embroidery, I'm going to do embroidery every Sunday and get a kind stallholder to sell it for me down the market. There's lots of kind stallholders, and they're nice reliable people as well. Either you come on the picnic, said Jamie, or you will get your bottom smacked, and this time I mean it.

'That's done it,' breathed Alfie, 'I bet there'll be a war now.'

Kitty began it by chucking a wooden spoon at Jamie. It bounced off his chest and he counterattacked. Kitty, yelling, fled from the kitchen and pelted up the stairs. She flung herself into the bedroom she shared with the twins and tried to slam the door in Jamie's face. Too late. He caught her.

Kitty, absolutely sure he really was going to smack her bottom, gasped. 'All right, I'll come on the picnic.'

'That's better,' said Jamie.

'Well, I've got to, ain't I, or you'll wallop me black and blue, won't you?'

'Probably.'

So she rode on the tram with them to Purley, and they walked from the tram stop to the Downs. But she didn't put her Sunday best on, just a blouse and skirt, and a boater. Alfie, Chloe and Carrie chased about and ran about, much as if they'd been released from a coiled spring. On the green Downs, amid the the laughter of the kids, Kitty had a strange painful feeling that this was going to be the saddest day of her life. They picnicked in the sunshine and played open-air games afterwards, Alfie a quick and lively boy, Chloe and Carrie girls of fun and giggles, Jamie an adventurous-looking man in his open-necked shirt and his air of physical energy. Kitty wandered about at times, looking at the views of Surrey in summer, its many shades of green patterned here and there with colourful nests of new houses.

'Where's Kitty?' asked Jamie at one stage.

'Up a tree,' said Alfie.

'Up a tree?' said Jamie.

'Yes, she climbed up,' said Chloe.

'By 'erself,' said Carrie.

'She said she 'adn't ever climbed a tree before, and that she ought to do it just once before the 'and of fate ended 'er life.'

'Cor strike a light,' said Alfie, 'I dunno what comes over women sometimes. I 'ope Mrs Fitch don't start climbin' lampposts.'

'Kitty said she ain't comin' down,' remarked Chloe.

'She said what?' asked Jamie.

'She ain't comin' down,' said Carrie.

'Oh, blimey, she ain't waitin' for the 'and of fate up a tree, is she?' asked Alfie.

'Where is she?' asked Jamie. The Downs were free of crowds. There were just a few people strolling in the distance, and a tranquil quiet prevailed. 'Which tree?'

'It's one over there,' said Chloe, pointing.

'Well, let's go and talk to her,' said Jamie, and Chloe led the rescue team towards a thick clump of trees and bushes. Kitty's voice was heard then.

'I don't need nobody, thanks, I'm all right up 'ere.'

Jamie advanced. There she was, standing on a lower branch about eight feet from the ground, her boater resting at the back

466

of her neck, its elastic around her throat. She looked mutinous.

'Come down,' said Jamie.

'No, I like it up 'ere,' said Kitty, 'and I can't get down, anyway. Still, never mind, it don't matter. You lot go 'ome and I might jump down and follow on later, if I don't break me leg.'

'Come down,' repeated Jamie. Kitty shook her head.

'Kitty, what we goin' to do if you break yer leg?' asked Alfie.

'We don't know any doctor round 'ere, do we, Chloe?' said Carrie.

'No, we don't know any,' said Chloe.

'Kitty, come down,' said Jamie yet again.

'I told you, I like it up 'ere,' said Kitty, holding an upper branch for support. 'I might stay all day and jump down when it's dark. Chloe and Carrie can get the tea when you all go 'ome.'

'Right,' said Jamie, 'I'm coming up to get you.'

'You better not,' said Kitty.

'What's up with 'er?' asked Alfie disgustedly. 'She ain't ever been in a mood like this before.'

'Well, it's bein' up a tree for the first time, I expect,' said Chloe.

'Oh, d'you think it's made her 'ead feel all funny?' asked Carrie.

'You'll 'ave to go up an' bring 'er down,

mister,' said Alfie. 'I'd go up meself, only I think she'd wallop me.'

'You Alfie,' said Kitty, skirt fluttering a bit, 'I've never walloped you in all your life.'

'I'll go up, Alfie,' said Jamie, 'and risk her walloping me.'

'I wish you'd all go 'ome and leave me to me fate,' said Kitty.

'I'll give you one last chance,' said Jamie, and lifted his arms. 'Jump,' he said, 'and I'll catch you.'

'Not likely,' said Kitty.

Jamie took a couple of strides forward, placed one hand on the lowest branch and looked up at her. Kitty gave a little shriek, quite certain he could see up her clothes. She used one hand to gather her skirt tightly around her legs.

'I'm coming up,' said Jamie, and began to hoist himself.

'I'll 'it you, I'll kick you,' said Kitty. She gave another little shriek. 'Oh, you're lookin'!'

'Now what's she talkin' about?' asked Alfie. His twin sisters glanced at each other and giggled.

'All right, I'll come down,' cried Kitty, 'but I'm not goin' to jump. Can't you go and find a ladder?'

Jamie, back on the ground, lifted his arms again.

468

'Jump and I'll catch you,' he said again. 'Or turn round and lower yourself to the next branch. That's the way you climbed up, probably.'

'Here, I'm not turning round,' said Kitty, fearful of her skirts.

'Come on, Kitty,' said Alfie, 'mister'll catch yer.'

'He'd better,' said Kitty, 'I'll really get ratty if I break me neck.' She edged forward. She slipped then, she slipped straight down, shrieking. Her clothes rushed upwards. Shapely legs, shining knees and Sunday stockings all presented themselves for a speeding second to Jamie's eyes before he caught her. Kitty blushed crimson as her feet touched ground and she found herself in his arms.

'No damage,' said Jamie, conscious of the warmth of her feminine body.

'Oh, look, d'you mind?' blushed Kitty.

Carrie gasped, 'Oh, 'elp, you didn't 'alf look naughty, Kitty.'

'Crikey,' said Chloe, 'no wonder she wanted a ladder.'

Kitty released herself and dashed her clothes into place.

'Sunday knees-up, that's what you just done, Kitty,' said Alfie, and the twins giggled again. 'You said you was goin' to do them in the parlour, not on a picnic. I dunno, you just can't trust some women.'

'Well, you can't always trust them when they're off the ground,' said Jamie, smiling. 'Kitty fell off a kitchen chair she was standing on a while ago. I had to catch her then.'

'Well, you'd better be careful, Kitty,' said Alfie, 'because next time you fall off anything, mister won't be there to do any catchin'.'

'No, 'e won't, will 'e?' said Carrie dolefully.

'Oh, bother it,' said Chloe, which was her way of showing what she thought about Jamie's imminent departure.

They took the long ride home on a tram. The kids were pink from a sun that had shone directly down on them instead of bouncing off rooftops. They had seen acres of green grass and what country views really looked like, all in company with a man who made them feel secure.

For the step-children of the late Henry Mullins, it had been a Sunday to remember.

Alfie, Carrie and Chloe ran home from school at midday on Monday to see Jamie before he left. They ran not in exuberance but to make sure they didn't miss saying goodbye to him. He had said he'd be leaving at quarter past twelve. He'd said goodbye to neighbours like Mrs Fitch and

Mrs Reynolds, and was ready now to take leave of Kitty and the kids, his suitcase standing on the doorstep. He was talking to Kitty, and Kitty's mouth was very set. He said hello to the kids and gave them a shilling each. Carrie and Chloe would have fainted with bliss if such a huge amount of pocket money hadn't been a farewell gift. They'd have given it back if only it would have made him stay.

Alfie, very touched by his own bob, said, 'I wish yer lots of luck, mister, you've been a real dad to us.'

'We won't ever forget yer, really we won't,' said Chloe.

'Will yer promise to send us picture postcards?' asked Carrie.

'Promise,' said Jamie, still fighting inner battles. 'Behave yourselves now, don't forget your respectability.' He kissed the twins. He shook Alfie's hand. He put his arm around Kitty's shoulders and gave her a squeeze. Her shoulders were stiff. 'Good luck, Kitty, I'll be in touch.'

'Yes, all right,' said Kitty, and it was an effort to get just those three words out.

He left then. They stood at the gate to watch him walk up the street towards the church and the Walworth Road, carrying his suitcase. He had come into their house at a time when their step-father had been a dark threatening cloud in their unhappy lives. He had brought a little bright light to them, and then, when their step-father died, that brightness had shone every day for them. He'd talked with them, laughed with them, and bought them rapturizing fish and chips. Now he was going. Chloe had a lump in her throat. Carrie was gulping. Alfie was biting his lip. Kitty was stiff, proud and silent.

They saw him reach the S-bend. He turned and waved. The kids waved back. Then he disappeared.

Swallowing, Carrie said, 'I don't feel very well.'

'I don't actu'lly feel unwell,' said Alfie, 'but I ain't exactly in the pink, like.'

'Kitty, ain't it a shame?' sighed Chloe.

'Don't you worry, loveys,' said Kitty, pulling herself together, 'we'll manage, you'll see.'

'I still don't feel very well,' said Carrie.

'I'll look after yer,' said Alfie. 'As soon as I'm a bit older I'll be a dad to all of yer.'

'That'll make us all not very well,' said Chloe.

'Let's go in,' said Kitty, 'and I'll get us something to eat.'

'I don't know I want anything,' said Carrie, 'I—oh, look, Kitty, 'e's comin' back!'

Jamie was striding towards them, vigour

and certainty in his step, his suitcase swinging. He had made a new decision. He'd had to. Perhaps he had known all along that if he couldn't manage a future in company with Kitty and the kids, he'd never be much of a man. He saw them, still at the gate, all four of them, and he knew every brown eye was turned his way. Kitty was a worker, he was a worker, and the kids would never go through life sitting on their bottoms.

He thought of his parents and what they would say to Kitty and the kids at a moment like this.

Workers of the world unite.

He might not use that phrase himself, but he could find other words, including special ones to Kitty.

Carrie, swallowing again, watched him coming up fast. She couldn't help herself. She ran to meet him. 'Mister, are yer comin' back to us, are yer?' she asked breathlessly.

'You'd like that? Come on, Carrie.' He took her hand and they reached the gate together. They all looked at him. All those brown eyes, with Kitty's as dark as burnt sienna. 'Listen, everyone,' he said, 'who'd like to come and live in Eastbourne with me? We can get furniture removers to collect all we need. Some stuff we needn't bother with, like old curtain poles, eh,

Kitty?' He let go of his suitcase, and with his left hand still holding Carrie's, he put his right arm around Kitty's shoulders and squeezed.

Kitty stared at him. He smiled, and she knew then that they had him for ever.

' 'Ello, 'ello, name of Mr J Blair?' enquired a fruity voice.

It was the postman, stout and hearty, with a midday delivery.

'That's me,' said Jamie, and the postman handed him a letter. Jamie looked at it, at the Belfast postmark and his mother's handwriting. It gave him an uneasy feeling. He still had the antics of Rosemary on his mind at times, and now there was the recent murder of Sir Henry Wilson. He ripped the envelope open, and Kitty and the kids watched him as he read the letter.

His mother had written to say she hoped he was still in good health, but that she and his dad had had a shock and a grievous disappointment. They couldn't get permission to go to Russia. They couldn't think why Comrade Lenin wouldn't let them in when they'd been loyal nearly all their lives to the cause of a workers' revolution. What with the shock of that, and then the Belfast police getting more spiteful, they'd decided to come back home to London. It's one blessing, knowing you'll be there, Jamie, said Mrs Blair, and perhaps there's room for us in your lodgings for a bit while your dad sorts himself out down at the docks. He's been promised a job there, like he had before and like he'd had in Belfast. We're both going to be a new help to you, Jamie, and perhaps we can all join the British Communist Party together. We're catching the night ferry on Monday evening and hope to be knocking on your door some time on Tuesday. We know you'll be consoling to your mum and dad in their bitter disappointment.

Jamie stuffed the letter into his jacket. Kitty saw a little grin on his face. She thought it was a little bit like a grin of relief.

'Oh, I thought there might be trouble for you in that letter, the way you opened it,' she said.

'There'll be a bit of aggravation at least, and for all of us, if we don't scarper off to Eastbourne as fast as we can,' said Jamie. 'My parents will be here tomorrow, knocking on the door and hoping you'll put them up for a while.'

'Oh, I wouldn't mind that, I wouldn't mind anything now that we're all still goin' to be together,' said Kitty.

'You'd mind the lot of us being badgered into joining the Communist Party,' said Jamie. 'We'd have to wave the red flag on Sundays and go on strike once a week. Nothing doing, Kitty. We'll leave the latchcord dangling, and I'll leave them a note. Right, then, who's for hurrying things up, who's for finding furniture removers able to do the job this afternoon and who's for buzzing off to Eastbourne before the day is out? It'll be work, work, pack, pack, with no time for a bite to eat or a drop to drink. Who's for it?'

'Us! Us!' The kids yelled in chorus.

'That means one of you taking a note round to your head teacher from Kitty,' said Jamie. 'If Kitty's in favour.'

'Course she is,' said Alfie, 'ain't you, Kitty?'

Kitty drew a deep breath.

'We'll do everything you say,' she said to Jamie. 'We don't mind where we go as long as you're with us.'

'All the way, Kitty,' said Jamie, and kissed her.

Kitty, turning pink, said huskily, 'Oh, on me doorstep and all.'

Alfie, Chloe and Carrie stared at her and blinked. Their strong enduring sister had little tears running.

'Oh, blimey,' said Alfie, 'you just can't tell with women. I 'ope Mrs Fitch don't cry 'er eyes out when she finds out I ain't 'ere any more.'

Three days later, Detective-Constable Hurst walked into the police station and button-holed his sergeant.

'They've bunked,' he said.

'Did I hear you say something?' asked Sergeant Watkins.

'That you did,' said Hurst. 'Kitty Edwards and her lodger and the kids have all done a bunk. I've just picked up the news. And what else d'you think? The lodger's parents are livin' in the house now.'

'Well, bloody good luck,' said Sergeant Watkins.

'But what if they've bunked with the loot?'

'Not their style,' said Sergeant Watkins. 'Case closed.'

The publishers hope that this book has given you enjoyable reading. Large Print Books are especially designed to be as easy to see and hold as possible. If you wish a complete list of our books, please ask at your local library or write directly to: Magna Print Books, Long Preston, North Yorkshire, BD23 4ND, England.

This Large Print Book for the Partially sighted, who cannot read normal print, is published under the auspices of

THE ULVERSCROFT FOUNDATION

THE ULVERSCROFT FOUNDATION

. . . we hope that you have enjoyed this Large Print Book. Please think for a moment about those people who have worse eyesight problems than you . . . and are unable to even read or enjoy Large Print, without great difficulty.

You can help them by sending a donation, large or small to:

**The Ulverscroft Foundation,
1, The Green, Bradgate Road,
Anstey, Leicestershire, LE7 7FU,
England.**
or request a copy of our brochure for more details.

The Foundation will use all your help to assist those people who are handicapped by various sight problems and need special attention.

Thank you very much for your help.